GREENGLASS HOUSE

GREENGLASS HOUSE

BY
KATE MILFORD

WITH ILLUSTRATIONS BY
JAIME ZOLLARS

CLARION BOOKS
HOUGHTON MIFFLIN HARCOURT   BOSTON   NEW YORK

Clarion Books
215 Park Avenue South
New York, New York 10003

Copyright © 2014 by Kate Milford
Illustrations copyright © 2014 by Jaime Zollars

For information about permission to reproduce selections from this book, write to
trade.permissions@hmhco.com or to Permissions, Houghton Mifflin Harcourt Publishing Company,
3 Park Avenue, 19th Floor, New York, New York 10016

Clarion Books is an imprint of Houghton Mifflin Harcourt Publishing Company.

www.hmhco.com

The text was set in Monotype Bulmer.

Library of Congress Cataloging-in-Publication Data
Milford, Kate.
Greenglass House / by Kate Milford ; with illustrations by Jaime Zollars.
pages cm
Summary: At Greenglass House, a smuggler's inn, twelve-year-old Milo, the innkeeper's
adopted son, plans to spend his winter holidays relaxing but soon guests are arriving with
strange stories about the house sending Milo and Meddy, the cook's daughter, on an adventure.
ISBN 978-0-544-05270-3 (hardback) — ISBN 978-0-544-05555-1 (ebook)
[1. Mystery and detective stories. 2. Hotels—Fiction. 3. Magic—Fiction. 4. Adoption—
Fiction.] I. Title.
PZ7.M594845Gre 2014
[Fic]—dc23
2013036212

Manufactured in the United States of America
DOC 20 19 18 17 16 15 14 13 12
4500576108

✳

*To my family, near and far, with thanks
for all my childhood Christmases;*

*To Raegan, Hadley, Phero, Oliver, Griffin,
and the one we call Amelia, adventurers all;*

*To Emma, who twisted my arm and
made me fix the things that didn't work;*

And to Grandmoo, because it's her favorite.

CONTENTS

one

THE SMUGGLERS' INN

There is a right way to do things and a wrong way, if you're going to run a hotel in a smugglers' town.

You shouldn't make it a habit to ask too many questions, for one thing. And you probably shouldn't be in it for the money. Smugglers are always going to be flush with cash as soon as they find a buyer for the eight cartons of fountain pen cartridges that write in illegal shades of green, but they never have money today. You should, if you are going to run a smugglers' hotel, get a big account book and assume that whatever you write in it, the reality is, you're going to get paid in fountain pen cartridges. If you're lucky. You could just as easily get paid with something even more useless.

Milo Pine did not run a smugglers' hotel, but his parents did. It was an inn, actually; a huge, ramshackle manor house that looked as if it had been cobbled together from discarded pieces of a dozen mismatched mansions collected from a dozen different cities. It was called Greenglass House, and it sat on the side of a hill overlooking an inlet of harbors, a little district built half on the shore and half on the piers that jutted out into the river Skidwrack like the teeth of a comb. It was a long climb up to the inn from the waterfront by foot, or an only slightly shorter trip by the cable railway that led from the inn's private dock up the steep slope of Whilforber Hill. And of course the inn wasn't only for smugglers, but that was who turned up most often, so that was how Milo thought of it.

Milo had lived at Greenglass House ever since he'd been adopted by Nora and Ben Pine when he was a baby. It had always been home. And he was used to the bizarre folks who passed through the inn, some of them coming back every season like extended family who showed up to pinch your cheeks at holidays and then disappeared again. After twelve years, he was even getting pretty good at predicting who was going to show up when. Smugglers were like bugs or vegetables. They had their seasons. Which was why it was so weird when the huge old bell on the porch, the one that was connected to the winch that drove the cable that in turn hauled the car up its tracks, started ringing.

The old iron bell's tone changed with the seasons too, and with the time of day. This evening, the first of winter vacation, was cold and brittle, and the snow had just begun to fall. Today, therefore, the bell itself had a brittle tone. It had a sound like a gulp of frigid air.

Milo looked up from the coffee table, where he was working on a math problem. He liked to get his homework out of the way right off the bat so he could enjoy the holidays without thinking about school. He glanced at his mother, who was sprawled across the rag rug in front of the big stone fireplace, reading. "Someone's coming up?" he asked incredulously.

Mrs. Pine got to her feet, tucked her book under her arm, padded across to the foyer, and peered out the window by the door. "Someone wants to. We'd better go start the winch."

"But we never have guests the first week of vacation," Milo protested. He felt a vague unease start to rise in his stomach and tried to swallow it down. Vacation couldn't possibly get spoiled so quickly, could it? He'd only stepped off the launch that ferried the Quayside kids to and from school a few hours ago.

"Well, not often, we don't," Mrs. Pine said as she laced up her boots, "but that's not because we have a rule about it. It's just because that's the way it usually turns out."

"But it's *vacation!*"

His mother shrugged and held out his coat. "Come on, kiddo. Be a gentleman. Don't send your mom out into the cold alone."

Ah, the all-powerful *gentleman* card. Still grumbling, Milo got to his feet, quietly whispering *"vacation vacation vacation"* as he slouched across to join her. He had just about finished his homework. That was supposed to be the end of responsibility for a while.

The bell rang again. Milo gave in to his frustration, stopped in the middle of the foyer with one boot on, and gave a single, furious yell with his hands clenched at his sides.

Mrs. Pine waited with folded arms until he was finished. "Got that out of your system?" she asked gently. Milo scowled. "I know this isn't the usual routine," his mother added, "and I know you don't like it when things don't happen the way you expect." She bent to hunt in the catchall basket beside the door for a flashlight. "But look, being surprised isn't always a bad thing."

The fact that it sounded logical didn't change the way Milo felt, of course. But he nodded and finished getting dressed for the cold. He followed his mother out onto the porch and across the lawn to a break in the dark wall of bare white birches and blue-green firs that covered the hillside. There, in a pool of deeper shadow, the grass gave way to a stone landing.

All his life, ever since he was really small, Milo had been very bothered by sudden changes of plan. More than bothered. Being surprised made him uneasy at the best of times. Now, tromping across the fresh snow in the bitter cold to haul a stranger up the hill, an unexpected stranger who was going to require him to work when all he really wanted was a quiet week or so with his parents and his house to himself . . . well, that made the uneasiness feel uncomfortably like panic.

The flashlight's beam pierced the pool of shadow, which flickered and melted into butter-gold; Mrs. Pine had turned on the light in the little pavilion hidden in the trees where the cable railway landed.

The railway began a hundred yards below, at the river. There were other ways to get to the bottom of the gorge, or to get to the top if you were down. There was a steep and winding stair that ran more or less parallel to the railway and led to the same pavilion.

There was also a road that snaked away from the inn and around the side of the hill down into the city proper, which was about a twenty-minute drive away. But only Milo, his parents, and the inn's chef, Mrs. Caraway, ever really used the road. Guests didn't come from the direction of the city. Guests came by river, sometimes in their own boats and sometimes by paying one of the dozens of old tars in the Quayside Harbors who'd ferry a person to Greenglass House in their equally aged boats for a few bucks. Given the option of being hauled up the steep hill in an antique conveyance that looked like a demented and oversized bumper car on rails or climbing three hundred and ten steps (Milo had counted), they always chose the former.

Inside the stone-floored pavilion were a bench, a shed, and the steel tracks of the railway. Mrs. Pine unlocked the shed, and Milo followed her inside to where the heavy cable that ran between the tracks looped around the giant spindle of the winch. Thanks to a complex mess of gears, once you got the winch going, it did all the work necessary to haul the single car up the slope. But it was old, and the lever tended to stick. Getting it moving was easier with two pairs of hands.

Together, Milo and his mother grasped the lever. "One, two, three!" Milo counted, and as one they hauled it forward. The cold metal of the gears whined like an old dog, and then they started to turn.

As Milo and Mrs. Pine waited for the railcar to click and clank its way to the top of the slope, he wondered what kind of person it was bringing up. Smugglers came in all kinds, and of course sometimes the inn had guests who were sailors or travelers and not smugglers at all. But not very often — and almost never in winter, when the Skidwrack and its hidden inlets were so often frozen.

While Milo was thinking, winding strings of glittering white firefly-sized lights came to life, outlining the pavilion and trailing off down the hill along the railing of the stairs. His mother straightened up from where she had just plugged them in.

"So what do you think? An elf on the lam from the North Pole? A popgun runner? Eggnog bootlegger?" she asked. "Best guess wins a brownie sundae. Loser makes it."

"What are those flower bulbs Grandma always sends you at Christmas that you love?"

"Paperwhites?"

"Yeah. It's a guy with a cargo of those. And stockings. Green ones with pink stripes." A low whine joined the creaking of the cable around the big spindle in the shed. You could tell where the railcar was by how the sounds it made changed. Milo pictured the misshapen old iron lamppost the car would be passing right about now.

"Green and pink stockings?"

"Yeah. He probably knows it was a bad idea, but now he's stuck with them. He was forced to take the cargo on — no, tricked into it — and now if he can't move it, he's ruined. He's already trying to figure out how to convince people to switch from baskets to striped stockings for Easter." Milo leaned over the pavilion railing and peered through the thickening snow falling amongst the birches and icing the pine branches, searching for the first glimpse of the car and its passenger. It was still out of view, but from the vibration of the rails, he knew it was being hauled up the steepest part of the slope now. "He's got meetings set up with people this week too. Magazine writers, some weird TV star, trying to see if he can make green and pink stripes a big fashion thing next year. And a sock-puppet company."

He leaned over the railing again, just far enough out that a few flakes of snow managed to make it past the roof onto his eyelashes. There it was: the blue metal nose of the railcar with its silver racing stripes (painted a few years back by Milo and his father along with its name, *Whilforber Whirlwind,* on the sides). And then, a moment later, its passenger: a lanky man in a felt hat and a plain black coat. Milo could just make out a pair of oversized glasses with huge tortoiseshell rims on his nose.

He wilted. The stranger looked disappointingly like somebody's grandfather. Maybe even a bit like a schoolteacher.

"I don't know," Mrs. Pine remarked, as if she'd read Milo's mind. "I could kind of believe that guy would take a chance on green and pink stripes." She ruffled his hair. "Come on, kiddo. Put on your welcome face."

"I hate the welcome face," Milo mumbled. But he straightened up and tried to look cheerful as the *Whirlwind* made its final ascent to the pavilion.

Up close, the stranger looked even more boring. Plain hat, plain coat, plain face, plain blue suitcase tucked in the boot of the car. Beneath the glasses, though, his eyes were bright and sharp as they flicked from Mrs. Pine to Milo and back.

Milo felt himself stiffen. It always started this way, whenever the Pines met someone new. You could just about see that person's thoughts: *One of these things is not like the others.* This stranger was hiding it better than most, for sure; there was no change in his expression, but that didn't mean he wasn't thinking it too. *How did a Chinese kid wind up in Nagspeake with that lady for a mom? Obviously adopted.*

The car came to a jerking stop at last, nearly sending the unexpecting passenger's face straight into the *Whilforber Whirlwind*'s padded dashboard.

"Hi." Milo's mother beamed as the man clambered out of the car and brushed the accumulated snow from his shoulders. "Welcome to Greenglass House. I'm Nora Pine. This is my son, Milo."

"Thank you," the stranger said, his voice just as boring as the rest of him. "My name's Vinge. De Cary Vinge."

Well, Milo thought sourly, he had an interesting name, at least. "I'll get your suitcase for you, Mr. Vinge."

"Oh, that's all right," Mr. Vinge said quickly as Milo reached for it. "Let me carry that. It's quite heavy." He grasped the handle and pulled. It must've been heavy; Mr. Vinge had to put a foot up on the side of the car and push off for leverage.

Which was when Milo's mother gave him a significant glance. Uncomprehending, Milo took another look at the stranger. Then he spotted it: one garishly striped sock, visible for just a moment before Mr. Vinge stumbled backwards with his suitcase. If anything, the orange and purple combination was even weirder than Milo's imaginary green and pink.

"Looks like maybe I owe you a brownie sundae," Mrs. Pine

whispered. Then, louder, "This way, Mr. Vinge. Let's get you in out of the snow."

———— ❄ ————

Milo's father was waiting when they reached the porch. "Hey there," he said, reaching out to shake Mr. Vinge's hand and taking his suitcase with the other. "Ben Pine. Rough night for travel, huh?"

"Oh, it's not so bad," Mr. Vinge replied as he stepped inside and shucked off his coat.

"You got in just in time," Milo's dad went on. "Weather report says we might see seven or eight inches of snow tonight."

De Cary Vinge smiled. It was a vague smile, a quick smile, but it was there for just a moment. Like he was pleased about getting snowed in, basically alone, in a remote lodge in a strange part of town. "You don't say."

Milo thought the smile was weird, but then again, the guy did have a weird name and he was wearing weird socks. Maybe he was an oddball after all.

"I put some coffee and hot chocolate on," Mr. Pine said as he led Mr. Vinge through the dining room to the stairs. "Let me show you to your room, then we'll be glad to send something up or you can warm yourself by the fire down here."

"How long do you think you'll be staying?" Mrs. Pine called after him.

Mr. Vinge paused, one foot on the bottom step. "I suppose that depends. Do you need to know right now?"

"Nope. You're our only guest at the moment."

Mr. Vinge nodded. "Then I guess I'll let you know."

Milo followed his father and their guest up the staircase. The inn had five main floors. The living room, dining room, and kitchen — all of them big, open rooms that flowed from one to the next — were on the first floor. The Pines' living space was on the second; the guest rooms took up the third, fourth, and fifth floors. The staircase that connected them was wide, with carved banisters on both sides. On each floor there was a landing and a turn so that the stair doubled back on itself, and each landing had a huge stained-glass window.

Mr. Pine led Mr. Vinge to the third floor, where the doors to the four guest rooms stood open. "Your pick, Mr. Vinge. Any preference?"

Their guest wandered down the hall, peering into each room as he passed. He paused at the end where the door to the old dumbwaiter was, then turned back to Milo and his father. Except Milo had the impression that Mr. Vinge wasn't exactly looking at them, but *past* them. Milo turned and saw only the stained-glass window and the snowy night beyond, tinged in shades of pale, pale greens: celery and celadon and tones like old bottle glass.

"This one will be fine," Mr. Vinge said after a moment, nodding at the room to his left.

"Sounds good." Mr. Pine set the blue suitcase just inside the door. "Want us to send up a hot drink?"

Before Mr. Vinge could answer, the brittle peal of the railway bell rang out again.

Milo stared at his father, shocked. "Another one?" he demanded before he could stop himself. Then he clapped his hands over his mouth, sure that had to have sounded horribly rude.

"I'm so sorry," Mr. Pine was already saying to the guest, shooting dagger-eyes at Milo. But Mr. Vinge didn't appear to have noticed Milo's faux pas. He looked just as shocked as Milo felt.

"Is that . . . is that the bell I rang?" he asked in a strange voice.

"It sure is," Milo's father said. "Sounds like we have another guest." He turned to head back downstairs, flicking Milo on his left ear as he went. Not hard enough to be painful, but just enough to let him know that even if Mr. Vinge had missed Milo's rudeness, his father hadn't. "Shall we send up coffee or hot chocolate, something to snack on?"

Mr. Vinge frowned, then shook his head. "No, thanks. I'll come down in a few minutes. I confess, I'm curious to see who else is traveling tonight."

Milo's father took the stairs two at a time and caught his wife just as she was about to go back out into the snow. "We've got it, we've got it," he said.

At any other time, Milo might've felt annoyed at being volunteered — never mind that if one guest threatened to spoil his vacation, two spoiled it for sure. But now, the sheer improbability of two separate guests showing up at this time of year made him more curious than upset.

Not only that, De Cary Vinge had been shocked when that bell rang. On one hand, he was *right* to be shocked that another guest was on the way. On the other hand, how could he possibly have known the inn was usually deserted at this time of year? Unless, Milo thought as he pulled on his boots, Mr. Vinge was here *because* he figured he'd have the place to himself.

That was the moment Milo first started thinking maybe there was something odd going on. But then his father opened the door and a knife stroke of windy night cut into the foyer. Milo zipped up his coat and stumbled out into the cold after his dad, trying to walk so that his steps matched the footprints Mr. Pine left in the accumulating snow.

They had to send the *Whilforber Whirlwind* back down the hill, Milo's mother having reasonably assumed it had made its last upward trip for a while. "What do you figure?" Mr. Pine asked as they watched the blue car disappear over the slope. "I gotta tell you — and don't tell your mom — I was really looking forward to a few weeks off. I'm not complaining, I'm just saying. I thought I was off-duty for a while."

"I know!" Milo exploded. "I already did my homework and everything!"

"What's the deal with Mr. Vinge? I didn't get around to asking what he does or what brought him here. Did you?"

Milo shook his head. "He's got some pretty crazy socks on, that's all I know."

His father nodded seriously. That was one of the many great things about Milo's dad: he always took whatever you said seriously. Milo didn't have to explain why it seemed meaningful that a guy who appeared to be so boring and normal wore such bizarre socks. His dad would get it.

The engine that drove the cable jerked to a halt: the *Whirlwind* had reached the bottom of the slope. A moment later, the bell rang again to signal that the passenger was aboard and ready to begin the trip upward. Mr. Pine disappeared into the shed for a moment to throw the lever.

Milo and his father leaned on the railing side by side in silence, staring through the trees and waiting for the first flash of blue. That was another great thing about Milo's dad: you could hang out with him and say nothing and still feel like you'd spent time together. Milo's mom wasn't good at that. Oh, she always had interesting things to say, and they had fun conversations every time they talked. But his dad was good at quiet.

The snow fell, trying to blanket trees and ground and night with silence while the winch and the cable and the rails and the car made their familiar mechanical noises, as if they were having a conversation while they brought up the new guest. And then, at last, there was the *Whilforber Whirlwind,* and inside it, hunched under a vivid blue umbrella topped with snow, was a lady.

As the railcar passed under one of the old iron lampposts, the light falling through the umbrella seemed to turn her hair blue too. She looked pretty young to Milo, or younger than his parents, anyway. She smiled and waved as the *Whirlwind* approached, and Milo found himself smiling and waving back.

The car came to a lurching stop, and the lady swung her umbrella over to one side, knocking off the snow and closing it up. Her hair stayed blue: a darker shade than the metallic cobalt of the railcar, but blue nonetheless.

"Hi," she said, her voice bright. "Sorry to drag you out into the snow."

"No problem," Mr. Pine said, offering a hand to help her out. "It's what we're here for. I'm Ben Pine and this is my son, Milo."

"Georgiana Moselle. Georgie," the blue-haired girl said. "Thanks."

"Can I carry your bag for you?" Milo asked.

She nodded, pleased, and pointed to a carpetbag in the boot of the car. "Sure thing. Thanks, Milo."

Milo hauled it out and started back through the trees to the inn. Before Mr. Pine followed, he paused to send the railcar back down the hill, muttering, "Just in case."

Inside, there were hot drinks waiting; Milo could smell cider simmering on the stove the second he opened the door. Mr. Vinge was waiting, too. As Mrs. Pine came to the foyer and introduced herself, he peered around the side of one of the big chairs in the living room, gave Georgie a curious look, then disappeared back into the depths of the chair.

"Let's get you a room first. Then there's coffee, tea, hot chocolate, and cider," Mrs. Pine said as their second guest stepped out of her green rubber boots. "Ben, what room did you put Mr. Vinge in?"

Georgie stopped dead in the act of pulling up her woolen socks and gave Mrs. Pine the oddest look Milo had ever seen. It was as if her face was divided in half: the bottom part was all innocent smile, but the top half was wide-eyed in unmistakable disbelief.

"You have another guest?"

Mr. Vinge leaned around his chair again, smiling blandly behind his oversized glasses. "De Cary Vinge. Just arrived myself."

"Georgie Moselle," said the young lady with the blue hair. The odd expression flickered on her face, like she really didn't want it there anymore but knew it would look weird if she stopped smiling right now. Neither she nor Mr. Vinge made any effort to shake hands. They just stared at each other as if each was trying to figure out something about the other.

Milo glanced over to see if his parents had noticed this bit of awkwardness, but somehow they seemed to have missed it. "Mr. Vinge is in Three E," Mr. Pine said to his wife, busy with his own coat and boots. "You don't mind showing Miss Moselle up?"

"Glad to. Milo, you want to bring that bag?"

"Sure." Milo watched the two guests continue to size each other up. Then Georgie turned away abruptly and followed Mrs. Pine toward the stairs. Milo trailed after.

"Third floor okay?" his mom asked. "Hardly seems worth it to make you hike up any higher, not when there's only the two of you."

"Oh, I don't know," Georgie said brightly. "How often does a girl get a whole floor to herself? Might be fun."

Fun? Why on earth would anyone want to walk up three flights if she didn't have to? Also, Milo knew from experience, having camped out in every room at some point or another, that it was pretty creepy being the only person on a floor. The inn made noises: floorboards creaked, old windowpanes rattled, hinges groaned . . .

But of course his mother was not about to tell a guest she couldn't hike up an extra flight of stairs if she wanted to. So they kept on going, up to the fourth floor.

While the stained-glass window on the third floor was done in shades of pale green, the one here was mostly blue: cobalt and robin's-egg and navy and powder and turquoise, with a few bits and pieces here and there that seemed, with the dark sky behind them, to match the guest's hair precisely.

Georgie Moselle beamed at it. "Look at that. Obviously I belong here."

Mrs. Pine waved an arm. "Any room you like, then. I forgot to ask, how long do you think you'll be staying?"

"Not sure. A week, maybe two?" After a quick look inside each, Georgie chose a room at the far end. Milo followed her to 4W and set the carpetbag on the folding luggage rack just inside the door. Or at least, that's what he meant to do. Instead, he dropped the bag into thin air and it fell three feet or so to the floor with a thud.

There was no mistaking the crunch of something breaking inside it.

Georgie was kneeling next to the bag before Milo had even decided whether to apologize or scream. "I'm so sorry," he babbled, staring from the bag to the luggage rack, which, for some inexplicable reason, stood to the right of the door rather than to the left, where it should have been. Every room with a W had a door that opened inward and to the right, so the luggage rack was always on the left.

"It's fine," Georgie was saying. "Don't worry about it."

"But something broke," Milo protested. Georgie was busy throwing clothes and toiletries that appeared to have been shoved randomly into the bag out onto the floor in search of whatever had broken. Milo stared in horror as the pile grew: jeans, pajamas, a jar of face cream, underwear. "I'll get . . . I'll get a towel or something," he said helplessly.

A book with a bent cover, a water-stained journal with loose pages escaping to flutter across the room, a plastic zipper bag of makeup and lipsticks, and then there it was. Georgie lifted two dripping pieces of broken pink faceted glass. The smell hit Milo a fraction of a second later: alcohol and something spicy, flowery. He'd broken a bottle of perfume.

"Oh, my God!" Mrs. Pine exclaimed from the hallway. "Oh, I'm so —" She gagged involuntarily and ran down the hall. A moment later she returned with a waste bin from one of the other rooms. "Throw it in here. We'll replace it, of course. I'm so sorry. I'll take anything that needs washing and do it up right away."

Georgie sighed and dropped the glass carefully into the bin. "It's not a big deal. Please don't trouble yourself about it. I don't know why I shoved the bottle in the bottom of the bag like that, anyway." She gathered her clothes up in her arms, dumped them on the yellow knitted blanket on the bed, and began to sort them into piles.

Milo's mother gave him a sharp, questioning look. He paused in the act of picking up the rest of Georgie's belongings. "The luggage rack's on the wrong side," he protested, jabbing an accusatory finger at the offending piece of furniture. "They're always opposite the way the door opens! Who moved it?"

"Milo." Mrs. Pine held out the waste bin expectantly. He sighed and deposited Georgie's things on the desk, which, fortunately, was right where it was supposed to be. Then he took the bin and escaped down the hall.

He'd gotten all the way to the utility closet on the second floor, where he emptied the bin of its flowery, vile-smelling, eye-burning contents, when he realized he still had Georgie Moselle's book under one arm. Great.

Well, he'd have to face her again sooner or later. Milo sighed and tried not to dwell too much on how the luggage rack not being where it was supposed to be, on top of vacation not happening the way it was supposed to happen, made it seem kind of like the world was trying to drive him crazy. He started back up the stairs.

Which was when the bell rang for the third time.

Milo turned abruptly and sprinted down the staircase to the main floor, past a staring Mr. Vinge, narrowly avoiding plowing into both his father and the silver coffeepot he was holding. "I'll get it!" he shrieked at the top of his lungs.

There were two of them this time. It was hard to tell who was least happy about that fact — the guests uncomfortably sharing the railcar bench as they got coated little by little with snow, or the *Whilforber Whirlwind* itself, which was definitely not meant to carry so much weight and was squealing abnormally as it approached the platform.

It wasn't that the guests themselves were exceptionally heavy. The boot of the car was stuffed full of so much . . . so much *stuff* that the pile of it was actually taller than the smaller of the car's passengers. It had to have been packed in there by a master, because

Milo couldn't rightly see how it hadn't all spilled out and tumbled straight down to the bottom of the steep incline. There were suitcases, briefcases, garment bags, something that looked like a telescope case . . .

Guests number three and four were scrambling to get out of the car before it had even come to a stop. They made Milo think right away of characters from a nursery rhyme, something out of Mother Goose or *Aunt Lucy's Counterpane Book: On a dark and rainy night, side by side, Mr. Up and Mr. Down had to share a ride.*

And much like Mr. Up and Mr. Down in the rhyme, these two looked like they'd be at each other's throats if they shared that ride even a minute longer.

The man Milo thought of as Mr. Down was short and dark-haired and looked like an angry schoolteacher. The other one, if Milo was honest about it, was probably too angular to really stand in properly for Mr. Up. Also, she was a woman. But she looked like an angry schoolteacher too, white-haired and haughty. Why did everyone look like schoolteachers while he was supposed to be on vacation?

Nonetheless, Milo raised a hand in greeting, regarding the two newcomers cautiously as they disembarked. They both looked about ready to snap. "Welcome to—"

Mr. Down pulled something from the car and the entire mass came undone. Baggage—most of it expensive-looking mauve brocade luggage—spilled down, bouncing across the platform and clunking onto the steel rails.

Mrs. Up, who had been about to come around to where Milo

stood, froze for a second. Her face went still; then it got red, then purple, then a shade something between gray and blue. Then she started yelling. Mr. Down straightened to his full diminutive height, his face already turning pink, and then he started yelling too. They continued bawling at each other, louder and louder, standing amid the ruins of the luggage tower. Milo wasn't even sure they were shouting in English. If they were, they didn't seem to be bothering to use real words.

"Excuse me," he said tentatively. The shouting went on as if he weren't there. "Excuse me," Milo said again, louder. Then, "EXCUSE ME!"

Without a pause, the two of them whirled on Milo and directed their yelling at him. He tried to listen. Then he tried to interrupt. Finally, he did what his mother did whenever Milo went on what she called "a tear" and couldn't be calmed down. He clasped his hands behind his back, made a face as if he was paying really close attention to whatever incomprehensible things these two were saying, and waited.

Amazingly, it worked. Little by little, Mr. Down and Mrs. Up ran out of steam. As the torrent of angry words subsided, Milo realized the whole argument seemed to be a matter of whose luggage had been taking up too much space in the boot. At last, they stood there silently on either side of the railcar, he with his arms folded across his chest and she with her hands balled into fists at her sides.

Milo smiled a big, welcoming smile and pointed to the path that led up to the inn. "Right this way," he said, as if he hadn't just had to wait out a storm of screeching. "Come right on up."

They each shot one last crabby look at the other; then Mrs. Up gave a noise like a growl and turned to the mess of gear strewn across the pavilion floor. She picked out an armful of mauve carry-on bags and strung them across her shoulders until she had mostly disappeared under them. "Young man, could I trouble you to bring my suitcase and my garment bag?"

Milo nodded and she made a face that was pretty close to a smile, then stamped out of the shelter, wincing with each step as her patent-leather heels sank into the snow.

Mr. Down waited with his arms still folded until she was out of earshot, then gave a giant, displeased sigh. "I was under the impression that this would be a quiet sort of place at this time of year," he said, looking at Milo as if he, personally, were responsible for giving out wrong information.

Milo shrugged. "You and me both. I'm supposed to be on vacation. Inn's that way. Can I help you with those?"

"No, thank you, I'll manage." The short fellow gave another sigh and collected the rest of the gear piece by piece. Then, looking like a pack animal, he started down the path too.

Milo walked once around the pavilion to make sure there were no forgotten bags or cases hiding in corners or lying on the rails before following the two combatants toward the inn. He slung Mrs. Up's garment bag over his shoulder by its hook and grasped the handle of her rolling suitcase. Then, just at the edge of the woods where the path reached the lawn, he paused and listened. There was a sound behind him, coming from the wooded hill. But not from the railway. This was a hollow sound, not a mechanical one. Even muffled by the snow, it was familiar, though Milo couldn't quite believe he was hearing it.

Someone was coming up the stairs. And, from the pace of the footfalls, that someone was coming up fast, practically sprinting up the last dozen steps. Milo jogged back to the edge of the platform and peered down into the snow swirling through the trees.

By the uneven glow from the occasional lamppost and the twisted strings of fairy lights, he saw that a dark figure was, in fact, approaching. And that figure was not merely sprinting up the stairs; he or she was taking them two at a time. Which, apart from being a fairly dangerous thing to do on snow-slick steps, seemed as though it ought to be physically impossible. There were, after all, more than three hundred of them. It was an exhausting climb under the best of circumstances.

He waited for the person to slow down. It didn't happen. The newcomer jumped the last three steps to land at the top, looking fresh as a daisy. A snow-covered daisy in a black knit cap, carrying a truly gigantic backpack on its shoulders. And wearing pink lip gloss.

"Hey there!" she said, grinning at Milo with only a little flush on her cheeks. "Didn't mean to startle you. Looking for the Greenglass House, supposed to be somewhere hereabouts."

"Yeah." Milo stared down the incline, still trying to figure out how she wasn't red-faced and dying of exhaustion. "Yeah. Right this way. Er — I'm Milo. My folks run the inn."

"Clemence O. Candler," she replied, holding out a hand with gray-painted fingernails. "My friends call me Clem."

Inside the inn, chaos had taken over. Mr. Down and Mrs. Up were still yelling at each other, only now they were doing so in the middle of the living room, he gesturing angrily with a telescope case held as if it were a sword, she with an embroidered bag clutched to her chest like a shield, and both with their wet shoes dripping slush onto the rag rug. Mr. Vinge stood in the corner, holding his mug defensively in front of his chest. Georgie Moselle sat on the hearth with her elbows on her knees and her eyebrows drawn up high on her forehead. It seemed they couldn't possibly go up any higher, but when Clem Candler trailed inside after Milo, they did. *Yes,* Milo thought grouchily, *another one. Get used to it. If I have to, you have to.*

Mr. Pine was trying unsuccessfully to get in between the two shrieking newcomers, and Milo's mother was pacing at the bar between the dining room and the kitchen with the phone to her ear. Clem Candler hung up her coat and arranged her shoes next to Mr. Vinge's without taking her eyes off the yelling duo in the next room. She took off her cap and shook out a headful of short red hair. "Pretty lively crowd," she muttered.

Meanwhile, Mr. Pine had had enough. Milo saw it coming, and braced himself. His father could yell when he wanted to. "ALL RIGHT!" Mr. Pine bellowed. His voice ricocheted off every surface in the room. Somewhere in the dining room a glass fell from its shelf and shattered on the hardwood floor. "That's enough from both of you!"

Mr. Down and Mrs. Up fell grudgingly silent.

"That's better. Behave yourselves like adults or I may just discover we're all booked up," Mr. Pine continued, fixing them, one by one, with a severe glare. "Do I make myself clear?" He waited for a reluctant nod from each, then gestured toward the wooden stand in the foyer where the guest register lay open. "You first, madam. Your name?"

"Mrs. Eglantine Hereward."

"And yours, sir?"

"Dr. Wilbur Gowervine."

"And you, miss?"

"Clemence Candler."

"And how long is everyone planning to stay?" The three new guests hesitated. Just like the first two, none of them seemed to have made up his or her mind. Mr. Pine sighed. "No matter. Milo, you want to do the honors?"

"'Kay." Milo kicked off his boots, picked up Eglantine Hereward's suitcase and garment bag again, and led the way up the stairs. Clem followed silently but cheerily in her stocking feet. Mrs. Hereward gave a grandiose sniff and trailed after them. Wilbur Gowervine made a big production of collecting his gear, then he followed as well, the long telescope case bouncing off the banister with each step.

Milo paused on the second landing under the pale green window and he and Clem waited for the other two to catch up. "This is the first floor of guest rooms," he said when Mrs. Hereward and Dr. Gowervine reached them. "You can pick whichever you like, except Three E. That one's occupied. It's the one with the door closed."

The three guests looked at one another. Clem waved a hand and gave the other two a dazzling smile. "You go ahead."

Mrs. Hereward gave her a curt little nod and stalked down the hallway. While she was examining the open room at the far end, Dr. Gowervine carried his belongings into the nearest open room and dumped them on the floor. "I'll take this one," he called.

While the tall old lady made a big production of deciding between the two remaining rooms, Clem leaned over and spoke quietly. "Say, Milo, I don't suppose there are upstairs rooms that are available, are there?"

"Well . . . sure, lots. Why?"

He supposed it wasn't really any of his business, but Clem didn't seem bothered. "I need my exercise," she explained. "I get a little stir-crazy if I don't get it, and what with the snow, I can't imagine I'm going to be putting in any runs outside anytime soon. Would it be a pain in the neck for your mom and dad if I took one on another floor?"

"Not at all. In fact, I don't think there's anybody on five. Two flights up? Five W has a really cool window with painted glass, if you like that kind of thing."

"Perfect."

Down the hall, Mrs. Hereward peered out the door of 3N, next to Mr. Vinge's room. "Young man, could I have the rest of my things brought up?"

"Sure, ma'am." Milo turned back to Clem, but she had already disappeared up the staircase.

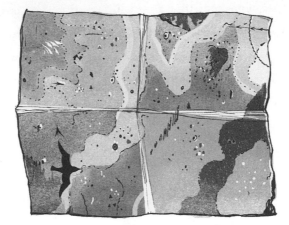

two

MEDDY

By the time Milo had squared away Mrs. Hereward's luggage, had checked in with Clem on the fifth floor, and had gotten himself a mug of hot chocolate from the saucepan on the stove and a few marshmallows to top it off, he was starting to feel out of control again.

It was late, and from throughout the inn came the sounds of strangers. The house's noises were different. Even the air smelled different. It should've smelled like winter and snow and fireplace and hot chocolate. Those aromas were still there, but they were buried now under the scents of Mrs. Hereward's wet wool coat, Georgie Moselle's broken bottle of perfume, and a faint whiff of tobacco from the pipe Dr. Gowervine had smoked out on the screened porch.

Milo slid onto one of the benches at the dining room table, where just a few hours ago he'd eaten a perfectly normal dinner before all the guests had started pouring in out of the snow. His mother muttered a goodbye into the phone she'd been glued to for the last twenty minutes, hung it up, and dropped onto the bench next to him. "How you doing, kiddo?"

He growled into his cup.

"Well, don't panic. That was Mrs. Caraway. She and Lizzie are coming back to help out. We're going to do our best to make sure you get your vacation."

"They are?" Mrs. Caraway was the inn's chef, and her daughter Lizzie, who owned a bakeshop, had come to help out once or twice before during especially busy times.

"When?"

"Tonight, if the roads are clear enough. But late. They're going to have to drive really slowly." She put an arm around his shoulder. "You want to stay up with me? I seem to recall owing you a brownie sundae."

Normally, Milo loved to sit up late with his folks in front of the fire. Sometimes they would read; sometimes they would play Scrabble or cards. Tonight, though . . . Milo peered over his mug into the living room. Mr. Vinge had gone back upstairs, Dr. Gowervine had done the same after his pipe, and Mrs. Hereward hadn't come down again at all, but Georgie Moselle and Clem Candler were both sitting there with hot drinks in green mugs. Blue-haired Georgie was curled up on the couch, her drink on the end table beside her elbow and a cigar box in her lap. She had a roll of black tape in one hand,

and she was wrapping it carefully around the edges of the box. Red-headed Clem sat on the rag rug, just barely within view from where Milo was: She had a roll of white tape, and she was wrapping up her ankles. Evidently, her climb up to the inn hadn't been quite as painless as it had looked.

Still, they were being quiet, and this might just be his last evening of peace. He could always go upstairs to the family's private space, but his parents would be down here taking care of the guests, and too much quiet and loneliness wouldn't make him feel any better. "I'll go get something to read. Be right back."

He was halfway up the first flight of stairs when he remembered that he hadn't returned Georgie's book, the one he'd taken accidentally from her room earlier that evening. He stopped, foot poised over the next step, and patted down his pockets. "Oh, no. What did I . . ."

There was really only one place he could have left it. He'd had it when he'd run out to answer the railcar bell. He didn't recall having it when he'd led the three new guests up to their rooms, or when he'd come back down to get Mrs. Hereward's luggage. Which meant it had to be outside. Probably in the pavilion.

Milo flung himself back down the stairs and into the foyer, where he grabbed his boots and ducked outside before anyone could ask him where he was going. He skidded across the porch, passing his father, who was busy stacking firewood under a tarp, and sprinted down the path and into the woods.

The fairy lights were still on along the roof and down the railing of the long staircase, but now they glowed under a half-inch glaze of snow. Milo found the paperback right away, wedged between the *Whilforber Whirlwind* and the edge of the wooden floor. He must have dropped it when the tower of luggage had come tumbling down.

He tugged the book free and tucked it in his back pocket, and he was just about to head back inside when he spotted something else on the steel tracks.

It looked like a blue leather wallet, only bigger. Milo climbed down onto the rails behind the car and picked it up.

And that's how he found the first map.

It was tucked into the left-hand pocket of the leather wallet, folded into quarters. The paper was old and green-tinged, the way the copper pots in the inn's kitchen were tinted green from verdigris —only Milo had never seen paper turn green like that. He unfolded it carefully with cold fingers. It was brittle and delicate and didn't look as if it could stand much more folding and unfolding, but he could tell it had once been thick and expensive. Milo held it up so that the light from the closest lamppost shone through, and he could just make out a watermark: it looked like a wrought-iron gate, but slightly warped and wrenched out of its original shape.

It was then, with the page lit up from behind, that Milo realized what he was looking at. He turned and hopped across the rails to the shed that housed the big winch, turned on the overhead light, and held the paper up again to get a better look.

It's a funny thing about maps: you don't have to know what

they're supposed to represent to know you're looking at one. A map is pretty much unmistakable. Draw one on a napkin, sketch one into the mud with the toe of your shoe, line up the flakes of your cereal with your spoon to make one in your breakfast bowl; maps come in all kinds, but they all still manage to look like maps. And the brittle, watermarked paper Milo was holding was definitely a map, even if it didn't look like any map he'd ever seen. At least, not at first.

There were no lines for streets, no boxes for houses, nothing to mark the features of a city or a town or even a lonely road winding through the countryside. Instead, there were shapeless washes of blue layered one on top of the other, so that in some places the paper was merely blue-tinged and in others the color deepened by degrees to china blue and ultramarine and royal and navy. Here and there, centered in the bands of shading, were groups of green ink dots, small clusters of two and three where the blue was lightest and larger clusters of nine or ten or more where it was darkest. In one corner was a group of nearly white curls, like slightly twisted triangles gathered together. In another corner was the shape of a bird with an arrow pointing away from one outstretched wing.

Milo knew a thing or two about maps. This, of course, came from twelve years of growing up around smugglers and sailors. And as he stared at the paper in his hands, he realized it reminded him of a very specific sort of map, one that he saw fairly often. It looked like a nautical chart, the kind that ships' navigators use.

Yes, a nautical chart. That was exactly what it was, with the shadings of blue and the green dots meant to represent the different depths of the waterway. The bird shape must be the compass rose, which would mean the wing with the arrow was supposed to be pointing north.

He turned the page so that the arrow pointed up, but that didn't make the waterway any more familiar. He turned it again and again, trying to find the orientation that would transform it into something recognizable: the Skidwrack River, or the Magothy Bay it emptied into, or one of the Skidwrack's inland tributaries. But no matter which way he held the map, it didn't look like any river or bay Milo knew of.

Then, outside in the pavilion, he heard a voice muttering curses. He put his eye to the crack between the door and its frame. A person wrapped in a heavy coat crossed Milo's view, head hunched low into the collar. A short, sharp breeze kicked up, swirling snow around the figure. It wasn't his mother or father, but between the snow and the twinkling lights, he couldn't quite work out which of the guests it was.

The person strode out of view and back in again, making a circuit of the pavilion, then hopped down onto the tracks inside it. Milo heard footsteps crunching over the stones between the steel rails.

He or she had to be looking for the leather wallet Milo had just found. The logical thing to do would be to step out and announce that he'd found it. It was, after all, the property of one of the guests, and at some point, he was going to have to give it back. Still, when the dark shadow swung itself back up off the tracks, something made

Milo edge deeper into the shed and tuck himself as far behind the winch as he could.

He held his breath and waited. Long minutes passed without any sound from outside. At last, Milo tiptoed back over to the door and put his eye up to the crack again. The unknown person was gone.

As quietly as he could, he refolded the map and tucked it into the leather wallet. He slipped it into his other back pocket, making certain it was hidden by his coat. Then, when he was sure, absolutely sure, that he was alone in the pavilion again, he crept out of the shed. Whoever it had been, he or she had left footprints, but already the swirling snow was busy erasing them.

Inside, the inn was basically just as he'd left it: his mom was at the dining room table; in the living room, Georgie Moselle was on the couch with her cigar box and Clem Candler sat on the rag rug, stretching her taped-up legs.

Mrs. Pine looked up from her book. "Milo, where'd you go?"

Milo yanked off his hat and looked around as he unwound his scarf, sure he must be missing someone. "Someone went outside after me. Who was it?"

Now Georgie and Clem looked up. "Nobody else came through this room," Georgie said. "We didn't see anybody." She looked at Clem. "Right? Or was I just not paying attention?"

"I didn't notice anyone leave. Not this way, anyhow." The red-headed girl stood and stretched. "Well, that's it for me, folks. See you in the morning." Then, silently, she ran up the stairs two at a time.

"What about Dad?" Milo asked, even though he was certain

that whoever he'd seen, it hadn't been his father. "He was outside, right?"

"He came in right after you went out. He's upstairs now." Mrs. Pine frowned. "What's wrong?"

Milo opened his mouth, then shut it again. "Nothing," he said at last, taking off his coat and boots and sliding onto the bench across from his mother. "Somebody was walking outside, that's all. Thought they must've come in this way."

"Good grief." Milo's mother slid off the bench and headed toward the foyer to put on her own cold-weather gear. "Guess I'd better make sure nobody's gonna freeze out there."

"Nobody's gonna freeze," Milo protested. "It's not like you can miss the house." But the door was already swinging shut behind Mrs. Pine, leaving Milo alone with Georgie Moselle.

For a few minutes, they ignored each other. Georgie continued messing around with her cigar box and her black tape, and Milo sipped his hot chocolate, acutely aware of the paperback tucked in his back pocket.

When he'd emptied his mug, he finally spoke up. "Hey — Miss Moselle?" he asked awkwardly. "Can I get you anything? More hot chocolate?"

"No, thanks," Georgie replied. "Don't worry about me. And you can call me Georgie, if you want."

Milo paused on his way to the kitchen and looked at the box she was occupied with. "What is that, by the way?"

She held it up. "Pinhole camera."

A camera? Made out of a cigar box? That was enough to distract him from both the empty mug in his hand and the book in his pocket. "What's a pinhole camera?"

"You can make a camera out of just about anything," Georgie said as she handed the box to him. "As long as there's an opening for light and a surface to capture it and turn it into an image. Do you know anything about photography?"

"Nope." Milo turned it over in his hands. Georgie had taped up all the edges, but there was a hole cut into the front of it. He tried to look inside, but all he could see was darkness.

"There's nothing to see right now," Georgie told him. "When I'm sure I've sealed up all the light leaks, I'll put photo paper in there. That hole will be the aperture." She took the box back and smiled at it. "I've always wanted to make one. I've just never tried before. Of course, this one isn't finished yet, but I think . . . yes . . . I think it'll work. It needs a name, though."

Milo laughed. "A name? For a camera?"

"Sure. All the coolest ones have great names. Hasselblad, Rollei, Voigtländer, Leica . . ." She held up the box between them as if her palm were a pedestal and declared, "I shall call it the *Lansdegown.*" She gave Milo a sharp, mock-accusing look. "Unless you think it doesn't *deserve* a name. Unless, in your vast cigar-box-camera wisdom, you think it's not *good enough.*"

"No, no, it does, it does." He forced himself to look solemnly at the box. "Lansdegown it is. What's it mean, though?"

"Lansdegown?" Georgie tilted her head. "Don't you know?"

He thought hard. "Nope."

"I bet you do," she said with a little smile. "I bet you've just forgotten. See if you can remember what *lansdegown* means, and then you can tell me if you think it's the right name for my camera."

Milo reached into his pocket and held out the paperback. Surely she wouldn't be angry. She would understand it had only been a mistake. "I took this when we were cleaning up — I didn't realize I had it in my hand. I meant to bring it back to you earlier," he said, "but I forgot. I'm awfully sorry."

"Aha! I thought I'd forgotten to pack it." Georgie smiled. "No problem. You ever read it?"

How odd. All that running around with this book, and he hadn't even noticed what it was called. The cover was plain, just heavy red paper with the title stamped on it in gray letters. "*The Raconteur's Commonplace Book,*" Milo read, pronouncing the unfamiliar word carefully. "I don't think so. What's a raconteur?"

"It's an old-fashioned word for a storyteller. This is a collection of folklore from hereabouts. You might know some of the stories." Georgie took the book and flipped through it, then handed it back open to the second chapter. "Know this one?"

"'The Game of Maps.'" Milo shook his head again. "I don't think so."

He held it out to her, but the blue-haired girl just waved her hand. "Read a few. See what you think. My feelings won't be hurt if you decide you aren't into it." She smiled again. "But maybe you wound up with it for a reason."

"Like what?"

She shrugged. "Don't know. Read it, then you tell me. I think you'll at least like the way it starts."

Milo looked down at the story Georgie had picked out and skimmed the first line. *There was a city that could not be mapped, and inside it a house that could not be drawn.*

Before he realized it, he'd read the whole page. He looked up to find Georgie Moselle grinning at him. "Good stuff, right?"

"Maybe." He set the book aside just long enough to go into the kitchen and refill his cup of hot chocolate. Then he hunkered down in one of his favorite places to go when there were guests in the house: a high-backed loveseat facing one of the huge bow windows that overlooked the grounds beyond the front porch. When he sat there, the back of the seat made a sort of wall that separated him from whatever was going on in the rooms behind him and provided just a little bit of privacy. Curled into one corner, he started reading, this time from the beginning of the book.

The rain had not stopped for a week, and the roads that led to the inn were little better than rivers of muck. This, at least, is what Captain Frost said when he tramped indoors, coated in the yellow mud peculiar to that part of the city and hollering for his breakfast. The rest of the guests sighed. Perhaps today, they had thought. Perhaps today, their unnatural captivity would end. But the bellowing man calling for eggs and burnt toast meant that, for another day at least, fifteen people would remain prisoners of the river Skidwrack, and the new rivers that had once been roads, and the rain.

No wonder Georgie had thought he might like it. Substitute *snow* for *rain* and subtract a few people and the author might've been writing about Greenglass House. In the book, however, one of the guests, a man named Phin, suggested that they pass the time by telling stories.

"In more civilized places, when travelers find themselves sharing a fire and a bottle of wine, they sometimes choose to share something of themselves, too," Phin told them. "And then, wonder of wonders — no strangers remain. Only companions, sharing a hearth and a bottle."

The wind and rain rattled the windowpanes as the folks gathered in the parlor looked from one to the next: the young girl in her embroidered silk stole; the twin gentlemen with the tattooed faces; the gaunt woman with her nervous gloved hands constantly moving; the other woman, gaunter still and hidden beneath two layers of voluminous shawls, whose red-brown skin showed in small flashes when her wraps did not quite move along with her.

"If you will listen," Phin said, swirling his glass, "I will tell the first tale. Then perhaps, if you find it worth the trade, you will give me one of yours. Listen."

The guests in the book agreed, of course, and in the next chapter Phin told the story of the Game of Maps. *There was a city that could not be mapped, and inside it a house that could not be drawn.*

Three stories later, the door flew open and a snow-covered Mrs. Pine tramped in, followed by more snow-people: Mrs. Caraway and her daughter Lizzie. Milo hunkered deeper into the loveseat and pretended to be so absorbed in his reading that he didn't notice them as they piled brown paper bags full of groceries on the dining room table and started peeling off coats and boots. He glanced at a little clock on the side table next to the loveseat: it was nearly midnight.

The couch where Georgie Moselle had been sitting was empty. Sometime in the past hour and a half, while Milo had been reading about the Unmappable House and the Maker of Reliquaries, she had disappeared. Milo had been so absorbed in the stories he hadn't heard her going up to bed or his mother coming in from the cold and going back outside again.

"Milo!"

It would, he thought sadly, probably be the last time in a while that he'd be able to read in peace like that.

He set the book down, sighed, and levered himself up out of his seat. "Yes, Mom?"

"Merry almost, kiddo." Mrs. Caraway, sock-footed, paused in the act of gathering up the bags again to give Milo a quick wave, then headed for the kitchen. Lizzie, who was twentyish, collected the rest of the groceries and followed her mother, giving Milo a smile and nod.

Mrs. Pine jogged into the kitchen after Mrs. Caraway. "Odette, I'll put that stuff away. You guys get some rest. Ben should have your rooms ready for you. Milo, can you take care of their suitcases?"

"Sure," he called after her. Then, before he could get up, he realized he was being watched.

Another girl, one about Milo's own age whom he had never seen before, was peering curiously at him over the back of the loveseat. This had to be Lizzie's younger sister, Meddy. Milo had heard plenty about Meddy but had never met her. "Hi," he said quietly, trying to tamp down his annoyance at being looked at so closely while he was in one of his special places. "You must be Meddy. I'm Milo."

Meddy Caraway looked as though she was just about as happy with this arrangement as Milo was. "Hello." She yanked off her knitted cap, and static electricity sent her short reddish-blond hair shooting out like a spiky halo around her red face.

Yay, vacation.

"So you're adopted, then?"

Arms full of suitcases, Milo paused on the second-floor landing and turned to stare at Meddy. "Excuse me?"

She looked at him curiously. "I heard you were."

He snorted, which he hoped made it sound like he thought this was just a stupid question, but his face was already going red. She'd *heard* he was? Of course, all you had to do was look at Milo and his parents and you could make a pretty good guess that he wasn't their biological kid. But Meddy was implying that someone had specifically *told* her he was adopted. That meant Mrs. Caraway and Lizzie had been talking about his adoption. It felt like a betrayal. The idea that people, people he liked and trusted, were discussing his family, his past, behind his back—

"Well?" Meddy peered at him as if what she was asking was just —was just *no big deal.* Which was *not* the case.

"Your room's this way." Milo spent the rest of the walk trying to decide how to answer if Meddy didn't get the hint.

There were two special guest rooms on the second floor that were only used for visiting friends and family. Milo opened the east-facing guest room, the one with the twin beds, and set Lizzie's bag down at the foot of the bed she usually took. "Did you bring a suitcase?"

Meddy gave him a long look, then shook her head. "Just threw my stuff in with hers."

"Okay, then." He waved his arm weakly in a vague gesture of welcome and left Meddy to make herself at home while he dropped off Mrs. Caraway's suitcase across the hall.

When he emerged, he found Meddy standing in the doorway of her room with folded arms. "You didn't answer me."

"Yes, I'm adopted," Milo said, exasperated. "It's none of your business."

She rolled her eyes. "Don't tell me it's a secret. It's pretty obvious. You don't look anything like your parents."

"I know exactly what I look like and what I *don't* look like!" he retorted. "It's personal."

Meddy shrugged, then turned and unzipped Lizzie's bag. "Where are you from?" she asked, peering inside.

"I'm from *here,*" Milo said evenly. "I've lived in Nagspeake my whole life. I was adopted when I was a baby."

"Yeah, but before that. Before you were adopted."

Honestly. It was as if he hadn't just told her this was personal. "I was adopted here," he said coldly, "from an agency here in town." He didn't mention having been a foundling. That was *really* none of her business.

"Yeah, but aren't you Chi—"

"*Yes, I am,*" he hissed. "And I said, it's *personal!*"

Milo turned and left her staring after him as he stalked back down the stairs to the loveseat by the window, where he'd left Georgie's book. He sank as far back into the cushions as he could, studiously ignored the adults in the kitchen, and tried to get back into the story.

A few minutes later, Mrs. Pine squatted down next to him. "Everything okay?"

"Fine."

"We thought we might have heard—"

"Everything's fine."

She nodded slowly. "What are you reading?"

Milo held it out so that she could read the title. "Georgie, the one with the blue hair, lent it to me. It's folktales about Nagspeake."

"I remember reading that book as a kid," Mrs. Pine said. "I remember liking it a lot."

"Yeah, it's pretty good."

"Are you sure you don't want to talk about anything?"

Milo stared at a paragraph he'd reread about three times. "Positive. I'm just going to stay up and finish this story."

His mother nodded and squeezed his hand once before straightening and turning back to the kitchen. Milo shifted, and in turn he felt the leather wallet shift in his pocket. "Mom?"

"Yep?"

"You didn't see anybody out for a walk when you went out again? The person I saw? Because nobody came in while you were gone."

She shook her head. "Not a single, solitary soul. Whoever it was, we probably just weren't paying attention when he or she came back."

———— ❄ ————

"If you beat the Devil," the tattooed twin called Negret began over the torrential rain beating upon the windows of the inn in the story, *"you can win your heart's desire. Everyone knows that, and some foolish folks probably think they could do it, too. But the Devil is a master gambler, and he makes his living off that sort of fool. It takes arrogance to dream of challenging him, but arrogance rarely helps anyone win; and the Devil, who is not usually arrogant, almost never loses.*

"Still, it's happened, though it's a rare and peculiar thing when it does. This is the tale of one of those occurrences, when the Devil got the worse of a deal.

"On the road between two remote towns, the Devil was walking alone at twilight when he came to a crossing of ways. And there, stopped under the finger post, was a scavenger's wagon. As the Devil approached, it occurred to him that this scavenger was a bit on the small side. Then, as the Devil's shadow fell across the ground before the scavenger and announced his diabolic presence, the small figure turned, and the Devil noticed two things. First, the scavenger had eyes the silver-gray of half-dollars or the full moon on the right kind of night. Second, the scavenger was small because it was a child — and not only a child, but also a girl."

Milo stayed in the living room reading until almost two, which was a truly unthinkable time to be allowed to be up. The fire had burned down to embers, the hot chocolate was cold, and outside the front windows the world was all shadowy snow and thick, deep night. *The Raconteur's Commonplace Book* sat open on his knee. The house, with its noises thrown off by all the strangers stashed here and there on the floors above, was just unfamiliar enough and the story he was stuck on was just creepy enough that Milo had about decided it was time to call it a night.

He shook himself awake for the fourth time and tried to make the words swimming on the page resolve themselves into sentences and paragraphs. It didn't work. He stretched and yawned — and then he spotted the dark blotch out in the snow. A darker shadow, a person-sized shadow.

The wind came pouring across the lawn and into the trees carrying a swirling cloud of white. When it cleared, there was no one there.

"Did you *sleep* down here?"

He came awake to find Meddy Caraway standing between the loveseat and the still-dark window with an incredulous look on her face. Milo stifled a yelp of surprise and tried to get up. The leg that had been folded under him all night was numb and he fell forward, straight out of the seat onto the floor.

He turned his head to regard the pink-fluffy-sock-encased toe of Meddy's left foot, and blew out a mouthful of air. He managed to shift the book, which had fallen from his knee and now lay under his cheek, just far enough to speak without chewing on paper. "What time is it?" His voice came out like a croak.

Meddy extended her left hand so that her wrist and the giant watch strapped to it popped out from under her sleeve. "Six. What are you doing down here?"

"What are *you* doing down here?" Milo retorted.

She turned and looked over her shoulder, frowning. "I heard a weird noise."

Milo followed her glance, then remembered the shadow he'd spotted outside before dozing off. He hauled himself to his feet and stared out the window, but there was nothing to see except the still-falling snow. "What did you hear?" he asked.

"If it was something I *recognized*," she said patiently, "I wouldn't have called it *weird*. But I can tell you this: it was inside the inn. Not out there."

"The house makes noises. It's old. Used to wake me up at night too." Milo rubbed his wrists, which were aching a bit from his fall, and shot Meddy a look over his shoulder. "When I was little."

Her eyebrows lowered. "Did it." She turned on her heel, heading toward the staircase. Then she paused, bent, and picked up something from the floor near his feet. Milo clapped a palm awkwardly to his back pocket. The blue leather wallet was not there, of course, because it was in Meddy's hand.

"Wait—" But she took out the folded map. "Careful, that thing's fragile," Milo protested as she opened it. He could almost hear the paper cracking.

"What's this?"

"Give it to me." Milo held out his hand, wiggling his fingers.

Meddy ignored him. "In a minute. What is it?" Milo wiggled his fingers more insistently. She waved him off, turned the page upside down, and frowned at it. "Oh. I see. A navigational chart."

Annoyed and mildly surprised that she'd identified the chart so quickly for what it was, Milo folded his arms. "Yeah. The dots are depths, probably, and the gull is the compass rose."

"I can see that. But it's not a gull, it's an albatross." She touched the bird almost reverently with one finger.

He didn't much like being told he was wrong, but Milo wasn't positive he knew exactly what an albatross looked like, so he decided not to argue.

She clearly wasn't going to give the chart back until she was ready, and he wasn't about to rip the thing by grabbing for it. "Can you be careful, please? It's old, if you hadn't noticed. Don't tear it."

"I'm not going to tear it," she mumbled. "This is really nifty. What's it a chart of? I mean, where? Doesn't look like the Skidwrack or the Magothy."

"I didn't think so either. I don't know what waterway it's for," Milo admitted reluctantly. "I sort of found it."

"What do you mean, sort of?"

"I think one of the guests dropped it. Just give it back." Exasperated, he reached for it again. Meddy took another long look at the page, then folded it up carefully and handed it over.

"Aren't you curious?" she asked. "Are you going to try and find out more about it?"

What he really needed to do, if he was honest with himself, was find out whose it was and just return the thing. Still . . . "How?"

It came out a little bit like a challenge, but Meddy didn't seem to be bothered by his tone. She tilted her head and peered off into space for a moment, then turned slowly, gazing around the empty rooms that made up the first floor: living room, foyer, kitchen, dining room. She considered the closed door to the screened porch at the other end of the living room, and she glanced at the wide staircase. Then she looked back at Milo, smiling an odd kind of half smile. "A campaign."

"A — a *what?*"

"Just listen. We're stuck here, right?"

"We — *I live here!*"

She gave him a sharp look. "You're telling me you're *happy* about this? Is this how you wanted to spend your winter vacation? Snowed in with a bunch of strangers underfoot?"

"Well, no, but —"

"Okay, well, I don't know about you, but if I'm going to be stuck here, I'm going to find something to do. I say we go in search of whatever this chart leads to."

Milo felt his temperature rising. It was one thing to be stuck with strangers and quite another to be stuck with Meddy. And for her to come barging in and telling him what to do — and with something *he'd* found — was completely not fair. "Who said *we* were going to do anything?" he grumbled.

She folded her arms. "What's your problem?"

"My problem is that you're right, I didn't want to spend my vacation this way, and that includes with *you!*"

"Right, I know what your problem with *me* is," Meddy said

patiently, "but what's your problem with my *idea?* I mean, we're here now. Might as well do something fun."

Aggravatingly, there didn't seem to be any good argument against that. Milo crossed his arms too. "Well, how, then? How do you suggest we begin? *If* I agree?"

Meddy nodded at the paper in his hand. "Well, for starters, before everyone comes down, why don't you tell me what you know about it? And then we should probably come up with a way of talking about it without everyone knowing what we're up to."

"Why?"

"Because the easiest thing to do would be just to ask around until we found out who the chart belongs to."

"Obviously."

"Yeah, obviously, except you haven't done that yet. How come?"

Milo hesitated, thinking of the person who had been out in the pavilion just after he'd found the chart, and how he'd instinctively hidden rather than given it back. "I don't know."

Meddy grinned. "I don't either, but I think it's interesting."

Milo opened his mouth, then shut it again. There was really no reason not to give Meddy's game a try. And he *was* curious. "All right."

They sat down side by side on the loveseat, and Milo told her how he'd found the chart, which led to him explaining how he'd wound up with Georgie Moselle's book, which led to Meddy demanding to know everything he could tell her about every guest in the house.

The sound of feet on the stairs made him pause. Meddy made *shut up* gestures, and Milo shot her a scowl in return and mouthed *I know.* "They're coming down from our floor," he added quietly. "It's not one of the guests, or we'd have heard the stairs way before." It was true. The sound of the fourth-floor flight in particular was unmistakable.

Sure enough, the person who appeared, feet first, was Mrs. Caraway, come down to start the first pot of coffee. She blinked blearily at Milo and Meddy. "You're up early. Want some hot chocolate?"

"Not me, Mrs. Caraway. I think I'm going back to bed for a while." He collected the chart in its leather wallet, and Georgie's book, and hauled himself up the stairs.

Milo's room was on the second floor. In addition to his room, his parents' room, and the two private guest rooms where the Caraways stayed, there was also a living room, a kitchen, and a dining room, all much smaller than the ones downstairs, so that Milo and his family could have privacy when they wanted it. He padded through to the far end of the living room and past the biggest of the house's stained-glass windows, a huge floor-to-ceiling panel in copper, wine, chestnut, verdigris, and navy. He continued down a very short hall to a blue door at the end of it. A big, round brass bell tied to his doorknob with a wide plaid ribbon gave a welcoming jingle as Milo turned the knob to enter and another as he closed the door behind him. He reached for a switch and the lights came on: a brass anchor lantern that hung beside the door that had once belonged to the ship his grandfather had served on, and a string of onion-shaped red silk lanterns embroidered with Chinese characters and hung with gold tassels that crossed the room diagonally from opposite corners of the ceiling.

He shut his eyes, stretched out the hand that held the book and the chart, and released them into thin air. Just as he knew they would, they landed squarely in the middle of his desk. He could tell by the quick, neat noise they made when they hit the leather blotter. Then, eyes still closed, he turned ninety degrees, took two steps to his right, tipped back on his heels, and let himself free-fall backwards. He landed, just as he always did, right in the middle of his bed.

Slowly, slowly, he felt himself relaxing. He swung up his feet and wriggled under his blanket — the knitted patchwork one his mother had made for him way back when she and Mr. Pine were still waiting to be matched with a baby — and in a few minutes he was asleep.

three

THE BLACKJACK

Milo's room had the best view in the whole house. It was a garret with a dormer window that looked out over the woods at a point where the slope down to the Skidwrack River was particularly steep, so on the right kind of day he could see all the way to the steely gray and blue water below. His window also had a fire escape, which was one of his favorite places to sit, particularly when the sun was going down behind the hill—although, strictly speaking, he wasn't allowed on it without supervision.

At the moment, however, it was morning, and there was no sky visible at all, just a thick gray overlay of cloud. It could've been any time of day at all. Milo, eyes still bleary with sleep, turned from the frosted window and reached for his alarm clock. Ten a.m.

The snow wasn't falling anymore, but from the thickness of the coating on the trees, it looked like it had to have been falling all night. It was the kind of sight that made Milo long for the ritual of warming up by the fire after an hour outside building something fortress-like and stocking it with an armory full of perfectly round, perfectly packed snowballs.

He changed his clothes, straightened the book and wallet so that they were neat on his desktop blotter, and left the room. He paused for a moment to tweak the bow that tied the jingle bell to his doorknob so that its loops were even, then headed down to the first floor.

In the dining room, breakfast was winding to a close — but Milo almost didn't notice. He was too busy thinking, *Boy, is it ever weird seeing them all in the same place.*

There was the nondescript Mr. Vinge swirling his fork in the last dregs of maple syrup on his plate. He was sitting at the near corner of the table with one ankle crossed over his knee, and this morning he was wearing yellow socks with blue polka dots about the same shade as Georgie Moselle's hair. There was Eglantine Hereward, watching with vague disapproval while Lizzie Caraway set a kettle on the stove to boil. Wilbur Gowervine sat at the end of the dining table, also eyeing Lizzie dubiously; evidently he and Mrs. Hereward had the same lack of trust in others when it came to the making of tea. In between glances at Lizzie, he examined the window that poured green tones across the surface of the table. Clem Candler, ankles still wrapped in tape, sat at one of the little breakfast tables by the dining room window, picking at a plate of pancakes and looking dreamily out into the snow. From where he stood at the bottom of the stairs, Milo could just see Georgie's blue head above the back of the loveseat by the window on the other side of the foyer, where Milo had spent the night snoozing. As he surveyed the scene, his father came stomping through the front door with an armful of firewood, awkwardly kicked his boots off, and headed into the living room.

"Morning," Milo mumbled to his mother, who was helping Mrs. Caraway start the dishes.

"There are pancakes in the oven," Mrs. Pine said. "Plenty for you to have seconds, too," she added as Milo's father came into the kitchen and stuck his hands under the faucet to wash up.

Milo piled up a plateful, sloshed maple syrup over it, and headed into the living room to have a little alone time before the day properly began.

Meddy had encamped herself in another of Milo's favorite places, the space behind the Christmas tree, where the corner of the room made a twinkly sort of cave. "Morning," he grumbled, not pleased to have another of his spaces overtaken, and sat on the hearth next to the tree.

"Morning. Ready to get started with our campaign?" Meddy asked, looking up from a pile of loose pages and a bigger pile of oversized hardcover books.

Milo stared in horror. The papers looked like homework, and despite their garishly illustrated covers, the books looked uncomfortably like textbooks. Warily, he chewed a mouthful of pancakes. "What's a campaign, exactly?"

"It's an adventure within a game world. Our game world is your house, and our adventure — our campaign — is going to be figuring out the mystery behind that chart."

"Okay . . . how?"

She beckoned Milo closer, and he clambered off the hearth to crawl down behind the tree beside her. "We're going to explore the house and investigate the guests," she explained, "and along the way we're going to look for clues. But first, you need a character."

"Why?"

She tilted her head. "It's part of the game. You make up a character and play as that person. Do you know anything about role-playing games?"

Milo frowned. "No. Like the kind with monsters and dungeons and dice with a million sides? That's what we're doing?"

"Yeah. But for a real game we'd need more people and a game master and all that stuff. We're kind of making up something of our own."

"Why do I need to pretend to be someone else, though?" Milo protested. "It seems a little . . . well, a little silly."

It also made him feel a little guilty. This seemed to be coming dangerously close to something he did in secret that he wasn't entirely proud of.

One of the problems with knowing nothing about the family you were born into was that you never really stopped wondering about it. At least, Milo didn't. He wondered who his birth parents were, where they lived, and what they did for work. He wondered if they were even still alive. He wondered how his life would be different if he had grown up with his birth family, how it would be different if he actually *looked* like his parents and people couldn't see immediately that he didn't belong. He wondered how *he* would be different —and sometimes when he did this, he imagined himself to be very different indeed, which sort of felt like imagining a character version of himself.

And sometimes, wondering all this made him feel he was being unfair to his mom and dad: to Nora and Ben Pine, who were his mom and dad as truly as the parents who'd given him life.

But what Meddy was talking about ... this was for a game, so maybe ... maybe it wasn't something he needed to feel guilty about.

"It's not silly," Meddy said patiently, her face tinted first green, then blue from the blinking lights on the tree. "Because for starters, that's how the game works. Second, you can make the character anything you want. It's fun. You can be anything, almost. You can be anybody."

Meddy swirled one of the stacks of paper around on the hardwood floor with her index finger so it faced him. It looked suspiciously like a move she'd spent time practicing. "These are your character sheets." She set a pen on top. "This is how we figure out who you are."

Who you are. Milo shifted uncomfortably and speared another bite of pancake from the plate balanced on his knees. "Who my character is, you mean," he muttered.

She shrugged. "In the game, you *are* your character."

Once again, Milo thought a little guiltily of all the times he'd secretly daydreamed about his biological family, or (extra secretly) other families he might have been matched with. Who he really was, who he might have been. But this was different, he reminded himself. This was a *game*.

"Okay." He set his food aside and picked up the pen. "Show me how it works."

"Well, tell me where you want to start. Actually —" Meddy held up a finger. She opened a battered and dusty old notebook to a clean page of graph paper. "Let's make this easier. A good adventuring party ought to have at least one each of four kinds of characters: a captain — somebody who has leadership and strategic capabilities; a warder — that's your big, hit-a-bunch-of-people-at-once offensive fighter, usually a wizard or magic-using type; a warrior — that's like your *best* fighter; and a blackjack, which is your trickster type. Our campaign will be different because it's just the two of us, but just off the top of your head, which of those sounds most interesting?"

"I . . ." Well, none of them sounded like Milo, if he was honest. All of those roles sounded like jobs for people who had things under control. "Probably the captain," Milo said finally. "Since I'm the oldest." Might as well aim high. "I am older than you, aren't I?"

Meddy leaned on her elbow, chin in her palm, and looked coolly at him over her knuckles. "Don't be an idiot. You don't get to be the leader just because you're older. Not even in the real world do you get to be in charge just because you got born first."

Milo opened his mouth to argue, but Meddy shook her head. "You're looking at this all wrong, you know. First of all, you *aren't* the oldest. Not in the game, I mean, not necessarily. I could decide I want to play a centuries-old dwarf or an immortal sage or something—"

"That's ridiculous," Milo protested.

"No, it's not!" she exclaimed. "Not in the game, at least. That's the whole *point*. In the game, you can be whatever you want. Look at it that way. I mean, there are rules about it, but—Milo, what do you *want* to be?"

What do you want to be?

Well, for starters, Milo thought, it would be nice to blend in for once, and not to have people stare because he looked out of place. And it would be nice not to feel so out of control whenever unexpected things happened. It would be cool to be more athletic, too.

"That's a good start." Meddy's voice jolted him to attention. She was nodding thoughtfully and jotting things in her notebook. With horror, Milo realized he'd been speaking out loud. *Blend In, Control In Unexpected Situations*, and *Athletic* were written in a column down one side of the page. Now she was drawing arrows and making notes in the margins.

"Blending in sounds like some class of blackjack, somebody who can disappear. Maybe a graffitist, or a kind of thief, like an escaladeur. Escaladeurs are masters at getting over walls and through fortifications and sneaking around things like castles and fortresses. They're reconnaissance experts, one of the types of characters you send to gather information." She jotted something at the pointy end of the first arrow. "The second part does sound like a captain thing. Grace under fire, right? I don't see you as a warlord or a whip, so maybe a schema or a fangshi . . . or a sortileger, even. A sortileger's a warder, but they have this whole divining thing based on deriving meaning out of randomness."

Milo blinked. "I have no idea what that even means."

She was scrawling in earnest now, drawing arrows all over the place. "Doesn't matter. I'll explain if we get to that point. Now let's think about abilities. If our campaign is this house, what skills would be particularly useful, do you think? Lockpicking, maybe?"

"Are we going to be breaking into rooms?" Milo asked warily. The guest room doors were the only ones that were likely to be locked, and his parents would kill him if he went into an occupied room just to poke around.

"Game world, Milo, not real world."

"Oh. Right. Then yes, probably. And . . . well, moving around quietly, for sure. It's a noisy house, especially when there are people in it."

"Good. This is all blackjack stuff, perfect for an escaladeur. I think we're getting closer to figuring you out."

"Hang on." Milo frowned at the page she was rapidly covering with notes. "What about you? Don't we need to figure out your character, too?"

She shook her head. "I'll build mine to go with yours. Whatever our adventuring party needs to round it out."

"That doesn't seem like much fun for you."

"Making up the character is only part of it. We'll be a team. My fun will be building the other half of that team. Now, back to you." She glanced up with a grin. "What else?"

Milo found himself thinking of one of the stories he'd read the night before, the one called "The Game of Maps." In it, a kid who took a bet to spend the night in a supposedly haunted house got lost inside it. Each time he tried to make himself a map of the rooms he'd been through so he could find his way out again, he failed — that, or (as the story seemed to imply) the house kept shifting around him. Only when he figured out how to listen to the house as it moved was he able to make sense of his surroundings.

"I want to be able to listen to the house," Milo said slowly.

Meddy pursed her lips. "I don't get it."

"Well, if we were in a — a forest or something, I could listen to the woods and the trees and the wind and figure things out. Like if we were being followed, or if there was a river, or whether someone built a fire somewhere . . . that kind of thing."

"Tracker stuff?"

"Right. Well, what would you call someone who had those kinds of skills, but inside buildings?"

"Ooooh." Now she sounded excited. She started flipping through the pages of one of the big books. "That could be a roamer — roamers have all kinds of weird knowledge gained from centuries of wandering through different places. As a roamer, you could understand how to listen to a house and read it because you've spent years and years learning how to do it in the course of your travels. Or you could be a savant. Like houses make sense to you because they just always have."

"Hey, what's all this?"

Meddy dropped her pencil as Georgie Moselle sat on the corner of the hearth and reached between them to pick up Meddy's notebook. Milo glanced at Meddy, not sure whether to be embarrassed. "It's for a game," he said awkwardly.

"Looks like a good list of skills for a thief," Georgie said in a voice that was just a bit too loud and just a bit too casual to sound natural to Milo's ears.

The room went so silent that the sounds of his mother and Mrs. Caraway doing dishes in the kitchen suddenly seemed ridiculously loud. Milo peered out from behind the tree and reddened. While he and Meddy had been making notes, the guests had begun to migrate into the living room, and now everyone in view was staring at him.

If Georgie noticed, she ignored them. "Blending in. Lockpicking. Athletic. Sounds like just what you'd need if you were some sort of cat burglar."

Meddy poked Milo. "Control in unexpected situations," she hissed. "Remember."

It was hard to feel in control when that many people were looking at you. "Actually," Milo said, his voice squeaking just a little, "it's for a kind of blackjack called an . . ."

"Escaladeur," Meddy supplied.

"An escaladeur. A reconnaissance guy."

Milo's father leaned past Georgie to add a couple of logs to the reluctant fire. "Since when do you play Odd Trails?" he asked with an eyebrow raised.

"What's Odd Trails?" Milo asked.

"It's the game all this stuff comes from," came Meddy's hissed answer from Milo's other side.

"I mean, I — I don't know," Milo stammered. "Some kids at school play it."

"Well, what do you know?" Mr. Pine said, pleased. "I used to play that as a kid."

"Really?"

"Sure! I used to be a tiercer-signaler. I was the guy who'd scout ahead and report back — kind of like an escaladeur, actually — but if things got tough, I was awesome with a sword. A tiercer usually carries a rapier, but it's too long a blade for a scout, so I used butterfly swords."

From the depths of the twinkling cave, Meddy made a quiet but definitely impressed humphing noise.

"Maybe we'll play sometime," Mr. Pine said, standing and dusting himself off. He ruffled Milo's hair with a hand that smelled like fireplace, then headed for the kitchen.

Meanwhile, the tension in the room had diminished. Milo glanced around and discovered that most of the guests had lost interest. Only Mr. Vinge was still flicking glances Milo's way from the chair opposite the tree.

Georgie handed the notebook back. "Neat. Sorry to interrupt."

As she got up, Clem Candler strolled over with a cup of coffee in her hand and crouched beside the hearth. "You know," she said cheerfully, "if you ever do want to make up a cat burglar, I can probably give you some pointers."

"You play too?" Milo asked, surprised.

"Nope." Clem grinned. "But I *am* a cat burglar." She winked at him. *Just kidding,* that wink said. When she straightened up again,

Milo saw her sneak a look over his head to Georgie Moselle. "Or you could ask Blue, there," she added. "Bet she has some thoughts too." Then she padded away, calling, "Is there more coffee?"

What was that all about?

"Boring." Meddy scooted back over next to Milo and fluttered her fingers at the note pages. "Let's get back to work. Let's talk ability scores. I'm going to suggest we rate you pretty high in dexterity, intelligence, and charisma. Those are probably going to serve you best."

Some time later, the two of them sat back, looking with satisfaction at the pages that were now covered with notes in both Meddy's scrawl and Milo's meticulous handwriting.

"Not bad," Meddy said. "In fact, this looks like a pretty cool character. What are you going to call him?"

"Call him?" Milo echoed. "Isn't he—isn't he sort of me?"

"Yes, but you should pick a name for the character too," she told him. "After all, it's a *character*. It's a different version of you. In the game, it helps to think of being different from the you that lives in the real world."

"But *our* game is *in* the real world."

"Yes, but . . ." Meddy sighed, exasperated. She tapped the page. "Look at all this stuff we wrote down. Be honest. When you read it, does it seem like *you?*"

"Of course not," Milo retorted. Hadn't that been the point?

"So give this person a name," she said patiently. "*Milo* doesn't think he has these qualities. But *this* person"—she tapped the page again—"*this* person has them. This person *needs* them. My character is going to need to rely on this person. I can't have him not come through because Milo's confused. So what's his name?"

Milo dropped his head into his hands and stared at the notes. She was right. Nothing on this page was like him. This was a character from a fairy tale, not from life.

He found himself thinking of names from *The Raconteur's Commonplace Book*. "Reever," he said, trying it out. "Or Negret." Those were the names of the tattooed twins trapped at the inn in the book. "Negret," he decided.

"Negret it is," Meddy said, writing the new name in the margin. She set down her pencil and stretched. "Well, that was a good morning's work." She tore the page out of her notebook along with several others and handed them to Milo. "I need you to do something for me. Make a floor plan of the house." She held out her pencil.

"The whole house?"

"Yes. A plan for each floor. Start with this one. We're going to need them."

She gathered the rest of the papers and the books into a neat pile, tucked them into the corner, clambered out from behind the tree, stretched again, and headed for the stairs.

Milo leaned out for a look at the clock on the mantelpiece. It was just before noon. He folded up his papers and stuck them in his pocket along with Meddy's pencil. "Negret," he said quietly, trying the name out. "Negret." It certainly sounded more like a blackjack than a twelve-year-old boy. Then he scrambled to his feet and rushed up the stairs in Meddy's wake. "Meddy?"

She popped out from behind the banister at the second-floor landing. "Yes?"

"What are we doing with this game, again?"

She gave him a disappointed look. "Trying to find out who lost that map, and what it's a map of. Obviously."

"Oh. Right." He scratched his head. All this talk about heroic, fantastic types, and he'd totally forgotten why they'd started the game to begin with.

"Milo."

"What?"

"You still have it, right?"

"The chart?"

"Chart, map, yes — Milo, do you still have it?"

"Of course I do," he retorted. Meddy held out her hand. "Well . . . I don't have it on me."

"Why on earth not? You just *left* it somewhere?" Meddy swooped down the stairs faster than he'd ever seen a kid move and glowered in his face. "Where?"

Milo shoved past her and stomped up to the second floor. He continued stomping until he reached his bedroom, Meddy close on his heels.

Then he stopped and stared at the door.

"What is it?" she asked, standing on her tiptoes to peer over his shoulder. "Is it open or something?"

"No, it's closed," Milo said slowly. "It's just like I left it."

Except that wasn't quite true. The plaid silk ribbon that tied the jingle bell to his door wasn't the same. The bow he had neatened when he'd left that morning was crumpled. Someone had turned the doorknob, and since Milo didn't make a habit of locking his door, that meant someone had probably been in his room.

The leather wallet and *The Raconteur's Commonplace Book* were still there on his desk, right where he'd left them, but once again, something was wrong. Milo had placed the red book on top, carefully lining up the book's bottom edge with a row of stitches on the wallet beneath it. The book's bottom edge was still parallel to the wallet's, but it no longer sat directly atop the row of stitches.

He moved the book aside, picked up the wallet, and flipped it open. The folded paper in the left-hand pocket was old and green-tinged, but Milo knew right away that it wasn't the same. He could feel Meddy watching him as he carefully eased out the page with two fingers and unfolded it.

It was blank. No washes of blue, no green dots, nothing.

"Somebody *stole* it?" Milo said, confused. A panicky feeling was coming up in his throat, but it wasn't the familiar anxiety he usually felt when things didn't happen the way he expected them to. This wasn't just some random surprise; this was legitimately *bad*. This made things different somehow.

"Well, I don't know if we can really assume it was stolen," Meddy said, reaching for the green page, which now dangled, forgotten, from his fingers. "If the person it belonged to took it, you'd sort of have to say they found the map and took it back."

Milo shook his head. "Somebody broke into my room," he said numbly. Because of course, that was what really mattered. In all his years of living at Greenglass House, in all the years of smugglers and what lots of people would call unsavory characters passing through, never had anyone invaded Milo's space. Never. Not once.

"Well, did you lock it?"

"It doesn't matter!" He stood with his shaking hands clenched in his pockets, stock-still except for his eyes, which darted to each nook and corner of his room, looking for anything else that might be disturbed. "I shouldn't have *had* to lock it! It's *my room!*"

"Okay, okay," Meddy said more gently.

Someone had been in his room. Milo's parents might have come in for some reason, or Mrs. Caraway, but given how much they were scrambling to stay ahead of the needs of five unexpected guests, he doubted they had time to worry about him at all. And of course, they wouldn't have taken anything.

Someone who had no business in his room had been there. And if one of the oddball guests was a thief for real and was after the chart for some reason, then this game they were about to start playing was turning into something more serious.

Someone had been in his room. Someone had been in his room. Milo forced himself to breathe evenly so he wouldn't have a panic attack.

He'd had panic attacks before. When he did, his mother usually told him to try to take his mind off it, to think of something else.

Like, for instance, a game.

"What's your name?" he asked Meddy.

"What?"

"In the campaign."

"Oh. Well, let's call me . . . let's call me Sirin."

"And who are you? You haven't told me anything about you yet."

Meddy scratched her head. "Well, there is a kind of character I've always wanted to play. It's called a scholiast. They're these winged creatures who follow angels around like familiars, and they're not supposed to act in ways that change the course of events. But they love adventures, and they never get to have any, so when you come across one — they're usually non-player characters, meaning you run into them and get information or clues or tools or something — you can almost always convince it to help. But I don't see why a player couldn't be one. I love the idea of a scholiast who's decided to have an adventure, even though she isn't supposed to. Do you mind if I try playing one?"

He shrugged, curious. "Why would I mind?"

"Well, for starters, Sirin would have to be invisible to all the non-player characters — meaning everyone but you."

Milo grinned. "I have to pretend you're invisible?"

"Milo," Meddy said sternly, "Sirin's an otherworldly creature who's not supposed to interact, just observe — unless ordered to do something by her angel. She'd have to be invisible to everyone but Negret. And that would make Negret the captain of our campaign. Sirin wouldn't be comfortable being in command. She'd just be excited to be able to join the adventure. But she might be very useful in terms of seeing things Negret can't. And she'd have unearthly powers that might come in handy."

"Powers like what?"

"Dunno. I guess we'll find out."

Meddy looked anxious, as if she was worried Milo might say no. He shrugged again. "Fine by me. Sirin it is. Sirin you are, I mean. Welcome to the campaign." He held out his hand, and they solemnly shook on their new identities. "Anything else I need to know before I start?"

Meddy blew out a mouthful of air. "Let's see . . . Always check for traps, left is always right unless there's a middle, always put your healer in the best armor and wear your magic rings on your toes instead of your fingers . . . What else? . . . Always have rope . . ." She counted these off on her fingers as Milo listened, wondering if any of it ought to be making sense to him.

"Never mind," Meddy said when at last she noticed his bewildered expression. "You'll figure things out as you go."

"All right." Milo-Negret leaned against the wall by the window and chewed on his thumbnail, relieved to discover that thinking about the game was helping the waves of anxiety subside. "Well," he said, "I don't think it was the map's owner who took it. If it was, he or she would just have taken the wallet and everything. There would've been no reason to make it look like it hadn't been disturbed, or to replace it with something similar. That only makes sense if the thief wanted to keep someone from realizing the chart had been taken for as long as possible." What they didn't know, he realized, was whether the thief was trying to fool the real owner of the chart or Milo himself.

He took the imposter map back from Meddy, or rather, *Sirin*, turned on his desk lamp, and held the paper up to the light, revealing the same twisted iron gate he'd seen on the original.

"It's the same paper," he told Sirin. "There's a watermark."

"So the thief somehow had another piece of that same old paper? That's weird. What are the chances of that?"

"I don't see how something like that could be coincidence. So the paper is important, maybe just as much as what was on it."

"That gives us three questions to answer," Sirin said, scratching her head. "What is it, whose is it, and who took it? Maybe the paper can help us with the *what* part."

There was another thing too, he realized. It had already seemed implausible that all these strangers would show up at the same place at such an unlikely time. And now it was clear that this map, if nothing else, connected at least two of them. "What if the guests are all here for the same reason, and the map is part of it? That would mean the map has something to do with . . . with Greenglass House, wouldn't it?"

Sirin looked at him with a strange expression—something like triumph—on her face. "Negret. What if there's some kind of—I don't know, treasure or something, a secret—hidden in the house? What if we had the map to it in our hands, just last night?"

Treasure? In Greenglass House? Milo wanted to scoff. Bizarre guests or no, this was still the same rambly-shambly house he'd lived in his whole life, and the idea that it concealed any secret at all seemed inconceivable. But to Negret, hidden treasure in Greenglass House was possible—just barely—and Milo felt a strange, brief flush of happiness. He was learning to think like his character.

"Well, someone else has the map now," he said. "I wonder if

whoever stole it knows how to read it, though. Maybe we still have time to figure this all out first."

"Hey, and what about all that stuff Clem was saying downstairs? She said she was a cat burglar, remember?"

"I thought it was a joke," Milo said. "But then she said something about Georgie Moselle, like maybe she was suggesting that Georgie was a thief too." He shook his head. "A real cat burglar wouldn't have made any mistakes." He pointed at the desk, where *The Raconteur's Commonplace Book* sat. "A real cat burglar would've noticed the way I'd left everything on the desk, and would've made sure to leave it exactly the same. And the bow on the door. Anybody would have seen the bell and made sure to keep it from ringing when he or she went in, but a professional would've left the bow just like I did."

As he spoke, Milo realized he was feeling a bit disdainful about the thief, whoever it was. "The thief thought he or she was being clever because of the decoy paper, but missed all the stuff that tipped me off even before we opened the wallet." He gave in to the game and his character completely and rolled his eyes. "Amateur."

"Well, to be fair," Sirin said with a little smile, "he probably didn't realize he was breaking into the room of the noted escaladeur Negret."

"No," Negret said, "I bet he didn't."

They set the paper on his desk and smoothed out the folds. Negret traced a finger over the iron gate, feeling the subtle difference the watermark made in the paper's surface. "Does it mean anything to you?" Sirin asked.

"There's no gate like this here. Not on the grounds of Green-glass House, not as far as I know." But even as he said the words, something made him pause. "Not on the grounds of Greenglass . . . Oh, wait, I *have* seen something like this before!"

He folded the paper, tucked it carefully in his back pocket with his game papers, and rushed out into the hall. Sirin followed him to the staircase, where he paused for a minute to listen. There were voices downstairs and quiet above. Good.

Negret and Sirin hiked up the stairs, and he found that his es-caladeur's feet instinctively sought out the quietest route: stepping far to the right on the third step, putting as little weight as possible on the fifth, skipping the sixth one altogether. All little tricks he'd picked up over years of creeping up and down the stairs of Green-glass House but never needed — not really — until now.

They reached the third floor, and Negret paused for a quick glance down the hall before making the turn up the following flight. This was Mr. Vinge's, Mrs. Hereward's, and Dr. Gowervine's floor, but none of them was in sight.

Up to the next landing they crept, the scholiast following care-fully in the escaladeur's footsteps. Negret motioned for Sirin to wait just before they reached the top, and he snuck ahead to make sure the fourth floor was as deserted as the third had seemed to be. The faint odor of Georgie's perfume still hung here, and the rooms lin-ing the hall were all open except the one at the end. Negret peered briefly into each until he reached Georgie's, where he put his ear to the door and listened. Nothing.

He returned to the stairwell and motioned for Sirin to join him.

Then he turned and looked triumphantly up at the huge stained-glass window that threw cold blue-tinted winter light onto the floor, scattered with the occasional gleam of green.

"Wow," Sirin said appreciatively. "All this time, and I never noticed it."

"Me neither," Negret admitted. Just to be sure he wasn't imagining the similarity, he pulled out the paper, unfolded it again, and held it up for comparison. Backlit by the window, the watermark shone through clear as day. "That's it, though. No mistaking it."

What had always looked to Milo like a churchy sort of mosaic revealed itself to Negret as a rendering of an iron gate. You had to look at the metal that held the glass together instead of the glass itself, but it was there. The window and the watermark were identical.

"What does it mean, though?" Sirin wondered. "Maybe there was an iron gate like this on the grounds once?"

"It's a really old house." Negret turned and looked around, taking in details Milo had lived with all his life. To Negret, however, they were new — or at least different: The rough old beams with their rich chocolate colors, the cream-painted pressed-tin ceilings in the halls, the sconces that had been converted to hold bulbs instead of candlesticks, the ivory and gold embossed wallpaper, so ancient that every once in a while Milo and Mr. Pine had to go around with a pot of thick glue and repaste the corners that always seemed to be peeling back from the walls. And, of course, the window itself, with the once-hidden gate that Negret couldn't *not* see any longer.

"The windows on the stairs are all a little different, but they're definitely a set," he said quietly, looking at the blue glass. "I wonder if the gate's somewhere in each one."

Sirin watched him with her arms folded. "What do you know about it? The house, I mean."

"My mother's parents bought it when she was a little girl. It was empty before that. Or, not empty — the owner hadn't used it as his main house in a while, I guess."

"And the previous owner was . . . ?"

"A smuggler. One of the famous ones, from ages ago, like the Gentleman Maxwell, only it wasn't him. I can't remember which one."

Sirin sniffed. "The Gentleman Maxwell wasn't ages ago. That was maybe right before you were born."

"Okay, but that's still way back, and the owner was someone from even before Maxwell's time."

"Doc Holystone, maybe?"

Negret snapped his fingers. "That's it."

"You're kidding! This house belonged to Doc Holystone?"

"Supposedly. My granddad bought it from his brother, after Doc Holystone was captured and died. That's how it came to be an inn for — well, for the kinds of folks who usually stay here. At first it was friends and shipmates of Doc Holystone's who needed a place to stay; then the word got out that it was a safe place for smugglers to put up when they needed some shore time. That's how my mom met my dad, actually. His father was on Ed Pickering's crew, and they stayed here a few times." Negret tried to keep the pride out of his voice. "He's not as famous as Holystone or the Gentleman, but he was fairly big once."

"That's pretty neat." Sirin looked around, impressed. "Then it wouldn't be surprising if somebody thought there was something hidden here. It would almost be weird if there wasn't."

"It might explain the nautical chart, too," Negret added.

Sirin scratched her head. "All I remember is that I didn't recognize the waterway. Think maybe it's not a waterway at all? It could be a map that only *looks* like a chart."

"Could be." Negret nodded. "If it was made by a smuggler — or anyone who lived on the water, really — it would make sense for that person to use the markings he or she was most familiar with. Or the person could've been actually trying to hide what kind of map he was making." He looked out the window at the azure-tinted snow that lay thickly over everything. "I hope the depth markings don't mean we have to dig for whatever it is. The ground under all that snow's got to be frozen solid."

Then he had a disappointing thought. "Or maybe the chart has nothing to do with the house at all. Just because the paper seems to doesn't mean what's *on* it does, too."

Sirin shook her head confidently. "It's connected. Apart from the watermark, one of the guests went to the trouble of bringing it here. When was the last time you packed something for a trip that you didn't think you'd use?"

"I guess."

She opened her mouth to say something more, but Negret stiffened and held up a hand. Someone had just stepped on the creaky stair halfway up to the third floor.

"That's one of the guests," Negret whispered. "Everybody else knows to skip that one. Come on. I want to take a look at the window upstairs, anyway."

The next staircase had four loud steps and two that murmured, all in a row. Negret showed Sirin how to avoid the noisy ones altogether by tiptoeing up the raised, ramplike base of the banister. They reached the fifth-floor landing without a sound, and after another quick glance down the hall (three more empty rooms with open doors, and one — Clem's — that was closed), Negret and Sirin stood before the big stained-glass panel.

This one was in shades of yellow and gold and deep green: jade and pine and hunter and emerald. Each window had a different pattern, and this one had always reminded Milo of chrysanthemums. Negret looked at it with fresh eyes and saw starbursts. *Not flowers,* he thought. Maybe it was all the talk of smugglers that made him think instead, *Explosions. Cannon fire.*

"There's the gate," Sirin murmured. Negret followed her pointing finger. It was much smaller and sort of tucked away down in the left-hand corner, but it was there. Now Negret could only see the starbursts as fireworks. It was as if the window were a painting of firecrackers exploding in the sky over the mysterious iron gate.

Another squeaky stair sounded, closer this time. So close it had to be Clem, since she was the only one staying on this floor.

There was no good reason for Milo to feel antsy about being found anywhere in the inn, as long as he didn't intrude upon the guests' rooms. Negret, however, didn't want to be discovered. Not just yet, and not looking so intently at a possible clue that he wasn't ready to share with anyone but Sirin. The two adventurers looked at each other. "Now what?" Sirin whispered.

There was one more flight of stairs stretching upward, which he knew would turn past one last stained-glass window and end at a door that opened into the attic. He also knew that even though the door would be locked, Negret would be able to open it if he wanted.

"We can wait on the attic stairs until Clem's gone," he suggested. "Or in the attic. I can get the door open."

Sirin nodded. "Good idea. If there's a secret hidden here, we need to know more about the house itself. Let's start right at the top."

The attic stairs were less familiar, so they hauled themselves hand over hand up the banister ramp all the way to the first landing, pausing only briefly for a look at the window before Negret led them on up the last flight to the door. He wanted to get into the attic quickly, before Clem reached the fifth floor. They could stop for a closer look at the glass image (more greens and a range of browns like the tones in a sepia photograph) on their way back down.

Much of the inn had been repaired or updated or replaced outright at some point over the years, but Negret figured the carved attic door had to be almost as old as the house itself. In the summer, when the wood swelled up, it had a tendency to stick, so that it took two people to get it open, and in the winter, it let drafts through that whistled down the stairs and made other doors swing, ghost-like, on the lower floors. It had a milky-green glass knob and hung from hinges that looked like they'd squeak if you so much as glanced at them wrong. Milo, however, knew that Mr. Pine kept them oiled because they were the only things about it he could control.

There was also a lock, but that was nothing for Negret the blackjack. Especially considering he knew where the key was.

The footsteps on the stairs below at last reached the fifth floor. "Just in time," Sirin breathed.

Negret nodded. Then he paused. He'd figured it was Clem who'd been on their heels, probably just going up to her room for something. But here it occurred to him that as far as he could remember, since the moment she'd arrived Clem had not once made a noise when she walked indoors, not even when she'd taken the stairs from the first floor to the second at a run.

Now that he'd spent some time trying to move quietly himself, Negret understood that the seemingly effortless, soundless way Clem had been moving didn't happen by accident. It took work, and practice, and awareness, and it probably wasn't something you just turned off like a light.

He also knew that he and Sirin hadn't been hearing the stairs at their loudest. They'd been too noisy for someone who knew how to move silently, but not noisy enough for someone coming up without caring about sounds they were making at all. Therefore, the person who'd arrived on the fifth floor was trying to be quiet, and wasn't doing it very well.

In other words, *not* Clem. Who, then? Why would anyone hike up an extra flight or two of stairs? And why try (however poorly) to be sneaky at it? He listened harder, and now he could hear something else: a slight wheeze. Whoever was coming was way out of breath.

"Hang on," he whispered. Then, as carefully and as quietly as only an escaladeur could, he crept back down the stairs to the landing under the green and sepia window. He peeked around the banister just in time to see the short, round shape of Dr. Gowervine disappear into Clem's room at the end of the hall.

Dr. Gowervine?

four

THE EMPORIUM

hat?" Sirin hissed from the landing above. Negret put a finger to his lips and stared at the open door. A moment later, Dr. Gowervine reappeared. Negret ducked out of sight and waited until he heard the door shut again with a soft click. Then quiet-but-not-silent Dr. Gowervine hurried back to the stairwell where Negret crouched out of view above and made his way back down. He was still wheezing a little. *Better cut back on the smoking if you wanna be sneaky,* Negret thought.

"Dr. Gowervine snuck into Clem's room," he reported breathlessly as soon as the shifty guest was out of earshot.

"Weird! Did he take anything?"

Negret blinked. "I . . . I didn't notice." *What an idiot,* he thought. He racked his memory, but if there had been anything in Dr. Gowervine's hands, he hadn't noticed — and he was mortified. Some blackjack.

Sirin came down the stairs and clapped a hand on his shoulder. "Don't beat yourself up. We've got an attic to explore, and it isn't like he's going anywhere."

"He must be the one who snuck into my room, too," Negret fumed. "He must have the chart. What the heck is he up to?"

"I don't know if we can assume he's the chart thief. All we know is that he went into Clem's room. We don't even know if he took anything. Really, Negret, the bottom line is this: we know nothing about any of these guys. We're going to have to find a way to figure out who they all are and why they're here." She looked up at the attic door. "But for now, my dear Negret, let's focus on where *we* are."

"Right." He reached for the potted plant on the sill under the window. It was fake, with paper-covered wire for a stalk and flowers made of pink glass, and underneath sat the attic key. "Here we go."

The lock turned easily and the door swung wide. Negret squinted into the dimness. "Stay here. There's a light someplace, if I can just find the string."

"Hold on!" Sirin grabbed his arm. "Check for traps first, remember."

Negret stopped dead on the threshold. "What traps?"

Sirin leaned past him and peered into the gloom. "I don't know, but it's never a good idea to just go barging into a strange room. You always should check for traps. Someone could be lying in wait, or there could be some kind of thing rigged up to decapitate the first person to step inside, or maybe there's a curse on the door so if you go through it—"

"You're talking about my house!" he exploded. "And you're being ridiculous. Curses don't exist and nobody's rigged a—a decapitation thingy in our attic."

Sirin shrugged. "Okay, Mister Lacking-in-Imagination. There could be a loose floorboard. There could be a spider web. I'm just saying, check a place before you go in."

Grumbling, Negret examined the door frame and discovered that there was, in fact, a spider web. Then he stepped inside and found the pull-string for the light. More accurately, he walked into it, the little round knob tied to the bottom of the string clunking him between the eyes. He gave it a tug, and a bluish-gray filament fizzled to life inside a glass bulb on the ceiling just inside the doorway. From the unimpressive circle of luminescence, Negret could just see a string hanging from another, still-dark bulb deeper in the attic. He pulled that one, and then another farther in, and then the next, but even once all four bulbs had carved out their individual pockets of illumination, he and Sirin were still standing in a mostly dim and indistinct space.

The attic of Greenglass House was slightly smaller than the lower floors, owing to the big sloping roof. It had probably once been a single open space, but over the long years of the house's existence it had been slowly partitioned into smaller sections, not by walls but by piles of things: here a collection of iron-banded teak chests piled up like a giant's discarded luggage; there a bank of chairs of all sorts, balanced precariously one atop the next; yonder a row of racks full of mismatched garment bags, moth-eaten fur coats, and several sets of embroidered silk pajamas that had worn paper-thin with time so that the embroidery was the only thing keeping them from disintegrating. The spaces between these makeshift partitions had been filled in little by little with the ephemera of years upon years, everything from dented brass musical instruments and keyless wind-up toys to tattered tablecloths and sweaters to precarious stacks of dusty books whose missing spines had been repaired with thick black thread. Above it all, the roof creaked in response to the wind's howls, and here and there frigid little gusts found their way in through hidden cracks and crevices.

"If I had something to hide, this is where I'd put it," Sirin said. "How are we ever going to look through all of this?"

"I don't know. Seems too obvious to me." Plus, the thing about attics and basements was, *everything* in there had once been a treasure to someone. Otherwise there'd have been no reason to keep it. If the chart's secret was somehow tucked away in this warrenlike room, it was just one secret among a thousand. Somehow, this spot didn't seem . . . *special* enough.

Still, an attic was an attic, and Sirin insisted that exploring rooms was a big part of any campaign. "It's not just about finding clues," she explained. "It's also about finding tools that might be useful down the road. Even if *it* isn't here — the thing the map leads to, whatever it is — there's got to be stuff that's useful to an escaladeur who listens to houses."

"All right. I think there's some cool stuff over —"

"Negret! We have to search the *whole place*. Don't skip around."

"Fine."

So Negret and Sirin began to methodically comb the attic. "How do you know if something's going to be useful?" Negret asked as he reached tentatively into the pocket of a fancy green coat with tails hanging down the back and gold braid looped at the shoulders. A piece of paper in the pocket fell to tatters when he brought it out for a look. The other pocket yielded a single mothball.

"Sometimes you don't know," Sirin replied from the other end of the rack. "I mean, when you're playing the game on paper, if it's important enough for the game master to tell you it's there, it's probably going to be useful. But I guess we'll just have to go with our guts." She drew the arm of a thin silk robe out away from the rest of the hanging clothes. "Perhaps a cloak of invisibility?"

Negret scoffed despite his best efforts to stay in character as Sirin took the yellow robe from its hanger and swirled it delightedly around her shoulders. "What's a . . . a . . . your character . . ."

"A scholiast."

"What's a scholiast need with an invisibility cloak?" he asked. "Aren't you already invisible to everyone but me?"

"I like it," Sirin replied simply as she admired the embroidery. "Plus, it has pockets! Gotta have a way to carry your gear on a campaign. I shall name it the Cloak of Golden Indiscernibility." She kept the robe on as she bent to start looking through the small boxes stacked on the bottom shelf of the rack. "Hey, try these on." With her top half hidden by the low-hanging coats, Sirin reached an arm back and held out a pair of black cotton slippers. "Think they'll fit you?"

"What for?" But even as he asked, Negret realized how they might be useful to an escaladeur: they had thick woven fabric soles. These would be very quiet shoes, without any of the squeaks of ordinary footwear, yet they wouldn't slip around on wooden floors or tiles like sock feet did. He'd managed to keep pretty quiet sneaking up here, but in these shoes, maybe he could be almost as quiet as Clem.

He toed off his sneakers and pulled on the slippers. With socks they were tight, but without them they fit perfectly. He took a few testing steps. "They're perfect. Thanks, Sirin."

"Don't mention it. Want one of these fancy coats?"

"Nah." The shoes looked nondescript enough that they might go unnoticed. An escaladeur needed to blend in. "I don't want to stick out."

He wandered over to a stack of wooden crates and lifted the lid off the closest one. It was full of old bottles wrapped in scraps of linen, and he'd just reached in for a closer look when something else caught his eye.

Wedged between the boxes and the wall was a door. Not a door *to* anyplace, although it must've been once upon a time. It leaned at an angle against the wall, its hinges unmoored and tarnished and sad-looking, and it was nearly identical to the heavy old attic door, down to the green glass knob. "Wonder where that came from?" he mumbled, trying to think of a doorway in Greenglass House that was without its door. Had it belonged to one of the many rooms in the house and just been replaced with a newer door at some point? Why had it been saved, then?

Negret leaned over the crates, reaching to touch a chipped facet on the glass knob, and as his fingers found it, something fell with a rattle to the ground. Stretching a bit farther, he could just barely make out a dull dark shape wedged in the angle between the bottom of the door and the boxes.

He eased backwards and landed lightly on his slippered feet, then squeezed himself between the stack and a pile of newer cardboard boxes that stood beside it. Then he bent awkwardly and worked his fingers along the edge of the door until he found the thing that had fallen. He didn't have to see the spiny, jangling spars poking out between his fingers as he picked it up to know what it was: a ring of keys. He must've knocked it loose from the lock below the knob.

There were five of them on a knotted loop of leather; old ones, the kind called skeleton keys. None of the doors in Greenglass House took that sort of key except the attic — not anymore. There was also a small hammered disc on the loop, misshapen and slightly convex, with an uneven hole punched in it for the leather to pass through. His heart gave a little jump. Four designs that looked like Chinese characters had been cut into the surface on one side. Negret brought it up for a closer look. He could identify an assortment of characters because the Pines were slowly learning Mandarin together, but they hadn't gotten far in their studies yet and these were not ones he recognized. He turned the disc over and found a rough spiked shape like a crown. He scratched with his thumbnail at a tiny bit of blue enamel that clung to the image.

Milo knew, of course, that no antique bric-a-brac in Greenglass House was even remotely likely to be connected to his own ancestry, even if it did have Chinese writing on it. *Negret,* on the other hand —*Negret* knew no such thing. Negret, he thought with a little thrill, could perhaps know the exact opposite.

Negret could know, for instance, that these keys had been handed down through his own family for centuries. Negret could even, maybe, remember the very day his father, a world-renowned blackjack himself, had passed the keys to his son. *I always knew you would follow in my footsteps,* his father might have said. *We all knew, the entire family, because you take after me so very much. We even look alike.* Negret gave in and pretended to remember looking in the mirror with his famous blackjack father to see the same nose, same mouth and eyes, same straight black hair as his own.

A strange pleasure crept into his heart. It lasted maybe thirty seconds before the wave of self-reproach he'd known was coming swept in and washed it all away.

He looked down at the keys. They might not open any locks left in the house—although he made a mental note to try them on the attic door—but certainly no self-respecting blackjack would leave behind a perfectly good set of keys. He tucked them into his pocket and ignored the lingering pangs of conscience. Quiet shoes and mystery keys. Not a bad haul.

"What'd you find?"

He turned and nearly jumped out of his new shoes. In addition to the yellow Cloak of Indiscernibility, Sirin had added a fur-lined hat with turned-up earflaps and a pair of old blue-lensed sunglasses with wire rims and a yellowed tag hanging from one earpiece by a bit of red thread.

Sirin pointed to the hat. "Helm of Revelations," she said, dead-pan. "Eyes of True and Aching Clarity," she added, indicating the glasses.

"Now you're just making stuff up," Negret protested.

"Obviously, though it's interesting that it was magic glasses that clued you in rather than the invisibility cloak." She grinned. "It's fun. Look." She took a pair of brown leather gloves from the pocket of her pants. "For you. Wildthorn's Crackerjack Gauntlets, for Pickers of Locks and Creepers Through Windows Needing Nimble and Foxy Fingers." She eyed the roof overhead, creaking under the weight of winter. "Also guaranteed to be useful when it's cold."

Negret took the gloves. "Thank you, Sirin." He pulled them on. Like the shoes, they fit perfectly, and as his fingertips warmed he realized how cold the attic was.

They moved on, rooting through boxes, riffling through books. Sirin added pieces to her costume, occasionally pressing something on Negret: a whistle that didn't seem to work, a ball of twine, because it was always a good idea to have rope, a dusty spiral pad that was empty except for the beginnings of a grocery list on the first page.

"Hey," Negret said as his eye fell on a cardboard box labeled ROLE-PLAYING GAME STUFF—AW in black marker. "Look at that! Role-playing game—isn't that what we're doing? This must be my dad's stuff. It could be useful, right?"

"We made up our own campaign," Sirin said, following Negret as he hurried to the box. "And like I said, we're not playing a proper RPG. It's not actually likely to be useful to us."

Negret opened it and peered inside. It was full of big hardcover books like the ones Meddy had had behind the tree that morning, and booklets and a few smaller boxes with labels that showed groups of adventurers dressed in elaborate costumes. Sirin crouched beside him and took out a booklet. "These are premade campaigns, games you would play at a table with a group and a game master."

He pulled a loose page of graph paper from the box. "A map from someone's game?"

"Looks like it." Sirin seemed entirely uninterested.

"Do you think there could be anything in here for the game my dad played? Odd Trails?"

"Maybe. Look, can we get back to *our* game?"

A little more rifling and Negret found it: a book with an illustration of a sinister-looking traveler beside a peddler's cart with the words *The Wayfaring Galleria* emblazoned on its side. Across the top of the picture was the title: *The Odd Trails: Scavengers, Peddlers, and Huntsmen of the Roaming World (Advanced Player's Handbook).* "Cool!"

Sirin sighed. "If you're going to bother with any of this stuff, why don't you at least take the one about blackjacks? That wouldn't be a total waste of time."

Negret set the book to one side. "How do you know there's one about blackjacks in here?"

" 'Cause I can see it. I know all these manuals." She leaned down and plucked another hardcover from the box. "Here. But don't forget, this is our game. Negret is *your* character. Nobody else gets to say what you can and can't do with him."

This book had a girl on its cover, walking on a wire over some kind of open-air bazaar. *Blackjacks of the Roads: Highwaymen, Sharpers, and Empirics (Advanced Player's Handbook).* "Awesome."

"Yes, but it's not a clue, Negret," Sirin grumbled. "Let's get back to the task at hand."

He moved on reluctantly, and found a few more useful things: a little round mirror with stains under the glass that he thought might be good for using to look around corners, an old tinderbox with a flint in it, a spade-shaped chunk of metal with a strange sort of jointed handle that he'd thought at first was a lock until he'd spotted the thick bit of charred wick coming from the hole in front. Not a lock, then, Negret decided. Some sort of old-fashioned lantern.

He located a red striped canvas rucksack to carry what he'd found and climbed to the top of a giant pile of sailcloth under one of the dirty windows to sit and organize his treasures. Sirin flounced over with her invisibility cloak trailing behind her and something cupped in her hand. "This one's for you," she said, scrambling up to join him. "You are not going to *believe* this find, Negret."

"What is it?"

"It is," she said dramatically, "a piece of that same paper."

Scrap was more like it; *corner* would've been even more accurate. Negret took the snip from Sirin's palm and held it up between his face and the flickering bulb overhead. The watermark wasn't visible, but a quick comparison to the page he still had in his pocket convinced him that the scholiast was right. The feel of the paper, its weight, the way the fibers ran, all of those things were the same. "Where'd you find it?"

"Over there, behind that big thing." Sirin pointed to a trio of

boxes that were stacked awkwardly against the easternmost wall behind a giant clump of machinery looped with thick old rope.

"I think that's the engine that ran the dumbwaiter back when it
worked." Negret slid down the pile, made his way to the machine,
and squeezed awkwardly past it, coating his fingertips with a mixture
of dust and congealed grease as he tried to maneuver. "Geez, Sirin,
you could've warned me." He wiped his hands on his knees, hoping he wouldn't have to explain the stains when Mrs. Pine did the
laundry.

"It's broken, whatever it was." Sirin peered over the engine as he
opened the topmost box and stood on tiptoe to peek inside. At first
he thought, irrationally, *Jewels!* He reached in to lift a piece into the
dim light: a not-quite-rectangular shard of glass that shone a dusty
sapphire color.

Negret picked carefully through the pieces. There were bits in
every conceivable shade of green. He eased the box to one side so he
could open the one beneath it. This one was full of golds and sunset colors. The third held russets and sepias that made him think of
varying shades of toast.

He picked a piece of glass from each box. "Let us call them the
Gems of Ultimate Puissance," Sirin suggested.

"What the heck does *puissance* mean?"

"Power and might. Gamers have lots of puissant objects." She
pushed her spectacles up onto her forehead and squinted at the
pieces he'd chosen.

"I bet they're left over from the really big window on the second
floor." Negret tucked the shards into his bag along with the rest of his

finds. "Mom said that one was made here because it was too big to get up the hill already finished."

"Perfect! These gems probably hold fragments of the power of the house itself," Sirin declared triumphantly, lifting one fist toward the roof, which chose that moment to drip something into her left eye.

"Wait, Sirin, where was the paper?" Negret asked, scratching his head.

She pointed at a piece of brown wrapping paper peeking out from under the bottom box. "It was stuck to that."

Carefully, Negret worked the wrapping out far enough to read the faded handwritten words on it. "Lucksmith Paper Merchants, Printer's Quarter, Nagspeake." He tugged, but it was stuck firmly under the box. "Lucksmith," he repeated. "Could be a clue."

They hunted for another ten minutes, during which time Sirin added a belt to the Cloak of Golden Indiscernibility and Negret found a pen he kind of liked. At last they stood under the string dangling from the bulb near the door and surveyed the space they'd just explored. "From now on, Negret, when we want to refer to this place, we'll call it the Emporium," Sirin announced. Negret gave her a dubious look—or tried to, but between the Helm, the Eyes, and the Cloak, it was a bit hard to keep a dubious look from morphing into a laugh.

Still. "This was fun," he admitted, slinging the bag over one shoulder. "An excellent morning's work, my dear Sirin." The bag knocked loose the papers and pencil he still had stuck in his back pocket, and as he picked them up, he remembered the assignment the scholiast had given him downstairs behind the tree. "Hang on. Before we go downstairs, let me draw the map for this floor."

Negret cleared a space on one of the old chests and started drawing. Sirin leaned over his shoulder and suggested corrections and additions until at last the two of them leaned back from the floor plan, pleased with their work. Negret wrote THE EMPORIUM across the top of the page in neat capitals. "There."

"That's a good-looking map," Sirin said admiringly.

"Thank you." His stomach rumbled hollowly and loudly enough that Sirin gave him a sharp look. "I wonder if it's lunchtime yet," he said, blushing. Then, on the way out the door, he paused. "Sirin? If we *are* making stuff up . . . if it's up to me what to do as Negret—or *with* Negret . . ." He hesitated. "Could I make up a different past for him? A . . . a family and everything, I mean?"

There. It was out.

"*Can* you?" Sirin repeated. "You totally *should*. Giving your character a history really helps you bring him to life."

He nodded, relieved, and reached into the rucksack to feel for the keys. It was for the game, so maybe it was okay, just this once, to pretend.

In fact, it was well *past* lunchtime. "Where on earth have you been?" Mrs. Pine demanded, eyeing the dusty pair as they came trooping into the kitchen.

"The att—I mean, the Emp—I mean, just messing around." Milo glowered at Meddy, who'd elbowed him twice during his answer but who was now looking innocently up at Mrs. Pine through the grimy blue lenses of the Eyes of True and Aching Clarity. Milo sighed and wondered how his mother was keeping a straight face. "When's lunch?"

"Lunch?" Mrs. Pine lifted an eyebrow. "Well, if you wash up—and I mean *really* wash up," she added with a dubious look at his hands, "you can make yourself a snack, but the rest of us had lunch hours ago." She pointed at the kitchen clock, and Milo gaped. It was past four thirty. "We'll have dinner ready around six. Don't spoil your appetite."

"Evidently there's some sort of a time warp in the Emporium," he muttered.

———— ❋ ————

Milo had read as far as the fourth story in the book, and someone was just about to kill a cat.

She had a good reason, the character called Nell. There were floodwaters rising throughout the city, and people were dying (including all of Nell's family), and somehow the cat was the key to making it stop.

When all that was left of the cat were its bones, she made her way to the river's swollen edge and set the bones on the surface. The frothing water took all but one. The remaining bone spun gently, as if it were caught in the mildest of eddies. Then it slid against the plunging flow, upriver and out of sight.

Milo took a distracted bite of his ham sandwich and read how, from that same direction, a strange man came walking toward the girl and asked why he had been summoned. Nell asked what could be done to stop the flood, and the strange man's reply began, *"There is a sort of magic called orphan magic."*

Milo sat up straight. It was hard to ignore that word, *orphan*, especially when you followed it up with *magic*.

"It is the magic of that-which-remains, of that-which-is-alone. It is, in many ways, the magic of desperation, but it is never the magic of chance. When one remains, it is the one that was meant to remain. It is the one that is special; it is precious because it is unique; it is powerful because that is how it survived. There is one bone in a cat that may call me, but it must be separated from the others to do its work. It has potential when it is connected to the rest, but when it is sundered away, its potential becomes power."

Very interesting indeed.

Night comes early in winter, of course, and the sun setting beyond the big hill behind the house was already sending deep shadows out across the white lawn. Milo sat cross-legged in the loveseat by the window, half watching the sunset colors and shadows through the rattling glass as they battled for control of the snowy grounds, half listening to the quiet sounds of people in the living room and the crackle of the fireplace. *The Raconteur's Commonplace Book* lay open on his knee, and he clutched the remnants of the sandwich in one hand.

Now that he was back among the guests, he had returned, mostly, to being just plain Milo. And while Negret was very curious about why Dr. Gowervine had snuck into Clem Candler's room, just plain Milo was still primarily bent out of shape about the fact that someone—maybe Dr. Gowervine or maybe someone else—had snuck into his own room and taken something from it.

He turned to glance at the stout man sitting by the fire. Despite his ongoing gripes at Mrs. Hereward—the two of them just kept on finding things to argue about—he was easy to overlook in a room that also contained blue-haired Georgie and red-haired Clem and, most especially, Meddy.

As if she'd heard him thinking about her, Meddy poked her head out from behind the Christmas tree. *What?* she mouthed. Milo shook his head and let his gaze wander. Mr. Vinge was there too, folded into his usual chair and sporting fresh socks (bright green and yellow argyle). He had a book open in front of him, but his eyes were closed.

We know nothing about any of these guys, Sirin had said. *We're going to have to find a way to figure out who they all are and why they're here.*

Milo took another bite of his sandwich, chewed thoughtfully, and closed the *Commonplace Book* again. From the rucksack at his feet he took the graph paper and started to work on a map of the first floor.

Meddy dropped onto the loveseat next to him and looked at the big rectangles he'd sketched out for the screened porch and the living room that flowed into the dining room that flowed into the kitchen. "Ah. Good. I was going to ask if you'd started a map for down here." She sat quietly for a moment while he added details: the stairs, the pantry, the fireplace, the foyer.

"If we're calling the attic the Emporium," Milo whispered, "what's our secret name for this floor?"

She considered. "Well, in lots of game worlds, the place where everyone comes together and gets information is a public house or a saloon or something. Some place where strangers meet for food and drink and conversation."

In *The Raconteur's Commonplace Book,* the inn where everyone was trapped by the floods was called the Blue Vein Tavern. "Let's call it the Tavern, then."

"Fine by me."

Milo added the first floor's new name in his precise capital lettering. He worked on the map for a few more minutes, then set it aside. His fingers bumped against the key ring as he reached into the rucksack again and dug out the big hardcover *Blackjacks of the Roads* guide. Then he took the keys out of the bag, examined them for a moment, and put them in his pocket. What advice would Negret's father offer to his son if he were here?

It is not merely our adversaries we must investigate, he imagined the old blackjack lecturing. *We must always work to know ourselves better, too.*

Fortunately, Milo had a whole giant manual to help him know Negret better. He opened *Blackjacks of the Roads* to the page titled "Overview" and settled back to read.

The Road is the greatest trickster of all, winding and forking and vanishing and reappearing across the wide country, making a mockery of maps and carrying even those who know it best into the unfamiliar. It shouldn't come as any surprise that the blackjack is the true child of the Road. Like the Odd Trail itself, the blackjack vanishes and reappears at will. No lock, no wall, no hidden thing is safe from him. No person, either: the blackjack's powers of intuition, persuasion, misdirection, and, often, pure thievery are the stuff of legend.

There was a lot of the overview that he figured he didn't need to know just now. Milo and Meddy had discussed what skills Negret might want, and Meddy had explained a little about ability scores, but there was plenty he still didn't understand: damages and levels and different kinds of exploits, hits and misses and modifiers. Also, a lot of the exploits—which seemed to be blackjacks' different powers or feats—had to do with fighting, which Milo couldn't see Negret needing in his and Sirin's game world, since all the other players were real people.

But there were a few things that looked useful, even though he didn't understand the specifics of how they worked in the Odd Trails realm. *Zephyr's Passage: your feet carry you as swiftly and invisibly as the wind. Irresistible Blandishment: you can entice even the most reluctant to do as you ask. The Fabulist: you weave lies and the world believes.* And then, *The Moonlighter's Knack: you can steal any object protected by anything that opens with a key or combination.*

Outside, the snowfall began to slow.

Dinner that night was awkward—or at least, it felt awkward to Milo. He was not only surrounded by strangers who weren't supposed to be there while he was on vacation—someone still owed him big-time for that—but more important, one of them was a thief and had been in his room. If that person *hadn't* been Wilbur

Gowervine, that meant there were *two* creepers at Greenglass House. And although Milo didn't like thinking of Clem as a thief, after her joke about being a cat burglar, he figured he had to consider the possibility.

It seemed to Milo that he ought to be able to catch the person who'd been in his room behaving differently toward him. That person had to be wondering if Milo had discovered the theft yet. And Dr. Gowervine — well, even if he wasn't the thief, he was still a creeper, and he ought to have the good grace to look at least a little guilty.

It would've been easier if Mrs. Caraway hadn't declared that it would be a buffet dinner. If they had all been sitting around the same table the way they did in those old British murder mystery shows Milo's mom liked, there would've been meaningful glances, forced conversation, dropped spoons, and, presumably, clues somewhere in the mix. But no; Mrs. Caraway and Mrs. Pine had made a roast with a bunch of root vegetables and egg noodles — a perfect dinner for a cold night — and everyone was eating it wherever he or she liked: at the breakfast tables, in the living room ... Nobody was actually sitting at the table but Milo's dad.

Milo scowled as he filled his plate. Those British detectives had it easy.

"Hey, kiddo." Mr. Pine's voice interrupted Milo's irritation. "Come sit by me."

He did, though he might have set his plate down just a bit too hard. "How are you feeling?" his father asked as Milo slid onto the bench next to him. "I feel bad that your mom and I haven't been able to spend much time with you."

"I understand," Milo said automatically. And he did. This wasn't some family reunion his parents had dragged him to.

"How are you feeling?" Mr. Pine asked again, reaching for the pepper.

Milo looked at his father, who didn't usually think he had to make conversation. Mr. Pine was examining his food and trying to sound as if what he was asking wasn't any big deal, but the fact that he had asked twice meant his question was important. "I feel okay, Dad," Milo said. "I wasn't happy about it, but everybody seems nice enough."

Somebody broke into my bedroom, though. Milo wasn't sure what made him keep quiet about that part.

Mr. Pine speared a forkful of parsnip and beef. "Well, look, I just want you to know we didn't forget that it's winter vacation. And we're still having Christmas, come hell or high water. Or, you know."

"High snow?"

"Exactly."

"Okay, Dad." Milo smiled down at his dinner plate. "And maybe we can play Odd Trails one day too. Now that I know you play. I found some of your old role-playing game stuff in the attic."

"You found my stuff? Weird. I thought I'd sold it at a yard sale years and years back."

"Nope. It's up there. So we can have our own game sometime."

"I'd like that. But listen, Milo, what I wanted to say is, if you need time with your mom or with me, all you need to do is tell us. I know you shouldn't *have* to tell us, but these next few days you might. Okay?"

"Okay."

"Okay." Mr. Pine swooped in to give him a kiss on the forehead as he stood up to get seconds.

Meddy clambered into the chair at the end of the table with the stained-glass window behind it. "Hey."

"Where's your food?" Milo asked, taking a huge bite of his own.

"I already finished. Listen, Negret. We've got to get these idiots talking." She looked around the room. "If they keep to themselves like this, we'll never find out what we want to know. We need *clues*."

"I know. I'm thinking. Do you have any ideas?"

Sirin shook her head. "All I know is, whatever we do, *you're* going to have to do the talking." She straightened the collar of the Cloak of Golden Indiscernibility, gave Negret a pointed look as Mr. Pine returned with his second plate of roast, and scooted out of the chair again.

Milo chewed, grumbling a little under his breath.

"Say, how's that book you're reading?" his father asked. "The one Georgie lent you?"

Milo swallowed. "Pretty good." Then he felt the beginnings of an idea. "That reminds me." He swiveled on the bench and looked around. Georgie Moselle was sitting at one of the breakfast tables with her back to him. "Excuse me, Georgie?"

She turned, fork halfway to her mouth. "Yessir, Milo?"

"How's the Lansdegown coming?"

Georgie flinched as the sharp clatter of cutlery bouncing off china rang out. Milo glanced into the living room. Most of it was out of his line of sight, but Clem was just visible in the chair at the end of the sofa, mopping away the gravy that had spattered across her cheeks when she dropped her fork. "What the heck is a *lansdegown?*" she asked.

"It's the name of the cigar-box camera," Milo said, wondering why Georgie now looked vaguely uncomfortable. "All the coolest cameras have names," he said, in case she was afraid somebody'd make fun of her for naming it. "Did you finish it, Georgie?"

"Sure did," Georgie said, giving him a grateful smile. "If you want, I'll bring it down later."

"Yeah, that'd be neat."

"I'd love to see it too," Clem said sweetly.

"As would I," Mrs. Hereward added. Both girls looked at her in surprise. "I dearly love photography," the old lady said, a bit defensively.

"And I really like the book so far," Milo added, getting up and carrying his plate of half-eaten food into the living room. "I think my favorite part's the way it's set up." He sat on the hearth and glanced around. Everyone seemed to be at least half listening, if only because this was the only conversation going on just then. "It takes place at an inn," he explained. "Sort of like this one. And the guests are all stuck there because it's raining and flooding and stuff, so every night someone — one of the guests — tells a story."

"You're reading *The Raconteur's Commonplace Book* or *The Holly-Tree Inn?*" Mrs. Hereward inquired.

"*The Raconteur's Commonplace Book,*" he replied. "You know about it? What's the other one you mentioned?"

"*The Holly-Tree Inn,*" she repeated. "Dickens. Or at least partly

Dickens. It has a similar structure. Some people think the fellow who collected the tales in *The Raconteur's Commonplace Book* modeled the idea after *The Holly-Tree Inn*."

Georgie set aside her plate. "Do you know much about folklore, Mrs. Hereward?" she asked politely, sitting beside her on the sofa.

"Some," Mrs. Hereward said, a note of hesitation creeping into the word. "Just a bit. I'm an old woman, and I've always loved to read."

That might well be true, Milo thought, but coming from Mrs. Hereward it managed to feel like a lie. He filed that observation away to think about later.

Irresistible Blandishment: you can entice even the most reluctant to do as you ask. He touched Negret's blackjack keys, which were still in his pocket. Surely Negret's father would've made certain his son could pull this exploit off.

"You know what would be fun?" he asked, trying to sound as if the idea had just occurred to him. "Maybe each of us should tell a story. We're all strangers together in an inn, after all. It would be just like in the books." He considered adding, *You could each tell the story of how you came to be staying here right now,* but decided that might be too specific. Something told him not everyone here was going to be willing to answer that question honestly. Maybe if they could pick any story, they'd all participate. And whatever story each person picked, Milo had at least a chance of learning something about the guest from the telling of it.

Worth a try, anyway.

"That's a lovely idea, Milo," Mrs. Pine said. "How about if Mrs.

Caraway and I make some punch while everyone finishes eating, and then we can have a story afterward? Or there's whiskey if anybody wants a hot toddy."

He beamed. "I'll help do the dishes, then." He ignored his father's shocked expression — Milo hated washing up. Negret, however, had a plan. As he passed from person to person clearing their plates, he'd have a chance to size up each guest's reaction to his idea.

He strolled through the room, a cheerful smile pasted on his face as he collected plates and cutlery. Behind the smile, though, the escaladeur was taking careful measure of each person.

Georgie was first, and her grin looked genuine. "I'm so glad you thought of that," she said as she handed over her plate with knife and fork neatly stacked to one side. "Maybe it'll help us act less like strangers. Might as well, since we're all here together, right?"

Mrs. Hereward seemed a bit flustered as she relinquished her own dish. "Now if I can only think of a story to tell," she said.

"You could tell what brought you here," he suggested, just to see what she'd say.

"Oh, no," the old lady replied immediately. She patted her hair nervously. "That's not interesting. I wished for a winter holiday trip and settled on this place. There's nothing interesting there."

Just like her answer to Georgie's question about whether she knew much about folklore, this had the feeling of a lie. *Well, not a lie, exactly,* Negret thought. *It might be true, but it's not the whole truth.*

Dr. Gowervine brought his dish over and added it carefully to the stack. He said nothing but gave Negret a thoughtful look as he pulled a leather pouch from his sweater pocket. He nodded once, took a pipe from the pouch, and went to the foyer to get his coat. Then he crossed the living room again and disappeared out the door to the enclosed porch at the side of the house to smoke.

Negret discovered his heart had sped up, and he took a deep breath to calm himself. *This man definitely has a secret.*

"What sorts of stories do people tell in the book?" Clem asked curiously. "Is there . . . I don't know . . . a right sort or wrong sort for this kind of occasion?" She scratched her head. "I don't honestly know if I've ever told a story before."

"You've never told a story?" Negret asked. "Not ever, not to anyone? You must have."

"Well, not like this," she protested. "This isn't the same as when you tell someone how your day went, is it?"

He opened his mouth to say that it wasn't quite like that, not exactly — but then he stopped himself. "It can be any kind of story you want. The point is that you share something with everyone. It's supposed to be a fun thing. I don't think you can do it wrong, if that's what you mean."

"It is fun, I suppose," Clem said thoughtfully. "Maybe tonight I'll just listen, and then I'll tell one tomorrow." She turned to Georgie. "Maybe you can tell us how you came up with such an interesting name for your camera, Blue."

Georgie smiled a bit sourly. "Maybe *you* can tell us how, Red."

"Maybe," Clem said thoughtfully. "Maybe I will."

"I would very much like to hear that story myself," Mrs. Hereward said with a very small, very strange frown.

Weird.

Mr. Vinge was last. He was still sitting in the chair in the corner, and he had his plate balanced on the arm. He gave Negret a very sharp looking-over before surrendering it. It was as if he somehow knew exactly what Negret was up to and wanted it understood that he knew, and moreover, if he decided to go along, it was for his own reasons.

Then he blinked and smiled a little lopsidedly as he adjusted his big tortoiseshell glasses, and Negret wondered if he hadn't been looking for meaning where there was just another bored, snowbound guest.

Mrs. Caraway met him where the dining room opened into the kitchen and relieved him of the stack of dishes. "Thanks, Milo. How about I make you a super-special hot chocolate for helping out?"

When the dishes were done, the after-dinner coffees and punch had been distributed, and plates of Lizzie Caraway's famous red velvet cake had been passed around, the eleven inhabitants of Greenglass House assembled in the living room. It had been an odd group from the start, but somehow with everyone here and staring at one another, they seemed even odder than before. Of course, now Milo was looking at them through Negret's eyes. That made a difference.

The mood in the room was stranger than before too. The group, taken as a whole, was giving off a tense combination of nervousness and expectation and curiosity and suspicion.

"So," Negret said at last, as innocently and cheerfully as he could. "Who's going first?"

The guests looked from one to the next. Negret glanced at Mr. Vinge, surprised to find he was really hoping the man in the argyle socks would speak up. But he was stirring his cup and looking mildly but pointedly down at his spoon. Clearly, he was not going to offer a story. Not yet, anyway. Milo looked to Dr. Gowervine, but he, too, kept mum.

At last, Mrs. Hereward gave her spoon a ringing tap against the edge of her mug.

"I suppose I can manage one," she said primly. All eyes turned her way.

"Mine is a very old, very venerable family." The old lady stirred her tea meditatively. "Perhaps one of what my father called our hand-me-down stories would be appropriate. I believe I'll tell you the one Papa called 'Only a Fool Scoffs at Destiny.' Listen."

"We *are* listening," Dr. Gowervine grumbled.

Mrs. Hereward opened her mouth to snap at him, but Georgie replied first. "No, Doc, that's how you begin a story in some of the old folklore traditions. It was how storytellers let their audiences know the tale was about to begin."

"Yeah," Negret said, realizing he knew what she was talking about. "Some of the stories in *The Raconteur's Commonplace Book* start that way."

Mrs. Hereward folded her arms. "If you're quite ready."

Dr. Gowervine rolled his eyes. "Excuse me for interrupting."

"That's fine," the old lady said loftily. "Now listen."

five

THE ROAMER AND THE SPECTER

*L*isten. There was once a young man who lived in a small town by the bay and worked up the coast in a slightly larger town to the north. The boy's name was Julian Roamer, and twice a day his walk took him six miles along a road that ran beside the water. There was the ocean, and then a ripple of high, seagrass-covered dunes, and then the road, which was badly paved along its whole length, with little stones that constantly got into Julian's worn shoes to abuse his feet. It was almost as if the stones themselves were embarrassed by the state of the road and wanted to escape it by any means they could."

"Roamer?" This time it was Georgie who interrupted. "As in *the* roamers?"

"I'm getting there," Mrs. Hereward said through clenched teeth.

"The roamers?" Negret asked. There was a story in *The Raconteur's Commonplace Book* called *The Roamer in the Nettles,* but he hadn't gotten to it yet. "What are roamers?" He had an idea that he ought to know, but he couldn't quite remember. Meddy had mentioned roamers when they were making up his character, but that was all that came to mind.

"In folklore they're this bunch of wanderers. Itinerants, living on the road. On special roads, usually." Georgie smiled cheerfully at the scowling Mrs. Hereward. "Sorry."

"Kindly don't spoil the story, young lady. To continue: One summer night, Julian was walking home under one of the most wondrous skies he had seen in ages. It was perfectly clear, and so full of stars that they seemed to have been spattered on like fine sprays of white paint. The night was so bright, Julian had even doused his lamp. The only thing spoiling the loveliness was a particularly painful stone in his shoe.

"He stopped and yanked off his shoe and muttered, 'I wish these stones would leave me in peace. In fact, I wish I were mayor of this town so I could fix this road.' It was the sort of thing anyone might say at any time without a second thought and without really meaning it. But it happened that at that precise moment, there was a shooting star in the sky.

"Everyone knows — or at least, was probably told as a child — that you can make a wish on a shooting star. Not everyone knows that the only way to be sure it will come true is to speak it aloud before the star disappears, and this is a nearly impossible feat to manage. But because the wish — the second wish — was on his lips just before the star began its descent, Julian managed to do it, even though he hadn't even realized there was a shooting star in the sky to wish upon.

"He shook out the pebble and was in the process of lacing the shoe back up when he heard a voice from the dunes. 'Young man,' the voice said. 'Would you repeat that, please?'

"Julian turned and found a strange, soaking-wet figure picking his way over the dunes. 'I beg your pardon?' he asked as the man approached. The stranger was wearing a silver tailcoat with black patches of burned fabric at the elbows and the collar. His trousers were a darker pewter color, and they were also burned at the knees. Every inch of him was sodden, as if he'd just picked himself out of the water.

" 'I asked if you could repeat your wish,' the man said, slapping a silver leather cap with earflaps against his thigh to shake the water from it. 'I didn't quite catch it, what with the airflow. Actually, I can't say I was listening all that closely to begin with. Nobody manages his wish well enough to get it all out in time. But I must say I'm grateful, and I'd grant your wish even if I weren't honor bound to do it. You saved my life, after all.' Then the stranger held out his hand. 'I'm Baetylus, and at the risk of stating the obvious, I'm a shooting star. What was your wish, now?'

"Julian stared, pop-eyed, but he understood this much: the stranger named Baetylus was offering to grant the wish he had just made. Julian looked down at the shoe he'd just put back on, and then at the long road ahead of him. 'I think I said something about being mayor so I could fix the road,' he said warily.

"Baetylus frowned. 'You'd like to be mayor? Really? And do you know anything about fixing roads?'

"Julian considered. 'Well, if I were mayor, I suppose I'd have someone working for me whose job it was, wouldn't I?'

" 'I suppose,' the shooting star said, looking disdainfully at the ground upon which they stood. 'Although frankly, this already looks like the kind of road you'd end up with if you had a mayor who'd wished his way into his job.' He wrung a few more drops from his hat and pulled it on, which made his head look like a bullet. 'Listen. Being mayor—well, certainly, I can give you that wish. But if you want to be a *good* mayor—there seem to be so very few of them—that must be the sort of thing you have to be destined for. And a wish that goes against your destiny . . . that's always a bad idea. Only a fool scoffs at destiny.'

" 'I think only a fool relies on it,' Julian grumbled. 'How can destiny decide what I'm going to be before I do?' "

Negret shifted where he sat on the hearth, suddenly vaguely uncomfortable as he considered the idea of destiny. It was the same kind of uneasiness he'd felt earlier that same day when she-who-was-now-Sirin had begun asking questions like *Who do you want to be?* Thoughts like this inevitably led to wondering what might have been if his life had started out just a bit differently. Or maybe, if there was such a thing as destiny, it didn't matter. Maybe he always would have ended up here at Greenglass House as part of the Pine family.

This train of thought brought on a gutful of guilt. Because if anyone had been able to hear his thoughts, that person would have to assume that Milo wished he hadn't ended up here. And that wasn't true. It was just that it was impossible not to *wonder* . . .

He turned his attention back to Mrs. Hereward. "The shooting star was apologetic about his criticism," she continued. " 'This is just my opinion from eons of observation,' he said. 'You're welcome to take it with a grain of salt. If you'd really like to be made mayor, say the word and I'll do it.'

"But by this time, Julian was already rethinking his wish. It had been a bit of an impulse anyhow. 'You're probably right,' he said. 'Honestly, I only said it because I had a stone in my shoe.'

" 'Look here,' Baetylus said, 'stone-proof shoes, that I can do. That's easy.'

" 'Seems like a waste of a wish.'

" 'Not at all. Stone-proof shoes that never wear out would be at once practical and completely impossible without the benefit of magic; just right for wishing. In fact, it's such a perfect wish that I'll give you that one for free, and the next time you and I cross paths, you can tell me what your real wish is. After all, you saved my life.' And with that, the shooting star reached into one pocket, took out a handful of dust, and sprinkled it over Julian's feet. Immediately the boy could feel the soles of his shoes stiffen, the laces tighten, even his socks thicken up between the leather and his skin. Then the peculiar man in his silver coat bent down and picked up a pebble from the road. He held it out to Julian.

" 'Was that the stone that was torturing me?' Julian asked.

" 'Not anymore,' Baetylus said, setting it in Julian's palm. 'Now it's a reminder of the wish you almost made.' He shook the boy's hand, and then the shooting star turned and headed up the road.

"When Baetylus had disappeared from view, Julian continued toward home, shaking the stone in his palm. He thought about what his real wish would be when Baetylus found him once more. *Well, I'm not going to wish to be mayor,* he thought, and tossed the stone over his shoulder. Aloud, he said, 'Perhaps I'll wish for enough money to pave the road myself.' And wouldn't you know it, Julian's luck was such that his carelessly thrown pebble fell into an old and forgotten well covered over by weeds. It happened to be a holy well — the kind they call in fairy stories a *wishing well.*"

"Who needs wishes with that kind of luck?" Sirin asked from behind the tree.

"Shh," Negret hissed. Then his cheeks went red as everyone turned to stare. "Sorry."

Mrs. Hereward gave a little harrumph before carrying on. "Julian, of course, didn't know this. He hadn't seen where his little stone had landed. He just kept on walking, looking at the stars and thinking of wishes, while behind him dark water began to bubble up out of the forgotten well, pouring over the mossy stones and running through the wind-twisted shrubs on the inland side of the road. It kept flowing up and out, more and more of it, all coming right toward Julian, who was blissfully unaware until the water splashed into the back of his shoes. Just then, a woman's voice called from the shrubs to the west: 'Excuse me, young man, you'll have to say that again.'

"Julian climbed onto a rock by the road-turned-creek and peered into the bushes just in time to see the owner of the voice haul herself out of the well and stride toward him. She wore a slate-colored dress, and her hair was the same silver as Baetylus's suit, but her skin was the dark of dark water — it might have been gray, or black, or brown, or green, or any one of them, depending upon the angle of the light that hit it. 'Could you please say that again?' she asked. 'I wasn't listening. My well is so old, and it's very rare that anyone finds it to make a wish in; I confess I don't listen as well as I should.' She held out the pebble he'd just thrown. 'I believe this is yours.'

"Only because he'd just met a shooting star did Julian manage to recover his poise at the sudden appearance of this strange woman. He introduced himself, and the woman in the beautiful dress shook his hand. 'My name is Wielle,' she told him. 'Would you tell me again what you wished for?'

"Once more, Julian had been speaking off the top of his head, and not because he really wanted anything. 'I wished for money,' he admitted, and then because that sounded quite selfish, he added, 'For paving the road.'

"Wielle looked critically at him. 'I'm not sure I'd suggest you make that wish,' she said at last. 'I'll grant it if it's what you truly want, but you seem like a nice fellow, and that sort of wish just never turns out well in my experience. Trouble comes when a person starts asking for money; it never does what they think it will do. And then there's the problem of destiny. Things never turn out well when you try to outwit destiny. Only fools do that.'

"Destiny again. Julian sighed. 'I don't know if I believe in destiny,' he said, 'but you're right, I didn't actually make that wish hoping someone was going to grant it. I was just thinking out loud.'

" 'Well, I'm not going back without granting a wish,' the woman protested. 'Do you know how long it's been since I've been out of that well? Give me something to do, I beg you. It's lonely down there. Moreover, if I grant a wish, I am allowed to stay out of the well for a decade.'

"There was nothing Julian particularly wished for — not really — but he didn't want Wielle to have to return to the well if she didn't want to. 'Let me see,' he said. 'I was only thinking of fixing the road when I made the wish before. Even getting rid of the broken paving stones would be an improvement.'

"Wielle considered. 'That's not a bad idea, you know. I could grant your wish for the broken paving stones to be gone for now, and then you could tell me your real wish another time.'

"Julian wondered for a moment why these strange wishing creatures were so eager to give wishes away and why they thought they were going to cross paths again — but Wielle was already walking toward him, her steps carrying her atop the little flood as easily as an insect skimming the surface. She took his hand, folded the pebble into it, and kissed his lips. When she stepped back, the broken pavement beneath the water was gone, without a single foot-piercing stone to be seen. 'Until we meet again, Julian!' she called, and then she too withdrew to the north, trailing the waters of the hidden well in her wake like the train of a fancy gown.

"With his fingers to his lips, Julian watched her disappear. Then, feeling a bit like he'd wandered off his usual road and into a dream, he started walking again.

"The dirt road was nicer than the broken pavement, but now that the well waters had receded, they had left a good deal of mud behind. Julian's improved shoes kept the sludge out nicely, but they didn't make the actual walking through it any easier, so after a few yards, he hiked off the road a bit, found a bush of blackthorn, and cut himself a walking stick. Then he returned to the road and continued on his way, muttering, 'Wishes, wishes, wishes,' as he walked. Now he had two saved up for a rainy day, and he was trying to figure out what sort of wishes Baetylus and Wielle would approve of. *Only a fool scoffs at destiny,* Baetylus had said, and *Things never turn out well when you try to outwit destiny* had been Wielle's advice. But Julian still didn't know if he believed in destiny at all. 'That would be a useful wish to make, maybe,' he mused. 'To know whether I have a destiny, and if I have, what it is.'

"He walked on in silence for a few yards, and then a new voice spoke up, a voice that seemed to come from incredibly close by. 'Say it properly, for goodness' sake! I can't do anything unless you say it properly.'

"Startled, Julian dropped his walking stick and turned in a circle, but there didn't seem to be anyone there. He looked toward the dunes, in case he'd inadvertently wished upon another star. He patted his hip and peered into the brush, but the stone was still in his pocket and there were no more strange waters rising to flood the road. Then he turned back around and saw a thin creature picking itself up out of the mire. Julian's walking stick had sprouted arms and legs and a narrow face and was now brushing mud from its bark-colored suit.

"'What on earth are you?' Julian asked, bewildered. Shooting stars and wishing wells he had at least heard of before, but a stick creature that granted wishes . . . well, that was something else again.

"'I am a wishing stick,' the thin man said with wounded dignity. 'You gave me life when you cut me from the blackthorn and made a wish upon me.'"

"A wishing stick?" Dr. Gowervine scoffed. "I've never heard of such a thing."

"Would you kindly stop interrupting?" Mrs. Hereward demanded.

Dr. Gowervine looked from Mrs. Hereward to Georgie, who he seemed to have decided was the closest thing they had to an authority on folklore. "Is that a thing, wishing sticks?"

Georgie shrugged. "Sounds like it is in this story, Doc. I mean, I've heard of wishing trees, so I don't know that wishing sticks sound all that preposterous. Also, it's a *story*," she said pointedly.

"'I'm Julian,' said Julian," Mrs. Hereward pronounced loudly, frowning at Dr. Gowervine. "'Sloe,' said the thin man. 'Pleased to meet you. Now, Julian, would you mind phrasing your wish in the *form* of a wish? Then we can get on with things.'

"'I suppose I wish to know if I have a destiny, and if I do, what it is.'"

Negret sat forward a little. *It's just a story,* he reminded himself. *It doesn't mean anything.* And yet he was as eager to hear the answer as if it had been his own destiny they were discussing.

"Julian prepared himself for a lecture from Sloe about what would make a better request. After his encounters with the other two wishing creatures, he was beginning to think he didn't have the knack for wishing at all. But when Sloe spoke, he said instead, 'That's two wishes. Pick one. If you really want to know, that is. I've never understood all this stock people put into destiny anyhow. Only fools rely on destiny.'

"'I agree!' Julian exclaimed. 'But twice tonight I've been told I'd be a fool to chance crossing destiny with a wish. How does anyone get anything done, worrying about destiny?'

"'I suspect they don't,' Sloe answered. 'Plus, if destiny exists, it doesn't seem it would be very functional if you could thwart it with a single wish. But tell me about these wishes you made before.'

"Julian did. The blackthorn man listened, nodded occasionally, interjected a question or two, and at the end, asked to see the pebble. 'Very interesting,' Sloe said quietly, turning the little stone in his twiggy fingers. Then he returned it to Julian. 'It seems to me Baetylus and Wielle gave you sound advice when they suggested you rethink your wishes, not because of destiny but because you yourself admit that you don't really want to be mayor and you don't really want money; you just want a better road. Perhaps they only mentioned destiny because they thought the idea might make you more likely to reconsider. Wishing creatures aren't supposed to argue about the wishes that are made to us, only we can't help having opinions.'

"'Do you have an opinion about what I ought to wish for?' Julian inquired.

"Sloe shrugged. 'Not really. But I owe you something for cutting me loose, so if you'd like me to give it some thought, I'd be glad to try and come up with something useful.'

" 'Yes, please.' Julian and the blackthorn man sat side by side on a piece of fence that had once held up the dunes. Sloe leaned his head on his palm and tapped his skinny fingers against his angular cheek. 'I suppose I think the problem with asking about your destiny,' he said at last, 'is that it can't possibly help you to know anything about it. Knowing would make you change your behavior somehow, and there's no way to be sure whether that would help or hurt your cause.' He turned to Julian. 'Let me ask you this: what do you really want?'

"This was a very good question. Julian hadn't given much thought to what he actually wanted. Except for one thing, of course.

" 'Sloe, could you fix this road, between the town I came from and the one I'm going to?' he asked. 'I mean *really* fix it, with new paving stones and drainage ditches and everything? Make it a proper road? That's all I wanted in the first place.'

"Sloe looked at Julian, then looked at the muddy dirt track. He nodded once and got back to his feet. 'I can do better than that. Give me one of your shoes.' The boy took off one of the shoes Baetylus had fixed up for him and handed it to Sloe, who cut a sign onto the sole with a fingernail tipped with a thorn. 'There,' Sloe said, pleased. 'Now wherever you walk in these shoes, good roads will follow.'

"Julian put the shoe back on and laced it up. It felt just the same as before, but when he stepped off the dune and onto the road, a neat surface of rounded cobblestones spread out beneath his feet like a stain. He took another experimental step, and the cobblestones poured forth, extending to the edge of the dunes, where they somehow seemed to sense that their work was done and stopped. The cobbles that had appeared under his first steps remained where they were. He stared at the new paving and then at Sloe.

"'Choose your paths carefully,' said the blackthorn man, 'and take off the shoes when you wish to feel grass or sand or water beneath your feet. But now when you wish to blaze a trail, you will always have the means. And while we're at it, why don't you give me that lantern, too, and your knife. The one you cut me free with.'

"Julian handed over his knife along with the lamp he'd extinguished earlier that night. Sloe scratched the symbol he'd cut into Julian's shoes onto the hilt of the knife and onto the underbelly of the lantern. 'Now you will always be able to cut a path, and you will always be able to light your way, as long as you have a flint. That stone that was giving you so much trouble would work nicely, I think.' Then he leaped down to the newly paved road and shook Julian's hand. 'Roam well, until we meet again.' And with that, Sloe also hiked northward and disappeared into the star-spattered night. And Julian walked home, marveling at the feel of the new cobbles that came up under each step."

Mrs. Hereward paused. "According to my father and his father and his mother and her father and his grandmother and so on and farther back, Julian was the first of the roamers, the great wanderers of the country, and the roads that he paved with his wish-magicked shoes became the most sacred of all the roads used by the creatures of their world, which is called in folklore the *roaming world*. And he always kept the shoes, the knife, the lantern, and the flint pebble. And ... well, that's it." Mrs. Hereward made a little bow over her mug and plate.

Milo's mother began to clap. "That was wonderful, Mrs. Hereward!" Everyone else very quickly joined in the applause.

Behind the tree, Sirin sat back and folded her arms. "All right," she admitted. "That was pretty good. That's what you call a creation story, Negret. I can probably use that in a campaign someday." She fished in her pocket, found a piece of paper and pen, and began scribbling.

Negret frowned and scooted off the hearth into the tree-cave. "But it was just a fairy tale," he whispered.

"I don't care. I liked it."

"But it doesn't tell us anything about why she's here."

At this, the scholiast peered up from her paper. She looked at Mrs. Hereward through narrowed eyes. "Doesn't it? Ask her what happened to the wishy stuff, the things the magic people gave Julian Roamer. Bet you're wrong."

"That's a bet. Mrs. Hereward," Negret called, leaning out from behind the tree, "what happened to Julian's things, the shoes and the pebble and stuff?"

The old woman gave him an oddly discomfited look. "Well, I'm sure I don't know, dear. Goodness, my tea's gone cold. Must see about some hot water." And she got awkwardly to her feet and bustled to the tea tray Mrs. Caraway had left on the coffee table.

Sirin looked up from her notes. "See? I told you."

"What just happened?"

"The logical grownup answer would've been to say it was just a story, and the wishy things didn't really exist. But that *isn't* what she said." Sirin grinned. "Here's a wild guess: I think Mrs. Hereward *doesn't* think it's just a story. And I think maybe she thinks there's some connection between it and this house."

"I see." The two of them watched Mrs. Hereward refill her cup with hot water, completely forgetting to add more tea.

Negret clambered back out into the open. "Anybody else?" he asked the other guests hopefully, climbing into the vacant chair on the other side of the fireplace.

Clem spoke up from where she sat on the rag rug before the hearth. "Can I make a request?"

"Sure, I guess."

"I'd like to hear a story about this house." All of a sudden, Negret was pretty sure if he'd dropped a pin in that room, it would've made a noise like the clash of cymbals. Did she mean she wanted *him* to tell a story?

His stomach gave a hard twist. Why hadn't it occurred to him that if he was going to ask everyone else to share, he might have to tell a story himself? In the book, the man who suggested the stories had told the first one.

But Clem beamed up at Milo's mom, who was leaning beside the grandfather clock that stood against the wall between the living room and the kitchen. "Would you mind telling us a bit about it?"

Mr. and Mrs. Pine glanced at each other. This was a tricky question, because while smuggling was a big part of the fabric of the city of Nagspeake and a huge part of life in the Quayside Harbors, the district Greenglass House overlooked, it was still, strictly speaking, illegal.

"I'd be glad to tell you what I know," Mrs. Pine said at last. "Of course, Nagspeake records . . ." She shrugged. "Well, everybody knows they're not great. I've lived in this house since I was about Milo's age. My dad bought the place, mostly furnished, from a family named Whitcher." She paused momentarily, probably, Milo figured, to give anyone who knew the name a chance to say *Wasn't that Doc Holystone's real name?* Nobody did.

"But now that you mention it," she continued, "I do know a story you might like. It's a ghost story, though — something that happened here. Is that going to bother anyone?"

Around the room, the guests shook their heads and waited.

"Okay. Well, it happened . . . let's see, Milo was a baby, so ten or eleven years ago? One of our regular guests — a fellow who'd stayed with us before — came down to breakfast and told us he'd seen a dead man from his window."

Milo nearly dropped his mug. *"What?"*

"You heard me." His mother wiggled her eyebrows. "And I'm sure you've all heard of Doc Holystone," she continued. "Along with the Gentleman Maxwell and Ed Pickering and Violet Cross, he was one of the great runners — runners being what smugglers call themselves — of the last half century. Doc Holystone was supposedly captured and killed when I was a little girl. But I'm from the Quayside Harbors, so I grew up hearing about his exploits. And some say he was captured right on the grounds of this house. Some say that his son was here at the time and saw it happen.

"Of course," she continued, "nobody said anything about that to my father when he bought the place. Folks didn't start talking about it until afterward, around the time my father opened the house as an inn, although certainly it was clear that something had gone very wrong — Holystone had vanished, and the surviving members of his family and crew had gone to ground so fast that the house hadn't even been cleared out. Years later, Ben and I inherited the inn, along with its regular guests. And then, one summer night when Milo was little, one of those guests . . ." She paused and looked at Mr. Pine. "It was Fenster, wasn't it?"

"That's what I remember. It was late for Fenster — that is, when he came to stay with us, it was usually in the early spring."

Smugglers and their seasons, Milo thought. He knew just who they were talking about. Fenster was a spring-season runner because he usually traded in illegal seedlings.

"Right. Well, maybe because it was summer, we put him in a different room than we usually did, one on the cooler side of the house." Mrs. Pine's eyes flicked over at Mrs. Hereward. Fenster must've been staying in 3N, and it looked as if Milo's mother was working out whether to tell the old lady that the events she was about to relay had taken place in her room. *Don't do it,* Milo thought. Mrs. Hereward flew off the handle too easily to be told she was staying in a haunted room.

"A different room in a creaky old house can be a little disorienting, even frightening, perhaps," Mrs. Pine went on, apparently coming to the same conclusion. "Milo can tell you something about that.

Milo's camped out all over the inn. How different is each room, Milo, in terms of the creaky-freaky factor?"

"Very different," he admitted. "It's not that they're scary, but you get used to the noises and drafts in one and they start to seem friendly and comfortable. Then if you move to another, they don't seem quite as friendly at first. You have to get used to them all over again."

"Exactly. So when Fenster came down the first morning and mentioned that he'd seen something strange, we all sort of thought he was just having that new-room adjustment. Something woke him up, he said, and then something outside the window caught his eye. No, he didn't know what had woken him — probably a sound of some kind — and no, he didn't know what he'd seen. Probably a flash of something in the trees, or in the sky. No, he didn't want to change rooms, he'd just wanted to mention it. Then he ate three helpings of pancakes and everything seemed to be fine.

"But the next morning it happened again: Fenster came down and said that he'd woken in the night and seen something from his window. This time, though, he said he'd gotten up and crossed the room to the window for a better look. And what he'd seen was the figure of a young man standing in the trees and staring up at the house.

"The man had been familiar, Fenster said. As I recall, he gave my husband a long look, like he was trying to figure out if maybe it had been him out there. But Ben hadn't gone outside that night, certainly not anytime after midnight, which is when Fenster figured he'd been up. Then he ate another three helpings of pancakes, and that was the end of it. Until the next morning, when Fenster came down and announced that he knew who the man he'd seen was.

"It had happened again, and this time Fenster had gotten right up and gone to the window, and there was the young man again, still standing near the trees, still looking up at the house. Something made Fenster raise his hand in greeting, and the fellow raised his hand in response. It was that gesture that Fenster had recognized. 'It was Doc Holystone,' Fenster told us.

"Everybody knows the Deacon and Morvengarde catalog company has always . . . *encouraged* the city to come down harder on the smugglers. Well, apparently, in the year before Doc Holystone's capture, Deacon and Morvengarde had put up Wanted posters around Nagspeake that showed Doc Holystone with one hand raised. Seems Fenster remembered those posters."

Milo hadn't heard this story before, but he knew Fenster Plum, and he knew it wasn't from a Wanted poster that Fenster had recognized the famous smuggler. Milo knew for a fact that Fenster had actually *sailed* with Doc Holystone, but Mrs. Pine would hardly be likely to tell a bunch of strangers that.

"So of course, we pointed out that Doc Holystone had been dead — supposedly — for more than twenty years. Certainly he hadn't been seen in Nagspeake since the night he was said to have been captured. I may have suggested that Fenster had been dreaming — maybe the unfamiliar noises in the room were to blame, or maybe the strange drafts. But Fenster insisted he'd seen him. And what made him so sure?

"Well, it turned out there was more to the story that Fenster hadn't told us. On the third night, after he'd raised his hand to the young man in the trees, it had finally occurred to Fenster that the window had been open each night when he'd woken, and *he* hadn't been the one to open it.

"Outside that room there's a fire escape, and Fenster had climbed out onto it for a better look. As he came to his realization about the window, he'd turned to look around and had discovered that he wasn't alone on the fire escape. Leaning over the railing next to him was a small boy. The boy was waving too. It was the *boy* that the young man had been waving to. And it must have been the boy, Fenster explained to us, who had been opening the window so he could climb out to look for Doc Holystone. The noise of the sash going up was what had been waking Fenster each night.

"Now, I don't know if I'd have had the courage to do this, but Fenster, who was half asleep and who is a bit of an innocent anyhow, actually spoke to the boy. 'Do you know who that is?' he asked. I don't know why he started with the man in the trees rather than asking the boy who he was or how he came to be in Fenster's room climbing out onto the fire escape — after all, there was no boy staying at the inn, and even if there had been, as you can see, guests here tend to get to know one another. Anyhow, he asked the boy if he knew who the man in the trees below was, and the boy nodded. And what he said, according to Fenster, was, 'That's my father. We must wave at each other now, because we didn't get to say goodbye then.'

"'And what is your father's name?' Fenster asked. 'He looks familiar to me.' The boy smiled proudly and answered, 'His name is

Michael Whitcher, and this house used to be ours.' Then the boy waved again at the man in the trees, and the man waved back, and then the two of them disappeared, leaving Fenster alone on the fire escape."

She paused once more, and this time the guests got it. "So Michael Whitcher was Doc Holystone?" Clem asked. "This house belonged to Doc Holystone?"

"Yup," Mrs. Pine said with a smile. "And at least once, according to Fenster, the ghosts of Doc Holystone and his son returned to say goodbye to each other. It's the only time we've ever heard of a haunting here."

"I like that story even better than the first one," Meddy said.

Almost immediately after Mrs. Pine finished her story, the rain started.

It flung itself at the windows in shining sheets that were lit peculiarly by the reflection of lightning on the snow, and from somewhere on the other side of the hill came the battering-ram sounds of thunder.

The sudden storm seemed to signal the end of the evening's storytelling. The first clap of thunder shook the room, and on the heels of a ghost story — even if it was a relatively pleasant one — the noise put everyone right on edge.

"Milo, I'm going to run up and grab that camera for you," Georgie announced, and disappeared up the stairs.

"Maybe I'll grab a sweater," Mrs. Hereward commented, and she headed up too.

Another slicing flicker of lightning. Another crack of thunder. This time, the white-glass chandelier over the table flickered and went out. It was only dark for a heartbeat before the lights came back on, but that was enough. What if the power went out?

Milo glanced around the room and knew everyone else was having the same thought.

"At least the rain'll melt the snow," Mrs. Caraway muttered. "Who needs more coffee?"

"Doubt it'll melt much," Dr. Gowervine said as he rose to go smoke on the porch again. He pointed outside the window at the icicles that hung from the eaves. "Those aren't getting any smaller. The rain must be freezing."

Mrs. Pine came to perch on the arm of Milo's chair, and he considered what his dad had said about the two of them feeling bad that they couldn't spend more time with him. He leaned his head against his mom's side as she put an arm around his shoulder.

"I think your storytelling idea was brilliant," she said. "How'd I do?"

"Perfect," Milo told her. "You were awesome. Have I heard that story before?"

"I think we must've told it to you at one point or another. Although I might've left out the part about the ghost boy, since that's the same fire escape that's outside your room. I might have thought it would freak you out." She ruffled his hair. "But I'm sure I was just being an overprotective mom. I'm sure that kind of thing would *never* freak you out." She tousled his hair again and stood up. "And hey, kiddo, is there anything special you'd like to do for Christmas

Eve day after tomorrow? Special dinner, special cake, special anything? My means are limited by this weather, but if there's something that would salvage Christmas for you, we'll give it a try. I mean, we'll do the Yule log and sing carols and stuff, definitely, but other than that. Think about it, and let me know."

"Okay, Mom. I'll think about it."

"Thanks, Milo." She looked around the room. "Anybody need anything from the kitchen?"

"I'd take another piece of cake," Clem called. "But I can get it."

"No trouble," Mrs. Pine said, and Clem, who'd already gotten to her feet, stopped abruptly. She dropped onto the hearth next to Milo's chair and leaned her elbows on her knees to wait. "Great idea, by the way."

"Thanks. Do you think you can tell one tomorrow?"

"I'll try and think something up." She looked thoughtfully at the stairs. "What's a *lansdegown*, Milo?"

Aha. He'd nearly forgotten about the odd exchange that had taken place between Clem and Georgie before Mrs. Hereward had started her tale. He sat up a bit straighter. "You mean, other than a funny name for a camera?"

The red-haired girl shrugged. "Most names mean something, or why would people give things the names they do? So what's *lansdegown* mean?"

"It sort of seemed like you might know what it means already," Milo pointed out. "Didn't you say something earlier about maybe telling a story about it?"

"I was just giving Blue a hard time," Clem said.

He gave her a dubious look. "That isn't how it sounded."

She waved her hand dismissively. "So you've never heard the word before?"

"Nope."

"You sure?"

First Georgie, now Clem. Why did either of them think he'd have a clue what some weird word meant? "Why don't you just ask Georgie?"

"I could, but I thought you might know something about it that she doesn't." To this odd statement, Clem added a conspiratorial wink. "Anyway, if you think of anything—"

"Clem?" Milo thought about what Negret would do, and decided just to put the obvious question out there and see if it got him anywhere. "Georgie asked me the same question, you know: if I knew what *lansdegown* means. Why do either of you think I know anything about a strange word I've never heard before? Is it because you think it has something to do with the house?"

Another direct question, thrown down like a gauntlet. Clem opened her mouth, then hesitated.

"Because, you know," Negret continued in his most reasonable tone, "maybe I would remember better if I knew more about it. I mean, if you told me what *you* know."

Clem gave him a shrewd look as footsteps sounded on the staircase. One set, light and quick: Georgie was on her way back down. Clem glanced in the direction of the sounds, then winked again. "Ask me another time," she said quietly. Then she got up quickly and headed for the kitchen to meet Mrs. Pine, who was on her way out with a slice of cake. By the time Georgie reached the main floor with her camera, Clem had settled herself at the dining room table and was chewing contentedly.

She kept on chewing as Georgie sat next to Negret and showed him the finished (*light-tight,* she said) cigar-box camera. Now and then he glanced at Clem out of the corner of his eye, but she didn't seem to be paying any special attention to them.

"Anyway, it's too dark now to try it out," Georgie was saying, "but maybe tomorrow I'll put it somewhere bright and take off the bit of tape that's covering the aperture and we'll see what we see. It'll take a long time for an image to form, but maybe by tomorrow night I'll have a picture to share."

Negret turned the camera over in his hands. Now he couldn't get the word *lansdegown* out of his head, but there was nothing about the object itself that gave any hints. It was just a thin wooden box wrapped up tightly with thick black fabric tape.

If he asked Georgie the same questions he'd just asked Clem, would she answer the same way? Would the answers change if he waited until Clem wasn't around? And then, out of nowhere, it occurred to him to wonder something equally interesting. *I was just giving Blue a hard time,* Clem had said. It had seemed strange then, and now Milo realized why. *Giving a hard time* was something you did to people you knew. So was giving someone a nickname, like *Blue.* But Clem and Georgie were strangers — or had been, until yesterday.

Unless for some reason they'd only been *pretending* to be strangers.

Interesting. He handed back the camera and smiled at Georgie. "Cool."

"Negret." Sirin climbed out from behind the tree and joined him, peering over the arm of his chair. She nodded at the stairs. Mrs. Hereward had at last returned to the main floor. She was wearing a sweater, and she carried a bag he vaguely remembered her holding while she was hollering at Dr. Gowervine just after they'd arrived at the inn.

"The bag," Sirin whispered. "Look at the *bag.*"

Now that Mrs. Hereward had opened the drawstring at the top to begin pulling red yarn from it, he could see that the bag was cylindrical, and it had a flat bottom, so that it sat sturdily on the floor beside her feet. It was made from thick canvas that seemed somewhat at odds with the delicate decorative stitching that covered the side. He hadn't paid much attention to the embroidered image before because when Mrs. Hereward was yelling, it was hard to focus on anything else. But now ... now he could see that it was a picture of a house—a bizarrely shaped hodgepodge of a house with green windows, set among dark pines.

Mrs. Hereward glanced up just then and caught him looking. Her face went redder than Clem's hair and she turned the bag quickly around so that the house was hidden from view. But that hardly mattered. On the other side was another image, one that Mrs. Hereward had no way of knowing he would recognize.

Picked out in gray-brown thread was a misshapen iron gate.

six

THREE THEFTS

The storm melted away the snow that lined the branches of the trees, and then the temperature dropped bitterly. Dr. Gowervine had been right — it didn't look like the rain had done much to get rid of the snow on the ground. When Milo woke up the next morning, the day before Christmas Eve, the only changes he could see out his window were that the icicles were longer and the trees were mostly bare.

Mostly bare, because it was snowing again.

Milo stretched and sighed and checked the clock: not quite eight. Plenty of time to laze around before he needed to drag himself downstairs. He had just picked up *The Raconteur's Commonplace Book* to finish the story he'd been reading when sharp knocking sounded on his door. Milo scrambled out of bed, yanked on his robe, and peered out into the hallway. Meddy stood there, barely managing to conceal her excitement. There was some sort of hullaballoo drifting up from somewhere below: at least three angry voices shouting over one another. "You better come down," Meddy whispered. "Sounds like you aren't the only blackjack in the house."

"Didn't we already know that?" he muttered, shoving his feet into his escaladeur shoes and grabbing his rucksack from the desk chair.

"Well, we suspected it, but now something's *really* gone missing."

Negret's blackjack keys were on his bedside table. He tucked them in his pocket, then followed her down the hall toward the noise at the bottom of the stairs. "Is it missing from Clem's room?"

She tossed him a dark look over her shoulder. "Nope."

Christmas season at Greenglass House. Usually so full of traditions — roaring fires and carols and hot chocolate and roast meats and pies and puddings. This year, it was also full of yelling adults.

Milo had begun to assume that any shouting in the house was likely to come from Mrs. Hereward and Dr. Gowervine, so he figured two of the voices had to belong to them. Once Meddy had mentioned theft, he'd guessed the third voice had to be Clem's — after all, they knew for sure someone had been in her room who shouldn't have been. But when he reached the bottom of the steps, he stopped in his tracks, shocked to discover that he'd gotten two out of three wrong. Yes, Mrs. Hereward was there, clutching a mauve dressing gown about herself, red-faced and shrieking, while Mrs. Pine and Mrs. Caraway tried to calm her down, but neither Dr. Gowervine nor Clem was anywhere to be seen.

Instead, there was Georgie, and also — Milo frowned — Mr. Vinge?

A familiar hand gently moved Milo aside. *"Knock it off!"* Mr. Pine bellowed as he stepped into the fray. "Everyone just *settle down.*" He glared from one fuming face to the next. "One at a time. What is the problem? You first, ma'am," he said to Mrs. Hereward.

The old lady didn't look like she could've held it in if he'd made her wait. Her face had gone the shade of one of the crimson poinsettias lining the stairs. "I have been *robbed!*" she wailed.

Milo's dad turned next to Mr. Vinge. "I am ... missing something," the tall man said carefully.

Georgie waited with folded arms until it was her turn. "Me too. Something's missing. I had it yesterday."

"Is it possible any of these items have just been mislaid?" Mr. Pine asked patiently.

"I suppose anything is possible," Georgie said reluctantly. "But I know where I put it, and it's not there."

Mr. Vinge spoke up next. "I don't like to accuse anyone of stealing, but the thing is simply gone."

"Not a chance!" moaned Mrs. Hereward. *"I have been robbed!"*

"Do you think one of them's talking about the map?" Sirin whispered. "Maybe whoever owns it didn't realize until now that it was missing?"

Negret shrugged. "When was the last time you saw ... the

missing things?" he asked the guests. "What *are* the missing things anyway?"

The three burgled parties looked suspiciously at one another. "I'm missing a book," Georgie said. "A notebook. I had it last night. I wrote in it before bed."

"Mr. Vinge?"

"A watch," the old man replied. "My pocket watch, which I was wearing last night during the storytelling."

"Mrs. Hereward?"

She folded her arms. "My knitting bag, which I was using yesterday evening. I sat up knitting until past midnight."

"Did you maybe leave it down here?" Mr. Pine asked, looking into the living room.

"No, I did not leave it down here! I took it up with me. I'm not in the habit of leaving my personal belongings lying around hotels!"

Interesting, Negret thought. Three missing things; none of them was the chart, and none of them had gone missing from Clem's room.

"Okay, okay." Mr. Pine rubbed his head and blinked. "Somebody make coffee and everybody keep it together. I'm sure we can figure this out."

Georgie huffed, stomped to the foyer, and started pulling on her boots. "I'm going for a walk. I'll be back when I'm calm." Mr. Vinge stayed where he was, right next to the stairs. He tucked his hands in his pockets and waited. Mrs. Hereward did not look much like she wanted to keep it together. She began pacing alongside the dining table. The *ca-click, ca-click* of her footfalls was nearly unbearable.

Negret tiptoed into the kitchen after his parents, trying to be unobtrusive as he got the milk bottle from the fridge and poured himself a glass.

"You don't really think anybody could've broken into their rooms, do you?" Mrs. Pine asked her husband quietly. "In our twelve years of running this place, even with our . . . usual guests, I don't remember ever having a theft."

"And they all seem to think they had the missing things when they went to bed," Mr. Pine whispered back. "Someone breaking into their rooms while they were sleeping? That seems awfully farfetched. Plus, the thefts don't make any sense. A watch I can see being stolen, but a notebook and a knitting bag? My guess is they put them away somewhere unfamiliar and now they don't remember where — or they may not even have looked that well, and when they came down and somebody suggested thievery, they all leaped at the idea."

"Well," Milo's mother grumbled, "we're going to have to find the stuff that's MIA. Lost or stolen, it's all still got to be here somewhere. Got any brilliant ideas?"

Negret carried his glass of milk into the living room and crept into the space behind the Christmas tree, where Sirin was already waiting. "The rooms are so small," he said thoughtfully. "How could the thief have snuck in and taken things while people were sleeping, without waking them up?"

"I was thinking maybe Clem could've managed it." Sirin scratched her head, knocking the Helm of Revelations askew. "Unless . . ."

Negret nodded. "Unless all three of them were out of their rooms at some point last night. So now we go from two potential creepers to *four?*"

"Looks that way. I wonder if any of them would admit to wandering around after everyone else went to sleep."

Ca-click, ca-click, ca-click. Mrs. Hereward's pacing was forceful, but she looked as though she was trying not to cry as she stalked back and forth in heeled slippers that matched her robe. "Is it weird that all of this began after they started telling stories?" Negret asked. "I can't stop thinking that if Mrs. Hereward was sneaking around, it had something to do with the story she told."

"So you think . . . what? That she was looking for something from that story?" Sirin frowned. "But it's — well, like you said. It's just a story."

"Yeah, but if that's really all it is, why'd somebody steal her bag?"

"What's her bag have to do with the story, Negret? She's obviously rich. Maybe it's worth something. That's the simplest answer."

"No, it has something to do with the story, I know it." He frowned and watched as Mrs. Pine approached the pacing lady with a cup of tea and maneuvered her to a seat at the table. "*This house* was sewn right there on the bag. You saw it. And the gate, just like in the windows and on the map."

"All right," Sirin argued, "but then if she's looking for something, what is it? What's the house got to do with an old story? 'Cause it's a *story!* It's *made up.*"

"So are Sirin and Negret," he pointed out reasonably.

"Do *you* think *she's* playing a game?" Sirin retorted. "I don't."

"No, it isn't that I think she's playing a game. But there's something about that story that's important to her, and somehow that's why she's here. Anyway, you're the one who said maybe Mrs. Hereward didn't think the story she told was just a story."

"All right then, fearless leader, where do we start?"

Negret looked at the old lady sitting forlornly over her tea. "I wonder if she'll tell us."

"If she'll tell *you*," the scholiast reminded him, pulling the Eyes of True and Aching Clarity down off her forehead and perching them on her nose. "I'm invisible, remember? Also, you're the one with the high charisma score. Charisma's what makes you persuasive. You're way more likely to get her talking."

"I still don't quite understand how these ability scores work."

"In a tabletop game? Chance and probability. The higher your ability score, the better your chances. You roll a die to see if you succeed. For you, here and now?" She grinned. "Believe you can do it and try hard."

Negret sighed. "Fine." He crawled out from behind the tree and headed for the dining room. But just as he was about to slide onto the bench next to Mrs. Hereward, his mom's voice stopped him.

"Hey, Milo?" she called. "I hate to ask, but would you mind giving Mrs. Caraway a hand with breakfast?"

He slumped for a moment, then obediently changed direction and padded into the kitchen.

"Thanks, kiddo." His mother leaned close. "Your dad and I want to talk right away to the people who are missing things and try and figure out what's going on."

"What do you need me to do?" Milo grumbled.

Mrs. Caraway patted his shoulder. "Could you put dishes and napkins and stuff out on the table? This is a big help, Milo."

Breakfast was soon underway. Clem came trotting down the stairs, then Dr. Gowervine emerged at a more stately pace. Both went right back up again after they heard the news, presumably to check their own belongings, and neither returned until breakfast was nearly ready. Mr. and Mrs. Pine chatted with Mrs. Hereward in the upstairs study, then Mr. Vinge. Just as Mrs. Caraway sent Milo to the table with the first of a seemingly never-ending procession of big covered dishes of scrambled eggs and sausages and grits and roast potatoes and fruit salad and sliced tomatoes with salt and pepper, Georgie returned from her walk red-faced from the cold and covered with a layer of fresh snow. "It's really coming down out there again," she announced.

Three racks of toast, crocks of butter, a pot of coffee and a pot of hot water for tea, and the table was set. The denizens of Greenglass House filed along the side of the table, filling their plates; evidently Mrs. Caraway had decided buffets were the way to go. It was still a very awkward breakfast, though. Even though they weren't sitting together, it was just what Negret had wished for the night before: each guest seemed to be trying to figure out everybody else. Now, if only he and Sirin could determine what clues, if any, were being dropped.

"You sit in the living room," she whispered. "I'll get my food last and eat at the bar by the kitchen so I can watch whoever stays in the dining room. Hurry!"

"How very odd," Dr. Gowervine was saying when Negret took a seat on the hearth. "Has anyone come up with a connection between the missing items?" The three burgled guests glared at him, Mrs. Hereward and Georgie from the sofa, Mr. Vinge from his usual chair. Apparently, it hadn't occurred to him that he, not having had anything of his own go missing, was automatically a prime suspect.

"No, Dr. Gowervine, we haven't," Mrs. Hereward said frostily. "*Is* there some connection between them? Please enlighten us, if you know something we don't."

Dr. Gowervine swallowed. "I was merely asking. I was trying to be helpful."

The old lady stabbed a potato slice. Her fork rang so hard against the plate that Mrs. Pine winced. "As far as I'm concerned, the only reason for anyone to steal an old knitting bag is kleptomania."

Clem wandered in from the dining room with her plate in her hand. "You must be very sound sleepers."

Mrs. Hereward glared at her. "Or the culprit was someone very, very quiet," she retorted.

There was an accusation there for sure, but Clem only shrugged. "That's a given. But even a very quiet person couldn't be completely silent, not in such small, creaky rooms." She blinked and glanced over her shoulder. "No offense. I just meant—"

Milo's mother replied from the dining room. "We know what you meant, Clem. None taken."

It was interesting, Negret thought, how quiet Georgie Moselle and Mr. Vinge were being. Mr. Vinge was working his way deliberately through his breakfast, saying nothing. Georgie seemed too upset to eat much. She picked at what little she'd put on her plate. When someone asked her a direct question, she answered, but Mrs.

Hereward was so loudly indignant that this hadn't happened very often.

Now Georgie was looking thoughtfully in Clem's direction. This was hardly surprising. Clem had to be considered Suspect Number One, even considering what Negret knew about Dr. Gowervine. She was not merely quiet—she was practically soundless. Plus, most everybody had heard her say she was a cat burglar, even though it had sounded like a joke. And Negret simply couldn't picture the short, gawky Dr. Gowervine in the role of a silent, sneaky footpad.

Then again, two days ago Milo would never have pictured himself as a silent, sneaky footpad—yet here he was, feeling more and more comfortable as the escaladeur Negret. Maybe Dr. Gowervine couldn't be ruled out quite that easily.

After breakfast, everyone went off on his or her own again. Clem announced that she was going to run the stairs for a bit, and disappeared. Dr. Gowervine went out onto the screened porch with his pipe. It was decided that the Pines would go up to their rooms with the burgled guests one at a time to double-check that the missing items weren't simply hiding in plain sight. Mrs. Hereward was first, of course.

Negret was torn. On one hand, it might be interesting to tag along under the pretext of helping out. On the other hand, he had a feeling his parents might prefer him out of the way. Plus, he realized as he looked around the living room that Mr. Vinge seemed to have gone upstairs too. Apart from Mrs. Caraway doing the dishes and Lizzie assembling baking ingredients in the kitchen, only he and Sirin and Georgie Moselle were left on the main floor.

Negret touched the keys in his pocket for luck, then gave Sirin a meaningful look and the two of them went over to where Georgie was sitting on the hearth. She was so deep in thought that Negret had to clear his throat before she noticed he and Sirin were there.

"Hey." Georgie scooted over to make room, and Sirin sat beside her. Negret perched on the coffee table. "So this is probably a bit more excitement than usual, huh?"

"You can say that again," Sirin muttered.

"A little bit, yeah," Negret agreed. "I guess this means you didn't get to set up your camera this morning."

Georgie smiled weakly. "No, I set it up. That was before I noticed the notebook was missing."

"My folks are hoping it turns up—that it was just lost, not stolen."

"I know, Milo. I hope they're right."

"Well, we—" Sirin kicked him in the knee and Negret corrected himself. "I thought maybe I'd see if I could help try and find it. I'm good at finding things."

Georgie looked at him closely, and for a moment he wondered if she thought maybe he'd taken her notebook. If he had, saying he'd found the things he'd stolen would be an easy way to turn them back in. He tried to keep his face neutral.

"All right," she said at last. "What do you need to know?"

Negret hesitated. "Well—I mean ... what does it look like, I guess?"

"It's about this big." She held up her hands and indicated a rectangle about the shape of a paperback book. "It's thin, like this." She made a pinching gesture with her thumb and forefinger less than an inch apart. "In fact, you might have seen it the day I arrived, when the perfume bottle broke and you helped me clean up my things."

"Was there anything special about it?" Negret asked casually.

"Well, obviously it was special to me," Georgie replied. "I made all kinds of notes in it that I'd rather not lose. But if you mean can I think of any reason anyone else would find it special . . . then yes, I suppose I can. And I guess it doesn't hurt to tell you," she added, more to herself. "Yes, I suppose it hardly matters now." But then she just sat quietly for a moment.

"What, then, for crying out loud?" Sirin demanded.

Georgie gave a resigned sigh. "The notes I had made were about this house," she said. "And about someone I thought might be connected to it."

"*Ha!*" Sirin erupted.

Negret's jaw dropped. "You're kidding!"

"Nope. But more than that I can't tell you," Georgie said, getting to her feet as the group that had gone to search Mrs. Hereward's room returned to the main floor. "I'm afraid I haven't worked out the connection yet."

"Georgie," Mr. Pine called, "shall we see if we have any luck in your room?"

"Why not." Georgie didn't sound as if she thought they were going to have any luck. Negret didn't figure they would, either. From the look on Mrs. Hereward's face, it was clear her bag had not magically turned up.

"You two go on ahead," Mrs. Pine said, heading for the kitchen.

"I'm just going to fix Mrs. Hereward some fresh tea. I'll catch up with you."

"Well," Negret whispered once all the adults had left the room, "*that* was interesting. Georgie's missing thing has to do with the house too. Just like Mrs. Hereward's bag!"

"I'm still not convinced her story has anything to do with the house-bag connection," Sirin muttered. "But I'm willing to have my mind changed. And now's your chance."

They waited until they heard the whistle of the teakettle in the kitchen, and then kept on waiting until they heard Mrs. Pine's feet trotting up the stairs. Then Negret and Sirin joined Mrs. Hereward at the dining room table.

Her hand shook as she stirred a spoonful of sugar into one of Mrs. Pine's thin blue teacups. Milo's mother almost never used them. They were old and brittle, and they had been her grandmother's. She usually only got them out when she said she needed cheering up, and if anyone needed cheering up now, Mrs. Hereward did.

Negret slid onto the bench opposite the old lady. "Hi, Mrs. Hereward."

She jumped, nearly knocking over her tea with her spoon. "Oh, Milo. Hello."

"Sorry to scare you. I guess your bag didn't turn up yet, did it?"

She shook her head. "No, I'm afraid the *thief* hasn't *returned* it."

"Er. About that." Negret leaned across the table and motioned for her to do the same. She gave him a dubious look, but after a moment she leaned down close enough for him to whisper. "We're

—I mean, I'm pretty good at finding things. I thought maybe I could look around and see what I can turn up. Maybe I can find your bag."

"What makes you think so?" she whispered back.

"Well, the thief would be a fool to hide it in his or her room, right? Eventually someone's going to suggest searching the rooms. Which means the best place to hide it would be someplace else in the house, and I bet I know all the good hiding places."

An expression of guarded hope crossed Mrs. Hereward's face. "Well, Milo, I'd be ever so grateful if you did. I suppose there's no harm in your looking around. It's your house, after all."

"Exactly!" Negret scratched his head. "The bag that went—that was stolen . . . it was your knitting bag, right? I was wondering why anyone would take it. Was it really valuable or old or something?"

"Well . . . well, yes, I suppose it's very old. Perhaps someone just assumed that since it was an antique, it must be worth something." Her reasoning made sense, but now she sounded a little evasive. Time to try his charisma, maybe. *Irresistible Blandishment. Irresistible Blandishment* . . . He touched the keys again for a little extra fortitude.

"I noticed it last night when you brought it downstairs," Negret said. "I liked it because I thought the picture looked like my house. Can you tell me anything about it? Anything might help."

"How would knowing about the bag help you to find it if you're just going to be looking for likely hiding places?"

"I don't know," Negret admitted. "But it seems like, if you're looking for something, the more you know about it, the better your chances are of finding it."

Mrs. Hereward pursed her lips. Then she smiled. "That's a very good argument, young man." She lifted her cup. "And I suppose there's no ignoring the fact that I'm not doing so well looking on my own. Maybe because I just don't know enough about this house."

Sirin, who had somehow managed to crawl under the table to listen, poked Negret in the knee. Now they were getting somewhere.

Mrs. Hereward sipped her tea. She was obviously thinking hard. Negret glanced around. Lizzie was in the kitchen baking something that was sending delicious aromas of nutmeg and clove and cinnamon and vanilla throughout the house, and she was making enough noise in the process that if they spoke quietly, there was no reason to think she'd overhear. Dr. Gowervine was still outside on the porch smoking his pipe, and Clem was still running the stairs, so they pretty much had the whole floor to themselves. For the moment, anyway.

"I inherited the bag," Mrs. Hereward said at last, very, very softly, "from my mother, who had inherited it from her grandmother, who had inherited it from hers. That woman, my great-great-great-grandmother, was the daughter of the woman for whom this house was built."

Negret blinked. "This house was built for someone in your family?"

She smiled sadly. "Yes, although neither that woman nor anyone else of her line lived here for long. There was tragedy in the family. The bag—they would've called it a ditty bag back then—was made for a girl who was meant to live in the house, before it became clear that she never would. But she kept the bag and used it, and much later, she passed it on."

"Did you come to stay here because of that connection to the house?" This made perfect sense. Milo would have happily planned a trip around visiting a house if it meant learning something about his birth family, even hundreds of years back.

"Yes . . . and no." Mrs. Hereward curled her fingers around her cup and tapped her ring thoughtfully against the blue china surface. Then she sighed. "I suppose this will sound ridiculous to you, but according to another ancestral story, before the house was abandoned by the girl and her family, a peddler came to the door and the girl bought one of the relics of Julian Roamer."

"What's a relic?" Negret asked. It was a word he'd heard before, but he couldn't quite remember what it meant. "Isn't it a religious thing?"

"A precious thing related to someone holy," Sirin said from under the table. "Usually an object of puissance."

"Well, it can be," Mrs. Hereward agreed. "A relic is a *trace* of something—something that survives or remains to remind us of something that once was. That's why some religious articles are called relics. They remind us of saints or martyrs. But anything can be a relic."

He thought back to *The Raconteur's Commonplace Book,* to the passage in the story in which the orphaned girl Nell had used a special bone to call forth the dark stranger who'd helped her stop the rising waters:

"There is a sort of magic called orphan magic . . . There is one bone in a cat that may call me, but it must be separated from the others to do its work. It has potential when it is connected to the rest, but when it is sundered away, its potential becomes power.

Maybe, Negret thought, when the man had been talking about *orphan magic,* he'd been referring to something like a relic.

"So . . . so you think not only that Julian Roamer was a real person, but that his wishy things were real things, and that one might be hidden in the house?" As he said this, Negret realized that in the story in the book, not only was the bone a relic, but so was the girl who'd used it.

Could I *be a relic?* he wondered. *Could I perhaps have some sort of orphan magic in me?*

"I suppose it sounds a bit fantastic," Mrs. Hereward admitted. Her face had gone pink again. "But . . . well, there you go. You probably think I'm just a silly old lady, but I got it in my head that it would be a bit of an adventure to look for Julian's relic, so here I am."

She stopped talking for a moment as Clem appeared on the stairs, reached the bottom, and did a neat about-face to start back up. *How can she stay that quiet even when she's running?* Negret wondered.

"Sillier yet," Mrs. Hereward continued when Clem had disappeared upstairs again, "I had no clues to follow except for the stories and the bag, and even the bag didn't really give me anything concrete to work with. But it's the only thing I own from those ancestors to link them to this house, and now it's gone."

To Negret's surprise, it didn't sound silly at all. It sounded as if perhaps, despite her hair-trigger temper and her constant tea drinking and the differences in their ages, Mrs. Hereward might actually be a sort of kindred spirit. They were both adventurers, after all, and they both wished for a link to their ancestry; Mrs. Hereward just seemed to have gotten stuck with a negative charisma score.

"I don't think it sounds silly," he said. "So what did you think you were looking for? His shoes?"

"His knife," Mrs. Hereward said, sounding a bit relieved. "I don't really know, actually. I always thought the girl who supposedly bought the relic from the peddler would've found a knife most useful; she grew up aboard a sailing ship sometime around the War of 1812, and while sailors didn't always wear shoes, they always needed a good knife." She looked up, hopeful. "Does that sound like anything you might ever have seen around the inn?"

"Not really. But then, I've never looked for anything like that before."

The old woman smiled. She reached across the table and patted Negret's hand. "Well, that's all right, young man. If you manage to find my bag, I'll be most grateful. I appreciate your looking."

"You don't mind adding this to our campaign, do you?" Negret asked as he and Sirin headed up the stairs. "Looking for the missing things, I mean."

"Not at all," Sirin replied. "Sometimes in a game you get rewards or find smaller treasures that help lead you to the big one. In Odd Trails, they're called *plums*." They paused on the second-floor landing. "Mr. Vinge's and Mrs. Hereward's rooms are on the third floor and Georgie Moselle's is on the fourth, right? What do you say we have a look on those floors?"

"Sure. You know what's interesting?" Negret reflected. "The girl who supposedly bought the relic grew up on a ship. That gives us two clues that have some kind of nautical connection; the girl the ditty bag belonged to and the missing chart."

"That chart paper looked awfully old, too," Sirin added. "Do you think it's from around the same time as the bag?"

"Well, Mrs. Hereward didn't mention anything about a chart, and I feel like if it was hers, if it had anything to do with her or to do with the relic, she'd have told us. I think she was being really honest about everything just now, don't you?"

"I guess."

"Then there's the gate on the bag, and the gate watermark. And the gates in the windows." Negret stopped on the landing and scratched his head again as he looked up at the green-upon-pale-green window with the iron gate worked into its design. "There must be a real gate like this somewhere on the grounds. It doesn't make sense otherwise, all these things connecting this house and that gate."

"Or there *was* a gate somewhere on the grounds," Sirin pointed out. "If the house goes back to the War of 1812, that's more than two hundred years for a gate to have been here, and then been moved."

Both he and Sirin looked up as Clem rounded the turn just above them. "How do you run so quietly?" Negret demanded. "Can you teach me how to do that?"

Clem paused, grinning and barely even breathing heavily as she jogged in place. "Long years of practice, my young apprentice. What are you up to? I saw you talking with Her Royal Highness downstairs. How'd you make your escape?"

"She's not so bad," he said. "Besides, I feel bad for her. Her bag's missing, and it was sort of a family . . . what's the word?"

"Heirloom?" Clem suggested. "Yeah, that's rough. You don't think anyone really stole it, though?"

"You tell me," Negret replied. "You're the cat burglar."

He'd meant it jokingly, but Clem's feet stilled and her face took on a pensive expression. "I'm not sure," she said perfectly seriously. "If it wasn't all three of them . . . Yes, I think if three things hadn't gone missing, I'd have said it was, definitely."

"You think three things missing means it *isn't* a thief? I thought that's what made it seem more likely that it *was.*"

Clem's forehead wrinkled. "Maybe it's more to do with *who* was robbed than how many were. Frankly, it's mainly Georgie's notebook that makes me think maybe it isn't as simple as garden-variety theft."

"Why? Because a watch and an antique bag make sense to steal, but not somebody's plain old notebook?"

Clem smiled vaguely. "No notebook of Georgie's is going to be a plain old anything," she said. "But yes, that's exactly it."

"You mean her notebook is valuable? But if it's valuable, then maybe it *would* be worth stealing!"

"Oh, I'm sure it was valuable, and definitely worth stealing to someone who knew what it was and how to make use of it. The problem is, the only person — other than Blue herself — who might possibly have any use for the notebook she lost . . . is *me.*"

Negret's jaw dropped. Clem looked at him and smiled even wider.

"Oh, I'm happy to admit that," she said easily. "The problem is, I didn't take it. That's why it doesn't make sense that it's missing." She nodded once and then she was off, disappearing around the next bend in the stairs.

seven

THE MOONLIGHTER'S KNACK

They stood under the third-floor window with its spectrum of soft and watery greens. The sole open door was at the end of the hall to the right: 3W, the only empty room on the floor. "Let's start there," Negret suggested.

"But anybody can walk in and out of that room. It wouldn't be a very secure spot to hide anything."

"Maybe the thief's counting on it not being a very likely hiding place," Negret argued. "And keep your voice down."

Just as he had the day before on the floor above, Negret examined the hallway with fresh eyes. Pressed-tin ceiling separated into sections by dark brown beams. Old wallpaper, although on this floor it was embossed with designs of swirling jade that matched the darkest pieces in the window. There were three sconces along the wall on each side, and at the far end, a little half-circle-shaped table with a potted white poinsettia on it.

Check for traps, Negret remembered. Maybe there wouldn't be any actual traps, but there was always the possibility of someone spotting what they were up to and asking questions. He paused, listening. All the residents of this floor were still downstairs, but Clem was somewhere on her way back up. Best to get out of sight before she passed by in the stairwell again.

He headed down the hall with Sirin a pace behind him and his eyes skipping over the walls, the floors, the three closed doors. Details that would have been so familiar as to be invisible to Milo might turn out to be clues for the blackjack Negret. Mentally, he made a list of what he saw on his way to 3W: one of the sconces needed a new bulb, and just like on the other floors, the heavy old wallpaper here needed fresh gluing. Also just like on the other floors, there was an old, sealed-up dumbwaiter at the far end. A part of him wondered whether someone might've hidden something in there, but the painted-over door looked the same as it always had. Nobody had gotten into the dumbwaiter this way in a long, long time.

Below the dumbwaiter door was the table. Moving the leaves of the poinsettia gently out of the way, Negret saw that it had been freshly watered; Mrs. Pine must've made the rounds with her watering can this morning. He winced at the quick whiff of spicy-sweet odor that the blossoms sent up, then checked the underside of the tabletop in case the thief had taped the stolen things to it. No luck.

"I hear Clem," Sirin whispered. Negret nodded, and they ducked into the empty room.

Just inside the doorway to the left was the luggage rack. There was a double bed with a folded blue and green striped blanket at the foot, a small desk and a chair, and a low dresser with six drawers. This room looked out on the wooded hill, and through the swirling snow — was it coming down even heavier now? — Negret could just make out the thickset shapes of some of the old outbuildings that lay scattered across the grounds.

"All shipshape?" Sirin asked.

"As far as I can see." He peeked under the bed — nothing but a couple of dust bunnies — and patted down the sheets and the pillows and the folded blanket. Nothing there, either, or in the dresser or the desk. They dragged the dresser a little ways from the wall, then took all the drawers out and looked inside its hollow skeleton. Nothing. Negret even boosted Sirin up for a closer look at each of the lighting fixtures. Nothing.

The room's bathroom didn't appear to be holding any secrets, either. Negret was feeling a little discouraged as he tried to neatly re-fold the towels after searching them without any luck. There was really no place else to hide anything in there. The toilet didn't have a tank, the medicine cabinet was empty, and the only other objects in the room were the soap and shampoo that sat on the bathtub shelf.

"Now what?" Sirin asked, leaning against the sink with cloaked arms folded.

"I'm not sure." Negret sat on the edge of the tub and neatened a crease in the paisley-patterned paper that wrapped the soap cake.

"Next floor? There are three empty rooms up—" He stopped speaking abruptly and looked at the little soap he'd been fiddling with. It was unused. The fancy paper wrapper should've been glued shut—he had helped put soaps and shampoos in rooms enough times to know that this brand came with the wrappers sealed—but it wasn't.

He picked it up and immediately he knew he was onto something. The weight of it was wrong. He turned it over and carefully unwrapped it. The soap cake fell into his hands, and his heart started beating faster. A little line ran around the edge of it. A seam.

Fumbling in his pocket, Negret pulled out the set of keys. *Remember,* he heard his imagined father, the venerable old blackjack, saying, *it isn't only locked doors that hide treasures.*

The flat hammered disc that hung alongside the keys was just thin enough to wedge into the seam. A gentle push, and the cake of soap fell open into two halves in his palm.

The center of the soap had been hollowed out, and in the cavity sat a gold pocket watch.

"Wow," Sirin breathed. "Wow, you're good."

The Moonlighter's Knack, he thought triumphantly: *you can steal any object protected by anything that opens with a key or combination, and also anything protected by hotel toiletries.*

"Wow," Negret echoed. The thief was lucky Mrs. Pine splurged on full-sized soaps rather than the tiny ones most hotels stocked, because the watch wasn't small. It was about the size of his palm, with a chain that ended in a straight bar. He pushed the knob at the top and it popped open. On the inside, opposite the face, was an engraved inscription.

To D.C.V., with high esteem
and thanks for a job well done,
from D. & M.

"D.C.V. must stand for De Cary Vinge," he said. "Well, there's no question about it. This is Mr. Vinge's watch for sure."

They stared at it for a moment. "So . . . what do we do?" Sirin asked. "Should we give it back?"

Negret's mind was whirling. "Eventually, yeah. But not yet. If the thief knows we found one of the stolen things, he might move the others."

"Do you want to leave it here? So he or she doesn't suspect anything?"

"No, 'cause he could move it again at any time." Negret took the soap to the sink, turned on the tap just a tiny bit, wetted the edges of the halves, and stuck them back together again. Then he rewrapped the hollow soap cake neatly and put it back where he'd found it.

"He'll know we're onto him if he even picks it up," Sirin observed.

"Yeah, but I bet he won't. Not for a while, anyway. He might peek in and check that it's still exactly where he left it, but he won't want to be seen poking around in rooms that aren't his. That might make people suspicious."

"What are we going to do with it, then? We can't get caught with it. They'll think we took it."

"My parents would never think that," he scoffed. Still, Sirin had a point. His parents might not think it, but the other guests would. They had to hide it somewhere safe until they could figure out when and how to give it back.

"I know!" Sirin snapped her fingers. "Let's take it to the Emporium! Here." She held out her hand. "I'll carry it. In case we're caught."

Negret grinned. "Why, because you're invisible?"

"Obviously," she replied, tucking the watch into the pocket of the Cloak of Golden Indiscernibility.

They crept back through the empty guest room and paused just inside the door to listen. Silence. Negret peeked out and found the hallway empty. "Let's go."

The two adventurers made it to the attic without any surprises or encounters. Negret unlocked the door, paused to check for traps, and stopped dead in his tracks.

"Another spider web?" Sirin inquired, peering over his shoulder. Then she saw it. "Oh, man. You think that means what I think it does?"

The big, elaborate web that he had almost walked through the day before hung in dusty tatters that swung gently in the cold air.

"Yeah, I think so," he answered darkly. "Someone else has been in the Emporium." Then he stepped back fast. "What if they're still in there?"

Sirin made a huffing noise. "If they are, they already know *we're* here, and they're going to be pretty embarrassed when they get caught." She leaned through the door. "You hear that, you sneak? You better start thinking up your excuses now."

There was, of course, no answer.

"Well?" Sirin asked. "Are we going in or not?"

Negret swallowed. "Yeah, we're going in." He stepped cautiously over the threshold and felt for the pull-string. The light popped to life. The next one seemed farther away this time.

Sirin pushed him. "I'm right behind you."

"Okay, okay." He took a deep breath and made himself walk to the next pull-string, and then the next. Miraculously, nobody leaped out of the dark. "Maybe it was Mom or Dad," he said as he pulled on the last light. "That would be the easiest explanation."

"No, it wouldn't," Sirin scoffed. "Your mom and dad have been dealing with the guests with the missing stuff all morning. There's no way either of them had time for some random attic trip."

"Well, they're gone now, whoever they were."

Sirin took the watch from her pocket. "How about I find a temporary home for this bit of treasure, and you look around and see if you can figure out what's been disturbed?"

"Like I'm going to be able to tell," Negret grumbled.

"We were just here," Sirin replied. "We went over the place pretty good. Maybe you'll get lucky and it'll be something obvious."

"I guess." He turned in a circle and tried to decide where to start looking for whatever it was Sirin thought he might notice. Then he remembered the map he'd made the last time they were here and dug it out of the rucksack. There were the garment racks full of clothes and the crates of old toys, the box of wrapped bottles, and the huge pile of dusty canvas he and Sirin had sat on to go through their haul, all where he had drawn them on the graph paper. There was the old door leaning against the wall, and the boxes of Gems of Ultimate Puissance half hidden behind the dumbwaiter mechanism—

Negret stopped, turned on one heel, and returned to the pool of light from the fourth lightbulb. Something . . .

Sirin popped up at his side. "What?"

"Shh." He stared at the map and then up again.

"Yeah, but what are you—"

"Shh!" He held up his hand for silence until she closed her mouth and crossed her arms and stood back. "Something . . . but I don't know what it is."

"Fine." Sirin walked over to the pile of canvas, climbed up, sat, and wrapped her arms around her knees. That's when Negret realized what was different.

"That's it!" he crowed. "Move." He shooed Sirin off the pile and started shifting layers of the fabric out of the way.

The day before, the canvas had been stacked so that when they'd sat on it, there had been room for both of them on top of the pile, plus space for Negret's rucksack between them. Today there was really only room for one kid.

The canvas was heavy and full of dust, but with Sirin's help Negret managed to shift it in huge folds until the pile became a grimy lake of sailcloth. And amid the waves in the lake was a misshapen bump sandwiched between the last two layers of fabric.

Negret crawled in between those layers, coughing and wiping cobwebs from his nose, until he reached the bump. Then he scrambled back out into the half-light of the Emporium with the thing in his hand.

"I don't believe it," Sirin protested as he emerged.

"I don't either." The two of them stared down at the embroidered canvas bag. There was the stitched-and-knotted image of Greenglass House, surrounded by blue-green pines. He turned it over, and there was the gate. It was unmistakably the same gate as the one in the watermark and the windows — but there was one difference. The gate on the bag had a detail the others did not: a little knot of bronzy-gold thread suspended from one side. A lantern.

"I want to give it back to her," Negret said. "I don't want to make Mrs. Hereward wait."

"Then we need to find Georgie's notebook. And I suspect, since the first two things were in different places, the notebook's probably going to be somewhere else too."

"Yeah." Negret kicked the edge of the canvas. "Here. Help me pile this back up."

"Where d'you want to hide the bag until we find the notebook?" Sirin inquired.

"I've got a pretty good idea." They muscled the canvas back into place and brushed off their hands. Negret picked up the bag. "Where'd you put the watch, by the way?"

"Buried it in one of the boxes of Gems of Ultimate Puissance."

"Go get it. I thought of a better place."

It had occurred to Negret just as he and Sirin had been trying to maneuver the heavy sailcloth back into an organized mass, which had reminded him of something else he had to do at some point that day, no matter what else happened in the house. That reminder had given him the idea for a perfect, *perfect* hiding place. "We need to get some stuff from our floor first, though."

And they still had to find the notebook, which could be anywhere. As they left the Emporium and Negret locked the door behind them, he began making a mental list of places to search next. The empty rooms on the fourth and fifth floors, the basement, under every rug in the house . . .

Then, just before he started down the stairs, Sirin grabbed his arm and mouthed, *Wait.*

There was a faint whispering in the hallway below. Negret and Sirin tiptoed to just above the turn in the stairs and hunkered down to listen.

"Don't be ridiculous," Georgie's voice hissed. "I know it wasn't *you.* If it had been, I'm sure I'd never have known it was gone, 'cause it would have been back before I'd noticed it was missing."

"Very true." That was Clem.

"I need your help." Georgie sounded reluctant and disgusted. "I need that notebook back."

"Why the heck didn't you hide it better?"

"Because I *thought* the only person I was hiding it from was *you,* genius, and there's not much point in trying to hide anything from you, not in quarters this close." Now Georgie just sounded angry. "Plus, I knew you wouldn't *take* it."

Clem chuckled. "Well, thank you, I guess."

"If you'll help me recover it," Georgie said with a sigh, "I'll share what's in it with you."

There was a pause. "No, you'll have to give me information that isn't in the notebook."

Now Georgie laughed, but it wasn't a funny laugh. It was resigned. "Of course. I should have assumed you'd found a way to read it already."

"Well? Do you *have* something that isn't in the notebook, Blue?"

"Oh, good grief. Of course I do."

Crouched on the stairs above, Negret wrinkled his nose. There was a smell in the stairwell, peppery and flowery at the same time, that hadn't been there before.

"Okaaay . . . what else do you have?" There was the sound of snapping fingers. "I know. Your little camera project." A pause. "Yes. I want that. I want your word that you'll show me the picture you took, when it's finished. The real one, not whatever ringer you're going to show the kid."

"It's just a—a lark, Clem! The kid seemed interested. That's all. It has nothing to do with Owen."

Owen?

"Baloney, Blue. Nothing you do is just a lark. I want to see the picture. No tricks."

Another pause, and then a noise that was half snort, half sigh. "Fine."

"And while we're being so chummy, was it by any chance you who was in my room yesterday?" Clem's voice inquired. Negret elbowed Sirin. She knew?

"Absolutely not. I'm not that stupid. I know my limitations."

"I thought it might have been you because whoever it was didn't touch anything, as far as I can tell. Whoever it was *did* know their limitations."

"Wasn't me, Clem. Look, do we have a deal or not?"

"Yeah, we do. I'll let you know as soon as I have anything to tell. And good grief, what the heck did you do, bathe in that stuff?"

"The kid broke the bottle in my bag. This is the only sweater I have. It has to be dry-cleaned, so Mrs. Pine couldn't just wash it, and this place is freezing today. You all are just going to have to deal." The perfume. Georgie's perfume, from the smashed bottle—that was the smell in the stairwell.

"Holy moly. I'll lend you one of mine. Hang on."

While Clem went to her room and retrieved a less odoriferous sweater for Georgie to borrow, gears turned in Negret's head. *What is it?* Sirin mouthed. He shook his head. There was something, something about the perfume . . .

Clem returned, Georgie thanked her, and Clem said something about what's a cardigan between moonlighters—which was odd, but not nearly as interesting to Negret just then as the elusive perfume thing. As the two guests headed back down the stairs, the pieces that had been nagging at him suddenly fell into place.

He grabbed Sirin's yellow sleeve. "Come on. I know where the notebook is!"

He took off down the steps with Sirin at his heels, not bothering to be quiet this time. After all, it didn't matter. He had the bag and the watch tucked in his rucksack, so there was nothing for the thief to go and rehide even if he or she did spot them.

"Excuse us," Negret said cheerfully as he passed by Georgie just as she reached her own floor.

"Don't you want to tell her?" Sirin whispered as they continued toward the third floor.

"Not yet," Negret whispered back.

"Don't you want to maybe tell *me?*"

"I'll show you." He stopped on the third-floor landing, rushed to the end of the hall, picked up the white poinsettia in its green ceramic pot, and crept back to run down the next flight as quickly as he could. Then he and Sirin hurried through his family's apartment to his own bedroom.

"Get my trashcan," he said as soon as the door was safely closed behind them. Then, holding the pot over the waste bin, he took the plant carefully by its main stalk and tugged it loose. As it came out of the pot, the wet soil held its shape for a moment before plopping away from the roots and into the bin. Something else fell into the bin, too: something in a plastic bag.

Sirin picked up the bag and opened it gingerly. The spicy-sweet smell that Negret had noticed on the poinsettia — and then again on the stairs near the attic — spread throughout the room as she pulled out a small, perfume-stained notebook with a bunch of loose pages stuffed into it.

"I should've remembered earlier," Negret said, beaming proudly. "Poinsettias don't really have any smell."

They sat on the bed with the three recovered items on the blanket between them: Georgie's sweetly reeking notebook, Mr. Vinge's gold watch, and Mrs. Hereward's embroidered ditty bag.

"Now what?" Sirin asked. "Can we just give them all back?"

"I'm not sure." Negret picked up the notebook and tried to hold his breath while he spoke so he wouldn't inhale any more of the perfume than he had to. "I'm still sort of afraid that if we do, they'll think we took them. If we found one thing, that would be different, maybe. But all three? I think maybe we have to be a little sneaky about it." He lifted the cover of the notebook. "Is it bad that I kind of want to look?"

"Look?"

"Through the notebook. To see what's in there that anybody would steal."

Sirin grinned. "Are you kidding? If you don't, I will. Especially after all that stuff Georgie and Clem were saying upstairs."

"It's just—" Negret hesitated. "It would be like reading somebody's journal or diary or something."

"Gimme." Sirin plucked the notebook out of his hands and opened it. Then she frowned, flipped a few pages, and frowned harder. "Good grief."

"What is it?"

She made an exasperated noise and tossed the notebook across to him. He caught it awkwardly and opened it to the first page. Lines of incomprehensible words marched across the page. He turned to the next page, and the next. There were arrows, boxes, cross-outs, and things circled and underlined, but not a single word on a single page was written in English. "What the heck language is this?"

"I don't think it's a language, Negret." The scholiast gave him a significant look. "Remember how she said she didn't think she'd be hiding it from anyone but Clem, so she didn't bother? She expected it to be found, but she didn't want it to be understood. I bet it's a *code*."

"An *entire notebook* in code?" He dropped it on the bed and stared at Sirin. "What on earth is going on with all these people?"

"I don't know, but maybe it's time we worked out what we know about them. Do you have something to write on?"

"That spiral pad from the Emporium's in my bag. On the floor by the desk. Should be a pen in there, too."

Sirin slid off the bed, rifled through the rucksack, and came back with the pad and pen. "Let's go in the order they got here," she said, scribbling a bit to get the old ballpoint working. "Mr. Vinge was first, right?" She wrote his name at the top of the page. "What do we know?"

"Weird socks," Negret said. "He reads a lot, but I didn't notice what." He popped open the watch again. "Write down the inscription: *To D.C.V., with high esteem and thanks for a job well done, from D. and M.*"

"What else?" Sirin tapped the pen against her chin.

Negret leaned back against the headboard and stared at the ceiling. "Can't think of anything else."

"We'll come back to him." She turned the page. "Who was next?"

"Georgie Moselle. Clem calls her Blue. They definitely knew each other before they got here. They don't seem to be friends, but they're still pretty nice to each other."

"Georgie said something interesting," Negret remembered. "When Clem said she wanted to see the picture from the cigar-box camera, Georgie said something like, *It has nothing to do with Owen.* Who's Owen? Maybe they just know each other a little because they both know this Owen person."

"There's also the camera," Sirin reminded him. "Georgie knows how to make cameras out of ordinary things, and Clem thinks she's taking a specific picture and the one she's going to show you is just a ringer — a fake."

"And she has a whole notebook in code." Negret picked it up again. "Want to write a little of it down?"

"Yeah." Sirin copied a few lines. "What else we got?"

"She loaned me *The Raconteur's Commonplace Book.*" He thought back to that first day. "She said she particularly thought I might like how it starts."

"Which is how?"

"Which is a whole bunch of people stuck at an inn, and someone suggests they tell stories. That's where . . ." He paused and frowned. "Well, that's where I got the idea last night, of course, but . . ."

Sirin was looking at him closely. "But what?"

Now he had another thought, although it seemed pretty far-fetched. "You don't think that's what she was hoping for when she gave it back to me, do you? That I'd try and get everyone telling stories about themselves?"

"Seems like that would be a lot to hope for," Sirin said. "But I don't know if it's any weirder than the rest of the stuff that's going on around here. Anything else?"

Negret shook his head. Then he snapped his fingers. "This morning, when we were talking to her downstairs, she said —"

"Yes, yes!" Sirin brightened. "When you asked what was in the notebook, she said she'd made notes about this house —"

"And someone she thought might be connected to it." He nodded. "The Owen person?"

"I bet it is. Can you ask your parents if they can think of an Owen?"

"Sure." Negret scratched his head. "Okay, moving on. Next were Dr. Wilbur Gowervine and Mrs. Eglantine Hereward." He smiled at the memory of the two of them wedged into the *Whilforber Whirlwind.* "They arrived at the same time."

"You know," Sirin pointed out, "if Georgie's right and Clem didn't steal these three things, that really only leaves Dr. Gowervine. And we know he snuck into Clem's room."

"Yeah, I thought of that," Negret admitted. "But Clem said nothing was touched, which makes it seem like he went in for some other reason than to steal things."

"Like what?"

"No idea," he admitted. "And the truth is, I really can't even think of anything else to write down about him. I feel like I know less about him than any of the others."

"What's he a doctor of?"

"Don't know."

"He's out on the porch a lot."

"Well, he smokes a pipe. I guess we do know that."

"Yeah, but I meant whatever his excuse is, he's out on the porch by himself a lot," Sirin said patiently. "We should probably look into that." She turned to a fresh page. "Mrs. Hereward."

Here they had a bit more information. They wrote down what they could remember about the old lady's story the night before, and what she'd told them that morning.

"Her ancestors were nautical folks. Maybe she has a connection to the chart." Negret picked up the bag and looked at the embroidery, then at the little lantern on the misshapen gate. "And the gate has to be a clue," he mumbled. "It keeps popping up everywhere."

Sirin turned the bag to the house on the opposite side, then turned it back. "I can't tell if the gate is supposed to be on the grounds of the house or if it's a whole separate picture."

"Yeah, it's hard to tell." Then he spotted something he hadn't before, on the house side. There was a design stitched onto the door: an arrangement of small straight lines that looked like symbols.

Negret shoved the bag at Sirin and took the blackjack's keys from his pocket. He examined the hammered disc on the leather key ring. On one side was the engraved crown with its specks of blue enamel. On the other side were the four Chinese characters. They matched the embroidered symbols on the door perfectly.

"What does it *mean?*" he howled at the ceiling. "This is so frustrating!"

"Mrs. Hereward might know what the symbols are," Sirin said, patting his shoulder. "We'll just ask her, once we give the bag back. Come on, stay focused." She took the key ring from him and copied the symbols onto Mrs. Hereward's page in the notebook. "Who do we have next?"

Negret sighed. "Clem. Clemence O. Candler. Fast and silent and joked that she was a cat burglar. Also, she implied that Georgie was a thief too." He snapped his fingers, remembering something else Clem had said. "I was thinking so hard about the perfume, I almost didn't notice! When she gave Georgie her sweater, she said *What's a cardigan between moonlighters.* And I read in that Odd Trails book about the Moonlighter's Knack, which is a —"

"An exploit. A blackjack skill that lets you steal almost anything," Sirin finished, nodding thoughtfully.

"Exactly!"

"Well, it could just mean they're both Odd Trails nerds," she pointed out.

Negret shook his head. "But she also admitted she'd have a reason to steal the notebook, which Georgie knew already."

"But even Georgie didn't think she was the one who did it."

"Well," he said, "Georgie told *Clem* she didn't think she did it. Maybe that was just — whatchacallit — misdirection?" Misdirection was, according to *Blackjacks of the Roads,* another key skill.

"Like maybe she was just giving Clem a chance to bring it back and pretend she wasn't the one who took it?" Sirin nodded thoughtfully. "Maybe. But didn't you kind of believe Clem when she told us that she didn't steal it?"

Negret *had* believed Clem, but he didn't know if that really meant anything. "Maybe she's just as good at lying as she is at sneaking around. I don't know if we can let her off the hook that easily."

"Fair enough. What else do we know about her?"

Not much else, it seemed. They decided to make a list of the remaining clues and questions they had, and came up with:

Nautical chart found outside, painted on paper with gate watermark

Map stolen with decoy left in its place (paper with gate watermark)

Piece of matching paper found in Emporium (Lucksmith Paper Merchants)

Gate is also on windows

Gate is also on Mrs. H's bag

Chinese characters on Mrs. H's bag match characters on Negret's keys

Who dropped the chart?

Is the person who took the chart the same person who stole the other missing objects?

Is Dr. Gowervine a thief, or was he in Clem's room for another reason?

They stared at the list, flipped back through their notes, discussed and argued, and came up with nothing new. But they both agreed that they needed to ask Mrs. Hereward about the symbols on the door — as soon as they could get the stolen things back to their owners without bringing any suspicion on themselves.

That much, at least, Negret was pretty sure he could manage. His idea about where to hide the bag and the watch before he'd found the notebook adapted beautifully into a plan for how to return them all.

He went into the second-floor study, where Mrs. Pine had been wrapping presents before all the guests had descended upon the house. He swiped two rolls of wrapping paper, a tape dispenser, a pair of scissors, and three identical boxes, and brought them back to his room.

"Excellent idea," Sirin said admiringly as the two of them placed the recovered items in the boxes, padding them with extra paper so they wouldn't slide around too much, then wrapped and labeled each one with an unobtrusive *w, n,* or *b* on an underside corner where the paper was particularly busy with drummers drumming. Then, since it just made sense to keep going, they switched to the second roll of paper and wrapped the presents Milo had hidden away under his bed for his parents.

He was knotting the bow on the last gift when someone knocked on his door. He shoved the spiral pad under the nearest present and called, "Come in!"

Mrs. Pine peeked in and smiled when she saw the pile of messily wrapped presents. "Lost track of time again?"

Milo and Meddy exchanged guilty smiles. "Yeah," Milo admitted.

Meddy looked at the clock on the bedside table. "Did we miss lunch?"

Mrs. Pine waved a hand. "I thought I'd try to keep you from going hungry today. Mrs. Caraway made macaroni and cheese and ham sandwiches, and we set some aside. Come on down before it gets cold."

"Be right there, Mom."

He waited until the door had shut behind Mrs. Pine, then packed the boxes he'd wrapped into his rucksack. "You coming?"

Meddy shook her head and took the notepad out again. "I want to think. Do you mind if I stay here where it's quiet and keep looking over our clues?"

That wasn't an easy question to answer. Did he mind leaving her in his room alone? Or at least—because yes, he definitely minded; this was *his* space—did he mind enough to actually say no?

She waited patiently while he considered. "I can go somewhere else, if you like."

In the end, it was thinking about the game that helped him make up his mind. They were partners in this adventure. If he couldn't trust her, he was all on his own.

"No, you can stay here," Milo said eventually. "But would you try and keep from moving anything? My stuff is right where I like it."

She nodded. "I promise."

"Okay, then." Milo opened the door and stepped into the hallway and took a deep breath. This was hard, but not as hard as he'd expected. "See you later."

eight

PLUMS

It stopped snowing and started raining again, and the rain immediately froze on every surface. By nightfall the sky had been swept clear of gray for the first time in days, and the moonlight glinted on a world that looked as if it had been coated with a layer of silvery glass. Then the winds started, and the glazed world began to groan and creak and even occasionally to crack, sending noises like gunshots echoing through the night.

Inside Greenglass House, everyone was looking considerably more nervous than he or she had looked the day before. It wasn't just the thefts, either. Milo knew his parents were worried about losing power when candlesticks began to appear, decorating spots where they didn't usually live. The house did have its own generator, and there was plenty of firewood, but the generator didn't start up automatically, which meant that if the electricity went out, there would be at least a short period of time without lights. The candles looked right at home among the Christmas trimmings, so the guests probably didn't even notice them, but to Milo, they stood out like sore thumbs.

So did the three packages under the tree with the secret marks identifying them as the stolen-and-recovered items. They were now buried under the pile of gifts Mr. Pine had added later that afternoon, but to Milo it was as if they had flashing signal lights on them screaming STOLEN THINGS! OPEN US!

Another meal, another buffet that scattered the guests all over. Once again, Meddy sent Milo to observe the living room. This time he took his plate to the loveseat. Sitting against the arm, he could peer over the back and watch. As a bonus, he could hear just about everything in the dining room, too.

Dinner was another awkward meal full of sullen looks and uncomfortable silences. Only Mrs. Hereward broached the subject of the thefts. "You've searched all of our rooms, to absolutely no avail," she burst out from the dining room as everyone was finishing up. The words erupted from her as if she'd been struggling to hold them in the whole time. She stalked into the living room and waved her fork back and forth between Dr. Gowervine and Clem. "What about theirs?"

Dr. Gowervine started sputtering indignantly. "You cannot possibly suggest that—"

"One of you did!" Mrs. Hereward's voice twisted up toward screech territory. "You're the only ones who weren't robbed! It has to be one of you!"

Clem finished chewing, set her fork down on the coffee table, folded her hands, and looked with maddening calm at the old lady. "You don't know what you're talking about. If you did, if you knew even the first thing about it, you'd know *that* doesn't mean anything."

Meddy dropped onto the loveseat and peered over the back with Milo. "What do you think she means?"

Milo shrugged, more interested in hearing Mrs. Hereward's response than in discussing Clem's.

"Maybe she's saying we're suspects too," Meddy grumbled. "That it might have been one of us, who belong to the house."

That was possible, of course, but Milo didn't think that was what she meant. It seemed to him that Clem could be implying that the thief might be *one of the three who'd been robbed.*

Now, that was an interesting idea. What if the thief was just pretending to have been robbed, to keep anyone from suspecting him? Or *her.* Clem was looking intently at Mrs. Hereward, as if she was pretty sure the old lady was behind everything.

"O — kay." Mrs. Pine hurried in and clapped her palms together. "How about coffee?"

Mrs. Hereward ignored her. *"Young lady,"* she said to Clem, "I'm sure you're not suggesting —"

"I'm not suggesting anything. I'm just saying you don't know what you're talking about, and by the way, I don't like being accused of funny business any more than you do." Clem folded her napkin, picked up her plate, and got to her feet. "Can I help with the coffee, Mrs. P?"

Mrs. Hereward opened her mouth, but Clem cut her off.

"You can search my room anytime," she said over her shoulder. "Search it now, if it'll make you happy."

Mrs. Pine held up her hands. "How about everyone calm down?"

"I'm perfectly calm, now that Miss Candler has offered to do the right thing." Mrs. Hereward didn't entirely sound calm, and her face had gone florid again. She turned to Dr. Gowervine, who had gotten up too and was passing by on his way to the kitchen with his own dishes. "What about you, Doctor?"

"This is ridiculous," he muttered.

Now the old lady discovered she was about to be alone in the living room and stalked after him. "Is that a yes, or a no?"

"How about everyone *calm down*," Mr. Pine repeated loudly from the kitchen. Everybody was either there or in the dining room now. Milo leaned farther out over the back of the loveseat so he could see.

Dr. Gowervine glared at Mrs. Hereward for a moment, then folded his arms, cleared his throat, and turned to Milo's father. "Mr. Pine, if you feel it will help this situation, I'm perfectly glad to have you look through my room and my things."

"Thanks," Milo's dad replied sourly.

Meddy frowned. "I think we need to give the stolen things back now, before this gets any uglier." She gave him a little push. "I'll do it. You go in there with everybody, then just say they aren't yours."

"What?" Milo whispered.

"Trust me. *They're not mine.* That's all you have to say."

"Okay, I guess."

Milo got up from the loveseat and crossed, unnoticed, into the dining room. He held his breath. A moment later, a delicate chaos of metallic ringing pealed through the inn. Out of sight, Meddy must've been shaking the branch on the Christmas tree where, according to Pine family tradition, Milo had hung Mrs. Pine's entire collection of silver bells all together.

"What on earth?" Mrs. Caraway demanded.

"I have no idea," Mrs. Pine answered. She and Milo's dad were already on their feet and heading back into the living room. "What's going on in there?" The rest of the guests followed, with Milo trailing last of all. When he arrived, Milo found everyone staring at the three presents that held the stolen items. They sat in a neat pile at the center of the rag rug.

Meddy tapped his shoulder and Milo whirled, opening his mouth to ask how she'd gotten out of the living room so quickly. She put one finger to her lips and whispered, "Shh."

Other than that shush, the house was silent.

Mr. Pine and Mrs. Pine looked at each other with wide eyes. "Ben?" Milo's mom said almost inaudibly.

"I have no idea." Mr. Pine squatted beside the three gifts and hesitantly picked up the nearest one. He looked around, then turned to his wife. "I don't recognize these. Do you?"

"No, they're not mine. Milo, honey, do you recognize these boxes?"

Just as Meddy'd instructed, he shook his head and said, "Nope. They're not mine."

"I could've sworn I saw you carry something like these down. And it does look like your . . . wrapping technique."

Milo made his way through the guests to look at the packages. He made a pretense of examining them closely, then went to the tree and unearthed the presents he'd wrapped for his parents. "These are mine," he said. "Two for you and two for Dad."

His parents looked at each other. "Well, someone thinks we ought to open them," Mr. Pine said. "What do you think?"

Mrs. Pine straightened and faced the dining table again. "Does anyone recognize these boxes?" Meddy stood with her hands innocently folded into the sleeves of the Cloak of Golden Indiscernibility and said nothing. "All righty, then." Milo's mom picked up the first box and tore off the wrapping. She lifted off the lid, pulled away some of the extra paper inside, and stared. "Holy cow."

"You're kidding." Mr. Pine reached into the box and lifted out the gold watch.

Mr. Vinge stiffened. "Good God. How on earth—" He stumbled across the room and reached for the watch. "I can't believe it."

Now Mrs. Hereward and Georgie strode forward. Milo's dad picked up the two remaining boxes and handed one to each. Mrs. Hereward started right in, ripping the paper away. Milo saw Georgie glance at Clem with a questioning look. Clem gave the tiniest shrug and shook her head.

Before Georgie could begin unwrapping the package, Mrs.

Hereward shoved the box she'd opened at her, grabbed the unopened one, and tore away the paper. Georgie fumbled the new box and dropped it. Wadded paper spilled out, and the perfume-stained notebook slid to the floor.

"Oh!" Mrs. Hereward flung away the box she'd grabbed and held up the embroidered ditty bag. Then she clasped it to her chest and dropped onto the sofa. A tear trailed down through the powder on her cheek. "I thought it was gone."

Georgie looked from her notebook to Milo's parents, then at Milo. "And we don't know where these came from? This isn't the result of your investigation, Milo?"

"Your investigation?" Mrs. Pine gave him a sharp look. "What investigation?"

Meddy made a zipping motion across her lips with her fingers and shook her head. He paused. Negret could call upon the exploit that would allow him to tell a perfect lie, but Milo discovered he didn't want to try the Fabulist out on his parents. He took a deep breath. "I went searching for the missing things, Mom. And I found them. But then I was afraid somebody might think I took them, if I just brought them back myself. So . . . so I wrapped them up, and I guess I thought maybe this way I could give them back without doing it myself." He glanced at Georgie, then at Mrs. Hereward, and then at Mr. Vinge. "I didn't take them, though. I swear."

Mr. Pine put his arm around Milo. "I know you didn't, kiddo. Of course we believe you."

"You . . . found them?" Mr. Vinge repeated, staring at his watch. "You just . . . But *how?*"

"I think we'd all like to know that," Clem said. "How, and where."

Milo glanced at his fellow adventurer. Meddy rolled her eyes and dropped her head into her palms.

"Can you tell us how you did it?" Mrs. Pine asked.

"Sure, I guess," Milo replied. "Can I have some hot chocolate first?"

"Of course." His mom squeezed his shoulder and headed back toward the kitchen. "Coffee and cake, folks? Help yourselves."

"This is a bad idea," Meddy grumbled, coming to stand next to him with her arms folded. "We should've stuck to the plan. Whatever," she said quickly as Milo began to protest. "Just don't drag me into it. It'll ruin our campaign." She reached into her pocket and took out the Eyes of True and Aching Clarity. "I'll watch everybody while you talk. See if I can pick up any clues." And she stalked away, muttering about how bad things happened when people went rogue and took stupid chances that put the whole team at risk.

He ignored her, too busy wondering whether it would be easier to explain everything to the guests as the blackjack Negret. Milo was already twitching a little at the thought of so many people listening to him talk. So Negret it would be.

Mrs. Pine came back with a mug of cocoa and sat next to him on the hearth. "It was really brave of you to tell the truth there, buddy. And I hope you know that *we* know you didn't take anything. Your dad and I trust you completely."

Outside the winds rose, whipping themselves up into a greater and greater frenzy. He leaned his head against her shoulder and said nothing as he watched the guests settle themselves in the living room with their desserts. Georgie gave him a wink as she dropped into one of the chairs. Mrs. Hereward passed by on her return to the sofa with a fresh cup of tea, and to his surprise, she squeezed his shoulder gently with her knotty hand. *Maybe they don't think I took them either,* he thought.

Mr. Vinge took his usual chair. He'd tucked his watch into an inside pocket, and now he regarded Negret over his coffee cup with a troubled expression in his eyes.

He might think I did it.

Clem sat next to Mrs. Hereward. Her face was cheerful, as usual. Dr. Gowervine stood near the door to the screened porch, looking uncomfortable.

When everyone else was seated, Mrs. Pine put an arm around Negret. "You ready?"

He nodded. "Yes."

Negret skipped the parts about the conversations he and Sirin had had with Mrs. Hereward and Georgie and began with how he'd thought the open guest room might be a good place to check. He told about finding the watch in the soap cake, how the unglued wrapper had tipped him off, how he'd known there was something wrong with it the minute he'd picked it up, and how he'd resealed the soap and decided to hide the watch somewhere else.

"I don't understand," Mr. Vinge protested. "Why didn't you just tell me you'd found it? Why didn't you give it back right away?"

"Because I figured if the thief knew I'd found one thing, he might move the other things," Negret said. "And that's why I took the watch to the attic."

As he told the next part about finding the bag, he said he'd noticed differences in the pile of sailcloth that led him to look there. It wasn't quite untrue, but he crossed the fingers of one hand in his pocket anyway, hoping no one would ask how one kid had been able to move a giant mass of heavy canvas sailcloth by himself. No one did. "Then I heard Clem and Georgie in the stairwell. I mean, I couldn't really hear anything you were saying," he added hastily, "but I knew it was the two of you. And I could smell Georgie's perfume, from the bottle I broke that first day. And that helped me figure out where your notebook was." He finished with the poinsettia, which, he realized with a guilty twinge, was probably at that very moment dying in his waste bin, where he'd left it. "And . . . well, I guess that's it."

The room was quiet for a moment. "I am thoroughly impressed, Milo," Mr. Pine said at last. "That was some pretty amazing observation. Thank you."

Georgie nodded and began to clap. Clem joined in, and Mrs. Hereward. "Allow me to refill your mug, Milo," Georgie said.

He smiled. For a moment he forgot entirely that Sirin was going to watch for clues, and he ignored the strained look that passed between his parents, who certainly had not forgotten that there was still a thief in their midst. He sat there with his hot chocolate and enjoyed the fact that, for the first time all day, the feeling in the house was companionable rather than suspicious.

It couldn't last, though. For one thing, the thief *was* still out there. For another, there was still the list of clues and questions they'd made earlier, and now that all the stolen things had been given back, it occurred to him that maybe this was a good time to cross one of those items off.

Georgie and Mr. Vinge had gone upstairs to put away their re-covered items, but Mrs. Hereward was still on the couch with the bag in her lap, running her fingers fondly over the stitching. Negret got up from the hearth and went to sit next to her. "Mrs. Hereward? Do you think I could ask you a question about that?"

She smiled. "It's the very least I can do, isn't it? What would you like to know?"

The side of the bag with the gate and its single golden lantern was facing up. "On the other side, on the door of the house, I noticed some symbols that look like Chinese writing."

Mrs. Hereward turned the bag over. "These."

"Yes. Could I ask you what they mean? If you know?"

She hesitated a moment, then smiled again. She glanced around —Dr. Gowervine had gone back out on the porch to smoke, and everyone else was in the kitchen getting more cake and refilling their mugs. She lowered her voice and said, "It's the original name of the house, Milo. Of *this* house. I don't know how to pronounce it properly, but in my family . . ." She looked around again to be sure they were still alone. "In my family it was always said *Lansde-gown.*"

His jaw dropped. "Just like Georgie's camera!"

Mrs. Hereward nodded with a half smile. "Indeed. I have been wondering how I might ask her where she came up with that name. I don't suppose she told you?"

Milo shook his head. "She seemed to think I might know what it meant. Like I might remember that I know if I think hard enough about it. Like maybe then I could tell her."

"Interesting," Mrs. Hereward murmured. "For the moment, I would be grateful if you didn't mention what I just told you to Georgie, Milo."

"Are you going to tell her?"

The old lady frowned. "I'm not certain yet. Let me think on it for a while."

Just then, a rending crack shook the night.

The wind and the frozen branches had been creating a clamor for hours, but this noise was different. It was *deafening*. "What was that?" Mrs. Hereward shrieked. "Good God, the house is coming down around our ears!"

"Would you *kindly* lower your *voice,* woman!" snarled Dr. Gowervine, stomping back inside from the porch.

Mrs. Pine rushed in from the kitchen. "It's not the house," she said soothingly.

Meanwhile, Milo's father hurriedly began pulling on his coat and boots in the foyer. It wasn't the house, but *something* had made that noise. He caught Milo watching him and grinned. "Just going to have a look," he said. "Sounded like a big branch. I want to make sure it didn't fall on anything. Want to come along?"

"Can I come too?" Georgie Moselle trotted over and reached for her coat. "I love winter at night."

Mr. Pine hesitated. "I don't know, Georgie. It's freezing out there."

"That's all right, Mr. Pine. I don't mind the cold." She swung her coat around her shoulders and zipped it up. "Lead on."

Plainly, his father didn't want Georgie coming with them. But instead of arguing he just shrugged, and the three of them trooped out into the night.

Milo hadn't gone three steps when he nearly landed on his backside. The porch was a slick of ice. "Whoa, there!" Mr. Pine caught his flailing arm and almost lost his own footing in the process.

"You sure the two of you can manage?" Georgie laughed. "And you were worried about me."

Clinging to the railings and inching along carefully, they made it off the porch without too much slipping and sliding. When Milo stepped down onto the snow, the surface crackled under his boot like the crust of sugar when you bit into a frosted cookie. His foot sank until only an inch of his green rubber boot showed above the white. Away from the shelter of the porch, the wind burned his cheeks, and the creaking of the trees sounded like a thunderstorm caught in a whiny mood.

"Milo, how about you and Georgie check the pavilion?" Mr. Pine suggested. "Watch the ice and stay away from the stairs. I'll check the woodshed and the outbuildings on the uphill side."

Georgie watched with a thoughtful look as Milo's father hiked through the snow around the back of the house. Then she seemed to remember that Milo was there, and turned to smile down at him. "Looks like it's you and me, pal." Milo figured either she didn't like being stuck with him, or she was thinking the same thing he was: what was Mr. Pine *really* going to check on?

Of course, he reflected, as the two of them stomp-stepped their way through the crusty snow to the tree line, there was no reason Georgie should know that the woodshed was made of stone and couldn't be hurt by a falling branch, no matter how big it was. As for the rest of the outbuildings . . .

Oh. Milo stumbled as he realized what the noise had been, and where his father was going.

Georgie took a huge pair of leaping steps to Milo's side. "What?" she asked.

"What?" Milo repeated, trying to look innocent as he resumed stomping toward the trees. Then he spotted something that made him stumble again, and he forgot all about what his father was up to.

There was a man in the woods ahead of them, stepping off the top stair onto the platform. He dropped the bag he was carrying with an explosive sigh and crumpled to the ground. Georgie made a strangled noise, then fell silent as she and Milo scrambled to reach him.

Gingerly, they picked their way to where he crouched. Georgie dropped to her knees. "Where did you come from?" she asked breathlessly. "Are you okay?"

"There's a bench over here, mister," Milo said.

"I don't think I can move a muscle," the stranger groaned.

Milo and Georgie looked at each other, then each reached for one of the man's arms. Carefully, they lifted him to his feet. Georgie slid her shoulder under the arm she held. "I'll help him to the house. Can you bring his bag, Milo?"

"Sure."

Leaning on the blue-haired girl, the man allowed himself to be half carried, half dragged toward the inn. Milo picked up the bag he'd dropped and staggered along in their wake.

He helped Georgie haul the stranger up the icy stairs—poor guy, Milo thought, after the hundreds of icy stairs he'd just climbed—and they somehow managed to get the door open. Milo glanced at the bell as they passed it, wondering why he hadn't rung for the railcar. The whole thing was frozen, a solid mass of metal and ice.

They maneuvered the newcomer inside and deposited him on the bench in the foyer. "Somebody bring blankets!" Georgie called. "*Now.*"

"*Mom!*" Milo added in his best *it's an emergency* tone.

Mrs. Pine was there in a flash, with Mrs. Caraway a step behind her. Milo's mother stopped short, stared at the man shuddering from the cold and his hike up the hill, then got right to helping Georgie get him out of his coat.

"It's going to be okay," Georgie said softly. "You're going to be fine. You're safe now."

"Who is *that?*" Mr. Vinge leaned over them, peering down his nose for a closer look.

"Don't know," Milo said. "He hiked all the way up from the waterfront, though. The bell isn't working."

"Clem," Mrs. Pine shouted, "bring some coffee!"

"My name's O-Owen," the stranger managed. "Thank you."

For the second time that night, Milo's jaw dropped. He looked at Georgie. She caught his eye and her face went redder than cold alone could account for. Yes, this must be the mysterious Owen she and Clem had in common.

"I'll get the blankets," Mrs. Caraway said, and disappeared.

He was youngish, like Clem and Georgie. His hair was dark, and so was his skin, kind of, now that the color was coming back into it. His eyes marked him as at least part Asian. *He looks a little like me,* Milo realized with a start. *Or at least, he looks more like me than anyone else in this room.*

"All right, coffee coming through. What's the big—" Clem Candler arrived in the foyer, took in the group huddled there, and stopped talking abruptly. The cup fell from her hand and bounced off the head of Mr. Vinge, who was crouched beside the newcomer. Steaming hot coffee spattered everywhere, and the mug shattered on the floor.

Mr. Vinge leaped away, clutching his head and howling, and backed into Mrs. Caraway as she came running down the stairs with an armful of blankets. Two adults and four quilts went flying. Mrs. Pine clapped her hands over her eyes, then pulled herself together and reached out to help Mr. Vinge to his feet. "I'm so sorry, Mr. Vinge. Come with me. I'll make up an ice pack."

Clem stood stock-still, staring down at the young man on the bench. Her face was pale and her eyes were wide. For the first time since she'd arrived at the inn, her easy poise seemed to have left her.

Milo followed her gaze back to the stranger, Owen. He managed a weak smile. "I told you I'd find you, Ottilie."

Georgie, who'd been watching this exchange just as closely as Milo, spoke one word softly, painfully. *"No."*

No one else appeared to hear her. Clem nodded slowly. "You win, Owen."

Georgie burst into odd laughter. So odd, in fact, that when she first made the sound, Milo was almost certain it was a crying noise, something like a sob. But no, she was smiling — strangely — when she spoke. "He calls you Ottilie? *Ottilie?*"

"It's my middle name," Clem said quietly.

Two shining lines of damp streamed down Georgie's face. "And I thought Clemence was ridiculous." She wiped her face on her sleeve, stood abruptly, and stumbled up the stairs.

The group watched her go, then turned their attention back to the half-frozen young man. Clem tucked layer after layer of blankets around him, then she and Mrs. Caraway got him carefully to his feet and maneuvered him to the sofa.

"You know this fellow?" Mrs. Pine asked from the entrance to the kitchen. Behind her Mr. Vinge watched with a tea towel full of ice held to his temple.

"Yes," Clem said. She took a steaming mug from Lizzie and wrapped Owen's cold hands around it. "Here." She helped him raise the cup to take a sip.

It has nothing to do with Owen. And here, as if out of nowhere, was an Owen who was on a middle-name basis with Clem. Georgie'd covered it up pretty well until the end, but it was clear she knew him too.

Meanwhile, Mr. Pine was somewhere outside, still investigating the noise. Milo was torn. On one hand, Owen, whoever he was, was a huge clue to . . . something. On the other hand, with all the ladies fussing around him, it wasn't as if he could answer any questions.

Still in his coat and boots, Milo slipped back outside and followed his father's footprints across the grounds. Just past the stone woodshed, the trail disappeared into the creaking woods. Mr. Pine's tracks were all but invisible in the darkness, but that didn't matter. Milo knew where his father had gone.

There was a scattering of old red stone outbuildings in the woods here, remnants of a long-ago time when the grounds on which Greenglass House stood had belonged to the monastery way at the top of the hill. Milo had turned one of them into a fort the previous summer. Another one had a spring in it that bubbled up out of the stony ground. Mr. and Mrs. Pine used another for storage, and had filled it with scrap wood and stone and old ironwork. The very oldest was nothing but three walls and two-thirds of a chimney, and it was pretty much held up by the vines that had grown around it. And then there was the one that hid the entrance to an abandoned subterranean railway line.

Nagspeake's failed railway experiment was called the BTS: the Belowground Transit System. Once, ages ago (or at least, before Milo was born), there had been a stop here called Sanctuary Cliff. And although the railway itself had been shut down, nobody had bothered to do much about the old stations that dotted the city. Most people, according to Milo's dad, didn't even notice them. Mr. Pine said that they'd been built to blend right into their surroundings, but Milo thought that if they were all like the Sanctuary Cliff station, the builders of the stations might actually have been trying to hide them. You'd never have spotted it if you didn't know what you were looking for.

The smugglers of Nagspeake had all sorts of tall tales about what they called "the old hole-and-corner railway." It figured into the legends about several of the city's most famous runners, and some of the ne'er-do-wells who'd stayed at Greenglass House even claimed it had never really been abandoned.

Most of them, though, had no idea how true that was. There was exactly one train that still ran on the old lines, and one conductor who worked on that train. Milo and his parents and the Caraways were among the very, very few who knew this, because that conductor was a regular guest at the inn and had come to trust the Pines somewhere along the way.

Milo hiked through the trees and up the hill until he reached the snow-rimed red stone of the Sanctuary Cliff station house. Two figures stood outside it, staring at the dark slab of the iron-bolted wooden door, which lay at an angle on a drift of snow. A third figure emerged from the darkness inside the station and reached a hand out to the other two, who helped him scramble up the slope of the door and out.

"Sorry, mate," said the third man, who wore a huge padded coat over gray coveralls, and a pair of leather-bound goggles pushed up on his forehead. "The lock was frozen solid." Between the weird accent and the goggles, Milo immediately recognized him as the conductor of the last running Belowground Transit train, Brandon Levi.

"Don't worry about it." That was Milo's father. Together the three men picked up the fallen door and pushed it back into place. "I'm just glad you didn't wind up stuck in there."

The tall conductor turned, brushing snow from his leather gloves. "Oy, Ben, we've got company." He waved. "Evening, Milo."

Milo waved back. "Hi, Brandon. Don't worry, Dad. Georgie's back at the house. And there's a new guy."

"A new guy?" Mr. Pine crunched across the icy snow and peered through the trees toward the house. "Since when?"

"He was coming up the stairs when Georgie and I got to the pavilion. His name is Owen," Milo said, "and it seems like he knows Clem Candler, but he called her something else. Ottery or something. It was a weird name."

"Good grief." Mr. Pine turned back to Brandon and the third man. Milo recognized him too: Fenster Plum, the short, scruffy plant smuggler who was a springtime regular at Greenglass House. The very same Fenster who'd sailed with Doc Holystone and had once seen his ghost.

"I think," Milo's father continued, scratching his head under his knitted cap, "you two had better come up with a story in case anyone asks what you do. Like I said, it's an odd bunch in there. There's a thief, at least, and while I don't think any of them look like customs agents or anything, I can't say for certain."

"No worries. I'll tell them the truth and just leave out the bit about the Belowground Transit," Brandon said easily. "Anybody wants to check with the fight houses on Morbid Street, there are plenty of people who'll vouch for me. Had a bout just last month." He winked at Milo. "Won it with a round kick to the other fellow's head, right on the button."

Then he and Mr. Pine looked at Fenster. "What?" the smuggler asked weakly. "I'll come up with something."

"Come up with something *now*," Brandon suggested with a scowl. "And try to stick to something you know about. You know what a bad liar you are."

"I am not," Fenster protested, which was so obviously a lie that even Milo rolled his eyes. "I know about flowers and bulbs and whatnot," he said defensively. "I can say I'm a gardener or something."

"That's not bad," Brandon said. "You could say you work at the monastery and got caught in the storm on the way home."

"Kind of a boring fake identity," Fenster grumbled. "I mean, if I'm going to have one, why can't I —"

"It's perfect," Brandon interrupted. "You can hardly get yourself into trouble with it, and that's what matters."

Instead of trooping straight for the inn, Mr. Pine led the little group on a roundabout route through the woods that brought them to a flat white swath that cut through the trees — the snow-and-ice-covered dirt road. Then, with a grumbling Fenster bringing up the rear, they hiked down it back toward Greenglass House. "So it'll look like they came in on the road, instead of through the woods?" Milo guessed.

"That's the idea." Brandon tapped the side of his nose. "The less said about the Belowground to strangers, the better." He glared at Fenster again. "Keep it in mind, will you?"

"I'm not an idiot," Fenster muttered.

They rounded a bend, and there were the giant snowy lumps of the Pines' truck and Mrs. Caraway's car in the inn's little parking lot, and the lights of Greenglass House glowing cozily through the aged glass windows beyond. Then, just as the four of them started across the lawn, a wind knifed through the trees downhill, sending everything in the world, it seemed, rattling and cracking even worse than before. The wind went on rushing uphill; there was a deep, rending noise somewhere among the evergreens; and barely a minute later, right before Milo's eyes, the lights of Greenglass House went out.

nine

THE TALE OF THE OTTER AND THE EYE

"Oh, boy," Milo said, staring at the house, which had suddenly been reduced to nothing more than a patch of gray.

"Good grief." Mr. Pine sighed. "I mean, I sort of figured this might happen, but still. Brandon, how about giving me a hand with the generator? And Fenster, you mind going with Milo and helping Nora get some temporary light in there? She's probably got a couple guests freaking out on her."

A couple at least. Mrs. Hereward and Dr. Gowervine were guaranteed to be panicking loudly. Milo didn't wait to hear Fenster's answer, just hurried as fast as he could toward the house.

He heard shouting before he even got up the porch stairs

(remembering at the last moment not to try to take them two at a time because of the ice). Then he opened the front door and all hell broke loose.

"It's just me!" Milo shouted into the maelstrom of voices that, once he listened for a moment, was really just the excitable pair and Mrs. Caraway and Lizzie trying hard to calm them down. The four stood at the center of the living room where the only remaining light, the glow of the fire, made their faces look monstrous. Mr. Vinge was nowhere to be seen. Georgie was still upstairs, maybe, and Clem and Owen seemed to have left the first floor too.

Mrs. Pine appeared in the light of a candle at Milo's shoulder, and she was furious. "Once things calm down, I will have some very loud and angry words for you about the way you disappeared like that on a night like this," she said tightly. "But obviously, they'll have to wait." She pressed a long grill lighter, the kind that works with a trigger, into Milo's hand. "Get to lighting candles. And—" She peered over his shoulder. "Is that *Fenster?*"

Fenster pulled off his cap. "Yes, ma'am. But incognito." He gave Mrs. Pine an exaggerated wink. "Just a humble monastery gardener, I."

She blinked, then sighed. "Fill me in later. Milo, where's your father?"

"Starting the generator." Milo beckoned her closer and lowered his voice. "Brandon Levi's with him."

"Also incognito," Fenster added, leaning in to whisper.

"Candles," Mrs. Pine ordered through gritted teeth. "*Now,* so maybe these two will stop thinking the world's coming to an end just because it's dark. I'm going down to the basement for the lan-terns. Actually, Fenster, could you give me a hand with those? And I should probably explain about this story I may have told everyone about you," she added as the two of them disappeared through the basement door in the kitchen.

Milo made a beeline for the candles his mother had artfully worked into the centerpiece on the dining room table earlier in the day. He squeezed the trigger and touched the flame to the trimmed wicks one by one. Meddy's face peered at him from the other side of the table through the candle flames. He jumped and heard himself give an involuntary squeak.

"Where've you been?" he demanded.

"Where've *you* been?" she countered. "I've been right here. Seemed like the best thing to do was just stay put until everything calmed down." She nodded at the living room, where, incredibly, the noise was rising. Mrs. Hereward and Dr. Gowervine had spotted Fenster passing through and were demanding to know who the new stranger in their midst was. "What's *with* those two?"

There were three unlit candlesticks on the kitchen counter. Milo gathered them and took them into the living room. He edged right into the middle of the yelling group, held up the lighter awkwardly, and clicked it alight.

Startled, the guests stopped shouting. Milo handed two of the unlit candlesticks off to Lizzie Caraway and lit the third. Then he shoved it at Mrs. Hereward, who took it more out of self-defense than any wish to be helpful. "That one goes on the table by the sofa," he said, and pointed.

Mrs. Hereward opened her mouth. "Right there," Milo added before she could get a word out. The old lady scowled but she did as she was told.

Milo took another candlestick from Lizzie, who was watching with a bemused look on her face. This one he lit and thrust at Dr. Gowervine. "This goes on the table by the front door. Over there, please." The doctor gave him a scowl too, but went without arguing. Lizzie handed Milo the last candle, which he passed along to the returning Mrs. Hereward before she could start yelling again.

"Thank you," Milo said, ignoring her obvious displeasure.

Mrs. Hereward looked at him, surprised. "Well . . . well, you're welcome."

"Why don't you sit and relax for a bit?" he suggested. "Take the candle with you. And, Dr. Gowervine, if you want to do something really useful, you could bring the firewood in for Lizzie." The short man stopped dead in his tracks in the act of following Mrs. Caraway into the kitchen to start yelling at her again. He glowered at Milo, turned on his heel, and slunk to the foyer to pull on his coat.

Milo smiled. *And I didn't even have to use Negret's Irresistible Blandishment,* he thought. *I just did it.*

By the time his mother reappeared with the handles of four kerosene lanterns looped over her arms and Fenster on her heels carrying a mountain of blankets and a few more lanterns that dangled from his wrists, the first floor was candlelit and quiet. Mrs. Hereward was knitting quietly on the sofa, Dr. Gowervine and Lizzie were stacking wood next to the fireplace, and Milo and Meddy were conferring in the corner behind the Christmas tree.

"Wow," Mrs. Pine said. "This isn't what I expected to find."

Georgie stumbled down the stairs and into the candlelit dining room. "Ah, I see it's not just my floor without light."

"Yeah, the house lost power, but everything's fine," Milo's mom replied. "How's the young man doing?"

Georgie shrugged and trudged into the kitchen. She looked miserable. "I don't know. I left them alone." Then she paused and roused herself out of her sadness long enough to glance curiously at Fenster. "I don't think we've met."

He gave a short bow that threatened to topple him along with his load of cold-weather supplies. As it was, two thick blankets landed on the floor just in time to nearly send Mr. Vinge sprawling as he returned to the first floor. "Fenster Plum, ma'am. And sir," he added, nodding to Mr. Vinge. "I'm a gardener. I work up at the monastery at the top of the hill, only what with the weather I got stuck on my way home. Home being down in Shantytown, miss, which is rather a long trip to take on such a wretched night. You can see how I wound up here. Nothing strange about it at all."

Georgie's eyes widened as she listened, but she nodded along as if there was nothing strange about gardening in the middle of a snowstorm, nor someone attempting a long trip home on such a wretched night, nor about Fenster's overlong explanation. Milo was pretty sure she wasn't fooled one bit.

Mrs. Pine gave Fenster a warning look. "Nope, nothing strange at all," she said.

"This wouldn't be the Fenster from your story, Mrs. Pine?" Mr. Vinge asked, picking up the fallen blankets.

"Why, yes!" Fenster said before Milo's mom could answer. "Nora said she'd told that tale!"

"You'll have to tell us your version of it," Mr. Vinge suggested as he placed the blankets back on Fenster's pile. "We've been telling stories."

"Glad to! Matter of fact, I can tell you now, right quick. It were April—"

"Not now, Fenster. My arms are killing me," Mrs. Pine interrupted.

It was Mrs. Hereward who came to the rescue, bustling out of the living room with a skein of green yarn dangling from one bony hand. "Oh, Mrs. Pine? I don't wish to sound hysterical, but by what means exactly are you going to keep us all from freezing in our beds tonight?"

"Well, the generator should bring the power back before long," she replied, sounding relieved at the change of subject. "But I'm going to take lanterns up to everybody's rooms now, and we have plenty of spare blankets and hot water bottles, too, just in case. It's true this is a drafty old house, but it's not built out of sticks and mud. It'll keep the heat in for a good long while before we have to worry about anybody freezing."

Mrs. Hereward looked skeptical, but Mrs. Pine just hustled Fenster toward the stairs and they headed up. Georgie went into the kitchen and poured herself a mug of coffee. "I've got one," she said. "A story, I mean." She took her mug into the living room and dropped into the chair opposite the one Mr. Vinge was settling into. "I'll tell the story tonight. Can I?"

"Sure," Milo said. "Why not?"

Georgie looked into her cup, then raised her face. "Milo, yesterday your mom said there was whiskey if we wanted hot toddies. You think I could have some for my coffee?"

"Sure." He went to the liquor cabinet, found the right bottle, and took it back to the blue-haired girl, who opened it and poured a generous amount into her cup. Then she handed the bottle back, stirred the whiskey and coffee together with her index finger, and took a long sip, wincing.

"Listen," she said at last. The night before, Mrs. Hereward had spoken the invocation like an order, but Georgie made it sound like a sigh.

"There were two moonlighters, two very famous thieves. One was a burglar who was called the Otter because of his acrobatic style and because he was known to be a spirited character. The other was a hacker called the Eye, because when he cased a target he saw everything and learned everything about it. Not one little slip of information was missed or went to waste.

"These two thieves knew of each other, of course, but they had never crossed paths. Still, by some quirk of fate, it happened that the Otter and the Eye fell in love with the same girl.

"This girl . . . well, it's impossible to say what makes a person fall in love, really, so there's no way to know how each of them came to love her. She was nice enough to look at, but that wasn't the reason. She was brilliant to speak to, and she had peculiar and fascinating ideas, which were definitely part of her allure. She was . . ." Georgie shrugged. "She wasn't the sort of person who would demand that anyone change who he or she was, and yet each thief felt in his secret heart that if by some miracle she loved him back, he might actually consider looking for gainful employment if she asked him to."

On the hearth, Milo groaned inwardly, wondering if after the promising beginning — moonlighters! — this was going to turn into a boring love story.

"Whatever the reasons," Georgie continued, "both the Otter and the Eye came to love her madly. And, being thieves, each immediately began to think about how he might steal her heart for himself."

Thank goodness, Milo thought. *Back to thievery.*

"Well, it's virtually impossible for two very elite thieves to make a play for the same plunder without becoming aware of each other, so before long, the Otter and the Eye — who you will recall had heard of each other, but had never met — discovered that they were questing for the same prize.

"If the way to the girl's heart had been as simple as the gift of any valuable object that could be taken from one person and given to another, the odds would have been so completely in the Otter's favor that the Eye would never have had a chance. The Otter was an expert in jewels and precious things, and unparalleled at the sort of work it took to steal them: the crafty sneaking-in and lifting-away and escaping without a trace.

"But the girl was not that sort of creature, and they both knew it. They also both knew that this put the Eye at an advantage. He was a master at the patient seeking of information, at knowing a mark so completely that, before long, that mark could not possibly keep secrets from him, and then at discerning which secrets were meaningful and which were not. If there was a single gift that could be given to the girl that might convince her of the devotion in the heart of a bandit, it was the Eye who had the best chance of finding it. But he knew the Otter would be watching, and that if he wasn't careful, the Otter would try to steal whatever he found before he could give it to the girl. And if what he found was anything that could be taken from him by stealth, even *he* would be hard-pressed to protect it from the Otter.

"Well, not to drag the story out, the Eye found what he was looking for deep in the archives of the city. The girl had been adopted as a child" — Milo sat up just a touch straighter — "and because of the dreadful state of the city archives, she had never been able to learn anything about her family."

"Her birth parents," Milo corrected instinctively. "The people who adopted her would still have been her family."

Georgie looked up at him apologetically. "Yes, sorry, Milo. She had never been able to learn anything about her birth parents, but she had always been curious. And while the Eye wasn't able to find anything about them specifically, he was able to track down some information about the one thing she had from before she'd been adopted: her middle name. *Lansdegown.*"

Milo stiffened, and on the sofa, Mrs. Hereward did the same. They glanced at each other across the room. Milo raised his eyebrows at her. Mrs. Hereward nodded, then tapped one finger to her lips.

Georgie didn't seem to notice the exchange. "The Eye discovered that the name was also the old, forgotten name of a house, and he determined to find out what this meant. He made no notes of what he'd found; for all he knew, the Otter was already sneaking into his lair every night and looking for information. The only physical clue he had was a chart, an artifact connected to the house from the days when it was called Lansdegown, and the Eye planned to follow that chart to its secret. To protect this clue, he created a decoy: a map very similar to the real one. Then he began to studiously consult that false map. When not pretending to pore over it, the Eye hid the false map as carefully as possible, as if it was precious and as if protecting it from thieving eyes was the most important thing in his life. And just as he'd expected he would, the Eye woke one morning to find the map gone as cleanly as if it had never existed. Knowing he had a very narrow window of time while the Otter was occupied with the false map, the Eye left for the house.

"It wasn't until after he had arrived at the house that the Eye discovered that he'd made a mistake and left the Otter a clue after all. He'd done a brilliant thing badly. When he'd made the false map, one of the steps he'd taken to be sure it would be convincing was to use the same paper as the real one, which turned out to be an antique stock he'd had to track down.

"Nothing stayed hidden from the Eye, not for long; it had taken him very little time to locate a box of the same old paper in an abandoned warehouse. What he hadn't known then—but what the Otter discovered once he had the fake map—was that the watermarked paper had been made specifically for the owners of the house, long, long ago. You see, when the decoy map itself had given the Otter no real information, he'd gone in search of information about the watermark, and despite all the Eye's efforts to throw his rival off his trail, it was the false map itself that led the Otter straight to Lansdegown House.

"The two thieves arrived only hours apart, and then, of course, it was a race to find the house's secret first. The thieves pretended not to know each other, and once they were introduced, they affected civility. But all the while, they were frantic, and watching each other in stealth and in silence."

Georgie and Clem, of course. Blue and Red. Never mind that she was pretending the story was about two male thieves. Milo nodded, thinking *I knew they were only pretending to be strangers.*

"Then the unthinkable happened." Georgie paused for another long sip of her doctored coffee. "The unthinkable was this: the girl herself showed up at the house. She turned up —" Georgie's voice made an odd, harsh sound as she broke off. She took one more sip, grimacing. "She turned up because she knew the Otter was there."

"How did she know?" Milo asked. "I thought she didn't know about the house. How'd she know they were looking for it?"

"She didn't. She didn't turn up there because she knew the thieves were looking there for a lost piece of her past. She turned up because she knew *they* were there. Specifically, she turned up because she knew the *Otter* was there. Not because she knew he was up to anything that had anything to do with her. Just because the Otter was *there.*" She looked dully at Milo. "You understand?"

He shook his head, and Georgie sighed. "All that time," she said in a voice that fell to a whisper as she spoke, "while Otter and Eye had been falling in love, the person they loved had been falling in love too. But only with one of them, of course. And Eye wasn't the one he fell for."

"You said *he*," Milo said. Then he realized what he'd actually heard her say. This time, Georgie had said not *the Eye*, but *I*.

As in, *and I wasn't the one he fell for.*

The coffee cup was shaking in her hands. Mrs. Hereward took it away gently. "You and Clem?" Milo asked, pretending he'd only just figured it out. "You're the thieves in the story, and you both liked the new guy, Owen?"

"Liked?" Georgie folded her hands in her lap and laughed shortly. "Yes, Milo." She took a deep, jagged breath, untwined her fingers, and reached for the cup the old lady was holding. "And he chose Clem."

There was a moment of quiet, then everyone jumped as a trumpeting noise cut through the room: Mrs. Hereward, blowing her nose. "I beg your pardon," she said, blinking rapidly. "Carry on." Was she *crying?*

Before Milo could process the strangeness of that, Meddy leaned out from behind the tree. She punched him in the shoulder with an exasperated look. "Stay focused," she whispered. "We need clues, Negret."

He rubbed his shoulder and got into character. "So . . . when you told me the missing notebook had stuff in it about the house and someone who might be connected to it, that person was Owen?"

Negret asked. Georgie nodded. "But you said the Eye—that *you* didn't make any notes because you were afraid they'd be stolen."

"I didn't, until I was on my way here and I figured it was safe."

"And why are you telling us all this now?" he asked. "After all the secrecy, all the hiding and sneaking and—"

"Because, Milo, *he chose Clem,* and not because of anything she did to steal his heart. She hadn't even gotten around to trying yet—I guess she didn't realize she'd already managed it *without* trying. He chose Clem, so it doesn't matter who finds the Lansdegown secret now." She drank deeply. "I'm done looking. It wouldn't do any good anyway. Not when he nearly froze to death trying to get to her. Maybe it's better if she finds it."

She looked down at her nearly empty cup, handed it to Negret, clapped her hands on her knees, and got unsteadily to her feet. She made an awkward little bow to the rest of the room—Negret and Sirin, Mrs. Hereward, Mr. Vinge, Dr. Gowervine, Lizzie, and Fenster and Mrs. Pine, who'd come back from distributing lanterns throughout the house toward the end of the story. "The end," she said softly. And with that, Georgie Moselle disappeared up the stairs.

"How sad for her," Mrs. Hereward said after a long, silent moment. "Poor lamb. Poor little blue lamb."

Fenster nodded. "I don't like seeing people sad. Somebody ought to make her a cake or something." Everyone turned to look at him. "Don't you think?" he asked. "Everybody feels better when there's cake. Darn it, I can probably do it myself."

"You can bake?" Sirin and Mrs. Hereward asked in unison.

"Well, not so's I could make a living off it," Fenster retorted, turning a little pink. "But I can measure flour and that, and I bet there's a cookery book someplace hereabouts. You have a cookery book, Nora?"

Mrs. Pine nodded with a little smile. "You bet, Fenster."

The old lady snorted. Then her face softened. "Why don't I give you a hand, Mr. Fenster? We'll bake one for her in the morning. We might even manage some blue icing."

"We probably can, at that, ma'am! I believe I have a blue pen someplace I can get open. First thing in the morning, then?" He made a sharp little salute. "Guess I'll head out and see how the generator's coming along."

Mrs. Hereward smiled politely until Fenster was out the door. "Milo, dear boy, you don't think Mr. Fenster was suggesting we'd use blue ink to color the frosting, do you?"

He winced. "Maybe." He glanced down at the bag she'd been clutching ever since it had been returned. "Mrs. Hereward? Do you think you might be willing to talk to Georgie about Lansdegown and what you know about the house?"

She hesitated. "I'm not sure. It doesn't sound like she wants to know any more, Milo. It might just be more hurtful."

"You could tell Owen," he suggested. "He must be the descendant of that first family somehow, if that's his middle name." He could hear his own voice rising and tried not to look as desperate as he felt. He shoved his hand in his pocket and clutched the keys, thinking of the imaginary old blackjack he had already grown so fond of. What a terrible injustice it would be if someone had information about Owen's past and didn't give it to him. It didn't matter to Milo that the young man was a perfect stranger. He had the chance to learn something about his heritage, and if Milo had anything to say about it, that chance was not going to be wasted.

"I'll think about it." Mrs. Hereward looked down at the symbols stitched into the door of the house for a moment, then turned the bag around, as if to say that the matter was closed.

Milo nodded and stood. Then he glanced at the bag again. "What about the gate? Was there a gate like that on the grounds back then?"

She frowned. "You know, I don't really know anything about the gate."

———— ❄ ————

He found Meddy later in the high-backed loveseat that faced the front window on the living room side. She sat with her back against one of the armrests, staring at the shadows cast by the flickering candelabra on the dining table, and she looked up as Milo sat down next to her. "Who's that new guy, again? Not Owen, but the other one?"

"Fenster Plum. He's a ... a *regular*. Cross your fingers he doesn't give himself away."

"I think I know him from somewhere," Meddy murmured. She sounded troubled.

"You might've seen him around the Harbors. He's been, well, *around* for ages."

"He's the one your mom told the story about, right? The one who saw Doc Holystone's and his kid's ghosts?"

"Hey, Milo." Mrs. Pine leaned down between them. "Everything okay?"

"Yeah, everything's fine."

"Good. I'm going to run out and check on your dad and Brandon and Fenster. They're taking forever. You going to be okay for a bit?"

"Sure."

"Come get me if you need anything, or just knock on Mrs. Caraway's door. She went to bed, but wake her if there's an emergency."

"Okay, Mom."

"You were saying, about Fenster," Meddy prompted when they were alone again.

"Oh, right." Milo lowered his voice. "Yeah, Fenster was the guy in Mom's story. She said he recognized Doc Holystone from the Wanted posters, but the truth is, Fenster *sailed* with him. It's a shame we can't ask him for a story. He tells really good ones."

"Hmm." Meddy looked at the flickering light on the table again for a moment, then pulled the glasses down over her eyes and turned to face him. "Back to business, Negret," she declared with a sharp look. "We have some new clues to sort through. For one thing, I think it's clear that Georgie was describing the map you found, so Clem must've been the one who took it."

He grinned, then shook his head. "No. If Clem's as good as Georgie says, then Clem wouldn't have made the mistakes the thief made, like not leaving my things the way I left them."

"Then who do you think it was?"

❋ 212 ❋

"I think . . . it was Georgie," Negret said slowly. "I think Georgie left it for me to find, back on the landing—"

"I thought you said someone had probably dropped it."

"I *did,* because that's what I thought *then.* But not now." He scratched his head, remembering Georgie's tale and how she'd described the Eye. "Now I think she left it for me. She dropped it on purpose. She *wanted* me to find it."

"But why?"

"Because . . . because she must've thought—or hoped—I would understand it. Maybe she was hoping I would know right away what it was a map of, and that I would follow it and lead her to . . ." Here he was at a bit of a loss, he realized. "To whatever it is she thinks is here. Something about Lansdegown."

"But what if Clem had found it instead?" the scholiast asked. "The map, I mean. Or if you'd mentioned it to her?"

"Clem wasn't here yet. But that's why Georgie stole it back, I bet! Once Clem turned up, she figured she couldn't have an important clue just lying around with me anymore."

"Shh." Sirin elbowed him. A moment later Georgie appeared on the stairs and shuffled tiredly into the living room. She collected her abandoned coffee cup, refilled it in the kitchen, then headed for the stairs again.

Mrs. Hereward made a loud coughing noise and looked pointedly from Mr. Vinge to Dr. Gowervine, who'd come back in from his smoke and now sat with his feet up on the hearth.

Mr. Vinge ignored her, but Dr. Gowervine spoke up. "Say, Miss

Moselle? Since you started it off, how about I tell the next story tonight?"

Georgie paused. Her eyes were red. "I don't know if I feel like staying up." She ran a hand distractedly through her hair. "I thought maybe I'd head out tomorrow. I should pack."

"Oh, come and listen with us," Mrs. Hereward cajoled, bustling over to the blue-haired girl. "Come take your mind off it for a bit, dear."

Georgie sighed and allowed herself to be led over to the chair nearest the tree. She curled her feet up underneath her, and for a moment she looked much younger than she'd seemed before. Negret couldn't help but feel sorry for her, she looked so miserable. Still, he was glad the storytelling wasn't over for the night. He turned and sat on his knees with his elbows on the back of the loveseat to listen.

Dr. Gowervine cleared his throat. "Well, I'm just a humble professor, and not much of a storyteller," he said, "so I hope you'll be patient with me." He looked thoughtfully at the arched window that topped the front door. Now and then a flicker from one of the candles reached it and illuminated one or another of the colored bits that made up the panel. "But in my work I do occasionally come across an interesting anecdote or two, and what I'm about to tell you is one of them. I suppose at least it's an appropriate story for where we are. It has quite a bit to do with stained glass.

"There was once a man who made windows," he began after a pause. "He was an artist with glass, but he was not a nice man. Or rather, he was not always nice. And he knew things. In fact, secrets were a sort of side business for him, the way secrets often are for people in Nagspeake. Or perhaps stained glass was the side business. Either way, he traded in both, and he was tremendously good at it.

"He worked out of a shop in the Printer's Quarter, making beautiful pictures with glass and metals and metal salts and occasionally taking charge of some morsel of secrecy, some crumb of mystery that someone wanted hidden away or brought to light or traded for another obscure and hidden thing."

He paused again as the front door opened and Mrs. Pine came inside along with a piercing swirl of frigid air.

"Sorry, folks," she said as she shucked her outdoor things. "They're still working. It's candles for us for a bit longer."

"Dr. Gowervine's telling a story," Mrs. Hereward announced.

"Whoops. Sorry to interrupt." She blew on her cold hands and headed into the kitchen.

"Those who didn't know about his secret business came to him for his glasswork," Dr. Gowervine continued. "Churches, architects, builders of libraries — even the mayor of the city came once, when it was time to rebuild after the city's archives had burned down. He asked the famous glazier for a window that would destroy itself with exceptional beauty the next time the archives were burned, and so interesting was the challenge, the glassmaker accepted. He was a strange man, with secrets of his own. His name was Lowell Skellansen."

Negret followed Dr. Gowervine's gaze back to the occasional flickers in the glass over the front door, wondering if perhaps the professor was building up to revealing that this famous artist had made the windows of Greenglass House, and that was what had brought him to the inn.

Apparently, he wasn't the only one who suspected as much. "Let me guess," Mrs. Hereward scoffed, waving a hand around so that her bracelets rattled. "Skellansen windows, every one of them? The house is too old for that."

Dr. Gowervine looked up coldly. "I know that," he retorted, and for a minute it seemed like whatever truce they'd called in the name of making Georgie feel better was about to be shattered. But the doctor just gave her an extra-vicious frown. "Yes, the house is old. And some of these windows are very old too. But unless I'm very much mistaken, and I'm something of an expert on the subject, so I doubt I am — many of them are quite a bit younger. Except for the ones in the stairwell, I suspect most were added after the house was built, much like the fire escapes and the side porch."

He adjusted his glasses and looked at the window next to the door to the screened porch. "These are beautiful windows, no question. But the difference between an exceptionally beautiful window and Skellansen's work is . . . well, it's a gulf. It's apples and oranges. Withered little crabapples and big ripe California oranges. Also, with one exception, none of the windows here looks to be more recent than, say, the very beginning of the twentieth century. Skellansen was making windows during my own lifetime."

"Except for one, you said," Negret reminded him. "Which one is that? Could that one have been from this Skellansen guy?"

"Ah, well. It's the enameled glass window. I imagine it's from sometime in the thirties. Still far too early for Skellansen."

"What's enameled glass?"

"Glass with color applied to it," Dr. Gowervine explained. "As opposed to when the glass itself is colored." He looked uncomfortable now, and abruptly Negret realized why. The professor was talking about the window in 5W. Clem's room. That was why he'd gone in there and touched nothing: he'd wanted a closer look at that glass. Fortunately for him, Clem wasn't around, and Mrs. Pine didn't catch the admission either.

He cleared his throat. "The point is, no, Mrs. Hereward, I'm certain these aren't Skellansen windows. But coming back to him: the story I want to tell began, as I suppose most things in Nagspeake do, with a smuggler. This particular smuggler was part of the crew of the famous Doc Holystone, and what he needed to move was a piece of information. So he went to the glassmaker who dealt in secrets."

Negret met Sirin's eyes. The famous Doc Holystone, who had once owned this house. That couldn't be a coincidence.

"For those who don't know," he continued, "Doc Holystone died thirty-four years ago after what seems to have been a somewhat reckless run, the details of which are still muddy."

Sirin frowned. Negret wondered what had caught her attention. Everybody knew that much of the Doc Holystone story.

"It does seem that agents of the Deacon and Morvengarde catalog merchants were involved, but then Nagspeake's customs agency is practically a wing of Deacon and Morvengarde, so that's hardly a surprise. It would certainly explain why the smuggler who came to Skellansen's workshop was in a state of panic, and afraid for his life. He knew the whole story, he said, and it needed to be told. But he couldn't be the one to do it. He didn't want Deacon and Morvengarde's enforcers after him. Could Skellansen help him find someone, perhaps at a newspaper, who would be willing to write about what had happened to Holystone?

"Well, Skellansen listened to the story and had a different idea. He would tell the tale himself. He would create a window that showed what had happened to Doc Holystone at the hands of Deacon and Morvengarde's agents, and he would put it where it would be sure to be seen. Skellansen had just accepted the mayor's commission for the window for the new city archives building, and he determined to make the smuggler's story his subject. There would be a big to-do over the unveiling, so even if Deacon and Morvengarde sent someone to smash the window the next day, thousands of people were guaranteed to see it at least once. It would be photographed and written about by journalists all over the city. It was perfect. Skellansen began sketching the minute the smuggler left his workshop.

"Now, this was not the only window the glazier was busy with at the moment, and it also wasn't the first time he'd combined his two livelihoods. He was crafty about it, but if you knew how to read his windows, there were whole worlds hidden in them, mysteries and secrets held together by glass and metal. And as it happened, somewhere out there in the city, someone else who'd had his secrets pass through Skellansen's hands had decided to put an end to the artist.

"You don't traffic in confidences and mysteries without knowing how to protect yourself, or without having some way to be forewarned when it's time to hide yourself away for a while. By the time the marauder with the knife between his teeth found his way into Skellansen's workshop, the glazier was long gone, and so was everything he'd been working on, including at least four windows it was known he'd been commissioned to make. The shop was not only abandoned, it was empty. Not a single piece of glasswork remained, and Skellansen has not been seen or heard from since."

"And?" Mrs. Hereward asked impatiently.

Dr. Gowervine looked at her, then back at the window beside the porch door, then back at the old lady again. "And he's still missing. Along with four windows, at least one but probably all of which hid secrets, at least one but probably all of which were enough for someone to want him dead. One of those windows had the secret truth about Doc Holystone's death encoded in it somewhere."

"And he supposedly made it to safety with four stained-glass windows while being stalked by a killer?" Mrs. Hereward asked skeptically. "That's a pretty incredible escape."

"Well, the workshop had been cleaned out. That's just a fact. But he wouldn't have needed to take the windows away intact," Dr. Gowervine said reasonably. "Most of us—people who study Skellansen—figure he escaped with either the cartoons, which are scale drawings used for measuring and cutting and laying out the glass, or possibly something called a *vidimus,* which is a sort of model made to show the customer. If he had the vidimus or the cartoon for any given window, Skellansen could reproduce it again."

He took another sip of coffee. The room waited. "And?" Mrs. Hereward said again.

"And what?" Dr. Gowervine demanded. "I don't know where

Skellansen went. I volunteered to tell a story because you said we needed to cheer the girl up, and all the glass in this place made me think of that one. Nobody said it had to be a story with an ending all neatly tied up like some ridiculous fairy tale. This story's true, and true stories don't have endings, because things just keep going."

Mrs. Hereward bristled at *some ridiculous fairy tale,* and Georgie snorted. "I didn't ask to be cheered up," she muttered. Despite her words, though, she was smiling.

Negret glanced at Sirin. She was still sitting stiffly, staring at Dr. Gowervine through narrowed eyes. Then she relaxed and ducked down behind the high back of the seat. "Well, that was interesting," she whispered. "What do you think?"

He hunched down to join her. "I think he's told that story before," Negret whispered in reply. "And I for sure don't think it just occurred to him to tell it because he's here and there happens to be a bunch of stained glass. It may be true that none of these windows are by that Skellansen guy, but that story and our windows must both have something to do with why he's here. And why he was in Clem's room." He explained the slip Dr. Gowervine had made about the enameled glass. "That doesn't mean he isn't also the thief, though. He's definitely looking for something."

"Agreed. So how do we find out what that something is? Are you thinking of all those glass pieces upstairs in the Emporium?"

"Yeah. But then I'm also thinking about what he said—how Skellansen wouldn't have had to escape with the real windows if he had the cartoons or the vi—vi—what was that word?"

"*Vidimus.*"

"Plus, if I was going to hide things that had to do with stained glass, hiding them somewhere that's already known for stained glass would be like hiding them in plain sight, right? Maybe Skellansen couldn't have hidden his actual windows here because they're so awesome they'd stick out. But his tools ... his models ... those might not be so obviously out of place."

Sirin was definitely impressed. "Wow, Negret. That's some good, sneaky thinking."

"Of course, it could just be that Dr. Gowervine's into stained glass and came here because we have a ton of it. He *could* be telling the truth about the Skellansen story just occurring to him. But there's also the Doc Holystone connection."

"Yes. That's interesting, isn't it?" She got that odd look on her face once more. "He didn't mention knowing this used to be the Holystone house, but do you think he did? Before he came here and heard your mom's story, I mean."

"There's an easy way to find out," Negret said. He turned to lean over the back of the seat again and raised his voice. "Dr. Gowervine?"

The professor looked up from his cup. "Yes, Milo?"

"About Doc Holystone?"

"Yes?" he answered guardedly.

Negret put on his most innocent expression. "Did you know this house used to belong to him? I mean before yesterday, when my mom told her story?"

Dr. Gowervine made a face that was probably supposed to look blank, surprised, guileless. It didn't manage to be any of those things. It looked like the expression of someone about to lie. "Goodness, no, I was completely surprised. Could've knocked me over with a feather."

"What a coincidence," Negret replied.

"Oh, yes, indeed," the professor agreed. "Quite a coincidence."

Negret turned back around and hunkered down again. "I don't recall him looking all that surprised at the time," he said quietly.

"So, not only did he already know," Sirin whispered, "but he *lied* about it. Why would he lie? It's not a secret, is it?"

"Nope," Negret whispered back, "but I bet if you were looking for something that someone went into hiding over, something that put someone's life in danger, maybe you'd feel a little nervous about it. Even if it all happened so long ago."

"So you think he thinks there's a ... a vidimus hidden here at the inn?"

"That, my dear Sirin, is exactly what I think he thinks. I think he thinks the secret of Doc Holystone's death is hidden somewhere right here." He let his character slip away for a moment and laughed, gazing out one of the two big windows that flanked the foyer. "This is so weird."

"Why?" Sirin asked, grinning back.

"Well, because. I mean ... this is my *house* we're talking about. Don't you think that's weird?" He shrugged. "I mean, yes, it used to be Doc Holystone's house too, but the day before yesterday I was just sitting here doing *math homework.*"

Outside, the snow had frozen in little drifts in the angles of the windowpanes. This window was plain Nagspeake glass: thick and air-pocked and about the color of the inside of a cucumber, so that everything beyond it was tinted pale green too. With so little light inside, the moonlit snow outside seemed even more luminous than usual. Glowing pale green snow, sloping away across the grounds to the tree line.

As he looked out toward the pavilion, Negret remembered the figure in the heavy coat who had appeared on the railcar landing two nights before. He'd assumed it had been the guest who'd dropped the map, but if he was right about Georgie dropping the map on purpose, maybe he'd been wrong.

Now it seemed possible that everyone had a reason to go snooping around Greenglass House.

As the candles burned lower, those who were still awake began to drift upstairs. Georgie was first, mumbling goodnight; then Mrs. Hereward and Lizzie and Meddy. Dr. Gowervine made one last trip out to the screened porch to smoke in the cold before he turned in. That left Mrs. Pine, Mr. Vinge, and Milo, who had moved to the hearth to read another chapter or two of *The Raconteur's Commonplace Book* by the light of the fire. His mother had stacked a few folded blankets on the brick, and with a minor adjustment or two Milo had turned the stack into a cozy sort of seat. The rucksack he'd found in the Emporium made a perfect footrest.

Mrs. Pine moved the fireplace grate and fed a pair of logs to the low flames. "You're a pretty quiet fellow."

Milo looked up, thinking she was talking to him, but his mother was smiling at Mr. Vinge. The old man shifted in his seat and crossed his ankles (green and blue argyle with what looked like a row of frogs hopping around them). "I suspect," he said with a chuckle, "anyone might seem a quiet fellow compared to some of the folks here."

"That's very true." Mrs. Pine replaced the screen and brushed her palms on her knees. "Mind if I ask what you're reading?"

He lowered his book. "A history of the Skidwrack and its environs."

"For work or for pleasure?" Mrs. Pine inquired. "You know, I don't think I ever got around to asking what you do. It got so busy, and you're so unobtrusive. Comparatively, of course," she added with a smile.

Milo kept pretending to read, but he was all ears. Mr. Vinge didn't answer right away. He seemed to consider the question for a minute before he said, "I'm retired."

If she wasn't satisfied with the answer, Mrs. Pine didn't let on. "That must be nice. Can I get you any more coffee or anything, Mr. Vinge?"

"No, no." He rose creakily and bowed. "I think I'll call it a night."

"How about you, kiddo?" Milo's mom asked. "Looks like you and I are the last two standing." She glanced out the window. "Inside, at least."

"I'm fine." He followed her gaze into the glittery night. "You think they're okay out there? Can I go check on them, maybe?"

Mrs. Pine smiled, but before she could answer, three bundled-up figures appeared from around the back of the house, plodding through the icy snow on the lawn. "Oh, crap," she muttered. "I guess this means no power tonight."

"Yikes."

The door opened, letting in yet another swirl of freezing wind, and Mr. Pine stomped inside, followed by Brandon and Fenster. All three of them looked frustrated, to say the least.

Mrs. Pine rushed over to help them out of their coats. "Milo, bring those blankets."

He gathered them up and carried them back to the three shivering men.

"Thanks, Milo," Mr. Pine said.

They wrapped themselves up, then trooped to the dining table while Mrs. Pine made a beeline for the kitchen, then reappeared and passed around steaming mugs. "No luck, huh?" All three of them looked at her with matching expressions of disgust. "I see."

"Naw, it's worse than that," Brandon grumbled. "You want to break the news, Ben?"

"Break the news?" Mrs. Pine repeated warily. "Please do."

Mr. Pine rolled his head on his neck. "My dear, you're not going to believe this, but we're ninety-nine percent sure somebody, somehow, went in and intentionally busted our generator."

"Somebody . . ." Mrs. Pine dropped onto the bench next to him. "You're kidding me."

"No, indeed. Sabotage," Brandon declared darkly. "Sure as if somebody shoved a wooden shoe in the bugger."

The old grandfather clock beside the sofa began to strike

midnight. Milo's father raised his cup. "So Merry Christmas Eve to us."

———————— ❄ ————————

His parents and Fenster and Brandon sat up for a long time discussing the generator problem, what to do about it and how to make sure the house—or at least the guests—stayed warm enough and the food didn't go bad and that sort of thing. Milo returned to the loveseat and picked up his book again.

He had been in the middle of the story about the Devil and the scavenger, but he couldn't quite get back into it now. There was too much rattling around inside his head. Negret and Sirin had recovered three stolen items, plus they'd figured out what had brought Georgie, Clem, and Mrs. Hereward to the house. All of that had been pretty cool. But Georgie, who had been really nice to him, had been crushed, which wasn't so much fun. Then there was Dr. Gowervine's story, which Negret suspected had also answered the question of what had brought him to Greenglass House.

What might the vidimus look like? And if Dr. Gowervine was looking for it, could he have stolen the three objects during his search? Georgie had told Negret her notebook contained information about someone connected to the house, and Clem had said she was the only other person who'd be interested in it—but what if Clem was wrong? What if Dr. Gowervine had somehow figured out that the notebook had something to do with the house and had swiped it for a look? Maybe that's what had happened with Mrs. Hereward's bag, too.

The only thing that didn't appear to fit was Mr. Vinge's watch, which didn't have anything to do with the house. Still, an old watch could be valuable, so maybe that theft had just been about . . . well, plain old theft.

Greenglass House back around 1812 . . . *Lansdegown House,* Milo corrected himself . . . Doc Holystone fortyish years ago . . . the gate, everywhere . . .

"Milo."

He jerked awake. Mr. Pine sat beside him on the loveseat, smiling tiredly. "How about heading on up to bed, kiddo? We're going to be up late here moving food and firewood and stuff." Milo nodded sleepily and gathered up his things. "Where'd you find that?" Mr. Pine asked, nodding at the rucksack.

"Attic."

"Very cool. That might be my dad's old city scout bag. I bet he'd love that you found it." He ruffled Milo's hair. "Do you think you're awake enough to take a candle up with you and blow it out before you fall asleep?"

"Yeah. Or — wait." Milo reached into the bag and felt around for the old metal lantern. "Can you get this going? I found it up there too."

His father took the lantern and looked it over. "Wow. What a weird old lantern. Hey, Nora," he called over his shoulder, "do we have any lamp oil?"

"Yeah, I think there's a bottle in the study that I bought for that funny pig lamp of yours."

"My pig lamp is not funny," Mr. Pine retorted. "Come on, Milo. Let's see what we can find."

Up in the study, Milo sat sleepily in one of the overstuffed chairs and idly turned the lamp over in his hands while his dad rooted through cabinets and desk drawers by the light of one thick candle. Then he sat bolt upright and awake.

"Found it," Mr. Pine said, waving a plastic bottle of colorless liquid and a box of matches. "It was on the liquor shelf, 'cause *that's* both logical and safe. Your mother, sometimes . . ." He regarded his son curiously. "What's that look for?"

Milo ignored the question. "Can you bring your light closer, Dad?"

On the bottom of the lantern was a pattern of curling scratches. He hadn't given them a second thought when he'd found it in the Emporium, but now, with two days' worth of stories and his growing collection of inexplicable clues, no detail seemed unimportant. *Now* he couldn't help but notice how much the curls looked not like a collection of random marks, but like . . . well, like something that had been scratched there *intentionally*. It almost seemed—he licked his thumb and rubbed at the spot. Yes. They were definitely meant to represent something. He turned the lantern one way, then another.

It was the candlelight that helped him see it, and just like the gate in the windows, once he did he couldn't un-see it. The curving, curling lines came together right before his eyes into the teardrop shape of a single lick of flame, and Mrs. Hereward's words from the night before came rushing back to him.

Julian handed over . . . the lamp he'd extinguished earlier that night. Sloe scratched the symbol . . . onto the underbelly of the lan-

tern. "*You will always be able to light your way, as long as you have a flint....*"

Milo reached into his bag again and took out the little tinderbox and flint he'd found near the lantern in the attic.

Mr. Pine was watching him with a bemused look on his face. "You going to let me in on the secret?"

"Dad," Milo said slowly, "remember Mrs. Hereward's story last night? The one about the roamer guy?"

"Sure." He glanced at the lantern again. "Oh, hey, I get it. There was a lantern in that story, wasn't there?"

"Yeah." Milo thought hard for a minute. "You know, she says her ancestors built this house."

"No kidding?"

"No kidding. She told me when I asked her about her missing bag. That's why she came to stay here. She said there was a family legend that her ancestor had one of the relics from that story."

"What do you know?" Mr. Pine was smiling now. "What are you thinking, Milo? You think this is the lantern from the story?"

"I was thinking," Milo said slowly, "that even if it isn't really magic, maybe this lantern would make her *think* of that one. It has a . . . a *something* scratched on it, just like the one in the story. And I found this, too." He held up the tinderbox. "I guess I was thinking . . . maybe she would like to have them. If it's okay with you."

Mr. Pine put an arm around Milo and hugged him. "That's the best idea I've heard all day. Let me make sure your mom doesn't object. I've never seen these before, and I don't imagine she has either, so I don't think she'll mind. But how about I ask her, just in case? I'll let you know what she says in the morning."

"Okay." Milo turned the lamp right-side up. "Can we try it first, though?"

"Sure." Mr. Pine uncapped the bottle of oil and poured some into the lamp, holding the cloth wick to make sure it didn't fall in. They waited a minute for the oil to soak the wick; then Milo held up the lamp by its chain and Mr. Pine struck a match. The wick caught fire immediately, turning from a red-gold flame to a deep blue.

"I'll be darned," Mr. Pine said. "Look at that blue! That definitely doesn't happen with my pig lamp."

———— ❄ ————

Milo awoke sometime later. It couldn't have been much later, because the blue flame of the lamp was still flickering on his desk, and his dad had said it could stay lit only until he came back with extra blankets.

The house was full of noises. There were the usual house noises, and the rattles of the windows and eaves from the wind that was still whipping through the trees and cracking icy branches outside. There were the sounds of adults moving and talking downstairs on the first floor. He could pick out his parents' voices, and Brandon's because his accent wasn't local, though he couldn't make out what they were saying.

But the noise that had woken him wasn't coming from downstairs. It was coming from *upstairs,* and not from the house itself. Milo had slept through enough nights with guests on the floors above to know what it sounded like when someone was walking around up there.

He swung himself out of bed and checked the clock on his desk. Its face glowed in the blue lamplight. Two a.m. Mr. Pine must have lost track of the time. He'd never intentionally have left Milo asleep with the lamp burning.

Milo slipped on his escaladeur shoes and instantly felt Negret yearning to sneak out and investigate. He looked longingly at the brass lamp, but wandering around a dark house in the middle of the night with an open flame just seemed like asking for trouble. He fished his flashlight out of his desk drawer and clicked it on and off. The beam was harsh and cold compared to the soothing cobalt light of the lamp.

From his rucksack he took the round mirror with the spotted glass he'd found in the Emporium, and from the bedside table he took the old blackjack's keys. He put one item in each of his pajama pockets, then, reluctantly, he extinguished the blue flame, opened his door, and crept out.

The second floor wasn't completely dark; someone had put a lantern on the kitchen table and another on the stand next to the stairs. Both were turned down low, so they only cast small pools of light, but it was enough to keep him from walking into things.

Negret paused by the stairs and listened again. The voices downstairs were still murmuring to one another. He tiptoed up the steps, remembering to skip the creaky ones. He figured the noise he'd heard had come from the next floor, since it had been loud enough to wake him. But now he couldn't hear anything.

There.

It wasn't the same as before, but he knew exactly what it was. It was the sound of someone turning one of the house's old doorknobs. Negret took the last few steps as quickly as he dared and reached around the turn of the stairs with the mirror in his hand. The reflection showed him an empty hallway, lit very softly by a battery-powered camp lantern that stood on the table where the poinsettia had been. It, too, was turned down low, but it cast enough light for Negret to be certain there was no one in the hallway. Every door was closed, except for the one to the unoccupied room in which he'd found the watch.

He tiptoed down the hall to the empty room, wondering what he was going to say if he found anyone there. There wasn't any particular rule against guests wandering around the house and poking their heads into rooms that weren't theirs — as long as nobody else was in them. Still, with the thefts and the broken generator, it seemed that anyone sneaking around might have some kind of nefarious purpose in mind.

Well, not everyone, Negret thought defensively. *I'm not up to anything nefarious.*

He stepped into the doorway, pointed the flashlight inside, and clicked it on. Cold light blazed into the room, throwing an indistinct circle of illumination on the dark window. Everything was just as he and Sirin had left it the afternoon before. Negret turned the beam toward the bathroom. Nobody. He tiptoed farther into the room, then over the bathroom threshold. Heart pounding, he swung the flashlight beam around the open door. Nobody. Heart pounding even harder, he flung aside the shower curtain.

Nobody. The room was empty.

There, again!

From out in the hallway, the sound of a doorknob turning. Negret fumbled with the shower curtain and scrambled out of the bathroom. Another knob turned, a different one, with a slightly different scraping sound. He misjudged the length of the bed and banged his shin against the footboard, which sent him sprawling, grasping for his lower leg as he stumbled the last few feet to the hallway. By the time he reached it and jabbed the flashlight beam out into the dark, the hall was empty once more.

But now he was sure something was afoot. Someone had left one room and entered another. He turned off the flashlight and tiptoed back toward the staircase. 3E, Mr. Vinge; 3N, Mrs. Hereward; 3S, Dr. Gowervine. Somebody was awake and moving around and was either in someone else's room or had just left it, but the closed doors gave no clues away.

At the stairs, Negret hesitated. With the flashlight still off, he squatted on the top step and waited, listening for Dr. Gowervine's telltale wheeze or Georgie's quiet but not silent footfalls.

And waited, listening for the swish of Mrs. Hereward's dressing gown, or the creak of Mr. Vinge's gaunt old bones.

And waited, knowing if it was Clem, he'd better not blink because there'd be nothing to hear at all.

And waited. And waited.

Nobody came out. Still, Negret waited. It was only when he felt himself swaying and realized he was about to fall asleep right there in the stairwell that he decided to give up the watch. He stood and nearly fell over again as both of his legs burst into pins and needles. The trip downstairs was not quite as soundless as the trip up.

Back in his own room, he relit the lamp and watched the blue flame dance. Did all this activity mean that in the morning someone was going to discover something else missing? Would the thief really try again, even after being thwarted yesterday? Or had he perhaps just gone back for the same things he'd taken before: a bag and a notebook connected to the house and a watch that wasn't? Why those things in the first place? What would Negret's blackjack father have to say?

He fell asleep without coming up with any answers.

ten

CHRISTMAS EVE

hristmas Eve dawned frigid. Milo woke up under three extra blankets. He rolled over and blearily looked at his clock. Seven a.m. The lantern was on his desk, extinguished. Whichever parent had finally come in with the blankets must've doused it after all, which meant that in addition to the lecture about running off that his mom was saving up for him, he was likely in for another one about not falling asleep next to an open flame.

Next to the lantern was his flashlight. The events of his late-night excursion came flooding back. Somebody — somebody other than him — had been sneaking around.

Outside, the sky was blue, but when he got out of bed and

crossed the room to his window, he could see a bank of steel gray sliding across the sky from the west. More snow coming.

He crawled partway under his bed and felt around until he found the spiral notepad in which he and Meddy had written their notes the day before. Sitting cross-legged on the floor, he flipped to the page with Dr. Gowervine's name, and across the top he wrote: Looking for vidimus for stained-glass window. Possibly linked to stolen bag and notebook. Probably in Clem's room to look at enameled window. Then he turned to the list of clues and added: Someone sneaking around night before Christmas Eve. Thief at work again? And then, after a moment's staring at the brass lamp: Possible that lantern from Emporium is a roamer relic? Small flame symbol scratched underneath. Lantern stitched on gate on Mrs. H's bag?

A knock sounded on the door. He got to his feet and shoved the notepad under his pillow.

Meddy stood in the hallway with a small, rectangular package wrapped in gold foil paper. "Merry merry," she said, holding it up. "This was on the floor outside your door."

Milo grinned as he took the box. "Mom and Dad always leave a present out for me to open on Christmas Eve morning."

He carried it back to his bed with Meddy following. They sat, and before he allowed himself to so much as untie the bow, he filled her in on the evening's events, from the discovery of the flame symbol on the lamp to the mysterious creeper on the third floor.

"What are we still doing here, then?" she protested, shoving him off the bed. "Let's get downstairs and find out what's missing! Get moving! Now!"

"Okay, okay." He grabbed his escaladeur shoes and his rucksack, paused to put his flashlight in the bag and the keys in his pocket, and with his Christmas Eve present tucked under one arm, headed for the door.

"Not gonna put on real clothes?" she asked, eyeing him skeptically.

"Nope." Christmas Eve, like Christmas Day, was traditionally a pajamas-all-day occasion in the Pine family. The guests were just going to have to deal.

Considering it was probably another post-burglary morning, the first floor was surprisingly quiet. Well, not quiet, exactly — but nobody was howling about thieves. Not yet, anyway.

Mrs. Caraway and Lizzie were sitting on either side of the dining table. Lizzie was only identifiable by the top of her blond head; her face was buried in her arms and her shoulders were shaking. At first Milo thought she was crying, until he saw Mrs. Caraway's face. She was definitely trying not to laugh.

Her eyes met Milo's. He must've looked puzzled, because she winked and gave a tiny nod toward the kitchen. And in the kitchen: shenanigans. Shenanigans in the form of Fenster Plum and Mrs. Hereward attempting to bake a cake.

"But . . . the power," Milo protested.

Mrs. Caraway shook her head. "The stove and the oven run on gas. They work just fine."

Both Mrs. Hereward and Fenster were wearing aprons that belonged to Mrs. Pine. Mrs. Hereward had chosen one with pink and white polka dots, the kind that hung around your neck and tied at your waist. Fenster's was the sort that covered only the lower half and looked like the front of a skirt. It was purple with a white lace ruffle all the way around it and a pocket that was embroidered with a lavender-colored flower.

"Fenster, dear," Mrs. Hereward was saying with exaggerated patience, "I promise you, one really does need to actually measure the ingredients when baking. Please stop throwing handfuls of things into the bowl."

"It looks like it needs more cinnamon," Fenster replied cheerfully. "I was just adding a pinch."

"A pinch is *called* a pinch because it's what you can pinch between your fingers, my dear."

"But that's barely anything!"

"That's exactly right. Also, that isn't cinnamon. It's pepper. Please put it down *immediately.*"

"Maybe it needs pepper," Fenster grumbled.

"It does not. I refer you to the recipe."

Brandon's muffled voice called from the living room. "Somebody make 'em stop."

Milo followed the sound to a pile of blankets on the sofa. "Did you sleep down here?" Milo asked the blankets.

"I did. Couldn't bring myself to climb the stairs. Oy, Milo?" One bleary eye appeared from under a hem. "Could you manage to sneak into the war zone over there and extract a cup of coffee with a bit of milk? You ought to find the milk in one of the coolers. Mrs. Whatsername might know which one if she's already had to find it for the . . . ahem . . . cake."

"I'll try." Milo dropped his bag, shoes, and present on the floor next to the sofa and made his way into the kitchen.

"Mornin', Milo," Fenster crowed. "We're making Miss Georgie a cheer-you-up cake, see if we aren't!"

"It rather remains to be seen whether it will turn out to be a *cake*," Mrs. Hereward said darkly. She reached across the counter, plucked a tin out of Fenster's hand, and returned it to the cabinet he'd just taken it from. "Thank you."

Milo edged his way around the counter where they were assembling the ingredients and found a metal coffeepot keeping warm on a little camp stove. The coolers Brandon had mentioned were lined up against one wall. "Mrs. Hereward, do you know which of these has milk?"

"The blue one, I think, Milo dear."

Brandon had emerged from his blankets and was adding logs to the fire when Milo returned with his mug. "Much appreciated."

"You guys were up late last night, huh?"

"Yep, and your mum and dad stayed up later than Fenster and I. No idea what time they finally turned in." He stirred the coals and gave Milo a half grin. "I heard you've had a fairly eventful holiday so far, kid."

"And it just keeps coming." He lowered his voice. "I heard

somebody sneaking around last night while you guys were still doing stuff down here. I expected something else to have been stolen, but maybe I was wrong."

Brandon shrugged. "Who knows? Still a lot of people who haven't gotten up yet. Plenty of time for today to go wrong." Just at that moment, the metallic sound of a stainless mixing bowl hitting the floor rang out, followed by some swearing from Fenster and a martyred sigh from Mrs. Hereward. "And it begins." Brandon took a long gulp of coffee. "Do us a favor, Milo. When your dad gets up, let him know I went out to get an early start."

"On the generator?"

"Yep. Hoping things'll look better in daylight. Also I figure if Fenster sets the house on fire, I'm safer in the genny shed." He clapped Milo on the shoulder and went to the foyer to start pulling on his cold-weather gear.

"Looks like no news until the rest of them get up." Meddy had been sitting quietly behind the tree. "You forgot your present, you know," she added.

"Oh, man!" He retrieved it from next to his rucksack and went to sit beside the tree on the hearth. Poor tree. Most of the Pines' Christmas customs were unaffected by the power failure, with the fire and all the candlelight and the stove still working to make sure there was no shortage of hot chocolate. All except for the tree, which looked sad and lonely without its lights.

But Milo had a shiny gold present to open, and presents trumped sad trees any day of the week.

He untied the bow and retied it carefully around one of the lower branches. Then he turned the box over and found a little envelope tucked into the seam where the edges of the paper came together. Inside was a card with a rocking horse on it, and inside the card was Mr. Pine's messy handwriting.

Merry Christmas Eve, Milo! We love you so much and we're so proud of how well you're handling all the unexpected stuff this year. We're also very proud of the excellent idea you had about the lantern. Maybe you can reuse this box when you wrap it up for Mrs. H.

Took me a little while to find this for you tonight. It never occurred to me that you might be interested. Enjoy!

Love, Dad.

Milo tore off the gold paper and slit the tape that held the box closed with his fingernail. Inside, a little blue velvet bag with a drawstring was nestled in silver tissue paper. He pulled it out, loosened the string, and turned it over above his palm. A metal figurine about the size of his thumb fell out into his hand.

Meddy leaned in for a closer look. "Wow. Your dad is *awesome*."

"What is it?" Milo asked. The little figure had been painted in colors that had darkened with age: a brown tunic and dark brown pants piped in blue the same color as the bag. It crouched low in a posture Milo immediately thought of as *sneaky*, and it held two odd, short swords in its pinkish-brown hands.

"I bet you anything it's your dad's Odd Trails character," Meddy said. "He told us he played a tiercer-signaler who used butterfly swords, just like these." She touched the weapons in the figure's hands carefully. "He might even have painted this guy himself."

"People play with little pieces like this?" Milo asked. Meddy hadn't said anything about figurines.

She nodded. "In tabletop games. Lots of people like to have player pieces like this. Helps them visualize where they are in relation to obstacles and enemies and stuff."

"Wow." Milo examined the little man's face closely. It didn't look anything like his dad, of course, but it definitely looked like a blackjack.

For just a moment, there it was: a twinge of remorse. He had made up a blackjack father in the game instead of simply imagining his real-world dad into the part.

I should just pretend it's Dad, he thought. Then, with a pang that hurt as much as the guilt had, he pictured the key fob with the Chinese characters and the parent he'd invented to go with them. *Negret is different from Milo,* he told himself. This soothed his conscience a bit as he slid the figurine back into its velvet bag and tucked it carefully into the inside pocket of his rucksack. "I'm going to wrap up the lamp for Mrs. Hereward. Be right back."

He gathered up the gold paper and went into the kitchen to find something to put the lamp oil in, doing his best to steer clear of the cake-baking insanity. A few minutes later, Milo was up in the study on the second floor carefully transferring the oil in the lamp to an empty vanilla extract bottle. Then he packed the lamp and the tinderbox and the bottle into the box, rewrapped it with the same gold paper, and carried it back downstairs.

In the kitchen the two aproned bakers were in the process of pouring batter into three cake pans. Meanwhile, Lizzie and her mother were watching wide-eyed from the dining room, and it looked as if it was taking every shred of their combined self-control to keep from swooping in and taking over. But at last Fenster managed to maneuver the pans into the oven and Mrs. Hereward twisted the dial on the tomato-shaped timer.

Lizzie and Mrs. Caraway began to clap slowly. Grinning, Milo joined in, then Meddy. Mrs. Hereward looked up with a scowl on her face, as if she thought they might be making fun, but Fenster beamed and took a bow. Surprised, Mrs. Hereward smiled awkwardly. Then she bowed too.

It was amid this applause that Milo's parents arrived on the scene. "What's the commotion?" Mrs. Pine asked blearily.

"I believe, with Mrs. Hereward's help, we have survived Fenster in the kitchen," Mrs. Caraway announced. "How about I take over and do the dishes?"

Fenster shook his head. "My mother, may she rest in peace, would never forgive me if I let you do that. Never leave a space you've used without you leave it shipshape."

"I quite agree," Mrs. Hereward added. "I'll wash, Mr. Fenster, and you can dry."

Mrs. Caraway sank back onto the bench. "So close," she mumbled. "So, so close."

Milo laughed and carried his box into the living room to put under the tree. A moment later, Mr. Pine came in and sat next to him on the hearth. "Did you find your present, Milo?"

"Yes! Is it really your Odd Trails character? The . . . the tiercer-signaler guy?"

"Sure is."

Mrs. Pine joined them a few minutes later carrying three mugs. She handed one to Milo and one to his father, then sat on the floor by the tree and listened with a smile while Mr. Pine reminisced about Odd Trails games he'd played as a kid, including one for which the cook on his father's ship had been the game master.

The fire smelled good, the tree smelled good, even the cakes (for the moment) smelled good. Milo sipped his hot chocolate and settled into a blissful calm. The house might be lousy with weirdoes, but for now, at least, he could still have Christmas Eve with his parents. Even Meddy seemed to sense he needed this time without her. Once he saw her peek over the back of the loveseat, smile, then sink away out of sight.

But the peace couldn't last long, of course. At last Mr. Pine clapped his hands on his knees and stood up. "I'd better go give Brandon a hand."

"Take the thermos," Mrs. Pine told him. She kissed Milo's forehead and got up too. "Odette," she called, "you ready to start breakfast?"

Mrs. Caraway peered into the kitchen. "I think so." She grinned. "Looks like the dishwashers are just wrapping up."

A few minutes later, the triumphant bakers emerged. The old lady held a cup of tea in one hand, and she'd ditched the polka-dot apron. Fenster went straight to the foyer and started pulling on his coat. He seemed to have forgotten the lacy purple monstrosity he was still wearing.

Mrs. Hereward sat on the couch, leaned back, closed her eyes, and sighed. Milo caught Meddy watching over the back of her seat again. They exchanged a glance, and she padded across to join him. Then Milo picked up the gold-wrapped present and went to sit next to the old lady. "Mrs. Hereward?"

She opened her eyes with a contented smile. "Yes, Milo?"

He held out the box. "I found this in my attic a couple days ago. I thought you might like to have it and my mom and dad said it was okay."

"Goodness, really?" She took the present hesitantly. "I really don't know what to say."

"Open it," Milo said, bouncing a little in anticipation.

She unwrapped it with agonizing slowness. Milo's mother was the same way — she acted like the world would end if the paper tore. He forced himself not to hurry her along. Then, at last, she opened the lid of the box and saw the lantern.

"What on earth —?" She lifted it out by its chain. "You . . . you found this?"

"Turn it over," Milo suggested. "Look on the bottom! It has —"

Mrs. Hereward spotted the flame symbol and breathed in sharply. "Oh, my."

"Remember in your story? How the wishing-stick guy scratched a symbol on Julian's shoes, and on his knife and his lantern?"

"Yes," she said softly, wonderingly. "Yes, I remember that part."

"And I thought . . . Well, there's that lantern on the gate on your bag. Maybe the relic your ancestor bought wasn't the knife, it was the lantern! A lantern would be useful on a ship, wouldn't it?"

Mrs. Hereward nodded. "It certainly would."

"Maybe it's not really Julian's, but I thought you might like it anyway." Milo reached into the open box and took out the bottle and the tinderbox. "And look. There's a flint in here, and some oil. We tried it out last night, my dad and I. The flame burns blue!"

"Blue flame," Mrs. Hereward murmured. "I don't think I even remembered to mention that."

"There's a blue flame in the story?"

She nodded. "In roamer tales, unearthly fire always burns blue." She shook her head disbelievingly. "It's impossible, of course — it was foolish to think there might be such things as relics of this nature in the real world at all — but . . . yes, Milo, I believe I will decide to say 'What if?'" She gave the chain a little twist. The lamp rotated slowly. "Anything is possible, isn't it?"

"Sure." Milo nodded vigorously. "Anything's possible."

"And you're certain your parents don't mind your giving this to me?"

Milo took his father's Christmas Eve card from his pocket and held it up with pride. Mrs. Hereward adjusted her glasses and read it. Then she sat back. "Well, if that's the case, I am honored and delighted to accept your gift. What a very kind thing to think of. I believe I will put it in my room so I don't lose it."

She put a hand awkwardly on his shoulder for a moment, then collected the pieces of her present and disappeared upstairs.

The smells of breakfast cooking brought the remaining guests down, one at a time: Georgie, still looking downcast; Mr. Vinge, sporting yellow socks with red zigzags; Dr. Gowervine, looking the same as always; and then, last of all, Clem and Owen. It looked like a good night's sleep had done wonders for the newcomer.

"Milo?" Mrs. Pine called. "Want to go out and tell the mechanics to take a break?"

Milo was much more interested in waiting to see if there had been a theft the previous night, but it didn't look like anyone was on the verge of that kind of announcement. With the exception of Georgie, everyone seemed to be in reasonably good spirits. So he suited up for the cold and slipped outside.

The slick of gray clouds had spread across most of the sky now, but there was still enough sunlight on the icy surfaces of the world to make Milo wish for a pair of sunglasses. He pulled his collar up, tucked his chin down against the biting air, and started around the side of the house, staying in the path his father, Brandon, and Fenster had stomped flat.

The generator lived by itself in a brick shed off the back of the house. Milo knocked on the door, just in case "working on the generator" involved anything dangerous that he shouldn't barge in on. The door opened and Brandon peered out. "Yessir, Milo?"

"Mom says can you stop for breakfast?"

Brandon smiled, then looked over his shoulder. "Oy, you two think we can break for chow?"

"I think so." Mr. Pine sounded pleased with himself. "Fenster, give it a go." A moment later a sputtering, choked noise made Milo flinch away from the door. He stumbled over his own feet and landed on his backside, crashing through the icy top crust into the softer snow beneath. As he picked himself up, the sputter settled into a rhythmic coughing, then into a low rumble. The three men filed out, looking satisfied. Milo's father scrubbed at his hands with a shop rag. "Let us go, gentlemen," he declared with a grandiose wave of the rag, "and claim our reward."

"What's that noise?" Milo demanded. "Does that mean it's working again?"

Mr. Pine winked. "Come along and we shall see what we see."

Their return was greeted with a standing ovation from the denizens of Greenglass House. The power was back on, from the curvy white glass chandelier over the dining table to the Christmas tree glittering warmly in its corner.

Milo left Mr. Pine, Fenster, and Brandon to their congratulations and plopped onto the loveseat next to Meddy, who was leaning over the back, staring thoughtfully at the tree and fiddling with the sleeve of her cloak. "Anybody say anything interesting while I was gone?" he whispered.

"If you mean, did anybody claim something went missing last night, then no." Meddy glanced over her shoulder. "But I think Mrs. Hereward's trying to be all sneaky and finish the cake before Fenster remembers it still needs frosting."

As if he'd overheard Meddy's words, Fenster broke away from the group in the dining room and made a beeline for the kitchen. Squabbling noises ensued. "Too late," Milo observed.

Mrs. Caraway managed to herd everyone to the table to load up their plates for the most cheerful meal the house had seen in days, frosting disagreements notwithstanding. Milo sat on the floor and ate at the coffee table, leaving Meddy to watch Mr. Vinge and Dr. Gowervine in the dining room. Then, out of nowhere, Mrs. Hereward leaned over to Georgie, who was sitting beside her on the couch, and whispered, "Are you quite sure it's all right, my dear?"

Georgie glanced across to the hearth, where Clem and Owen were sitting. Even Milo could see how blissfully happy they were to be sitting next to each other — so much so that he almost felt embarrassed for them. It was as if they couldn't hide how much they liked each other.

The blue-haired girl took a deep breath. "Yes, Mrs. Hereward. I'm quite sure. Thank you. Go ahead."

Mrs. Hereward patted her lips with her napkin, picked up her fork, and tapped it gently against her juice glass. "Excuse me for interrupting, but, young man — it's Owen, isn't it?"

Owen looked up. "It is, yes, ma'am."

"Of course, you understand that last night we were all very curious about you, but we didn't want to bother you while you were so very ill, or bother Miss Candler while she was attending to you," Mrs. Hereward said a bit apologetically. "However, I couldn't help but notice that Georgie seemed to know you as well, and in the course of the evening she happened to mention your middle name."

"My . . . middle name?" He looked at Georgie. "I didn't know you knew it."

She smiled sadly. "Surprise."

Mrs. Hereward patted Georgie's hand. "Not what you'd call a common name, Lansdegown. Have you ever run across anyone else who has it?"

"No, ma'am. Frankly, I've tried to track down information on it, but"—he spread his hands—"city records are bad to start with, and the records from my adoption don't include information on my birth parents. I was a foundling."

Just like me, Milo thought, leaning in to listen even more closely. Those who'd eaten in the dining room were drifting in now.

"Well, young man, I can help you. Would it astonish you to know that you and I might just turn out to be related?"

Now everyone was staring. Milo could understand why. It was the same reaction the Pines got now and then when they told someone that Milo was their son.

"Yes," he admitted slowly, taking in Mrs. Hereward's pale skin and blue eyes. "Yes, that would be very astonishing."

"I thought as much. So let me tell you a little story. I mentioned to Milo that an ancestor of mine built this house. There were two children in the family. The elder was a girl called Lucy. Her father was a British privateer who had remarried after her mother's death, and his second wife was a Chinese lady." She paused for a sip of orange juice. "They had a son, Lucy's half brother, whose name was Liao. Until he was about six or seven, Liao and his mother lived in China while Lucy and their father lived aboard their ship. Then, sometime around the beginning of the War of 1812, the captain decided it was time to bring his family together in a place he hoped would stay out of the conflict. So he built this house and brought his loved ones to Nagspeake.

"It was the two children who came up with the name for the house. The privateer's surname was Bluecrowne, and at Lucy's request, the little boy Liao translated as best he could the two parts of the compound name — *blue* and *crown* — into Mandarin. Lucy, who was also very young at the time and who knew very little of the language herself, wrote it down phonetically. I could not possibly tell you how to pronounce the words properly, but the result, the name with which the family christened the house, was *Lansdegown*."

Owen was listening wide-eyed and rapt. Milo couldn't blame him. This was exactly the kind of thing he'd always longed to know about his roots.

"I imagine, therefore," Mrs. Hereward finished, "that you might well be descended from Liao's branch of the family; or perhaps someone of Asian heritage married one of Lucy's descendants. That may be impossible to know. But in any case, that's where the Lansdegown name comes from. Two small children translating the surname *Bluecrowne*."

The young man shook his head. "This is amazing," he murmured.

Milo blinked hard and tried not to cry. Emotions were welling up inside him that he didn't quite understand. It wasn't as if he'd learned anything about his own ancestry, and he didn't feel jealous of Owen. He felt happy for him — wildly, indescribably happy, just knowing that someone who hadn't known *anything* about his heritage could now know *something*.

He wasn't the only one trying not to cry. Clem—plucky, poised Clemence O. Candler—had already lost the battle. She looked at Georgie with tears on her cheeks. "She asked if you were sure," Clem said. "She asked your permission before she told. You knew?"

Georgie was blinking hard too. "I told my—*our* story last night, after you went up. I mentioned the name, and Mrs. Hereward put it together."

"Milo thought I ought to tell you," Mrs. Hereward said to Owen, "and this morning Georgie convinced me he was right."

"After . . . after everything, though," Clem stammered, her voice cracking. "After everything you and I . . . This is what we were both . . . Why didn't *you*—"

"Because look at the two of you!" Georgie's voice broke as she lost control of her own tears. "There was no reason for me to try and beat you to it anymore."

Clem got to her feet and stumbled across the room, and before Georgie could do more than stand up, Clem threw her arms around her and hugged hard. "Thank you, Blue," she whispered. Georgie stood frozen for a heartbeat, then she put her arms around Clem and hugged her back.

For his part, Owen looked as if he couldn't decide which to lose his cool over: the new information about his ancestry or the strange behavior on the part of the two girls. He didn't seem to have a clue that they had been competing for his heart all along.

Meanwhile, Milo sat stock-still on the floor, just barely keeping the tears at bay as his heart galloped painfully. *Bluecrowne.* He forced his white-knuckled fingers to set his plate down on the coffee table and reached into his pocket. His fingers found the leather key ring, and for the umpteenth time he ran his fingers over the characters on the disc. He took it out, turned it over, and looked with a lump in his throat at the image on the other side.

He pictured Negret's father, Chinese like his son, who had handed these keys down as they had been handed down to him. Meddy's game had for the first time given him an excuse to imagine a birth parent into his life without feeling like he was being disloyal to his mom and dad, and Milo discovered that he had very rapidly grown to treasure these keys and their pretend history. *It's real history for me,* Negret's voice said in his mind.

Yes, Milo replied silently, sadly. *But for Owen, it's more than real. It's true.*

He wiped his eyes, forced his face into something like cheer, and got to his feet. He crossed the room full of surprised silence and tugged on his father's sleeve. He showed him the ring of keys. He whispered a question.

Mr. Pine glanced at his wife and chuckled. "I think Milo's working on cleaning out the attic." To Milo he said, "Sure, kiddo. Why not?"

Milo cleared his throat. "Excuse me, everybody, excuse me." His voice shook a little, but hopefully not enough for anyone to hear. Thirteen pairs of eyes turned to him. He turned to Owen. "Mr. . . . Owen, I found this the other day. I kept it because I thought it was neat, but I think you should have it." He held out the key ring.

Owen took it and examined the disc that hung among the keys. Milo watched him run his fingers over the Chinese characters, then turn it over to find the engraved crown with its spots of blue enamel. *Bluecrowne.*

"I . . . I don't know what to say." He looked at Milo with an expression full of emotion. Milo recognized that emotion immediately, even though he didn't have a word for it. "I would treasure it," he said quietly. "May I really have it?"

Milo nodded solemnly. "I asked Mom and Dad first."

The young man curled his fingers around the keys. "Thank you, Milo. You don't know what this means to me."

"I do, I think," Milo admitted. "I was adopted too."

Then he sat down on the floor again and picked up his plate from the coffee table, ignoring the eyes he could still feel on him. Negret had lost his only memento of his father. But when things were passed to you, you were supposed to pass them on to someone else eventually too. Perhaps, he thought, perhaps when the old blackjack had given the keys to Negret, he had said something like, *I am giving these to you and someday you will give them to someone else. Maybe that person will be your own son, but maybe not. It could even be a stranger. You'll know the right person when you find him.*

And so both Milo and Negret made peace with letting go of the blackjack's keys. Milo discovered to his surprise that only the slightest ache remained. He took a deep breath and released it slowly and turned his attention back to his pancakes.

A few bites later, Georgie sat down beside him and elbowed him gently in the side. Her eyes were red, but she looked almost happy. "You did good," she whispered. "Thank you for that, and for what you said to Mrs. H."

"Even though it doesn't make him like you best?" Milo whispered back.

"Sure." She hesitated, then nodded. "Yes. Even though. You've given a truly important gift to someone I love."

Milo elbowed her back. "I think you did good, too."

It wasn't precisely what he'd been thinking of when he'd read about *orphan magic,* but it was still kind of magical, and he, Milo, who had once been an orphan, had done it.

"Thanks." Georgie clapped her hands on her knees and stood up. "Mrs. Pine? Can I talk to you?"

Milo's mom, who had been circling the living room with the coffeepot, nodded and joined Georgie over near the tree. "I think I'll get under way today," the blue-haired girl said quietly. "The ferryman who brought me over gave me a card and told me to call if I needed him again."

Mrs. Pine shook her head. "The phone lines were strung right up with the power lines. They'll be down until the city sends a lineman out for repairs."

Georgie sighed. "I thought as much. I don't suppose there's any other way to call a launch, is there?"

"We have a flag we can raise." Mrs. Pine made an apologetic face. "Of course, there's no knowing how long it will take anyone to answer. I wouldn't like to hoist the emergency colors unless it's an actual emergency."

"No, of course not." Georgie scratched her head. "But yeah, would you send up a flag for me?"

"Sure, Georgie, if that's what you want."

"Thank you. I'm . . . I'm sorry to put you to the trouble. How will I know if someone's coming? How long do you think it'll take?"

"In this weather?" Mrs. Pine considered. "They'll likely have shut down the ferry dock, so it'll depend on how long it takes somebody to see the signal who's also willing to make the trip. Could be five minutes, or there could be no answer at all until the weather starts to settle down. If the dock's still open, they'll hoist a reply, not that we'll see it if the snow starts up again. If it's closed, but if someone out there wants the work and doesn't mind the weather, he or she'll just turn up and ring the bell. In any case, whoever shows up will charge you an arm and a leg, you know."

Georgie gave a careless wave. "That doesn't matter. No offense, but I'm almost willing to risk hypothermia and hike out of here. Almost," she added when a wave of concern crossed Mrs. Pine's face.

"Okay, Georgie." Mrs. Pine squeezed her shoulder. "I'll ask Ben to send up the flag right away."

Things were calm for a while after that. Milo finished his breakfast, and when he carried his plate into the kitchen his mother swept him up into a giant hug. When she let go, Milo saw with surprise that her eyes were a little red, as if she'd been crying too.

"What's wrong?" he asked.

"Nothing, Milo." She squeezed him again. "Just proud."

He returned to the living room, still awash with feelings. As he crossed to the tree in search of Meddy, Owen spoke up from the hearth. "Hey, Milo, you got a minute?"

"Sure." Milo sat beside him. Owen held up his hand. In his palm was a carved, bone-colored figure about the length of the young man's thumb; a serpentine creature with clawed feet and a ferocious, fanged face.

"A dragon?"

Owen nodded. "As a kid I was obsessed with them because of all the dragons in Chinese mythology. I collected . . . oh, probably hundreds of dragons. Paintings, books, stuffed animals. And tons of little guys like this one." He held out the figurine and Milo took it gingerly. It was heavier than it looked. "That was my favorite," Owen continued as Milo turned the dragon over in his fingers. "I found it at a flea market when I was ten. Turned out to be real ivory and an antique, but mainly I just really liked his little face. So when I outgrew stuffed animals and didn't have room anymore for every picture of a dragon that's ever been drawn, I kept that guy and carried him everywhere." He hesitated. "This probably isn't going to sound as weird to you as it might to someone else, but . . . well, that was kind of my way of connecting to my heritage. A way of carrying it in my pocket even when I wasn't sure how I felt about it, or sure of my place in it. Does that make sense?"

Milo nodded, staring hard at the dragon and trying to keep his emotions in order.

"I even made up stories about it," Owen said with a little laugh. "Sometimes about the dragon and its adventures, and sometimes about the figure itself and where it had come from. Even now I pretty much never go anywhere without it. But listen, Milo, it never occurred to me that in a million years I would ever have something that's *actually* linked to my ancestry that I could carry around in my pocket instead. And now that I have that, thanks to you, I'm thinking maybe it's time to pass my dragon on." Together they looked down at the creature. "I'd like to give him to you. If nothing else, maybe he'll bring you luck."

Milo opened his mouth to say *thank you* and discovered he couldn't speak. The two of them sat there for a long moment. Milo went on staring down at the dragon so that he could pretend he wasn't crying. Owen sat quietly beside him, looking at the dragon too. He didn't ask if Milo was okay, or if he needed a tissue, or if he wanted to be left alone for a little. He just stayed there and kept Milo company.

Finally Milo wiped his eyes with his sleeve and nodded. He hiccupped once. "Thank you," he whispered.

Owen nodded once. "Bye, little guy," he said to the dragon. Then he got to his feet and left the living room.

When at last he thought he could look up without everything he was feeling rushing across his face, Milo took a deep breath and wiped his eyes again. His mother wandered in and pretended to straighten the throw blanket on the sofa. She gave him a quick, fake-casual glance and raised her eyebrows. *All okay?*

Milo nodded and smiled.

Then came the sound of feet barreling down the stairs. "What on earth is wrong with you people?" Dr. Gowervine bellowed.

"Oh, no," Mrs. Pine muttered.

"Here we go," Milo whispered, sliding the ivory dragon into his pocket. "Here it comes."

"What's wrong, Dr. Gowervine?" Mrs. Pine said with only

a touch of exhaustion in her voice as she hurried out of the living room. Milo followed.

"What do you *think* is wrong?" he snarled. "I've been robbed!"

Milo's father had only just come in from sending the signal flag up the pole behind the house and de-icing the bell in case someone actually came in response. He put a hand to his wind-burned face. "You're kidding. This can't be happening."

"*I am not kidding!*" Dr. Gowervine was starting to sound hysterical.

"Okay, okay. He didn't mean that." Mrs. Pine took the professor's arm. "I'm coming up with you. Let's have a look."

Grumbling, Dr. Gowervine allowed himself to be led back upstairs. Meddy swooped over to Milo and grabbed his arm. "Let's go, Negret."

He ran back to the sofa to put on his escaladeur shoes, then they took the first set of stairs slowly so they could talk without Mrs. Pine and Dr. Gowervine overhearing them. "This messes everything up," Sirin muttered. "I was sure it was him."

"I thought so too," Negret said. "I thought maybe he figured the bag and the notebook might have clues to where the vidimus thing he's looking for is hidden, since they're all connected to the house. I just couldn't figure out the watch."

"Maybe it was a decoy," Sirin suggested as they turned the corner on the second-floor landing. "You know, the watch was stolen to throw us off track and to keep us from figuring out what he was really after."

"Except now he's off the hook, 'cause he was robbed too. Unless . . . yeah! Unless that's another decoy. So nobody'll suspect him?"

"Not bad, Negret. Not bad." They reached the third floor. It sounded as if having Mrs. Pine search his room with him wasn't calming Dr. Gowervine down much.

"When was the last time you saw it?" Mrs. Pine asked with superhuman calm.

"I don't know when the last time was—I know I checked on it when everyone else had things stolen, and it was fine. But since then . . ."

"And what does the bag look like?"

Dr. Gowervine exhaled hard enough that Negret and Sirin heard it all the way out in the hall. "It's a large satchel, brown leather with red contrast stitching, brass hardware with my initials engraved on it. It's lined with plaid satin, mostly red."

"Now he's just being fussy," Sirin muttered. "Don't you think 'brown satchel' would've done the job?"

"Shh."

"Can you tell me what was in it?" Milo's mother asked.

"It was that damned story!" Dr. Gowervine exploded. "I knew I shouldn't have said anything about it! I *knew* it! But that harpy convinced me to tell one to take that girl's mind off some . . . some stupid *boy* trouble, and it was all I could think of. I knew I should've just kept my mouth shut."

"Dr. Gowervine," Mrs. Pine said with the kind of patience that only moms seem capable of, "what was in the satchel?"

There was a pause. "My work," Dr. Gowervine said quietly. "All of it. Everything I had on Lowell Skellansen. The entirety of my research was in that bag."

The conversation inside the room trailed off as the actual searching got under way. Negret nodded toward the stairs, and he and Sirin tiptoed down to the second floor. In the bedroom, he took the spiral pad from under the pillow, opened it to Dr. Gowervine's page, and wrote, Missing after breakfast: brown leather bag with all of Dr. G's stuff about stained-glass guy. "How do you spell *Skellansen*?"

"Doesn't matter." Sirin leaned against the window with her arms folded. "So regardless of whether somebody else took it or he's faking it, the satchel won't be in his room anymore. He'd have known your parents would want to search the room with him because that's what they did yesterday. And he said it was a *big* satchel. Where could he hide something that size?"

Negret was thinking about the noises he'd heard the night before, but if there were clues in the sounds of doorknobs turning and someone sneaking around in the silences in between, if there was a pattern there that could give some hint about where the thief had hidden the missing bag, Negret couldn't see it. "Plus, he could've moved it," he mumbled. "The thief had all morning to hide it."

Three quick raps sounded on the door. Negret closed the notepad and hastily shoved it under his pillow again. "Come in."

The door opened and Georgie Moselle peeked in. "Hey, sorry to interrupt. Your dad said you might be up here. Can I talk to you for a minute?"

"Um. Sure." He slid off the bed and joined Georgie in the hallway.

She looked much better now, and she carried a plate of blue-frosted cake. "I wanted to say thank you for what you did today." With her free hand, she held out a thin, rectangular packet wrapped in paper patterned with blue snowflakes.

"A present? For me?"

"A present for you." Georgie waved it at him. "You gave one to Mrs. Hereward, and you gave one to me — and to Clem, too — when you gave those keys to Owen. It's not much, but I'd like you to have it."

"Thanks, Georgie." He took the parcel. "Should I open it now, or save it for tomorrow?"

"Go ahead. I don't plan to be here tomorrow. Open it carefully so you don't tear what's inside."

He unwrapped the gift gingerly, trying not to rip the paper. Inside was . . . more paper. Brittle, textured green paper. He recognized it right away.

"The chart!" He stared up at Georgie. "I *knew* it was you! You left it for me to find, didn't you?"

"I thought it might make for a good experiment," she replied. "That was before everybody else in the world showed up, of course. It was an impulse, I guess. I didn't think it all the way through. And yes, I'm the one who took it back. I'm sorry about breaking into your room, but once Clem got here . . . well. But I thought maybe you'd like to keep it. You can keep the little leather thing I left the decoy in, too."

"I love it!" Negret unfolded the chart carefully. "Do you know — whoops!" Another piece of paper — thicker, almost like cardboard — slipped from inside the folds and fluttered to the ground. He and Georgie nearly banged heads as they both reached to try and catch it.

She got her hands on it first. "Should've mentioned that. Here you go."

It was a photograph in tones of off-white and gray. It was blurry and smudgy and grainy, and the image was more or less circular, darkening to black at the corners. Even without color, Negret knew what he was looking at. "It's the window on the fourth floor!"

"Bingo. It's the picture I took with the cigar-box camera yesterday."

"But what does that have to do with Owen or Lansdegown or anything?"

Georgie shrugged. "I needed to make Clem think I was looking for answers in places I wasn't so she didn't notice what I was really up to. The camera was what you'd call a red herring. A fake clue. It doesn't have anything to do with anything. Still, it turned out nicely for a first attempt, didn't it?"

"It sure did. Thanks, Georgie. This is a really great present."

"I'm glad." She turned to go, then paused and came back. "You started to ask a question."

"Oh, yeah. The map — do you know what it's of?"

She shook her head. "I never did find out. I checked it against all the local waterways I could find. The paper's old, obviously — I guess it could date back as far as the time of the original family Mrs. Hereward was talking about. Except for one thing." She tapped the cluster of curved white marks in the corner. "I think that paint's newer. I don't know how *much* newer, but a lot newer, anyway. Maybe the compass rose, too."

Negret peered at the bird-shaped compass and the white paint of the curvy things to the north of it. "How can you tell?"

"I'm a thief, Milo," she said with a little lift of her eyebrow. "You know that, right?"

"Yeah," he replied slowly. "So . . . ?"

"I'm an expert in a lot of things that might surprise you, but that are critical to my . . . job. Forgery is one of them. A big part of creating a good forgery is making certain that there are no parts of the work that stand out from the rest. Everything I know tells me this paper is a couple hundred years old, and that the ship and the seagull at least were painted on it much, much later. To my eyes, they stick out like sore thumbs."

"The *ship?*"

"Yup, the white thing there. Pretty sure that's meant to be a ship under full sail, seen from above. I could be wrong, though."

It was like the flame symbol on the lantern; now that she'd pointed it out, Negret couldn't see anything in the white curls but the shapes of sails. "No, I think you're right. What was it about this chart that connected it with the Lansdegown name?"

"I found it in a stamped envelope with 'Lansdegown House' on the front. Just the name of the house. No address. Figuring *that* out . . . well, that's a story for another time. And all along I could have just followed that stupid watermark." She shook her head ruefully. "Anyway, plenty of mysteries left for you." Georgie gave him a little salute. "Enjoy, Milo, and thank you."

"You're welcome. And, Georgie? You probably shouldn't eat too much of the frosting."

She looked down at her plate. "Yeah, Mrs. Hereward said the same thing. Something to do with ink that didn't totally make sense to me."

Sirin was fairly bouncing up and down when Negret closed the door behind him. "Tell me, tell me, tell me!" she demanded.

He'd just handed over the chart and the photograph—and winced at Sirin's very un-scholiast-like squeal of delight—when another battery of knocks rang out against his door. "Good grief, now what?" He crossed the room and opened the door. This time it was Clem.

"Hey, Milo." She held out a small cylinder wrapped in the same blue snowflake paper. "For you."

"Really?" Two presents in less than ten minutes? From people who'd known him a grand total of two days? This was crazy.

"Really." For the first time, Clem's face was very serious. "Thank you."

"Well . . . you're welcome."

"Well, open it!"

Normally Milo didn't need to be invited twice to open a gift, but now he hesitated. "Clem, Georgie said you came to Greenglass

House because you somehow worked out from a piece of water-marked paper that this is where she was coming. That you followed the watermark itself, which was a picture of a gate."

Clem nodded. "Yes, I did."

"How did you know the gate had something to do with this house?"

"Ah." She put her hands in her pockets. "You know, I had a piece of incredible luck. I found the gate itself in an antique shop."

"You found the *actual gate?*"

"The actual gate. Well, half of it, anyway."

"Did you . . . steal it?"

She laughed. "It was pretty heavy, Milo. No, I didn't steal the gate. I was actually there . . . well, for something else. *Looking* at something else," she added sharply. "But I recognized it right away, and fortunately, proper antique shops — as opposed to the dodgy ones down on the Harbors and in Shantytown — are supposed to know the provenance of the things that they sell."

"Provenance?"

"The origin of the thing. Where it came from, and who owned it before. And according to the shopkeeper, the gate came from this estate. I guess the spot where we all came up the hill wasn't always the main way up. There was a different route when the house was first built, farther east along the ridge. There was a clearing there, and the gate stood at the top."

Where on earth could anyone have gone down to the river, except where the *Whilforber Whirlwind* now ran? The rest of the ridge was steep and rocky and dangerous, and all of it was covered in trees and undergrowth. "Where could that have— Oh." There was no other route down, but there *was* a place where there was a break in the woods.

"You know where that would've been?" Clem asked.

"I know where there's a clearing. But there's no way down from there. It's a garden now. I didn't think of it because it's not just steep; it's a real cliff. We had to put up a fence, and Mom's always saying one of these days even the fence is going to go right over the side."

Clem nodded. "Well, a lot can change in a couple hundred years. Rivers, hills ... probably part of the slope did collapse. Maybe that was the spot; I don't know. I only know the shopkeeper said the gate was the original entrance to the grounds, and that it stood in a clearing in the trees, and when the sun set, it shone through the iron and looked like another one of the house's stained-glass windows. I recognized it as the same gate as in the watermark." She shrugged. "And that's how I found my way here. Now, open your present! What's wrong with you? When I was your age I couldn't resist a present for ten seconds."

He grinned and turned his attention to the package. When the paper came away, he was left holding a piece of leather tied into a cylinder by a knotted cord. "What is it?"

"Good grief, open it!" Clem blurted, all seriousness gone again. "I'm dying of anticipation."

He picked loose the knot in the cord and unrolled the leather in his palm. Inside was a collection of little metal sticks. Each one had a handle at one end and a long, thin middle. He pulled a few out of their pockets and saw that each had a different shape at the other end. One was hooked, one had teeth like a key, another had a triangular bit. "I still don't know what it is."

"It is," Clem said dramatically, "a lockpick kit."

Negret blinked and stared at the thing in his hand. "A *lockpick kit?*"

She shrugged. "I figured you're going to need something for getting locked doors open, considering you gave Owen your keys. Plus, every blackjack needs a lockpick kit. That's just basic provisioning."

"But"—he frowned—"won't you ... I mean, won't you need it again?"

Clem waved a hand carelessly. "Worry not, my young apprentice. I have plenty."

A real lockpick kit. *Wicked.* "Thanks, Clem!" He rolled the kit back up and put it in his pajama pocket. "Um—do you think you can show me how to use the different pieces?"

She held up her hand. "One, they're called *picks,* except there are also a couple torsion wrenches in there, which are called, well, torsion wrenches. And two ... maybe." Clem winked, and then, silently as ever, she padded away.

eleven

TRAPS

Do you think the thief probably avoided the attic and the spare rooms this time?" Sirin asked after Negret had repeated Clem's information about the gate and they'd spent ten minutes or so taking each pick and wrench out of its leather pocket, examining it and speculating on its function. "Now that he knows we're onto the places he hides things?"

"Probably. If it was me, I'd try to find a better spot. Especially since the satchel is bigger. It'll be harder to hide." Negret was already running through the possibilities. The basement . . . maybe the covered woodpile outside . . .

"Still, I'll feel better if we check," Sirin remarked. "I don't like the idea of leaving rooms unexplored. It's bad reconnoitering."

"That makes sense." Negret put the spiral notepad and the lock-pick kit in his rucksack and slid Georgie's map and photograph into one of its pockets. "Let's start with the empty rooms, then."

Different rooms were empty now than had been yesterday. Last night Clem had asked to switch to a room on four so she could be across the hall from Owen, which had prompted Georgie to move up to an empty room on five. Then, after breakfast, Brandon and Fenster, who had slept in the living room, had taken rooms on the fifth floor too. All of this shuffling left Negret and Sirin four rooms to go through, after Negret had taken a few minutes to draw a floor plan that looked like a house-shaped layer cake and noted where everyone was now staying. They needed to double-check the still-empty room on three, then properly search two rooms on four and one on five.

They started on the fifth floor, in the gold and green light cast by the window in which starburst fireworks erupted over the ever-present gate. "You know," Sirin observed, "if Dr. Gowervine's right about the windows having been brought here from somewhere else, then the gate must have come from wherever these windows came from. If it's important, it's probably important because of something to do with that original house."

"Maybe," Negret agreed, "but I still want to take a look at the garden."

Sirin shrugged. "It'll be covered in snow. There'll be nothing to see."

"Okay, but I don't want to *not* look at it. Like you said, it's bad reconnoitering, right?"

"I guess," she grumbled, and turned to look down the hallway. "But I don't know what you're hoping to get from it, except cold and wet."

Judging from the doors that were open, Brandon and Fenster had chosen the two rooms closest to the stairs. Once again, Negret tried to be extra observant as he and Sirin headed down the hall. The same wallpaper, the same carpet, the same sconces, the same ceiling. The same painted-shut dumbwaiter door at the end of the hallway. The table under it was square, and the poinsettia on it was red.

Clem's old room was 5W at the end of the hall. It was just like all the rest: bed, dresser, desk, chair, luggage rack, bathroom. She'd tugged the linens into place before she'd left, but Negret could tell nobody'd been in to make the bed up fresh. They found nothing interesting there.

On the fourth floor, the two doors closest to the stairs were also closed, so Negret and Sirin headed for the end of the hall and started with the room Georgie had vacated. She'd left her bed unmade, but the room was just as lacking in items of interest as Clem's. Negret started to move the luggage rack to its correct place on the other side of the door, then realized that the rug underneath it sat unevenly against the wall. He decided maybe his mother had put the rack there on purpose to hide the crooked edge and, with effort, left it where it was, even though his sense of order was still disturbed. Then he and Sirin crossed the hall to the last empty room.

Negret pulled the door to 4E mostly closed behind them, just as he had in the other rooms. It seemed like a good idea to avoid drawing attention to what they were doing, even though, apart from some heavy snoring on five, the adventurers hadn't seen or heard a single person during their search.

They looked in all the likely hiding spots — nothing — and were just about to call it quits when the door swung shut.

It happened so quietly that if Negret hadn't been facing the door, he might not have noticed a thing. But as it happened, he not only saw the door swing shut, he saw the knob turn at the very last moment, accompanied by a soft click.

"Draft?" Sirin asked, following his stare.

"I . . . guess?" But it hadn't moved the way doors usually did in the old house's drafts. And drafts definitely didn't turn doorknobs.

Then a second soft click got him on his feet and reaching for the knob himself. It wouldn't turn.

"No," he said, incredulous. He rattled the doorknob. "No *way!*"

"It's locked?"

"It's locked!" He stepped back and stared. "I don't believe this."

"From the outside? You can't unlock it from in here?"

"I could if I had the key," Negret said patiently. "These all lock with keys, from the inside or the outside."

"So . . ." Sirin bent and put an eye up to the keyhole. "So that means . . . ?"

"Yeah." Negret aimed a kick at the heavy, old wood. "Somebody locked us in. With a key. On purpose." He dropped to a seat on the luggage rack. "You know what we didn't do?"

"Check for traps?"

"Yeah."

Sirin examined him thoughtfully. "You're taking it pretty well."

"It only looks that way. I promise you, I'm not happy about it." He set his rucksack down beside him on the rack, opened it, and took out Clem's lockpick kit. "Do you think there's any chance at all I can make these work?"

She shrugged. "It would probably be silly not to try."

He unrolled the packet and looked over the picks. *Gotta start somewhere,* he thought. He reached back into the rucksack and found his pair of Wildthorn's Crackerjack Gauntlets, for Pickers of Locks and Creepers Through Windows Needing Nimble and Foxy Fingers, pulled them on, then chose a pick with an end that looked like the teeth of a key. He slid it into the keyhole. *Now what?*

Come on, Moonlighter's Knack. Presumably it was good for getting past locks and combinations even if you weren't out to steal things. He wiggled the pick. He poked around with it. He tried rotating it as if it *were* a key, but that didn't accomplish anything either. Negret repeated this process with one pick after another until he'd gone through the entire contents of the roll. Finally he slid the last pick back into its spot, folded his arms, and slumped against the wall. "Some escaladeur," he grumbled. "I've actually got lockpicks, and I still can't open the door."

Sirin patted his shoulder. "Don't be too hard on yourself. You don't know how to use them. It's not like there were instructions in there." She turned around. "Come on, Negret. I guess we could always bang on the door until someone hears us, but do we have any other options?"

"Let's hope we don't need any." Together they set to banging on the door and hollering at the top of their lungs. Long minutes passed. No one came.

"Unbelievable." Negret stared at the locked door in frustration. "Somebody must've taken one of the passkeys. The guest keys only work for their own doors."

"So there's another key for this room somewhere?" Sirin asked.

"Sure, in our study on the second floor, not that it helps us."

Sirin looked at him sharply, opened her mouth, then closed it again. "No, of course it doesn't. But maybe . . ." She took him by the arm and shoved him at the door. "Look closely, Negret."

"I am."

"No, closer." She gave him another push, shoving him right up against the wood and somehow tripping him in the process so that he fell smack into it.

"Ow!" Milo shook her off and rubbed his nose. "What's wrong with you?"

She sighed. "Sorry. Clumsy me. So how do we get out of here?"

"What did you want me to look closely at?"

"Just the lock. You're the escaladeur, after all."

Milo gave her a suspicious look, then turned to the lock. "I don't see anything. We'd need either the room key or one of the passkeys to open it." So the thief hadn't just been poking around on the guest floors. He or she had been sneaking around on the second floor, looking through his parents' stuff, too.

It made sense, of course—most people locked their doors when they were sleeping, so the thief had to have had a way to unlock them. Still, it was maddening to know his family's private space had been violated again. And not only had something been stolen from their private space, it had been used against him. He was incensed. On top of that, surprisingly, he felt the sting of wounded pride. Negret was not pleased to have been out-blackjacked, even if there was really no way he could've seen this coming.

"Negret." The scholiast waved a hand in front of his face. "Stick with me. You've got to get us out of this room."

"All right, all right." He focused and looked around. "Fire escape." He crossed the room to the window, which opened without difficulty. A frigid, whistling wind shoved its way inside, flinging a spray of snowflakes against the screen. "We're going to have to take this out."

The lockpicks proved perfect for popping the screen free from the window, even if it wasn't their intended use. Sirin craned her neck and peered out, then recoiled, shaking her head hard with her hands pressed to the wall for support. "I don't like the looks of that. Not at all."

Negret leaned out next to her. "Uh-oh."

Climbing onto the fire escape would be easy. It was so easy, Milo's parents had specifically forbidden him to do it, except in an emergency or with their supervision. The red metal stairs attached to the outside of the house were steep. They had railings, but they were rickety and they swayed with every step. And then there was the snow and ice that lay thick on every surface. A fall from the fire escape would mean a drop of anywhere from two to five stories.

The wind blustered through the nearby trees and sent up more unholy creaking.

Only in an emergency, his parents had said. Well, this counted, didn't it?

"Do you actually think you can get down without slipping?" Sirin asked dubiously.

Negret bit his lip. "I really don't know."

Just then a huge icicle fell onto the steps below the window and shattered. The noise was loud enough to make them both wince. They looked sharply at each other.

"We could—"

"Yes. But if they didn't hear us banging and yelling from inside, will they hear banging from outside?"

"If anyone's in the kitchen, they will. The fire escape ends right above the kitchen window, and it'll carry the sound right down. We need something metal." He thought for a minute, then snapped his fingers. "I know what."

Negret sprinted to the door, folded up the luggage rack, and carried it awkwardly back to Sirin. Together, they maneuvered it out the window. It was just wide enough, and the fire escape just narrow enough, for them to rest one end of the rack on the sill and clang the opposite end against the ice-coated bars.

And it made a *spectacular* clanging. *Clang clang clang clang clang!* Like an out-of-tune church bell. *Clang clang clang clang clang. Clang clang clang clang clang!*

A minute passed. Then two. Then five.

Clang clang clang clang clang!

Then, at last, a figure came running around the side of the house: Milo's father, looking completely bewildered.

"Oh, thank goodness." Negret gave the luggage rack one more clang for good measure, then leaned around its edge and waved.

Mr. Pine stared up at them. "Milo? What on earth are you doing?"

"We're locked in!" he shouted back. "The fire escape's too icy to climb down. Come up and unlock the door!"

A look of disbelief flashed across Mr. Pine's face, then he disappeared around the side of the house again.

Not long after, the sound of a key in the lock announced his arrival. "What on earth is going on?" he demanded as he opened the door.

"Somebody locked us in on purpose." Negret squeezed past him into the hallway and looked around. "We were looking for the satchel, first upstairs, then here . . . then somebody locked the door."

"Hang on, I'm confused—"

Negret ignored him and poked his head into Georgie's old room. "We must have been getting close to something that the thief didn't want us to find."

"But we searched in here," Sirin protested, peering around Negret for another look. "We were thorough."

Mr. Pine scratched his head. "We were?"

But the room appeared exactly the same. If the thief had moved something while they were locked in, that meant they had missed something before. But what?

"Milo," Mr. Pine was saying, "I'm totally at a loss here."

Negret opened his mouth to respond, then stopped. The little ripple in the carpet, the one he thought the luggage rack had been hiding, was gone now. The carpet lay smoothly against the wall.

He moved the rack aside, pulled the lockpicks from his bag once more, fished one out of its pocket, and slid it between the edge of the rug and the wall. With a little levering, he managed to make enough space to get his fingers in.

"Milo, what are you— You're going to— Don't pull up the carpet!"

"It was already like this, Dad," he protested. "The rug was messed up earlier, but now it's not. Somebody smoothed it out. I bet *that's* why we were locked in. To check that we hadn't found whatever's under here, and make sure this spot wouldn't stand out if we came back for another look."

"You keep saying . . ." Mr. Pine shook his head and stopped asking for explanations. "Milo, there could be tacks—be careful, okay?"

Negret heard the warning, but it barely registered. His fingers had just found something that wasn't carpet and wasn't floor: heavy paper, folded.

He drew it out carefully. He expected it to be more of the greenish, gate-watermarked paper, but it wasn't; it was thick and cream-colored. Official-looking. The kind of paper you'd type an important letter on.

The first thing he saw as he unfolded it was the seal of the City of Nagspeake printed in blue at the top of the page. Then, some equally official-looking typed words:

Be it hereby known and confirmed throughout the
City and Beyond that the Bearer of this Letter
has been deputized by the Customs Department of
the Sovereign City of Nagspeake . . .

Sirin gasped.

"Oh, no." Mr. Pine, who'd squatted to look over Negret's shoulder, took the page from his hand. He read it through, turned it over and back, read it again. "Oh, boy."

"What's it mean, Dad?"

"It means somebody here's not who they say they are, and that Fenster really needs to not blow his cover." Mr. Pine folded the letter and tucked it in his pocket. "This was Georgie's room, wasn't it? I would never have pegged her for a customs agent." He looked out the window and into the swirling snow. "I wonder why she has us calling a launch, not that I think anyone's coming. You think you can keep mum and pretend you don't know anything about this? I gotta go talk to your mom."

"Sure, Dad." Georgie Moselle, a big-time thief *and* a customs agent? Could you be both of those things at the same time? And if you could . . . did that mean she'd locked them in? Did that also make her the person who'd been stealing from the other guests? None of it seemed like Georgie. "I think she was telling the truth about wanting to leave. Plus it's weird she'd have left that paper behind when she moved rooms, isn't it?"

"Maybe she decided she didn't want it to be found with her stuff, if anybody went looking," Mr. Pine said.

"Who'd go looking?"

"In this group? Who *wouldn't*," Sirin retorted.

"I dunno, Milo. Listen, I have to take care of this. Try not to get yourself into any more trouble, and try to act normal, okay?"

Mr. Pine didn't seem concerned about the details. Negret could understand that. Customs agents were the archenemies of smugglers. The first worry, knowing there was a customs agent in the house, was that Fenster might get himself arrested. The second worry, he figured, had to be that the Pines themselves might get in trouble somehow. They'd said Fenster was a regular, after all.

"Okay." He and Sirin watched Mr. Pine hurry down the hallway.

"You don't think it's Georgie, do you?" Sirin asked.

"No, I don't. I'm not sure who it is." He grinned. "But I do think I know where Dr. Gowervine's bag might be. Come on."

———— ❄ ————

The second floor was still empty when Negret and Sirin slipped into the study, but he figured his parents would be there soon. He also figured they'd want him out of the room while they were talking about the customs papers because they wouldn't want to worry him. Which meant he had only a few minutes to find Dr. Gowervine's satchel.

Sirin looked around. "Why here?"

Negret shrugged. " 'Cause it makes sense. With this many guests, Mom and Dad don't have time to hang out here and relax; they've got too much to do. So it would be easy for someone to slip in and out unnoticed. You start looking. I want to check and see if I'm right about the keys."

His parents' innkeeper stuff had its own shelf in a cabinet below a glass-fronted bookcase. Everything looked as if it was in order: there was the cash box and the ledger, and there was the little pegboard that held the keys. It had three rows with four little hooks apiece, one hook for each guest room. Of course, only four keys hung there now.

Below the hooks was a wire tray that held the extra passkeys. There should have been two — since the closest locksmith was all the way down in the Harbors, the Pines kept plenty of spares — but there was only one.

"There's definitely a key missing," he reported. "And I think we should keep the other one, just in case." He tucked it into his rucksack. "Until I figure out those lockpicks, anyway."

"Anything else in here the thief might've taken?" Sirin asked.

"Well, we never have much money in the cash box." He peeked inside it just to be sure. There were a few small bills and some change, which was more or less all that was ever in it.

The ledger, which contained the names and visit dates of almost every guest, would probably be interesting to a customs agent. Negret took it from the cabinet and flipped it open. Familiar names marched down the pages — familiar, but almost entirely false. Fenster Plum, for instance, usually signed in as Plum Duff Collins. Even in the safety of Greenglass House, smugglers were a cautious bunch. If the customs agent (he still couldn't bring himself to believe it was Georgie) had gone through the ledger, he or she wouldn't have gotten much from it other than a bunch of made-up monikers.

He put the ledger back and closed the cabinet. "All right. Help me look around."

"No need." Sirin was standing with her face right up against the window. She pointed out. "Look."

At first he couldn't see what she was talking about. Then, smooshing his face a bit more awkwardly against the glass and following the direction of her pointing finger, he spotted a brown lump out on the fire escape, half covered in fresh new snow. "Is that what I think it is?"

"I bet it is." She reached for the locks, and together they slid the window open.

Negret clambered halfway out and managed to get one hand on the lump. He brushed away wet snow, got his fingers around the handle, and dragged it back into the study. It was definitely a satchel, although at the moment it was a patchy muddy color, stained with wet. It had red stitching and shining brass hardware, just as Dr. Gowervine had described.

"If we'd only looked, I bet we could've seen it from the fire escape we were banging on," Negret said.

"I bet from upstairs all we'd have seen was the snow on top of it. Are we going to open it, or just turn it in?"

"I guess we should just give it back. But maybe, since we found it," Negret reasoned, "we've earned a look at what the thief was after, right?"

Sirin nodded her approval and flipped up the latches. The satchel opened to reveal a flurry of papers and notebooks. One particular item caught Negret's eye. He reached in and withdrew a square black-and-white photograph.

There it was again, that funny thing about maps: how you

couldn't mistake them for anything else. Even when they looked like nothing more than doodles on a foggy window. Or, more accurately, like a *photo* of doodles on a foggy window, which was exactly what Negret seemed to be holding.

The window had six panes all fogged up with condensation, and it took up most of the picture. There was a rectangular shape drawn at the bottom, cut in half by the line of metal separating the panes. The shape was surrounded on all sides by roughly triangular peaks that swooped up over it like mountains drawn by a little kid, and a single line ending in an arrow meandered through them to point at the right-hand side of the rectangle they surrounded.

"There's something weird about this," Negret said, scratching his head. "I kind of feel like I almost recognize it. Like I almost know what it's a picture of."

"What about all the rest of this stuff?" Sirin asked. "It would take us hours to go through all of his notes."

Just then, two pairs of footsteps came rushing along the hallway. Negret got up and stuck his head out the study door just in time to make his mom nearly leap out of her shoes with fright. "We found it," he whispered, and waved them in.

"This is ridiculous," Mrs. Pine said, staring at the open satchel. "Well, I guess Dr. Gowervine'll be relieved, anyhow." She and Mr. Pine exchanged a look. "Milo, you want to take it to him? Your dad and I need to chat."

"Okay." Reluctantly, he closed the bag.

"No messing around this time, though, okay? Just take it straight to him. He's freaking out."

"One of the passkeys is missing too," Negret added. "I have the last one. Just in case."

Both of his parents immediately felt in their pockets and took out their own key rings. "Got mine," Mrs. Pine said, looking at her husband. "You?" He nodded. "All right, I suppose." She herded Negret out the study door. "If you see Brandon or Fenster come down before we do, think you can get them to come right up here without giving anything away?"

"Sure."

The door closed gently behind the adventurers, and they started down the hallway toward the stairs. "You keep an eye on everybody," Negret whispered to Sirin. "See how people react when we come in with the bag."

The first floor went silent when they arrived. "Whoever keeps taking things," Negret announced, "better knock it off. You are no match for our thing-finding skills." And he held up the water-stained satchel with both hands.

"That's my—" Dr. Gowervine shoved out of his chair and dashed to where Negret stood. "Where on earth— Good grief." He took it gingerly. "What happened to it?"

"The thief put it out on the fire escape," Negret told him. "You better make sure everything's in there, I guess."

The professor took the bag to the dining table, pulled handfuls of papers from it, and began to separate them into piles. "Er, thank you, Milo."

"No problem." He watched the sorting for a moment. Then he

caught Sirin's eye and nodded toward the loveseat by the window as the rest of the guests, most of whom had come in to see what the fuss was about, returned to what they'd been doing.

Georgie sat at one of the little brunch tables by the dining room window, retaping the cigar box she must've opened to get at the photograph of the fourth-floor window. In the living room Clem and Owen were sitting very close together on the couch. One of her hands was tucked into his, and they were talking so intently that Negret thought they might not even have noticed him return the bag to Dr. Gowervine. Mrs. Hereward sat in one of the other chairs, knitting peacefully. Mr. Vinge settled back into his usual chair, and as Negret watched he picked up the book on his knee and went back to reading.

"Did anybody react?" he whispered to Sirin when they were hidden by the high seat back.

"Everybody looked up, but as soon as they saw the satchel, pretty much all of them went back to what they were doing. Except for Dr. Gowervine, of course."

Negret eyed Mr. Vinge, and the book he'd been working his way through since the night he'd arrived. "A history of the Skidwrack and its environs," he said thoughtfully. "Hey, Sirin? Now that we know why Georgie brought the chart with her and since her secret's out, do you think we need to keep the chart itself secret anymore?"

Sirin frowned. "Well, in general I'm for keeping secrets as long as possible," she said reasonably. "After all, other people are still keeping them. Why?"

"I'm still curious about what it's meant to show."

"Georgie said she checked it against everything around here, though."

"Yeah, I know, but I'm thinking about what Clem said about the gate. How in two hundred years, the landscape could've changed. Erosion, weather, tides and floods . . . maybe our chart shows a part of the river as it was, not as it is." Over in his chair, Mr. Vinge turned a page. "He's reading a history of the river and the land around it. I bet there are older maps in there. Maybe we can find a match."

"Georgie knew the paper was old, though. If she's as good a researcher as she says, she probably checked old maps."

"Not necessarily." Negret shook his head. "Because remember, she said she could tell that parts of the chart were newer than the paper. What if the ship and the compass are new, but the waterway and the depths aren't?"

The scholiast considered this. "I wouldn't show it to him. But if you can get him to let you have a look at the book without telling him why, I don't see the harm."

Just then, Mr. Vinge stretched his long legs, balanced the book open flat on the arm of his chair, and got creakily to his feet with his mug in one hand. Negret all but vaulted over the back of the loveseat. "Excuse me, Mr. Vinge?"

The old man pulled his glasses down toward the tip of his nose with one finger and looked at Negret over the top rim. "Yes, Milo?"

"If I promise not to lose your page or bend anything, could I take a look at your book?"

"At my book?" Mr. Vinge repeated, surprised. "Whatever for?"

"I heard you tell Mom it was about the Skidwrack," Negret said, thinking fast. "We're doing a unit on the river in Social Studies. I thought maybe if I found some interesting facts to take back to school after the holidays I might get some extra credit."

Mr. Vinge pushed his glasses back up and gave him a long, considering look through them. "Certainly, then. Please help yourself. I'll rest my eyes for a bit." He took a few long steps and paused. "I've read several books on the history of the river," he said. "If you have any questions about what you read, I may be able to answer them."

"Thanks." Negret made a beeline for the book, marked Mr. Vinge's place carefully with his index finger, and carried it back to the loveseat. For the next ten minutes, he and Sirin went down the index of illustrations, checking the chart against every picture in the book. None seemed to bear any resemblance to the blue and green shapes on the paper.

"How are you coming along?"

Negret and Sirin all but jumped out of their skins. Mr. Vinge stood behind the loveseat, peering mildly down at the two of them. Negret folded the chart up as nonchalantly as he could manage. "Fine, thanks. I guess you want your book back."

"There's no hurry. Have you found any good facts for your classroom?"

"Well . . . " Negret scratched his head. "Actually, I sort of got caught up looking at the pictures." He closed the cover and held it out. "But I think I'm done. I might go outside now, before it gets too dark. Thanks, though."

"Suit yourself." Mr. Vinge took the book and turned back toward his chair. Then he paused and raised a finger in a gesture that made him look like a teacher about to give a lecture. "Here's a fact you might appreciate, since you're reading *The Raconteur's Commonplace Book*," he said. "Once upon a time, cartographers wrote *hic sunt dracones* in the margins of their maps to indicate places that were dangerous or unexplored. It means *here be dragons*. But Nagspeake cartographers wrote *hic abundant sepiae,* which means *here are many seiche.* Have you gotten to the story in the book about the seiche, who come ashore but can only stay if each finds a human willing to take his place under the river?"

"Yeah." Negret grinned. That had been a creepy one.

Mr. Vinge smiled back. He looked like he was out of practice at it, but the smile seemed genuine enough. "Does your secret chart there have a warning?"

Negret shook his head. "Wish it did. That would be cool."

"Sometimes the warning wasn't written out. Sometimes it was just a picture of an otter."

"Nope, no otters. Just an albatross. Ow," Negret yelped as Sirin elbowed him. "No otters," he repeated firmly, glaring at her.

"Ah, well." Mr. Vinge adjusted his glasses again. He sounded a touch disappointed. "It must be a map of very safe waters, then." And he went to fold himself back into his chair with *The Skidwrack: A Visual History* open on his knee.

Negret rubbed his rib cage. "Did you have to wallop me that hard?" he hissed.

"Just reminding you to stick to the plan," she replied airily. "Keep our secrets, Negret. Where are you going?"

He tucked the chart into Georgie's leather folder and tucked that into his bag. "Out for a look at the garden, like I said before. Keep an eye on things."

"Now?" Sirin protested. *"Now?"*

"Yeah," he retorted quietly. "It'll be too dark later. Plus I told Mr. Vinge I was going to, and it'll seem weird if I don't. You want to come?"

"No, and I wish you wouldn't waste your time with it either. We have real clues to follow." The scholiast took the Eyes of True and Aching Clarity out of her pocket and perched them on her nose. "But don't mind me."

Negret slid off the loveseat. "I'll be right back. It's just across the lawn." Ignoring the glare she was directing at him through her blue lenses, he headed into the kitchen, where Mrs. Caraway was slicing carrots. "I'm going for a walk outside. Will you tell my folks if they ask?"

"I don't know, Milo. You probably shouldn't go by yourself. It's freezing out there, and the snow's getting heavy again."

"Just a short walk. I won't even leave the lawn." Negret smiled with as much confidence as he could muster. "You'll be able to see me from the window."

Mrs. Caraway looked dubious. Milo followed her eyes to the

window and saw that, in fact, you couldn't see far across the grounds at all. "Got a watch?" Mrs. Caraway asked at last.

"No. Why?"

"Here." She wiped her hands on her apron and unbuckled her own wristwatch. "Borrow mine and be back in ten minutes, or I'm sending Lizzie after you. Deal?"

"Deal." He strapped it on as he headed for the foyer, then bundled up and stepped outside into the freezing afternoon.

Each footstep crunched as Negret walked, his boots sinking deep into the white. He shaded his eyes against the whirling snowflakes and tromped across the lawn toward the clearing in the trees. Just as he'd told Mrs. Caraway, it was a straight walk from the front door directly across the lawn. Through the whirling eddies of snow the clearing didn't look particularly clear at all, but it was there, a white-on-white space between two banks of snowcapped pines.

As he walked he wondered what his parents would decide to do about the customs agent. It simply couldn't be Georgie. It couldn't be.

A shadow moved somewhere off to his right. Negret glanced sharply toward the railcar pavilion as a cascade of high-piled snow slid free from one corner of the roof. He stared for a long moment, but there was nothing more to see and nothing more that moved.

He frowned, but a glance at Mrs. Caraway's watch reminded him that he didn't have time to waste on rooftop avalanches. Not only that, but it was too cold to stand still. So he turned back toward the clearing and kept on walking.

It made sense, he thought as he arrived at the foot of the little rise that led to the garden. It made perfect sense that this would once have been the entrance to the grounds; it basically lined up with the front door, unlike either the pavilion or the current road. Somewhere under the snow was a short set of three stone stairs that led up to what was now the little garden that Mrs. Pine — who was many wonderful things, but definitely not a gardener — planted every year and tried to keep alive for more than a few weeks. There were two stone benches like parentheses, one on either side of the space. Beyond those was a box hedge that had once been neatly trimmed, and on the other side of that hedge was a split-rail fence meant to keep anyone from venturing too close to the cliff.

Negret dug the seat of one of the benches mostly clear, then decided the stone was too cold to sit on. Under the bench, though, there was a shadowy space where the snow had blown and collected into drifts, leaving a neat little oblong cave just big enough for a smallish boy to climb into. It was the kind of secret, hidden place he could never resist. He climbed under the bench and discovered that not only was the space exactly his size, but it was warmer in there than it was out in the open.

If the gate had once stood here, Negret couldn't tell where. Either way, he didn't have long to stay and think about it. Mrs. Caraway's ten minutes were almost up.

He crouched there for another long moment, absent-mindedly running his fingers over a bit of old graffiti cut into the cold stone by a former owner or perhaps by some long-ago guest: RIP AW ADDIE

WE HARDLY KNEW YE, over a badly carved picture that looked like some kind of bird with a hooked beak. An owl, maybe, although it was impossible to tell for sure.

Maybe Clem was right and the place where the gate had stood had crumbled into the river long ago. Maybe Clem was wrong, or the shopkeeper had his facts wrong. Still . . . he leaned out and looked back at the house that faced this garden so perfectly, and up at the sky toward the invisible sun that could have made the gate look like a stained-glass window to someone looking up from below, andNegret felt certain that even if he couldn't prove it, Clem was right.

Then: "Milo!" Mrs. Caraway's voice pierced the cold from somewhere on the lawn. Negret checked the watch and discovered that he was late by two minutes. He crept out of the cave under the bench and sprinted for the house and the figure standing before it with her hands on her hips.

Fortified with a mug of hot cider after being chastised for not following instructions and (to hear her tell it) practically dying of hypothermia right before Mrs. Caraway's eyes, Negret found Sirin in the living room, waving from the glimmery cave behind the Christmas tree.

He retrieved his rucksack from the loveseat and crawled in beside her. "Well?" she demanded. "Was it everything you hoped?"

Negret shrugged. "I couldn't tell if Clem was right or not, but I believe her."

Sirin narrowed her eyes. "What else?"

"Nothing else. I just wanted to see if that could be the place.

You're the one who said it was a bad idea to skip searching places that could be important."

"But you didn't *learn* anything else," she pointed out.

"Fine. You were right and it was pointless," he said, exasperated. "Why are you hounding me about it?"

"I'm not hounding you."

"You are." In a bit of a huff, Negret got his notepad out of the rucksack. "Fine. Let's get back to real clues. Did *you* learn anything while I was gone?"

"All right, I'm sorry. And no, I didn't."

"Then we both wasted ten — twelve minutes, and we're even. Let's get back to it."

"Okay." Sirin sat back and drew her knees up under the cloak. "Is the customs agent connected to the thefts, Negret? Are we looking for one person or two?"

"I think they're the same person, but I'm not positive." Negret flipped the spiral pad open. "So let's pretend they're separate people. First, the thief. Either it's Clem, because she's the only one who wasn't stolen from, or one of the others faked being robbed to throw off suspicion."

Sirin took the notepad and fished a pen from her pocket. "Argument for it being Clem — we already know she's a thief."

"Sure. Clem's the simplest answer, definitely."

"So I guess let's move on to the complicated one." She began listing the names of the thief's victims, and next to them what was taken. "What's the complicated one, Negret?"

The pen stilled. He looked at what she'd written.

Georgie – Notebook with Lansdegown research in it

Mrs. Hereward – Ditty bag with Greenglass House on it

Mr. Vinge – Gold watch with engraving in it

Dr. Gowervine – Satchel with Skellansen/Doc Holystone research in it

"I'm not sure yet," Negret admitted. "Other than it's one of those four."

"Fair enough." Sirin turned the page. "Now the customs agent. The simplest answer is it's Georgie, since the paper was in her room."

"And the complicated answer: someone hid it in her room so that he or she wouldn't be connected to it. Misdirection."

And then, all at once, Negret saw it. There was only one way the complicated answer worked here, and boy, did it *work*. He reached across Sirin and turned the page back to the list of stolen things. Yes. *Yes.* One of those things was not like the others. He grabbed the notepad and turned more pages until he found a note from the day before. Then he sat back, stunned. Not only was one of those things not like the others; one of those things contained the clue that proved Negret right.

"They're the same person," he whispered. "And I know who it is."

"Well, don't keep me in suspense," Sirin hissed. "Who is it?"

But just as Negret opened his mouth to answer, Mr. and Mrs.

Pine came into the living room with Brandon and Fenster in tow. Brandon looked casual enough, but Negret could see a sharpness in his eyes and a slight difference in how he was moving. Apart from being the Belowground Transit conductor, Brandon was a professional fighter, and it looked as though he was holding himself at the ready in case he had to throw down.

Fenster was a different story. His eyes darted around the room, like those of a wild animal caught in a corner. He stumbled on the rag rug before the fire, and Brandon caught him with a cautionary look and whispered something that had to be a warning to keep it together.

"Who's hungry?" asked Mrs. Pine with painfully fake cheer. "Late lunch? Early-afternoon tea?"

Negret grabbed the notepad from Sirin, slid out from behind the tree and made his way as casually as possible toward the kitchen. Fenster winked at him. Brandon elbowed Fenster. "Cut it out with the signals!" he muttered. "Honestly."

Mr. and Mrs. Pine had gone into the kitchen and were exchanging a few hurried words with Mrs. Caraway and Lizzie when Milo reached them. "Mom," he whispered. "Dad, can I talk to you guys? It's important."

He didn't wait for an answer, just grabbed his mother's sleeve and pulled her toward the big pantry under the stairs, motioning for Mr. Pine to follow.

"Milo, what on earth —"

"I know who it is," he interrupted when they were more or less alone.

Mr. Pine frowned. "You mean you think it's not Georgie?"

"I'm *sure* it's not." He lowered his voice. "The thief and the customs agent are the same person."

"Milo, I know you don't like the idea," Mrs. Pine said gently, "but Georgie could be the thief too. She could just have *pretended* to be robbed."

"That's exactly what the thief *did,* but it wasn't Georgie."

"Then why was the affidavit — the paper you found — in her room?" Mr. Pine asked.

"It was just like you said, Dad. To keep it from being found in the real agent's room. Misdirection, just like with the stolen things. Only it wasn't Georgie."

"You think someone was trying to throw suspicion on her, then?"

"No, I think when the agent put the paper there, he thought he was hiding it in an empty room." He looked at his mother. "Remember how I dropped Georgie's bag on the floor and broke her perfume because the luggage rack wasn't where it was supposed to be? That's because the customs agent had *already hidden the paper under the carpet* and moved the rack for a little extra cover."

"But then ..." Mrs. Pine frowned and looked at her husband. "That would make it ..."

"Yes!" Milo nodded feverishly and held up his notepad. "And look. Here's what was stolen. Everything has to do with the house and why people came here, except for one thing."

One thing: the only thing that was both an obvious item to steal and completely out of place on a list of objects having to do with Greenglass House and what had brought the guests there.

The thing that belonged to the only person who could've thought Georgie's room was just another empty room: the person who'd arrived before her. The very first guest of all.

Mr. Vinge.

He watched his parents figure it out too. Time for the last clue, the ultimate proof. He turned the page again. "You never saw the stolen things close-up, like I did. Look. This is what was engraved inside the watch."

> To D.C.V., with high esteem and
> thanks for a job well done,
> from D. & M.

"D. and M. stands for Deacon and Morvengarde, doesn't it? Is it true, what Dr. Gowervine said yesterday, that Deacon and Morvengarde are in league with the customs people?"

"Well, it's true that about the only thing that's harmed by Nagspeake smuggling is Deacon and Morvengarde's business," Mr. Pine said quietly, looking back into the kitchen to be sure nobody was listening in. "Without the smugglers, D. and M. would practically have a monopoly on goods coming into the city. Whether they and the customs agency are actually in league together — nobody's been able to prove it, but yes, everyone suspects it."

"So you believe me?" Milo demanded.

"Once all the others showed up, he must've decided to investigate who they all were and their connections to the house." Mrs. Pine nodded slowly. "You just might have hit the nail on the head, kiddo."

"Well, then, what do we do about it?"

"That's a tougher question." She looked at her husband. "Apart from helping Fenster keep a low profile until we can get him back on the Belowground and out of here, I don't much know what we can do. If Mr. Vinge is with customs—and if he's here on a job—he may be looking for confirmation of illegal activity."

"Well, we don't do anything illegal, do we?"

"No, but we also don't call the authorities and turn in evidence. We aren't smugglers, but we might be considered *accessories* to smuggling." She squeezed his hand. "But I don't want you to worry about that. I just need you to try and keep it together and not get in trouble and"—she laughed a little—"try and enjoy Christmas Eve. Can you manage that, and let your dad and me worry about the other stuff?"

"I'll try, I guess." But he was pretty sure he wouldn't have much success.

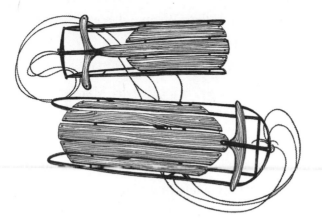

twelve

MR. VINGE'S TALE

For the rest of that day, it was very, very hard not to stare at Mr.
Vinge. Milo couldn't figure out how his parents managed it
either.

First, they tried to get Fenster out of the house and away to safety
on the Belowground Transit System. He and Brandon and Mr. Pine
bundled up on the pretense of double-checking that their fixes to
the generator were still holding and disappeared into the snow, but
instead of going around the house, Milo saw them hike uphill toward
the woods and the hidden entrance to the BTS. Half an hour later all
three were back again, looking more like icicles than men. Milo was
standing next to his mother in the kitchen, waiting for a cup of hot
chocolate, so he heard Mr. Pine's whispered explanation. "Control

system's frozen solid and there's some damage. Brandon thinks he can fix it, but not quickly."

"Damage?" Mrs. Pine repeated warily. "Damage like the generator damage?" By *like the generator damage* Milo was pretty sure she meant *sabotage*.

"Not sure. I mean, he doesn't think so, thank goodness. If it is, someone did a way more convincing job this time around."

For the rest of the day, while Brandon came and went, Milo's parents made sure one of them was always in the same room as either Mr. Vinge or Fenster. They didn't tell Fenster who they thought the agent was, which was probably a good idea. Fenster would never have been able to keep it together if he'd known. He'd have stared, for sure. As it was, he was acting more and more paranoid as the day progressed.

Christmas Eve day wore on toward Christmas Eve night, and despite all the excitement in Greenglass House, it proceeded just as slowly as it seemed to every year. The snow kept on and the wind kept whipping it into the corners of windows, and now and then Milo forgot about Mr. Vinge and Fenster and even Negret and fell dreamily into thinking of frosted windowpanes and silver bells. The smells of baking ham and pies and bubbling cranberry sauce with orange drifted through the first floor to mingle with the pine and bayberry and peppermint scents of the candles. And just as the light outside began to dim, Milo's father came down the stairs with three patchwork stockings with bells on their toes.

Mr. Pine hung the stockings from their customary hooks on the mantelpiece, then turned to Milo, who was curled up with his book in the loveseat by the window. "You know what we haven't done?

Any sledding. What do you say we get out of here for a bit, just you and me? I bet with all the ice under the snow it'll be perfect sledding out there. If we hurry, we can probably get an hour in before full dark."

They suited up and headed out into the whistling cold, making their way carefully down the porch steps. Then Milo followed his father toward the section of woods where all the outbuildings were. They walked in their usual companionable quiet, except when Mr. Pine hummed occasional bits of "Up on the Housetop." It was Christmas Eve, it was snowing, the lights of home were glowing behind him, and Milo was going sledding with his dad.

The structure they called the garage had never actually held a vehicle. Milo's dad regularly vowed that one of these days he'd clean it out so they could finally put a car in there, but Milo doubted he'd ever get to it. It was the largest and closest of all the outbuildings, a big square of red brick with two wooden doors, which stood just inside the trees. Mr. Pine had taken the shovel from the porch, and now he dug away the drifts piled against the front of the building. Then he brushed the snow from the latch, and together they managed to shove the left-hand door open just far enough to squeeze through and get inside.

A pop and a sizzle, and a bulb very much like the ones in the Emporium fizzled to life overhead. "The sleds are in here somewhere," Mr. Pine said, surveying the space. "Where'd we put them last year?"

"Probably under everything," Milo grumbled. "We keep saying we need a place for them, but we never find one."

"This year, then. Without fail. You search that side and I'll take this one."

Milo picked his way along the right-hand side of the space while his father started down the opposite side. The sleds would be easy to spot, Milo figured, and he wasn't disappointed. One of them turned up right away, up on top of a pile near the back. The green metal rails and polished wood stuck out like a sore thumb among the rest of the junk, which was mostly lumber and stuff that fell into the broad category of *parts:* an old engine, several drawers that didn't seem to have furniture to go with them, sections of picket fencing that had once been painted yellow, that sort of thing.

"Found one, Dad." Milo tugged on the front of the sled, but the back half wouldn't budge, and he wasn't tall enough to see what was holding it fast. "Stuck, though."

"The other one's over here. Hang on." A moment later Mr. Pine appeared and climbed onto a heavy old headboard. As he yanked the sled free, the headboard shifted under his weight and the whole pile lurched. Mr. Pine leaped down, fumbling the sled in his arms. It fell, bouncing off something metal with a *ploing*. "Darn," he grumbled, examining the runners. "Chipped the enamel."

Milo ignored him. He bent for a look at the thing the sled had banged and did a double take. It was mostly hidden under the headboard. "Dad, can you help me lift this?"

"What for?"

"I want to see the thing that's under it."

Mr. Pine shrugged but did as he was asked, and together they managed to lift the headboard just enough. And there it was, rusted and twisted and with several bits of ancient dead ivy clinging to it here and there: the very same gate Milo had been seeing images of everywhere he looked for the last three days. Half of it, anyway. Clem's antique dealer had at least been telling the truth about where his half had come from.

He reached out to touch it where several flakes of green enamel from the sled's runners clung. It was smaller than he'd expected somehow: just about his own height. He'd assumed all the pictures were showing the kind of gate that was the size of a door, something at least as tall as an adult. But this was like a small garden gate, the kind you might lean on to talk to your postman as he passed on the sidewalk. Nonetheless, it was the same one. It had to be. There was even a hook for a lantern just where the stitched gate on Mrs. Hereward's bag had its little knot of golden yarn.

"Milo," Mr. Pine grunted. "Gotta let go of this now. Heavy."

"Dad," Milo said when Mr. Pine had lowered the headboard again, "where's that gate from?"

"Don't know. It's like the attic and the basement—half the stuff in here is from before your mom's and my time. Why?"

"It's the gate in our windows. Each one in the stairwell has that gate on it somewhere. Haven't you ever noticed it?"

Mr. Pine frowned. "I think you'll have to show me later."

"Yeah, I will." Maybe it wasn't so surprising that his father hadn't noticed the gate hidden in the stained glass before. Milo hadn't noticed it either, not until he'd seen the watermark on Georgie's map.

Found the gate, found the gate, he sang silently as he and his father hiked along, each trailing a sled behind him. Who knew what it meant, or if it meant anything at all, but still, he was delighted. It was a piece of the house's history, which meant it was a piece of Milo's history, and every bit he managed to collect was precious.

The place they were headed was only a little ways from the building that hid the entrance to the Sanctuary Cliff Belowground Transit System stop, so they went first to check on Brandon's progress on the train repairs. Then they tramped on to the sledding spot, a slope of clear, unblemished white.

Mr. Pine was right; the icy snow was perfect. He shoveled some into a barrier at the bottom of the hill so they wouldn't go barreling into a tree; then they hiked up and raced down and overturned their sleds on the barrier-snowdrift and did it all again and again until the light was gone from the sky. Then Mr. Pine took a pair of flashlights from one of his pockets for the walk home.

They left the sleds and the shovel on the porch and trooped inside, red-faced and snow-covered and grinning. "Have a nice time?" Mrs. Pine asked, waiting with a steaming mug in each hand while they fought their way out of their coats and boots.

Mr. Pine kissed her cheek. "Just what the doctor ordered. Am I right, Milo?"

"Yup." He took his mug and inhaled. The hot chocolate had a sharp peppermint bite to it, and there was whipped cream on top — the homemade kind that had to be dolloped on with a spoon and took longer to melt.

"Everything's stable, but the train's still down and Brandon's called it a night," Milo's mom said quietly to his father. "And there was an answer from the ferry dock, just after you two left. If I read the signals right, they're shut down but looking for somebody to come out. I couldn't put a reply together before dark, though. Just about an hour to dinner," she added, louder.

Milo crept back into the cave behind the tree with his mug. He leaned against the wall, put his feet up on one of the larger presents, and took a sip of hot chocolate. The fire was crackling away, the house was as calm as it had been in days, and even Fenster (visible through the branches if Milo leaned just a bit to his left) seemed to have settled down. He and Lizzie and Brandon and Georgie were playing some kind of card game — girls against boys, by the look of it. Dr. Gowervine must've been out on the porch smoking again; there was just the faintest scent of pipe tobacco in the room. And Mr. Vinge didn't appear to have moved the entire time Milo and his father had been gone.

The rucksack was still under the tree where Milo had left it when he'd rushed out to tell his parents what he suspected about Mr. Vinge. He opened it up, took out *The Raconteur's Commonplace Book,* and flipped to the story Mr. Vinge had mentioned earlier.

I've never yet found anyone who could tell me how the two things came to be associated with each other, a quiet young man named Sullivan was saying, *but for as long as any oldster on the Skidwrack can remember, superstitious folk have always crossed themselves when they see river otters, for fear of the Seiche. Except, of course, for the odd foolish romantic who actually thinks he wants to meet one. The Seiche are supposed to be beautiful, after all.*

"Hey." Meddy crept into the tree-cave.

Milo closed the book reluctantly. "Where've you been?"

"I don't know, upstairs? Were you looking for me?"

"Not really," Milo admitted. He'd sort of fallen under the spell of Christmas Eve and had been enjoying having some time to himself. It hadn't even occurred to him to wonder what Meddy had been up to, despite his discovery on the sledding trip (which, he thought guiltily, he should probably have invited her to join). "But listen! I found the other half of the gate!"

"The gate? *Our* gate? Where?"

"Out in the building we use for storage. I found it buried under some stuff at the back. Dad says it's probably from before he and Mom took over the place, just like Clem said, but he doesn't know anything about it. It's smaller than I thought. Do you think it means anything?"

Meddy looked up as a rush of cold air spiked through the room. Clem and Owen must've gone for a walk, and were just now returning, all smiles and pink cheeks. "No idea," she said, "but it's neat that it's there."

Mrs. Caraway's voice rang out from the kitchen. "Dinner, folks!"

"Guess I'll take the living room again." Milo tucked *The Raconteur's Commonplace Book* into his rucksack, slung the bag over his shoulder, and crept out from behind the tree with Meddy on his heels. The card players sitting on the floor around the coffee table were still at their game. "Who's winning?" he asked.

"Who do you think?" Georgie replied with enough relish that Milo suspected it was the girls.

Meddy liked to get her food last in order to observe everybody, so she held back, and Milo and Dr. Gowervine were the first to the table.

"Was anything missing from your bag?" Milo asked him as he picked up a plate from the stack.

"Hmm? Oh, no, nothing. It's so strange," he said. "Why on earth do you think anyone would go to the trouble of stealing notes on such an obscure thing?"

"Don't know." But certainly the thief was interested in *plenty* of obscure things. Milo was pretty sure it was what those things had in common — Greenglass House itself — that the thief was really intent upon.

That *Mr. Vinge* was intent upon, he corrected himself silently. That the *customs agency* was intent upon. Was he just after as much information about the house and its history as possible, trying to figure out its connections to smuggling? Or was there something more?

"Young man," Mrs. Hereward said, smiling at Owen as they took their places in line, "you may be called upon to tell a story this evening. I do believe it may be you and Mr. Vinge."

Owen smiled. "It's the least I can do, ma'am. Everyone's been so hospitable."

"I believe I can manage one as well," Mr. Vinge added. He sat at one of the little tables by the bow window, waiting for the others to finish filling their plates. "I've been considering and I believe I have just the one."

"I think we'd all love to hear it, Mr. Vinge," said Milo's mother.

"That's right," Brandon agreed, reaching for the bowl of potatoes. He sounded casual, but there was a hard edge to his words. "Give us a tale, Mr. V. In fact, I'll help wash up after supper so we can hear it sooner."

Mr. Vinge smiled, and Milo wondered if the smile was really as cold as it seemed, or if he was imagining it. "I'll do you one better, Mr. Levi. How about I tell it right now?"

"Er. All right, spectacular," Brandon said warily.

"It's very interesting that we've already heard two tales about Doc Holystone this week." Mr. Vinge leaned his elbows on the table in front of him, steepling his fingers together so they came to a point under his chin. "Holystone was one of the great smugglers of my youth, of course, and one of the most famous for leading Deacon and Morvengarde — and the city customs agents, of course — on a merry chase."

Fenster looked up sharply from filling his own plate. "What other story?" he asked. "There was the one about the window maker yesternight, I remember."

"Why, the one about you, Mr. Fenster," Mr. Vinge said, surprised. "Did Mrs. Pine not mention she'd told the story of you seeing the ghosts of Doc Holystone and his son?"

Fenster relaxed. "Oh, right. She told me, I just forgot. Only you got it wrong," he added, speaking to Mrs. Pine. "But I guess that doesn't signify. Sorry to interrupt, Mr. Vinge. Carry on."

Mr. Vinge looked at him through narrowed eyes for a moment. Then he continued. "It was said that Deacon and Morvengarde had made Holystone their top priority; this, in a city in which they already had more agents than any other."

"You can say that again," Fenster muttered. Brandon, who was standing next to him, moved one long leg in what looked like a perfectly innocent motion. Fenster yelped. Brandon must've kicked him under the table.

"Sorry," Fenster mumbled. "They did say that, though. Everybody knew it," he added a bit defensively. "Not just ... well, you know. Not just the runners."

Milo cringed inwardly, and he suspected the rest of the Greenglass House regulars — Milo's parents, Lizzie, Mrs. Caraway, and Brandon — were doing the same. Only the smugglers themselves called one another *runners*.

"Shut up," Brandon said through gritted teeth. Then he nodded at Mr. Vinge. "Carry on, mate."

Since no one so far had left the dining room, Milo took his plate to the bar, where Meddy was sitting rigidly, waiting to be last to the buffet. "He's going to give himself away," Milo muttered. "It's just a matter of when." Meddy nodded tightly but said nothing. Her face was stony.

Meanwhile, at his little table by the window, Mr. Vinge smiled an odd half smile. It was hard to tell whether he'd noticed Fenster's slip. He cleared his throat and continued. "So. Doc Holystone, as I'm sure everyone knows, managed to hide his identity for many, many years. It wasn't until the very week he was killed that anyone knew for certain who he was."

Fenster frowned, and Milo could tell he was about to say something stupid. He thought maybe he knew what it was too, so he cleared his own throat and spoke up first. "Lots of people must've known," he interrupted. "His crew, for one thing. Plus all the people he did business with. Just, they would never have informed on him. You mean none of the customs people or catalog agents knew." Fenster gave a satisfied nod.

"Yes, of course," Mr. Vinge said, a bit tightly. "None among the law-abiding citizens of the city knew his name, I should've said. Criminals, I'm sure, will protect their own. Yes, there were plenty who knew. They did not come forward."

Now everyone stiffened, serving utensils momentarily stilled. Even the unflappable Clem and the lofty Mrs. Hereward looked unsettled at the harsh way Mr. Vinge pronounced the word *criminals*. Brandon caught Fenster's eye and shook his head slightly, warningly. And Milo's parents were looking very, very uncomfortable. *Criminals will protect their own.* Did letting smugglers stay at your inn count as protecting criminals?

From the hard look on Mr. Vinge's face, Milo was pretty sure *he* would say it counted.

It had always seemed to Milo that most folks in Nagspeake, if you asked them and they answered honestly, were more on the side of the smugglers than the customs agents or Deacon and Morvengarde. But Mr. Vinge, perhaps, wasn't most folks.

"The agent in charge of Deacon and Morvengarde's investigation," he continued, "discovered the truth not long after he finally found a member of Holystone's crew willing, at risk to his own life, to give evidence."

"To give evidence after being beaten to within an inch of his life, you mean." This time it wasn't Fenster but Dr. Gowervine who spoke up. When Mr. Vinge looked sharply at him, the professor stared defiantly back. "Oh, please. I've studied the case of Doc Holystone for fifteen years. I've seen pictures of that crewman after Deacon and Morvengarde got through with him. The smuggling community itself raised the money to pay the costs of all the medical bills the poor man racked up after his run-in with the Deacon agents. That, in itself, is evidence that he was tortured for his information."

"You know an awful lot about it, do you?" Mr. Vinge asked casually. Dangerously, Milo realized. *Something's happening here.*

"Meddy?" he whispered, but she was still staring at Mr. Vinge, as unmoving as if she were made of stone.

"I want to hear what he has to say," she said grimly. Something about her words made him jump. Everyone else in the room jumped too; maybe because Meddy had never spoken that loudly or that authoritatively to anyone but Milo. Even Mr. Vinge looked up momentarily with a strange expression on his face. Or maybe it wasn't Meddy's words at all but the sudden chill that cut through the dining room that made everyone pause. It was as if there were a window open somewhere that had let in a sharp gust of wind. But there was no open window, and the front door was shut tight.

"Tell them," Meddy said to Milo, more quietly. "Tell them you want to hear too."

Confused, he did as he was told. "I want to hear what he has to say. Finish the story." Mr. Vinge eyed Milo for a long moment. He stared back, a little defiantly. "Go on."

"The smuggler showed the agent a map," Mr. Vinge said slowly, holding Milo's gaze. Milo swallowed, suddenly certain he knew what was coming next. "A map," Mr. Vinge continued, "on which the details of Doc Holystone's next shipment were hidden, encoded in groups of dots meant to look like soundings." He smiled, and the smile was cruel. "A shipment of weapons that would be arriving aboard Doc Holystone's ship, the *Albatross,* in a week's time."

Meddy's fingers dug into his arm. "That's a lie," Fenster protested. "Everybody knows Doc Holystone never ran weapons!"

"Every smuggler runs weapons at some point or another," Mr. Vinge said, his eyes still on Milo. "Every. Single. One. Doc Holystone especially."

"You're a liar!" Fenster snarled.

Mr. Vinge grinned. "Why do you think everyone was after him? Because he smuggled books, because he ran black iris bulbs, because he brought the city meaningless trinkets and antigravity pens? Don't be absurd. Nobody cared about that."

This time Georgie snorted. "Deacon and Morvengarde did. They care about anything they don't get a piece of the profit on."

"That's right! Quit hitting me," Fenster snapped at Brandon, who was still trying to get him to shut up. "The man's a liar who says Doc Holystone ever ran weapons. He never did, not once."

Another hard slice of cold stabbed through the room. *"I want to hear what he has to say!"* Meddy snarled. "Say it," she hissed to Milo. The fury in her voice was frightening.

"I want to hear what he has to say," Milo repeated, shaken.

Mr. Vinge took a sip from his cup and spoke deliberately. "Despite all their efforts, the investigating agents were thwarted. Someone had tipped Holystone off, and the man wouldn't be the legend he is if he weren't capable of pulling off some fairly miraculous getaways. This was one of those escapes. It was . . ." He shook his head and made a noise of disgust. "Well, it was something. So the smugglers escaped with their cargo —"

"Which it was copper pipes," Fenster snarled, ignoring warning noises from Brandon and both of Milo's parents, "because there was a shortage thanks to price hikes in that infernal catalog, and none of the Quayside contractors could afford —"

"— running away like the little mice they were —"

"Now you're just being a — *Stop hitting me, Brandon!*"

"And that might have been the end of that episode if not for one thing," Mr. Vinge went on, taking another calm sip from his mug. "The mice were gone, but there was still a chance to capture the rat who led them. The agent in charge was certain that Doc Holystone must have avoided the act of putting things on paper like the plague. He guessed that when Holystone had to resort to pen and paper, there must have been some signal to prove that those very rare written messages came from him. So while his colleagues had been busy setting up the raid on the weapons drop, the agent had turned his attention to the map. He discovered a watermark. The age of the paper led him to an equally old and venerable papermaker, and from there to a house that now, two hundred years later, belonged to a man called Michael Whitcher, who had found the old paper stock in his attic."

According to Georgie, this was very nearly the same way Clem had tracked the Lansdegown name to Greenglass House. Milo glanced at the red-haired thief. Her face was dead pale. Meanwhile, Mr. Vinge took a folded brown sheet from his pocket and unfolded it. Milo wilted. It was the wrapping from Lucksmith Paper Merchants that Negret and Sirin had found in the Emporium along with the scrap of watermarked paper.

And I showed him Georgie's chart. If Mr. Vinge was right, then Doc Holystone himself might have made it. Milo was acutely aware of the bag that still hung across his chest. He'd taken it from behind the tree so he'd have it wherever he sat to observe the guests during dinner, but now he wished he'd actually gone to hide it.

"Now, back to the raid. As far as Holystone probably knew, this was just another failed attempt on the part of customs. The fact that one of his crewmen had come forward was still a closely kept secret. The agent who'd found the watermark guessed that, having come so close to capture, Doc Holystone would go to ground once he'd shaken his pursuers. And there was no reason for him to suspect his identity had been compromised. So the agent left the rest to the raid and waited for the great smuggler to return to his true sanctuary." Mr. Vinge paused and looked around the room dramatically. "A house full of stained glass that stood high on a hill overlooking the river."

Beside Milo, Meddy was holding her breath. Her fingers were still digging into his arm.

"And this is where he hid the most important piece of the cargo he'd nearly been captured bringing into Nagspeake. A weapon, like the rest of the cargo, but a legendary, deadly, and unbelievable weapon. Something the city of Nagspeake could not permit to remain in the smuggler's hands. Something the city had been seeking for more than a century."

"Doc Holystone never ran weapons," Fenster howled. "Never!"

"Fenster!" Brandon looked as though he was trying to figure out whether he should just wrestle Fenster to the ground and choke him out or knock him unconscious for a while, for his own good. He glanced at Milo's father. But before Mr. Pine could say a word, Fenster had stumbled around the table. He pointed a finger at Mr. Vinge's impassive face and blurted, "The customs spooks have always used some mysterious deadly weapon as the reason for their raids, and it's never been real. It's always been a lie! It's *always* been an excuse for coming down on the runners. The weapon you're talking about — it never existed. And even if it did, Doc Holystone would never have touched it with a ten-foot pole, do you hear me? Never! He was a *patriot.* He believed in changing things, but he didn't think weapons were the answer. Good God!"

Fenster shoved his quaking hands in his pockets and swallowed hard. When he spoke again, his voice shook. "Do you know how much money he could've made if he'd agreed to run weapons? Do you think nobody ever asked him to? People tried to hire him to run guns and explosives and war engines *all the time!* And all the time, every time, he said no."

Mrs. Pine stepped up to the quivering smuggler and put an arm around his shoulders. "Fenster — Fenster, come with me."

He tried to shake off Milo's mother, but Brandon stood with her now and Mr. Pine, too, and between the three of them they managed to haul him away from Mr. Vinge and out the side door onto the screened porch. Milo could just make out Fenster's dark shape through the stained-glass window in the living room as he squatted on his haunches and dropped his head in his hands. Mrs. Pine crouched next to him and put an arm around his shoulder.

Meddy squeezed Milo's arm even harder, and he felt her nails cut his skin. He was just about to repeat her words again when Georgie Moselle spoke up.

"Well, Mr. Vinge, you're some kind of good storyteller," she said angrily. "Are you just trying to wind that poor fellow up?"

"A necessary unpleasantness," Mr. Vinge said carelessly, leaning back in his chair. "I'll finish when they come back."

"I think we've heard enough," Dr. Gowervine grumbled, striding toward the porch. "I know I have. Doc Holystone was no gunrunner, no weapons-monger. I know not everyone agrees about whether he's the hero I think he was, but —"

"Sit down, Dr. Gowervine." Mr. Vinge's face was neutral, but his words — that hadn't been a request. It had been an order. "Sit down," he repeated when the old man looked at him in surprise. Mr. Vinge stood, reached into his pocket, and took out a folded rectangle of leather. He flipped it open to reveal a bronze-colored badge and tossed it on the dining table between two serving dishes. "Sit. Please. In fact, everyone please take a seat."

"What is that?" Mrs. Hereward demanded, squinting at the badge.

"Deputy customs ID," Georgie said coldly. She looked up at Mr. Vinge. "Is that thing real?"

"I found a customs agency paper hidden under the carpet earlier today," Milo said quietly, glaring at him. "Right after Dad let us out of the room you locked us in, Mr. Vinge."

"Yes, yes, you're better at hide-and-seek than I am," the customs agent retorted. "I'm sure we're all very proud of you."

The side door opened and Mr. Pine stalked across to the dining table. "What's this about?" he demanded. "Do you have a concern you'd like to discuss privately?"

"Not privately," Mr. Vinge replied. "Sit down, Mr. Pine."

"I'm fine," Milo's father snapped. "Let's go have a word, you and I."

Mr. Vinge put a finger on the badge in its leather folder and spun it to face Mr. Pine. "I said, have a seat, sir. I need a few words with everyone. That includes you and your wife and Fenster out there."

The door opened again, and Mrs. Pine stood uncertainly in the doorway. Milo thought he knew what was going on. His father had come in to get Mr. Vinge out of the way before they let Fenster back in. They weren't going to let the two of them be together in the same room anymore if they could help it.

Unfortunately, it seemed Mr. Vinge had other ideas. He ignored the looks passing between Mr. and Mrs. Pine, strode into the living room, and called to Fenster, who was pacing furiously on the porch. "Fenster! Set something straight for me."

Fenster pushed past Milo's mother into the room. "You bet I will, you flipping liar."

"When you said Mrs. Pine got your ghost story wrong, what did you mean?"

The smuggler stopped in his tracks and frowned. "What's that matter to you?"

Mr. Vinge shrugged. "You say I'm a liar. I say, if I'm mistaken, help me correct my errors. What did Mrs. Pine get wrong about your ghost story? Was it, perhaps, the part where she said you recognized Doc Holystone because you'd seen Wanted posters with his image on them? Isn't it true that you recognized him because you sailed with him? Because you were part of his crew? Isn't that the part she got wrong?"

The smuggler's hands balled up into fists.

"Fenster," Mrs. Pine whispered, putting a hand on his arm.

He shook her off. He stared at Mr. Vinge for a moment, red-faced. Then the tension went out of him and he actually grinned. "No, sir," he said, tucking his hands into his pockets. "No, sir, that's not the part she got wrong. She said I saw Doc Holystone's son, when everybody knows Doc Holystone had a daughter. Addie, she was called." He elbowed Mrs. Pine gently. "Which it was a fairly silly mistake to make." Still smiling, he looked at Mr. Vinge with a defiant glitter in his eyes. "And that's all Nora got wrong, bless her."

Mr. Vinge forced a smile in return. "Well. Thank you for clearing that up. Now perhaps you'll clear up something else for me. You, or perhaps our intrepid hosts. Certainly one of you must know the answer. I'm finished with these games."

There was a long moment when nobody moved, and then Mrs. Pine stepped forward and crossed her arms. "Please explain yourself, Mr. Vinge. Explain why you're ordering my guests and my family around, and while you're at it, please also explain why you stole from my guests and why you locked my son in a room. Actually," she snapped, "don't bother. Please just pack up your things and go. You'll have to figure out how to contend with the weather on your own."

Mr. Vinge chuckled. "No, no, Mrs. Pine. At the moment I represent the law in this house, so I believe the orders are mine to give. Here's all the explanation I feel you require: Doc Holystone's final cargo is here in the house somewhere, and I think either you or your husband or Fenster knows what it is and where. Obviously, Holystone's legacy is alive and well here, or your son wouldn't be running about with one of those watermarked maps. Especially not one that just happens to have an albatross on it. Not exactly the kind of thing that turns up just anywhere, is it?"

Georgie gasped. "No, no," she protested. "*I* brought that map! *I* gave it to Milo!"

"*The cargo is here!*" Mr. Vinge roared. "And I don't intend to leave without it. I've waited nearly forty years to be able to close the book on Doc Holystone. I'll leave when I have that cargo. Not before."

"Milo," Meddy whispered, "get ready to run."

"*What?*"

"You heard me," she hissed back. "When I say so, run for the stairs. Not outside; you can't hide outside or you'll freeze. Run for the stairs. Run fast. Run for the Emporium."

Milo opened his mouth to demand to know what the heck she was talking about, but Mrs. Pine spoke first in a voice that shook with fury. "Mr. Vinge, you are *not* the law, and you will have to leave."

"I'll throw you out myself," Brandon growled, stalking forward.

Then two things happened. Mr. Vinge pulled a gun from his vest and leveled it at Brandon, and two strange men burst through the front door into the house.

"Run!" Meddy yelled. Milo launched himself off the bench and sprinted for the stairs. *Zephyr's Passage,* he thought wildly to himself. *Your feet carry you as swiftly and invisibly as the wind.*

"Stop," Mr. Vinge snarled. "Get that kid back here!"

The two strangers leaped after Milo and Meddy, but before they had even crossed the room, Clem was on the move. In a series of motions that looked like something out of a kung fu movie, she took three steps that carried her from the bench to the corner of the bar that divided the dining room from the kitchen, and then she pivoted and took a flying leap straight into the nearer of the two strangers in pursuit of Milo. Down he went, with Clem on top of him.

Owen had none of Clem's acrobatics, but he was only a few steps behind her. The second stranger was just about to grab Clem when Owen tackled him. Milo and Meddy reached the stairs, and then they were on the first landing.

There was an explosive boom from below. Milo stumbled. "Was that—"

Meddy grabbed him by the collar and threw him forward. "Keep going!"

He obeyed and sprinted up until the green glass knob of the door to the Emporium was turning in his palm. He fell over the threshold and sprawled across the dusty floor. Meddy slammed the door shut behind them. The first overhead bulb sputtered to life.

That was when Milo realized he'd just run away and left his parents in the living room with a man holding a gun. "That was a *gunshot,* what we heard, wasn't it?" He yanked off the rucksack and burst into tears.

Meddy crouched on the floor next to him and patted his shoulder. "Pull it together, Milo," she said in a comforting tone that didn't match her words. "Your mom and dad would want you to get out of the way of that gun."

"I . . . I *left* them there," Milo sputtered. "I just *left* them! What if he . . . what if he . . ."

"Vinge doesn't want to hurt your mom and dad." Meddy sighed. "I should've recognized him," she added bitterly. "I should've known."

Milo wiped his eyes. "Known what?"

"That he was from Deacon and Morvengarde. He just looks like an agent."

Milo wasn't sure what she meant by that, but the evasive tone of her voice made him stop and think. "You said you should have *recognized* him," he said slowly, getting to his feet. "Why would you have recognized him?"

"I meant recognized him as an —"

"Plus, you were acting really weird when he was talking," Milo continued, looking closely at her. "Something's up. Something you're not telling me. Why would you have recognized him?"

Meddy folded her arms and considered him for a long moment. "What I'm going to tell you is going to sound crazy, but I need you to believe me, okay?" He shrugged and waited. At last, Meddy sighed. "He was talking about himself. He's the agent in the story," she said. "It happened here at the house. He's way older now; that's why I didn't recognize him, but that's the guy." She pointed a finger viciously at the attic door, as if Mr. Vinge were standing on the other side. "He's the guy who captured Doc Holystone, and he's the guy responsible for his death, too."

I've waited nearly forty years to be able to close the book on Doc Holystone, Mr. Vinge had said. It certainly sounded like Meddy might be right. Still . . . "How could you know for sure?" Milo demanded, eyes wide. "How could you *possibly* know?"

She swallowed, and all the poise and anger drained from her. She swallowed again, and Milo realized she was about to cry.

"Because I saw it," she whispered. "I saw *him,* with Doc Holystone. I was there."

"That's not possible," Milo said, confused. "That was forty years ago, Meddy."

She smiled weakly. "Wrong on both counts, Milo. First of all, it was thirty-four years ago. Secondly, my name's not Meddy. Not even when I'm not Sirin."

Milo opened his mouth, then closed it again. "Meddy. Short for Madeleine or something."

"*Mrs. Caraway's* daughter is called Meddy," she replied deliberately. "If you told her you've been playing with her daughter for the last few days, she'd think you were off your rocker. Meddy Caraway isn't here. She never was. But I introduced myself to you at about the same time as the Caraways arrived, and you assumed I was Meddy, and I just never corrected you." She scratched her head. "I kept thinking you were going to say something to someone that would make me have to explain things to you, but you never really did."

And it all came together. As Milo stared in shock, a series of recollections flashed through his memory.

It's like the attic and the basement — half the stuff in here is from before your mom's and my time.

ROLE-PLAYING GAME STUFF — AW.

She said I saw Doc Holystone's son, when everybody knows Doc Holystone had a daughter. Addie, she was called.

ADDIE WE HARDLY KNEW YE.

"You're . . . Addie Whitcher," Milo said slowly.

She smiled hesitantly. "I never really liked Addie, actually. I'm sort of partial to Meddy, now that I've gotten used to it."

"And Doc Holystone . . . was your father?"

She nodded, looking steadily at him.

Milo nodded back numbly. "And you saw Mr. Vinge capture him thirty-some years ago?"

"Thirty-four years ago, almost exactly." She smiled crookedly, then put her hands in her pockets and looked down at her feet. For the first time, Meddy — Addie? — seemed very, very young.

His head was spinning. The math didn't work. "But you're not old enough. You're my age."

"I *was* your age," she said deliberately. "Thirty-four years ago."

RIP AW.

In his mother's story, Doc Holystone's child had been a ghost. And Fenster had said apart from that child being a girl, the rest was true.

"You're a ghost?" Milo murmured, not daring to believe his own words.

"Thirty-four years ago," she repeated softly, rubbing the toe of one shoe against the heel of the other. "I'll never forget that day, you see, because it was the same day I died."

thirteen

COMBAT ENCOUNTERS

They stared at each other. Milo couldn't decide whether to laugh or consider believing it. The latter was guaranteed to lead to him freaking out. Meddy looked as though she knew he probably wouldn't believe her story but was holding on to a tiny shred of hope that maybe, just maybe, he might surprise her.

"Can you prove it?" Milo asked.

She sighed. "If you need me to." And without further warning, she flickered like a lightbulb about to die. She was there, and then she was not, and then there she was again, and then she was gone.

Milo stood alone in the attic. He turned in a circle with his blood rushing, heart thudding in his chest. "M-meddy? I mean, Addie?"

And there she was again, right in front of him, as if she'd been there all along. Her arms were crossed over the Cloak of Golden Indiscernibility. "Meddy's fine. I'm used to it."

So she was . . . a ghost. He dropped to a seat on one of the crates. He felt dizzy, suddenly.

Well, for starters, Sirin would have to be invisible to all the non-player characters — meaning everyone but you.

"You weren't just pretending to be invisible, were you?" Milo asked when his heart slowed back down to a reasonable speed. "Nobody else *could* see you, could they? Not ever. Not the whole time."

She shook her head apologetically. "No."

"They couldn't hear you either? And you just let me go around acting like you were there? I must've looked like I was some kind of crazy person, talking to myself," Milo grumbled.

"I think only people I show myself to can hear me. But I'm sure you looked less crazy than some of the other nutters here," she offered. "If that's any consolation."

"There's a memorial to you carved into one of the benches in the garden," Milo said. "Is that why you didn't want me to go? Not because it was a waste of time, but because I might have figured out the truth if I'd found it?"

"It's my headstone," she said simply. "Not just a memorial. I suppose they thought, with what had happened with my dad, it was better to keep my grave secret. Hidden. And it isn't that I didn't want you to know the truth, but I thought it might . . . distract you. Maybe even scare you."

"I'm not scared!"

"But I can see how the unexpected upsets you," she said gently. "And you were so upset every time your space was invaded: your room, your floor, the inn itself when all these guests started arriving. I really couldn't imagine how you'd feel about *me*. *And* I thought it was a waste of time," she added gruffly, sounding (thankfully) a bit more like Meddy again. "That much is true."

Milo nodded. There was a lump in his throat and he felt the stirrings of panic start to swirl in his middle. She was right — suddenly, his own home felt like an alien place.

He looked at his friend. She still looked the same. "What should I call you?" he asked helplessly.

She thought for a moment. "Meddy. We can't have you wasting time trying to figure out who I am when you talk to me. Okay?" There was a hopeful note to her voice. "And 'cause I'm the same person I've been all along, Milo."

He nodded again. The sickness twisting his stomach didn't let up. "My parents," he whispered. "He . . . he has a gun."

Addie — *Meddy,* he thought firmly — shook her head. "Mr. Vinge doesn't want your parents. He doesn't want Fenster. He wants something he thinks my dad or someone else came back to hide. If we can find it, we can get rid of him and no one will get hurt."

"Somebody could've been hurt already," Milo protested. Then he brightened. "Meddy, if you're a — a — if nobody else can see you, can't you . . . I don't know, sneak up on him and take the gun or something?" He scratched his head. "Could you even do that? Take something from . . . from . . ."

"Someone living? Sure. You've handed me things. But taking

Mr. Vinge's gun . . ." She shook her head. "I thought about that, but I don't have any magical powers that I know of that would help me get a gun away from him. The only difference between if *I* grab for the gun and if *you* grab for the gun is that no one can see me, so maybe I'd have surprise on my side."

"Surprise might be enough!"

"I don't think so. Would you know how to wrestle a gun away from an adult? 'Cause I wouldn't. Plus, he's probably used to guns, and I'm not. Anything could go wrong. Those other guys could have guns too. Someone could get really badly hurt. Or killed."

She fell silent, and Milo remembered that Doc Holystone hadn't just been *captured* that day so many years ago. "Did you see it?" he asked.

"You mean, when . . . ?" Meddy shook her head and looked down at her feet. "No. I only saw Mr. Vinge try to arrest him."

She sat next to Milo on the crate and they were silent for a moment.

"He came home late that night," she said at last. "He came from the cliff. There was no railcar then; there wasn't even a proper stair. It was a set of hidden toeholds, that's all. If you knew where they were, you could make your way up, but there was no railing, and it had been raining, so I'm sure it was slippery on top of being a difficult climb to begin with." She took a deep, shuddery breath. "He'd probably been running for hours before that. Running, climbing over rocks, taking the best route he could find to come home fast without being followed."

Milo patted her shoulder awkwardly.

"I like to think he was coming to get me," she went on quietly. "That we were going to run away to sea until things cooled off for him. Really he was probably just coming to say goodbye, and to tell me where to go to be safe. He must've known that having found him, the D. and M. agents wouldn't stop until they *caught* him. He wouldn't have wanted to put me in harm's way, even if it meant we'd have to be apart."

"Where was your mom?"

"Died when I was little."

"So you were all alone here, when he was away?"

"Not usually. We had Mrs. Gallick for a cook and her nephew to keep the house up." Meddy smiled sadly. "She used to think she was in charge when Dad was gone. I let her believe it because she and Paul—that was her nephew—played Odd Trails with me. That night, though—that night I was by myself. It was unusual, but it happened once in a while."

"How could he have left without you, then?" Milo demanded, indignant. "What if something happened to him? You'd really be alone. You'd be—"

Meddy raised her eyes and looked at him evenly. "An orphan? Like you?"

"Well, yes!" But the second the words were out, he regretted them.

"You're not an orphan, Milo," she said, sounding a little irritated.

"No, I'm not," he mumbled.

"You have a family. You have *two*, even if one of them is a mystery. And how do you know that the first of those families, the one you were born into, didn't do exactly the same thing my dad did, which was to do the best thing they could figure out to do for you, and which for some reason happened to mean you couldn't be together?" Now she sounded angry. "And by the way, it didn't exactly turn out badly for you, did it?"

Milo shook his head and put his hands over his ears. "I know, I know, I know! Stop, okay?"

"It turned out *great* for you," Meddy snapped, pointing at the world on the other side of the attic door. "You're here, with two people you love and who love you. I—" She stopped, swallowed. "I *died*."

I died.

"The bell at the bottom of the hill was there," she continued, the sharp tone leaching out of her voice. "He rang it before he started up the cliff, I think to wake me up. I climbed out onto the fire escape to watch for him. And from the fire escape—"

"You can see that part of the woods," Milo finished. "Where he'd come into view if he came up the cliff."

"I was watching when he appeared. I waved. He didn't see me—he should've known to look for me there, I thought, but he was looking the wrong way. He was looking across the grounds at the front of the house—"

"Toward the hill road?"

"Yes. Because that's where Mr. Vinge was waiting. I couldn't see him, but I saw my dad see him. He turned back toward the cliff and disappeared into the woods. A minute later, there was Mr. Vinge—a younger Mr. Vinge, about the same age as my dad—running for the woods. Then he disappeared into the trees too. I was so scared. I held my breath. And Mr. Vinge came out again. Without my dad."

Milo held his breath too.

"Another man, not as fast a sprinter, I guess, crossed the lawn toward Mr. Vinge at the tree line," Meddy continued in a voice that was nearly emotionless except for an occasional little shake. "I leaned out as far as I could to try and hear what they said. Mr. Vinge was lighting a cigarette." She licked her lips. "And I . . . I knew then that my dad had fallen. He'd lost his footing, and he was lying at the bottom of the cliff. And Mr. Vinge had seen him fall and knew he was dead. Because if he hadn't seen, if he didn't know for sure, he would've followed. And the other man reached him, and Mr. Vinge blew cigarette smoke at the sky, and he opened his mouth to say something, and I leaned even farther . . . I thought — I hoped — that maybe I was wrong, that maybe he would say *He got away,* or *We'll get him next time* . . . I leaned out to try and hear his words and I . . . and . . ."

Milo watched her with wide eyes. "You fell?"

She nodded silently.

"And you died."

She nodded again.

They sat side by side without saying another word for a long moment. Milo tried to imagine the moment she was describing and felt a thick lump form in his throat. "I'm sorry."

"Time goes by strangely for me." She looked around the attic. "I don't know if I've ever haunted this house before, or if I did, for how long. I remember snippets of the time between . . . between when I fell and a couple of days ago when I met you. I remember people repairing things, replacing things, loud noises. I remember a man hanging the ship chandelier in your dining room, for instance. I remember when you and your grandfather and your dad built the track for the *Whilforber Whirlwind*. I remember seeing Fenster Plum a few times after your parents moved here, although I certainly saw him plenty with Dad before, so I might be remembering wrong. I remember the time your mom told the story about, at least, when he saw me on the fire escape, but I don't recall how long ago it was. Time goes by strangely.

"Things looked . . . new . . . to me when I came into the house this time," she continued after another moment. "Everything looks new, even what I know was here before." She fingered the sleeve of the yellow robe. "Like this robe. Like that door, where you found the Lansdegown keys. They must have been around when I was alive, but they're still new to me."

"What made you come back?"

"I had to." Meddy frowned. "Mr. Vinge arrived. I knew something was wrong in the house, but I didn't know it was him. It takes time for me to figure things out. It's like remembering the middle past, the part after I died, but before this. I can get to it, but it takes time. When he came back . . . and one by one the rest of them arrived, I could feel the *seeking* in the house. Everyone was seeking something here. But" — she waved a hand — "they're all looking for different things. I could feel the searching, and I could feel the wrongness. I couldn't find the place where the two . . ." She frowned and laid one palm over the other.

"Where they overlapped."

"Yes." She scratched her head. "And I couldn't figure it out on my own, because I couldn't talk to them. Well, I suppose I could have, but I didn't want to. I didn't trust any of them. I needed help, and I decided on you. I came up with the game. I thought maybe we could find the thing, the reason for the seeking, before the wrongness got too strong."

Milo nodded.

"And you were so good at it," Meddy continued, peering into his face. "You figured all this stuff out. You were so good at being a blackjack, and you figured out the answer to every puzzle we came up against. You found the Lansdegown keys, you found the roamer relic thing . . . I know you can find what Mr. Vinge is looking for." Her voice took on a more pleading tone. "I know you can, Milo, and I can't do it without your help. If we can manage it, we can get rid of Mr. Vinge. This is all he wants."

"And you're willing to give it to him?" Milo asked dubiously.

"I hate the idea," Meddy said miserably, "but I don't know what else we can do."

Something was nagging at him. "Meddy?" It felt strange, using a name he now knew wasn't hers, but her face brightened immediately when he did. "You said when your dad came back, to get you or to say goodbye, he didn't make it all the way to the house." He felt his face flush as he realized what he'd just said. "I mean . . . he didn't actually come into the house."

"I know what you meant," she said softly. "Yes, that's true."

"Then why does Mr. Vinge think he hid a weapon here?"

She snorted. "Fenster was right. Dad never touched weapons. The customs people made that story up, so Mr. Vinge must know there's no secret weapon to be found. Either he's after the same thing Dr. Gowervine is and he just doesn't want to admit it, or he's convinced himself that things happened differently that night than they actually did and thinks Dad managed to hide *something* before he died. But if there's something, *anything,* hidden here, if we can find it, I bet that'll be enough to get rid of Mr. Vinge. I bet he doesn't know exactly what he's looking for either."

Milo shook her by the shoulder. "Think, Meddy! Even though it's hard. Think! What might it be?"

"No, no, no," she protested, "I don't know anything about it, whatever it is. *If* it is. If Dad had really hidden something here at some point, he wouldn't have told me. He didn't tell me details — that was supposed to keep me safe. I didn't even know about the watermarked paper. No," she said, shaking her head. "It wouldn't have been Dad. It must've been afterward. After my . . . after I . . . Someone must have come back afterward. Skellansen, if Dr. Gowervine is right, or someone he sent."

She got to her feet. "Listen, I'm going downstairs to check on things. Cross your fingers. Maybe we'll get lucky. Maybe they ganged up on him and kicked him out and the problem is gone. But you'd better start thinking about what clues we have, just in case." She hesitated. "You know, Negret's parents aren't down there. Maybe Negret would find it easier to focus than Milo. Just a thought."

"Maybe." He retrieved his rucksack and opened it. It was a little harder to shift into Negret mode now that this was so clearly not a game anymore. Then another thought occurred to him. "How do you carry things, anyway? How come nobody's seen a phantom yellow robe flying around the house?"

"No idea." She smiled weakly and glanced at the open box of role-playing game supplies. "In some games, different worlds and different beings exist on different planes. Maybe I have my own plane and I pull things I can wear or carry over to where I am."

"Like you can turn things ghostly?"

"Maybe, temporarily. But it only seems to work for little things — although I did manage to take some of my books downstairs to the tree that morning we created your character. But remember when we were locked in the guest room and I shoved you into the door?"

"Yeah." Negret rubbed his still-sore nose.

She shrugged. "Let's call that an experiment that didn't work."

"But you could've gone and gotten the key and brought it back?"

"I thought about that," Sirin admitted. "But that would've meant passing through the door, and I didn't want to give myself away unless I had to. And as it turned out, you came up with a way out yourself. But speaking of keys, is your spare passkey in your bag? Can I borrow it in case he's locked everybody up somewhere?"

"Yeah." Negret located the key and handed it over. "It'll only work for the guest rooms, though."

"Okay. I'll be back as soon as I can." She smiled weakly and disappeared through the door. Negret swallowed hard. It really was true. He willed his heart to slow down to its normal pace and forced himself to focus.

By the time Sirin returned, Negret had the clues laid out on a flat-topped trunk.

"Everyone's fine," she said breathlessly. "Nobody was hit. But what's the room at the back of the house by the kitchen?"

"Laundry room. Or the pantry. They're both there. Why?"

"I think Vinge and his guys have people locked in the laundry room."

"What?"

"One of those strangers is watching that door, and there's yelling coming from the other side. Mr. Vinge has your parents and Fenster in the living room, and he's grilling them about my dad and the house. I heard him say something about them being under arrest. And Mr. Vinge's other guy is on the second floor. I think he's looking for you. So we have to hurry."

"My mom and dad are *under arrest?*" he protested. "Can customs agents even *do* that?"

"I don't know, but he seems to *think* he can. He has the key to the laundry room door, too. Is there more than one?"

"I don't know. I've never seen my parents lock that door." Milo dropped his head into his hands. "This is awful. Can't you get them out without a key?"

"How? If I could pick locks, don't you think I'd have done it when we were locked in the guest room before I tried shoving you through the door?" She shook her head sadly. "I'm not magic, Negret, I'm just . . . not like you. I can pass through walls, but *you* can't, and neither can the people locked in your laundry room."

"Can't you do *anything?*" he snapped before he could stop himself.

"Not much," she snapped back. "That's why I needed you!"

"Sorry."

"It's okay. It frustrates me, too. But look—I brought these." From her pocket Sirin took a small paperback book titled *Works, Being the Fifth Catalog.* She laid it on the trunk next to the blank decoy paper and the chart they'd gotten back from Georgie. "I ducked into Dr. Gowervine's room and checked in that satchel." She pointed at the bottom edge. "Look: *Skellansen.* I think this is a catalog of his stuff. I thought it might help us to see some of his work. And I brought that funny foggy-window map picture."

"Good idea."

He picked up the Skellansen catalog. "Guess we have to start somewhere." It was hard to care about the pictures he was looking at as he flipped through it. *Focus,* he thought. *There could be a clue here, and if there is, Mom and Dad need me to find it.*

Stained glass and more stained glass. Round church windows and vaulted church windows, windows that showed cheerful monks brewing beer, windows with beautiful ladies dancing, windows with ships under sail slicing through blue water with white foam at their bows. And there was more. Tables with mosaic tops. Fireplace screens with glass set into them to catch the light of the flames and send it flickering throughout the room. Glass chandeliers and glass candelabra and glass lamps.

Negret tossed the catalog aside. "I don't know what I'm looking for." He picked up Georgie's chart, then Dr. Gowervine's photo. "I can't figure it out if Dr. Gowervine couldn't. He spent his whole life trying to discover whether there's a hidden vidimus. This is hopeless."

"It's not hopeless," Sirin insisted. "Quit grousing and think."

"I am!"

"You're complaining, is what you're doing." She picked up the chart again. "Remember what Mr. Vinge said? That my dad and his crew used to hide information on charts like these."

"Yeah. Encoded in the soundings. I'd have to be a codebreaker to read them." Codebreaking was not an exploit he possessed.

"Maybe the information we want isn't in the dots. Remember, it was the ship that caught Georgie's attention."

"The stupid ship thing." Negret took the chart and looked at the curls of white painted on the page.

"I mean, my dad was captain of a ship. It's not totally impossible that it has something to do with—"

"Wait." He touched the compass rose. "It's an albatross. That was the name of your dad's ship, right? That's what Mr. Vinge said."

"Yeah . . . so?"

"Compasses are for navigating. To show the way, right? Well, this compass is pointing us to a ship. Literally." He touched the arrow, which he'd thought was meant to indicate north. It was directed at the puff of curling sails. "Maybe the shape of the compass is meant to tell us what ship it is."

"Well, if whatever it is is hidden on the actual clipper, we're out of luck," Sirin said dubiously. "I don't know what became of the *Albatross*."

Negret shook his head. "You said something before about a ship chandelier."

"Yeah, the one in your dining room. I don't know if that's what it's supposed to be, but I always thought it looked like one."

He looked at the sails on the chart. "And you said you sort of remember when it was hung."

"Sort of. It was in the afterward." Her eyes widened. "You think . . . ?"

Negret was already flipping through the catalog again until he came to a page of glass chandeliers. "Skellansen made them, too. Look." Some looked like traditional chandeliers, the kind with faceted beads dripping from upturned arms of glass or brass. Others, though, were more fanciful. There was one with curves of red and gold that looked like a graceful ball of fire. Another was made of carved and engraved pieces that looked like glittering, silvery stars that seemed to be hanging in thin air. Milo pictured the cluster of cream-colored glass that hung over his dining room table. It would look right at home on this page. "Could be . . ."

"But didn't Dr. Gowervine say it was a story window?" Sirin protested. "Something that had information to give? What can a chandelier tell anybody?"

"Yes, but that's just what he suspects. Maybe he's wrong." He tapped the catalog and the map. "The more I look at these and the more I think about it, the more I'm sure we're onto something."

Sirin lifted the photographic map she'd taken from Dr. Gowervine's satchel, the one that appeared to have been drawn in the condensation on a window. "Okay, Negret, I have an idea. Keep the ship chandelier in mind now, and look at this again."

What was she talking about? It looked the same as it had before: the best he could figure was that it showed a path through mountains to a rectangular building, and he said so.

"Not mountains," Sirin said. *"Sails."*

"Which would make this rectangle thingy what?" Negret asked. "A deck?"

"Could be."

"So . . ." Now he thought hard, trying to remember whether the chandelier downstairs had anything that could approximate a deck. It didn't, as far as he could remember, but maybe he was thinking too literally. "So you think this picture was meant to show someone where to look in the chandelier — in the ship — for something that's hidden there?"

"I think we should find a way to check."

"That means going back down there where Mr. Vinge and his gun are."

She nodded soberly. "I know. We need a plan. Negret, it's time that you and I talked about combat encounters."

"Combat?" he repeated warily. "You aren't saying we should actually try to *fight* them, are you? Three men with at least one gun, probably more? Where'd they come from, anyway?" But even as he asked the question, he remembered the times when he'd thought he'd seen shadowy figures moving on the grounds. Maybe they'd been there all along, hiding somewhere out in the cold. Maybe in one of the old outbuildings deeper in the woods, where they could camp without being seen or heard.

"Yes, that's exactly what I'm saying," Sirin said. "But not fighting like you're thinking. We can beat him, if we're smart. And we *are* smart. Smarter than he is. Look at all the stuff we figured out while he was sitting around with those stupid socks."

Negret swallowed. One boy and one girl—one dead girl who admitted there wasn't much she could do—against three men with guns. And he wasn't sure they were smarter, or even whether that really mattered. When it came down to adults versus kids, adults always seemed to have the upper hand, even without firearms being involved.

Well, maybe not always, he thought, remembering one of the stories he'd read on the first day of vacation. *The Devil, who is not usually arrogant, almost never loses. Still, it's happened, though it's a rare and peculiar thing when it does.* If the Devil could be beaten, surely an old man in ridiculous socks could be beaten too.

He scratched his head. "Okay, so we're smarter, even if we're smaller and we don't have weapons. What do we—" He stopped abruptly and tilted his head, listening. "Hang on." It was the attic door, shifting just a bit on its hinges. "Someone's opening doors on the next floor down. The air's moving and rattling this one."

"That's probably the guy I saw on the second floor," Sirin whispered. She rushed to the door. "Can we lock this?"

"It doesn't lock from inside." Negret met her eyes and grinned. "You can't unlock the door from in here either, you know."

Sirin's face broke into a wide smile. "I see where you're headed with this, my dear Negret. And I like it."

After a hurried discussion of strategy, he crept down the attic stairs and peered around the landing into the fifth-floor hallway. "Ready?" he whispered over his shoulder.

"Ready."

A moment later, one of Mr. Vinge's thugs emerged from 5N. Negret kicked his heel gently against a step. The agent looked up. Negret gave an exaggerated jump as if he was horrified to have been caught, then sprinted back up into the attic. He kicked the door closed and ducked behind the garment rack just inside it.

The agent's feet hammered up the stairs and the door opened. "Kid," he said, "nobody's going to hurt you."

Sirin peeked out over one of the trunks farther in, just enough for the top of her head to be seen. The thug took a step in her direction. Milo wasn't sure what was different, but the agent had definitely seen her. She ducked down behind the trunk again. "Promise?" she called.

His eyes narrowed and he stalked deeper into the attic. "Yeah, promise. Come on out and let's get you back with everybody else."

"I don't know," Sirin said warily. Negret waited. The agent took another step, then another, toward the trunk where Sirin had been. Just a bit farther . . .

"Come on, now. Can't have you running around while we're trying to get things settled. Throws everybody off his game. That's how people get hurt."

"Okay, then," Sirin sang cheerfully. "Here I come!"

Even to Negret, who knew what was coming, it was a shock to see her appear right out of thin air. Suddenly, she was standing on top of a crate not two feet from the stranger. He stumbled back, then recovered himself and made a grab for her.

Negret was already on his feet and rushing for the exit with his rucksack bouncing against his back. The moment he was on the other side, he flung the door shut and shoved home the key from under the potted plant. *Click* went the lock just as the agent's bulk thudded against the door.

"He forgot to check for traps," Negret scoffed as he pocketed the key and Sirin materialized on the stair beside him.

"Amateur," she agreed. "Congratulations, Negret. You just won your first combat encounter. One down, two to go."

The agent began banging furiously on the door. Negret led the way down to the next floor and into the nearest open room. "We can't just go down the stairs. They're going to be watching, if they sent that guy up after us."

"They might hear him banging, too, if he keeps it up," Sirin pointed out, dropping onto the luggage rack with her elbows on her knees. "They'll probably send the other guy up after him when he doesn't come back down. We shouldn't hang around here much longer. What next?"

Negret looked at the window and the snow-coated red staircase outside it. "Hey, Sirin, this counts as an emergency, right?"

"I'd say so." She eyed the fire escape.

Negret scratched his head and peered out. The snowy steps ended just above a sloping roof. "That's the generator shed. We can climb down from there, and then we'd be right by the kitchen door at the back of the house."

"Which is next to the laundry room where everybody's locked up, right?"

"Yup."

"Sounds like a plan, then."

"Yup."

She looked at him, frowning. "You think you can manage the climb?" There was a fearful note in her voice. "All it would take is one slip and . . ." She trailed off. "Well, one slip and you and I would have a lot more in common than we do now," she finished.

Control in unexpected situations . . . Athletic . . . High in dexterity, intelligence. Negret reached into the rucksack and pulled on Wildthorn's Crackerjack Gauntlets (also guaranteed to be useful when it's cold).

Of course, it was one thing to pretend to be an escaladeur and another to try to climb down four windy, real-world stories of icy fire escape, jump from there onto a roof, and then somehow get from that roof to the ground.

In the real world he wasn't a blackjack. He hadn't been trained by a famous blackjack father who'd always known his son would follow in his footsteps. He was just a kid who didn't know where he came from and hadn't had any say in where he'd ended up. But, he told himself, he *did* get to decide what he was going to do from here. Just as he'd decided who Negret was, he got to decide who *Milo* was. He got to choose who and what he was going to be from now on.

It must be separated from the others to do its work. It has potential when it is connected to the rest, but when it is sundered away, its potential becomes power.

He got to choose what he was going to *do* with whatever potential, whatever power, he possessed.

"Negret? . . . Milo?"

He nodded. "I'm going to try. If it means I can help my parents and get these creeps out of the house, I've got to."

He opened the window, and Clem's lockpicks made short work of the screen. Wind and snow swirled into the room, and cold sharp as a knife.

"I'll be with you," Meddy said. "I'll be right behind you."

Milo nodded. He swallowed, and then, as carefully as he could, he swung one leg over the windowsill, and then the other, and then he was outside.

He grasped the railing and stood up. The metal was freezing, even through the gloves, and it felt as if the entire fire escape was swaying in the wind, as if it might pull away from the house at any moment.

"It won't come down," he said to Meddy through chattering teeth. "Dad has it checked every year. It just feels that way."

She nodded and eased herself out after him, but she looked worried. "You okay?"

The snow was soaking through his shoes. He picked up one foot, testing the slick surface beneath it.

Abruptly, the window came down behind them. "Get down," Meddy whispered. Milo hunkered down as far as he could while still holding on to the railing, and he could just make out the shape of one of Vinge's thugs passing by in the hallway. A heartbeat later, the second one peered into the room. But he didn't seem to think anything of the screen Milo had left propped against the wall, and it didn't occur to him to look outside, beyond the room itself. He disappeared into the hallway, apparently satisfied.

"Our captive seems to have been let loose," Meddy said softly.

"M-m-maybe that's good," Milo replied numbly. "M-maybe they'll waste time looking for us. Right now, Mr. Vinge doesn't have backup."

But for how long? Milo moved his other foot carefully, testing. With all the snow, it was almost impossible to see where the edge of the stair actually was. *There.* A little give as the snow crumbled, and his foot found the first step.

He eased his way down, still clutching the railing. *Ignore the wind,* he thought. *Ignore the way the metal rattles against the wall. Ignore the way your feet slide a little each time you move.*

And then, suddenly, instead of another step there was a wide, flat space. He'd reached the fourth floor.

"Wait." Meddy slipped past him — of course she didn't have to worry about falling — and peered through the window. "All clear."

Down and down and down, feet testing, gloved hands clamped tight to the railing. Move one foot. Move one hand. Move the next foot. Move the next hand.

It was freezing. He couldn't feel his feet anymore. And then, another open space, and they had reached the third floor.

"And ... and all clear." Meddy looked down. "One more floor, then the shed roof. You still okay?"

Milo nodded, teeth clicking together convulsively. "One more floor."

"You're doing great," Meddy said. "Come on. One more. Let's go."

It was harder to get his feet moving this time, but somehow he got down the last flight of stairs without freezing or falling. Here, instead of more stairs down to the ground, there was a ladder with a latch on it. In good weather, you could just release it and the ladder would slide down, leaving only a short drop to the ground. But now the mechanism that held it in place was frozen solid.

They were up too high to simply jump to the ground, but the roof of the generator shed was closer, and the bottom of its slope was low enough to leap from. "All right," Milo said through clenched teeth. "All right." Carefully, he climbed over the railing and stood with the metal bars at his back, clasping them tightly.

"Want me to count?" Meddy asked. Milo nodded. "Okay. Ready? One . . . two . . . three!" She looked down at his hands, which had simply refused to let go. "Want to try again?"

Milo shook his head and jumped.

His feet shot out from under him as he landed on the angled roof. Just like on the fire escape, under the snow was a layer of ice, and it was as if he had landed on an oiled slide. Down he slipped, scrambling helplessly for a grip on something, anything—but there was nothing to hold on to, and before he could even yelp he was tumbling off the roof and into a snowdrift.

He lay in the snow for a moment, trying to determine if anything was broken. Meddy perched on a drift beside him. "All in one piece?"

"I think so."

"Then get up before you catch pneumonia. Let's go!" She pulled him up by his elbow and pointed at the back door. "We're almost there."

"Yeah." He got to his feet, brushed himself off, and felt to make sure the rucksack hadn't come open on the way down. Together he and Meddy crept to the kitchen door.

She peeked through its little curtained window. "I see Mr. Vinge's back, but the other agents must still be looking for us upstairs. Before, one was sitting in a chair in the kitchen guarding the laundry room, but there's no one there now." She looked back at him. "You ready? We probably don't have much time."

"I'm ready." Milo rubbed his frigid hands together and reached for the doorknob.

But the door only opened partway, and it gave a tremendous protesting squeal in the process. Mr. Vinge rushed into the kitchen to see what the noise was. His eyes went wide. "You!"

Milo slammed the door shut and leaned against it. "What now?"

"Well, now —" The door flew open again and he went flying into the snow. One of Vinge's thugs towered over Milo for a moment, then grabbed him and dragged him inside. Meddy followed, wringing her hands. "I guess I was wrong about these guys still being upstairs," she whispered apologetically.

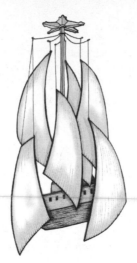

fourteen

DOC HOLYSTONE'S FINAL CARGO

Sneaky, aren't we?" Mr. Vinge observed as the man carried Milo into the living room and dropped him unceremoniously onto the rag rug before the fireplace. "Just keep your seat," he snapped at Mrs. Pine, who was on her feet and reaching for her son. Reluctantly, she dropped back onto the couch between her husband and Fenster Plum.

"You all right, Milo?" Mr. Pine demanded. "These guys didn't hurt you, did they?"

"No, Dad, I'm okay. Just cold, is all," he said as reassuringly as he could manage through chattering teeth.

Milo and Meddy looked at each other. "Remember the plan," she said. "Find what he wants and get him out of here, Milo. Okay?"

"Okay." He got to his feet and faced the three customs agents. "Mr. Vinge, you said you came for Doc Holystone's last cargo. If I tell you where it is, if I give it to you, will you leave? Will you leave us all alone?"

Mr. Vinge eyed him with interest. "*You* know where it is?"

"Like you said, I'm better at hide-and-seek than you are. Plus you practically told me where it was yourself." He folded his arms. "Is it a deal or not?"

"I suppose," Mr. Vinge said, taking his gun casually from his pocket, "I could just point this at your mom and tell you to take your deals and shove them." Then he smiled grimly. "But yes, it's a deal. All I want is the cargo."

"All right, then." Trying not to think of the gun or the threat that had just been made, Milo got up shakily and went into the dining room.

Please, let us be right. Please, please, please.

He took one of the tall stools from the bar between the dining room and the kitchen and put it up on the table, right under the pale glass chandelier. His feet were still a little numb, so he was extra careful as he clambered onto the table and then onto the stool for a closer look.

The piece that connected the glass structure to the brass tube that held the electrical cord was also brass, and shaped like a square on top of a rectangle. Looking closely, Milo could make out slightly raised blocks along the side of the rectangle. *If this is a ship,* he thought, *those are the gunports.* The top square sat roughly where the quarterdeck of a ship would be, and a very faint seam ran along its edge, as if it had once had a lid that could be removed.

Milo took the lockpick kit from his rucksack and selected a tool with a thin, triangular spade at the end. Carefully, he wedged it into the seam and gave it a twist. The top of the square box popped off easily, although the entire piece gave a little lurch to one side as it did, twisting on the brass tube from which it hung. Milo reached inside and felt soft fabric.

"There's something here," he whispered.

The stool shot out from beneath him. Milo flailed for something to hold on to, but the glass sails of the chandelier just fluttered and clicked out of reach and he went down hard, twisting his ankle and landing on his hip on the table. Meddy clapped her hands to her face with a squeal; and in the living room, Mrs. Pine shouted his name. "I'm fine," he groaned. "Oww."

"I'll take that." Mr. Vinge tossed the stool aside and climbed onto the table himself, shoving Milo carelessly away with one foot. He reached into the chandelier and stepped down from the table holding a blue felt bag in one hand. He worked open the drawstring and dumped the contents into his other palm, frowning.

Milo couldn't see what had fallen out of the bag, but whatever it was, it wasn't what Mr. Vinge had been expecting. He glared at Milo. "Is this a joke?"

"Is what a joke?" Milo snapped, rubbing his ankle. "What is it?"

Mr. Vinge shoved the thing in Milo's face. It was a little painted figurine, very similar to the one Mr. Pine had given Milo that very morning, only this was a girl — or at least, it had a girl's face. The rest of it was shaped like a bird of some kind. An owl, maybe.

"Can I have a look?" he asked.

Mr. Vinge snorted and tossed the figurine to him. It was incredibly detailed, with individual feathers painted on its arched wings and minute scales on its legs and claws, which were curled around a branch. Its eyes looked more like an owl's eyes than a girl's. Milo turned it over. There was one word painted on the base. *Sirin.*

Well, there is a kind of character I've always wanted to play. . . .

"It's a figurine for role-playing games. It's — it's a type of character called a scholiast." Milo flinched as something ran down his face. He touched his cheek and discovered he was crying. "It was for his daughter," he said. "It's a character she always wanted to play."

"It's a *toy?*" Mr. Vinge snarled. "A *child's toy?*"

Milo nodded. He looked at Meddy, who was standing beside the table, unseen by everyone but him. She stared at the tiny owl-girl with wonder on her face. "He must have brought it back from a trip for her."

"That can't be all there is," Mr. Vinge protested. "All the subterfuge, hiding it like that — why would anyone go to all that trouble for a *toy?*"

Fenster spoke up from the sofa. "Ain't got any kids in your life, have you?"

"But she wasn't *their* child! Not the child of anyone who was involved in actually bringing the thing back here and hiding it." Mr. Vinge looked truly and utterly perplexed.

"But he was our captain, and she was our captain's daughter,"

Fenster snapped. "And it weren't me who put that critter there, but I bet I can tell you what was going through the mind of the fellow who did: *If I can't do a thing for Doc, I can do this one thing for his little girl.* Or for her memory, I suppose. By then, of course, she was gone too." He frowned, and it looked for a minute as if Fenster Plum was trying not to shed a tear himself. "I wish I'd thought of it. I wish I'd known."

Mr. Vinge stared at the figurine, utterly flummoxed. Then, all in a moment, the confusion fell away from his face. "In that case . . ." He held out his hand. "I'll take that, Milo."

It was exactly what they'd planned all along, but now that Mr. Vinge was standing there reaching for the miniature Sirin, Milo clutched the treasure to his chest. "No way. What do you care, anyway? You were looking for a weapon, or a secret or something. This is nothing to you."

"It *is* something to me," Mr. Vinge retorted, "because if Doc Holystone cared that much about it, then it's what I came here to find." He took a step toward Milo, who scooted away and off the table on the other side. "It may have been part of his life, but I won't have it become part of his legend."

Fenster jumped to his feet. "You'd take it and hide it away just out of spite? A *toy?*"

Mr. Vinge whipped out the gun and pointed it at him. "What kind of fool are you? It won't be enough to hide it away. *He's* proof of that." He gestured at the laundry room door. "Our Dr. Gowervine spent his *life* looking for this. You think he's the only one? No, it has to be destroyed, even if it really is nothing but a piece from a game."

"Milo," Meddy began hesitantly, "don't go rogue on me. Don't take stupid chances. Give it to him before he does something with that gun—"

Milo ignored her. "I won't let you," he said. "It's hers, even if she never got to have it herself. It's not about Doc Holystone; it's about a guy and his kid who didn't get to say goodbye to him." He wiped his fist angrily at the dampness on his face. "It's a treasure, and you can't have it."

Mr. Vinge sighed. "Please don't make me use this gun, Milo."

The room erupted with protests. "No!" Milo's mother and father and Fenster stumbled over one another as they leaped to their feet, but before Mr. Vinge could turn his weapon on them and warn them to sit still, the air in the inn changed.

The chandelier rattled, and so did every window on the floor. The dying fire sent up a puff of sparks, and the string of lights on the Christmas tree flickered.

"Stop this."

And everyone in the room, every single person, turned to look at Meddy. For the first time, the rest of them could see her.

There was nothing different about her that Milo could see. She was still wearing the ridiculous yellow robe and the blue glasses, but other than that she looked like a normal kid. There was no halo, no sudden glow, nothing you'd think would signal to folks that there was, suddenly, a ghost in their midst.

But then, maybe it was enough that there was suddenly a *girl* in their midst—a girl who, as far as the rest of them knew, had appeared right out of nowhere.

Everyone — Milo's parents, Fenster, Mr. Vinge and his two thugs — was staring at Meddy, but she only had eyes for Mr. Vinge.

She walked straight up to him and reached for the gun in his hand.

Mr. Vinge flinched. Sweating suddenly, he pointed the gun. He squeezed the trigger.

Milo screamed.

Meddy stopped short and looked down at her stomach. Then she turned to look at the bullet hole in the floor just behind her. "You *shot* at me. I might be dead, but I'm still a kid. You shot at a *kid*." She shook her head in disgust. Then, before anyone, including Milo, could so much as blink, she was standing centimeters from Mr. Vinge's white, sweat-streaming face. No, not standing — because they were eye to eye, even though Mr. Vinge was nearly six feet tall and the ghost of Addie Whitcher was shorter than Milo.

"I'll take that," she said with a voice like ice floes cracking in the river. "Before you shoot someone you can hurt." And then the gun was in her hand and she was small again. Mr. Vinge collapsed back against the table, both hands over his heart.

"Hey, boss?" the taller of the other two agents asked uncertainly.

"You were asked to leave this house before," she went on in a deadly calm voice. She looked from Mr. Vinge to the agent who had spoken, then shifted her gaze to his partner and back to Mr. Vinge. "*I'm* not asking. *You will leave this house.* You will leave my friends in peace. And you will do the same for my father's memory."

Mr. Vinge glanced up, and despite his obvious fear, for a moment it looked as if he might be on the point of arguing. Before he could open his mouth, though, Meddy was huge and nose-to-nose with him once more, and this time, her face was so angry it looked almost disfigured.

"You will leave this house!" Her voice came out something between a wail and a scream. Milo clapped his hands over his ears, and he wasn't the only one. It was a painful sound, full of misery and sadness. And fear, Milo realized. Meddy was scaring herself. But stronger than the fear, stronger than the misery, was the rage of Addie Whitcher. It burned white-hot on her face, revealing her furious heart the way spreading daylight illuminates the landscape. And in the face of that rage, there was nothing, *nothing* for Mr. Vinge to do but run.

He dashed out from between the table and the screeching ghost girl who still held his gun dangling at her side and flung himself at the foyer. He fought his way through the door and the buffeting wind that slashed its way in, and disappeared into the snow and the night. Despite the wind, the door swung shut with a bang. Then it opened again, and a gust picked up one of the coats hanging on pegs in the vestibule and whisked it out into the night.

Through the windows, Mr. Vinge's dark shape could be seen darting clumsily across the grounds toward the road. His coat rushed along after him until he spotted it and panicked. The coat tackled him. After a moment, Mr. Vinge got awkwardly back to his feet, picked up the coat, stared at it, pulled it on, and started running again. And then he was out of sight.

Meddy looked from the open door to the two remaining agents.

"What are you waiting for?" she asked frigidly. "Do you want me to get *your* coats? Or do you need me to make the ghost face again?"

They looked at each other; then they too sprinted out into the night.

Meddy held the gun as if it were a dead rat as she walked back into the living room. She set it carefully on the table and looked at Milo's parents. "I think someone had better put this somewhere safe."

Milo's mother nodded shakily. She picked up the gun gingerly, looked around for a moment, then made a beeline for a little drop-front desk in the kitchen that could be locked with a key. Mr. Pine rushed across the room and collected Milo into a huge and quaking hug.

"I'm okay, Dad," Milo assured him. "You should probably let everybody out of the laundry room."

Mr. Pine made a sound that was sort of like a laugh and sort of like a giant sigh of relief. "Right-o," he managed. "Probably have to break the door down. One of Vinge's creeps had the key."

"I've got it," Mrs. Pine said from the kitchen. "There's a spare in the junk drawer."

Meanwhile, Fenster was staring at Meddy. "Addie?" he said uncertainly. "Addie Whitcher?"

Meddy smiled at the old smuggler. "Hi, Fenster. It's nice to see you. Thank you for the nice things you said about my dad." Then she smiled at Milo. "And thank *you*, except what did I tell you about going rogue and taking stupid chances? We had a *plan*. He really could've hurt you, and I didn't know I could do all that stuff until I tried. It could've gone really wrong." She still looked a little freaked out.

"The plan?" Mr. Pine stared from his son to the ghost girl. "You . . . you two . . . had a plan?" He rubbed his face. "Milo, when I figure out what's going on, you're going to get a serious talking-to about what to do when someone has a gun, but at the moment I just don't know what to think about anything."

"No kidding," his mother added.

"Be free," she said, unlocking the laundry-room door and throwing it open. "We won. Or rather, Milo and his friend did."

This, of course, required much explanation, and more introductions.

"So let me get this straight." Dr. Gowervine stared at Meddy. *Everyone* was staring at Meddy. "You—Milo, you found Doc Holystone's cargo, in order to get Mr. Vinge to leave, and then you changed your mind?"

Milo nodded. "I should've done what Me—Addie said. She told me to hand it over." He held out the figurine to her. "But it's yours. It should be with you. It's important. It's from your dad."

Meddy took it with both hands. "It's really beautiful, isn't it?" She held it up so that Dr. Gowervine, who was hovering nearby, obviously hoping for a look, could see it. "Isn't it beautiful?"

"It *is* a scholiast," Mr. Pine said, peering at the little painted owl-girl and then at Meddy. "So you're the reason Milo knows all about Odd Trails all of a sudden, huh?"

She nodded. "Think maybe the three of us could play sometime?" Milo asked. "Or . . . do you have to leave now? Now that you have your present and Mr. Vinge is gone?"

She considered. "I don't know. I don't . . . feel like I need to leave." She looked at Mr. and Mrs. Pine. "I guess you probably don't want your house haunted, though."

Mrs. Pine shrugged with an exhausted smile. "Sounds to me like it's been haunted for a while now. Not to mention, it was your house first."

"The truth is, I don't really know how it works," Meddy said. "It's like I told you before, Milo. Time passes and I don't know what happens to it. So I don't know if that means I'll keep on finding myself here or not. But if you don't mind, it would be nice to be able to say hello when I am. And maybe play Odd Trails."

Milo's father still looked shaken, but he managed a smile too. "We'd be delighted to have you."

Dr. Gowervine, meanwhile, had taken the painted figurine for a closer look. "Not to sound too disappointed, but this is really the thing I've been looking for all this time?"

"We thought maybe the chandelier was Mr. Skellansen's work," Milo said. "Could that be?"

"Yes, yes, I think you're probably right about that. If I hadn't been so focused on something that . . . well, that could tell a story, something more like an actual window, I probably would've realized it myself." He frowned. "But all my sources really did seem to indicate that Skellansen had chosen Doc Holystone as the subject of his window for the archives." He held the figurine out awkwardly to

Meddy and pulled his hand back a little too quickly when she took it, as if he were afraid she might bite. "Although, of course, I think Milo is right and it's a treasure in its own right," he added hastily. "And so is the chandelier. There are so few pieces of Skellansen glasswork in the city, it's quite amazing to find one here. Just . . . well, you understand."

"They're not *your* treasures," Meddy said.

He nodded a bit sadly. "Indeed."

Milo looked up at the chandelier. Then he picked up the stool Mr. Vinge had yanked out from under him and set it back up on the table. "Dad, can you hold this for me?"

Mr. Pine gave him a wary look, but he held the stool steady while Milo climbed up again. Holding his father's shoulder, he stood on tiptoe and reached again for the rectangular brass hull. It had turned a little, he remembered, when he'd jimmied off the lid that had formed the top of the quarterdeck. Now he gave it an experimental twist, and it moved without resistance. Turn by turn, Milo unscrewed the piece from the brass wiring tube until the hull came loose in his hand. It was heavier than he'd expected, and he nearly dropped it before he managed to hand it off to his dad. Then he looked inside the tube.

There was something wrapped around the inside, so tight against the inner surface that it would've been easy to miss if he hadn't been looking for it. He reached in carefully and worked it loose until he was able to draw it all the way out.

"Wow." He looked up from the cylinder of paper in his hand. "Dr. Gowervine, do you want to look first?"

The professor didn't have to be asked twice. He rushed to the table and took the roll carefully, reverently. As Milo climbed down, Dr. Gowervine set the paper on the table and gently, very gently, began to unfurl it.

"Oh, my," he whispered.

The paper unrolled to reveal a stunning painting.

"Oh, my," Dr. Gowervine said again. "Oh, my. Do you think . . ."

Mrs. Pine hurried into the kitchen and returned with clean coffee cups. Carefully, the professor weighted down the corners with them. "Oh, my. Oh, *my.*"

A small clipper ship was cutting swiftly down a river. Carved into the prow in place of a figurehead was a winged shape Milo thought he recognized from the old chart's compass rose: an albatross. It was a beautiful ship, and from the motion of its bow wave and the billow of the sails, it appeared to be the kind of vessel Milo's grandfather would've called a "weatherly, sweet little sailer." There was another ship behind it on the river, but that one wasn't nearly as weatherly; it seemed to be struggling to keep up, and its sails weren't nearly as trim.

The man at the helm didn't seem worried about being followed. He wore a brown tarpaulin hat with a gold pin stuck through the band that ran around the crown. His chin was clean shaven, but his sideburns were red-blond, just exactly the same shade as Meddy's. He was younger than Milo had expected, younger than his own parents, but he had the stern, determined face and blazing eyes of a hero. This was someone who was intent upon important things, difficult things, and who would be a force to be reckoned with if you tried to stand in his way. All of that was clear from his face and the way he gripped the tiller. And from the people gathered on the riverbank, waving and cheering with all their might, it seemed that he just had to be a force for good. You almost didn't need to know who he was to want to cheer him on too. But of course, they all knew exactly who he was. Captain Michael Whitcher, the smuggler who'd called himself Doc Holystone.

Dr. Gowervine had called this kind of drawing a cartoon, and it did look a bit like one, in that the shapes had thick, dark outlines that Milo figured must represent the metal that would join the pieces together in the final glasswork. But it was not at all *cartoonish*. The colors were subtle and varied, and the forms the shapes built were fluid and seemed to have motion of their own, from the frothing water at the bow of the clipper to the sails billowing in the wind. The only other place Milo could remember seeing people done in stained glass was in a church, and the face of the man at the helm did not look at all like the stylized, immobile figures of saints Milo was used to. He looked as if he might turn his head at any moment from the river before him and look right out at you.

It was staggeringly beautiful—a work of art all on its own, even though the piece of glasswork it was intended to become had never been made. It was almost hard to imagine the final window being any more stunning.

Meddy reached out and touched the painted face. "That's my dad," she said softly. "That's just how he looked to me."

"It's just how I pictured him too." Dr. Gowervine's face, which had been so pinched and tight and aggravated ever since he'd arrived, had relaxed at last into a look of contentment. "What a treasure. This house is so full of treasures."

"Boy, is it ever," Milo put in.

Mrs. Pine spoke up. "You said you'd been looking your whole life for this. What did you plan to do if you found it?"

"I don't know." The professor couldn't tear his eyes from the cartoon. "I suppose before I told the story I hoped you might not know what you had, that perhaps I could convince you to sell it to me. But of course, you must keep it," he added with complete sincerity. "It belongs here, with you. With his daughter's . . . memory."

"What if . . ." Meddy hesitated. "What if you borrowed it?"

"Well, then I'd take it to the university, have a copy made by a glassmaker I trust — an apprentice of Skellansen's, actually — and perhaps, if you think it proper, ask him to go on and create the window it was meant to be. I suspect the university might display it if I asked." He touched one edge that had been worn from rubbing up against the wiring in the tube. "And perhaps I might go ahead and have this mounted for you. For preservation."

"That sounds like a pretty good plan," Mr. Pine said. "What do you think, Milo?"

"I think it ought to be up to Meddy," Milo said. "Addie, I mean."

Milo's mother nodded. "I agree."

"Then I think you should borrow it," Meddy told the professor. "Take care of it and don't let anything happen to it. But I'm really glad other people will get to see this picture."

"Your father was my hero, you know," Dr. Gowervine said. "Perhaps, sometime later, you and I could talk about him."

Meddy beamed. "That would be great."

There it was again, that joy, the same feeling Milo had when Mrs. Hereward had told Owen the Lansdegown story. Meddy's family was gone, but here was someone who could share what he knew about her father, and who would cherish what she told him.

Mrs. Pine came around to where Milo stood and put an arm around his shoulders. "Not a bad Christmas, all things considered? Even if it wasn't what you were expecting?"

Milo looked around the room. With Mr. Vinge gone, those who remained were either old friends or those who had come looking for something and had found it — or something enough like it to be content — and had given something to someone else. Mrs. Hereward, who had found a lamp and given Owen a piece of his past; Georgie, who had found an answer (even though it wasn't the one she had been looking for) and who had helped convince Mrs. Hereward to tell the Lansdegown story; Owen, who had come seeking Clem and who had given Milo his childhood treasure; Clem, who had come seeking the key to Owen's heart and who had helped Milo escape so that he could rescue everyone else; Dr. Gowervine, who had come seeking his hero and would be able to give Meddy new knowledge of her own family.

"I think it turned out *better* than I was expecting," Milo admitted. "And it's not even Christmas yet."

Into the contented hush that followed his words came the frosty peal of the railcar bell.

fifteen

DEPARTURES

It was late; full dark, by the time the grizzled ferryman had downed a cup of coffee and had his scarf and gloves warmed in the dryer and declared himself ready to sail again. One by one the guests began drifting downstairs with packed bags. "Are you sure you want to leave now too?" Mrs. Pine asked when Clem and Owen came to pay their bill. "It's so late, and it's going to be freezing out there. Where will you go?"

"Owen lives in the Quayside Harbors," Clem said. She winked at Milo. "We'll be home before Santa gets anywhere close. And we'll pass the word for some reliable lawmen to come up when they can, if you like. I know one or two who won't let customs bully them around, and you might feel better about all this if you talk to someone."

"Well, I won't lie, that would be wonderful," Mr. Pine admitted, "but only if you're sure you really want to go. And of course, we hope you enjoyed your stay."

All four of them burst into laughter.

"You didn't get to show me how to use the lockpicks!" Milo protested as Clem and Owen made their way to the door with Mr. Pine and Mr. Ostling, the ferryman. At the mention of lockpicks, Milo's parents both looked over at him with similar questioning expressions, but neither said anything.

"You're right, I didn't." Clem sat on the arm of Milo's chair. "Tell you what. When I get home, I'll send you a book to start with. Then one of these days, I'll see if I can't stop back by and see how you're coming along. Fair?"

"Fair."

Owen held out his hand. "Thanks again, Milo, for everything. It was really nice to meet you and your family."

Mrs. Hereward came down next, followed closely by Dr. Gowervine. She turned to Milo. "Young man?"

Milo sat up straighter in his chair. "Yes, Mrs. Hereward?"

She fixed him with a stern look. Then it crumbled away and she smiled as she held out a flat box wrapped in red striped paper. "Merry Christmas, dear."

"For me? Thank you!" He tore off the paper and opened the box. Inside were a scarf and a pair of mittens, dark green with white snowflakes dotting them here and there. "Are these what you were knitting all this time?"

"Yes, but I confess I didn't realize they were for you until today." She patted his shoulder. "You were very good to all of us, Milo, and we certainly didn't give you any particular reason to be. Whoever said this house is full of treasures was right, and I think you're the biggest treasure of all." She patted his shoulder again and rearranged her face back into its sterner configuration. "Now I think that's quite enough of my being sentimental. How about putting on those mittens and helping me with my things?"

Milo bundled himself up while Mr. Down and Mrs. Up settled their bills with his mother, then he collected as much of Mrs. Hereward's baggage as he could manage and made his way carefully out the door, down the stairs, and across the lawn to the butter-yellow light in the pavilion and the fairy lights that glowed golden under their white frosting.

Mr. Pine was there with his hand on the lever that started the winch; from the sound of the rails, the *Whilforber Whirlwind* and its two smitten passengers must've been about two-thirds of the way down the cliff.

"Mrs. Hereward and Dr. Gowervine are coming too," Milo said, huffing a little as he set down the bags.

"Clem told me." Mr. Pine tugged on his son's new scarf. "Present from the knitter?"

"Yeah. These, too." He held up his mittened hands.

"Nice."

The pitch of the rails changed, and Mr. Pine hauled the lever to its neutral position. A moment later, the bell rang below: a single crisp, half-frozen metallic note. Mr. Pine pulled the lever to start the *Whirlwind* back up the hill, and he and Milo stood in silence, watching the rustle of the trees in the wind sending down tiny flurries of snow. The fairy lights twinkled as the wind shifted them, too, and at last the blue nose of the railcar appeared at the top of the slope just as Mrs. Hereward and Dr. Gowervine arrived at the platform.

"It's been a lovely stay," Dr. Gowervine said. He patted the tube Milo had thought was a telescope case, which now held the precious Skellansen cartoon of Doc Holystone. "Truly. Thank you." Mrs. Hereward just nodded to Mr. Pine and patted Milo's shoulder once more, and then they, too, were off down the hill.

"Let's go see about some hot chocolate," Mr. Pine said when the bell rang again from the bottom to let them know the railcar had delivered its passengers safely.

They met Georgie on the porch. "Taking the ferry with the rest of them?" Mr. Pine asked, ready to head back to the landing.

Georgie shook her head. "No, after all the noise I made about wanting a boat, I'm hopping the train instead. Brandon's giving Fenster a ride into town and I asked if I could tag along. Less ... crowded," she said with a sad smile. "Mrs. Caraway and her daughter are coming too. They should be out in a minute."

Milo blinked. The Caraways had known about the BTS, just as the Pines had, because Brandon was a friend of the inn. But Georgie? "He told you about the Belowground?"

She gave him a wry look. "I'm the Eye, Milo, remember? I didn't need to be *told.* I just needed to convince him I wouldn't tell anyone else, and that's the kind of secret a thief just doesn't share."

"Wow. *How* did you know?"

Georgie smiled. "Thieves also don't usually share how they get their information, Milo. But I will tell you that there was a big clue in *The Raconteur's Commonplace Book.* Never overlook folklore if you want to really know about the place it came from."

"I must not have gotten to that story," Milo said, searching his memory. "But that reminds me — don't forget your book. I'll go get it now. Be right back."

"Well, wait, you haven't finished it?"

"Not quite. Almost."

"Do you want to?" she asked.

Milo considered. "Yes. I like it a lot."

"Then keep it. Lend it to someone else when you're done, okay?"

"Cool. Thanks, I will." He fidgeted while they waited for Brandon and Fenster. "I feel bad," he said at last. "Everybody else got something important to them. You didn't."

"Not true," Georgie protested with a grin. "I got a blue cake. A very delicious blue cake," she added as the door opened and Fenster came out onto the porch with Brandon a step behind him.

"Which it was my pleasure," Fenster said gallantly. "Even if Mrs. Hereward was a bit stingy with the cinnamon."

Georgie took the old smuggler's arm. "She says it was pepper, you know."

"Just a pinch, that's all I wanted to put in," Fenster grumbled. "Just a pinch. How far by the lee could it have gone?"

Brandon shook Milo's hand. "See you in better weather, mate. Happy Christmas."

Hugs from Mrs. Caraway and Lizzie, and then the whole caravan trooped away into the woods with Mr. Pine toward the red brick shed that hid the entrance to the Belowground Transit System. Milo watched them until they were gone.

"I'm going to go too. For now, anyway."

Milo turned to find the ghost girl standing beside him on the porch. "You don't have to, you know."

Meddy—Milo still couldn't quite manage to think of her as Addie—nodded. "I know that, and I'm grateful. But you should have your Christmas with your family, now that all the guests are gone. That's all you've wanted the whole time, isn't it?"

"It was," he admitted, "but I don't mind anymore. Not about you. You're welcome to spend Christmas with us." And rather to Milo's own surprise, he meant it.

"Nah." She smiled happily. "Not this time. That's something I can give you, after all you did for me. Anyway, I'm sure I'll be back." She grinned. "You know, since I have all the time in the world."

Milo looked at his new friend. "If you're sure."

"I'm sure."

"Then . . . well, Merry Christmas, Meddy-Addie-Sirin." Awkwardly Milo held out one hand, and the two of them shook solemnly.

"Merry Christmas, Milo-Negret." And then, just as she had in the Emporium, Meddy flickered once and was gone.

For a moment Milo stood shivering in the swirling snow and looked at the place where she had been. Then he went inside.

Mrs. Pine was standing at the window. She held out an arm, and Milo went to stand beside her. The house felt empty, and it was so quiet the crackle of the fireplace seemed unnaturally loud.

"How you doing, kiddo?" Mrs. Pine asked.

"Fine. Tired, I guess."

"And your friend?"

"Gone," Milo said, looking out into the night. "Gone for now."

"Think she'll turn up again soon?"

"I think so. I hope so."

"Is she the reason you had such a good time these past few days even though it wasn't what you were hoping vacation would be?" Mrs. Pine asked. Milo nodded, and his mother hugged him tight. "Then I hope so too." They stood in silence for a moment more. "Milo, you know your dad and I know you still think about your birth family, right?"

Milo stiffened a little, but only for a minute. "I guess so."

"And you know we understand that? We recognize that it doesn't mean you don't love us. And we would never want you to feel guilty about loving your birth parents too, and wanting to think about them."

A knot began to form in Milo's throat. "I understand."

"I guess I just thought," she said carefully, her eyes on the window, "that with all this talk about . . . oh, everything, the past of the house, Doc Holystone and his daughter, that fellow Owen being adopted too, and learning something about his ancestry . . . and of course that wonderful gift he gave you . . . I guess I thought you might be feeling something. Sad, or glad, or just *something*, even if you didn't know what that something-feeling was. And maybe you might want to talk about it. With me, or with your dad when he gets back. Or not. That's fine, too."

Stupid tears. Milo wiped his eyes with the collar of his pajama top. "Okay." Across the lawn, Mr. Pine was stomping back through the snow toward the house. "Maybe not tonight, though. Maybe tonight we can just have Christmas Eve."

"Of course. Anytime you want." She gave him one more hug, then Milo's dad was back and kicking off his boots and Mrs. Pine put on one of her mother's old holiday records and little by little, Greenglass House changed from an empty inn back to Milo's home at Christmastime.

They stayed up late, because they were by themselves at last, and there was hot chocolate to drink and snickerdoodles and the puffy white cookies Milo's mother called *forgottens* to eat, and by the time his parents sent him stumbling up to his room, it was well past midnight.

Milo clambered into bed and pulled the patchwork blanket up to his chin. Normally it took forever to get to sleep on Christmas Eve, but tonight his eyes seemed to slide closed all on their own.

The wind shivered through the trees and sent pale clouds sailing across the dark winter sky. All around him the house murmured its familiar good nights, and Milo Pine drifted off to dream of blackjacks and smugglers and scholiasts and houses full of treasures and secrets still to be found. The last thing he saw before he fell asleep was his Odd Trails figurine, the one his father had given him, standing where he'd put it on his bedside table along with Owen's ivory dragon. But now the painted tiercer and the dragon weren't alone. Between them stood the little Sirin owl-girl.

"Good night," Milo whispered. "See you soon."

Author's Note

In 2010, my husband and I decided to begin the process of international adoption. It wasn't a question of infertility (something we've found ourselves explaining since the birth of our first child, Griffin, in 2013). The truth is that there were a lot of factors involved in our decision to adopt, and although we did ultimately decide to pursue a pregnancy as well, having already begun the adoption process, there was no question of abandoning that unknown member of our family on the other side of the world.

We chose China because we both had an interest in the culture and history. We began studying, both on our own and with our adoption agency, and among the many topics we read about and discussed were questions of identity and family and culture and heritage. If you've read my book *The Broken Lands* you might be thinking now about Jin, and the speech Liao gives her atop the Brooklyn Bridge. It probably won't surprise you to know that Jin evolved from a secondary character into a co-protagonist at right about the time that Nathan and I decided to adopt.

I began writing *Greenglass House* in the summer of 2011, during a spell when my critique group decided to play a game in which we gave each other prompts meant to inspire new projects. Lindsay Eland was responsible for mine: *stained glass*. Back then, I was thinking all the time about adoptive families and what ours might be like. Out of these musings and the many hours of reading and study we spent preparing for our adoption came Milo and Nora and Ben Pine. I didn't want the story to be specifically and only about adoption, just as I don't imagine the experiences of every child who came to his or her family in this way are forever and always about adoption. However, when I chose the makeup of the family who ran the inn, it meant adoption would be part of the story. A lens — not the only one, but an important one — through which Milo views the world.

No two children are alike, so I have no way of knowing whether our Chinese son or daughter will have the same questions and secret concerns that Milo does. But every kid has a birth family, so I know that his or her birth family will always be part of my child's life in some way (even though, as in Milo's case, the chances of ever knowing anything about that first mother and father will be very slim). I would be very surprised if he or she didn't wonder about those parents frequently. I hope he or she will not feel in any way uncomfortable about those wonderings, and will feel secure talking to Nathan and Griffin and I about them. But kids are kids — you're secretive little critters. You suffer in silence when you shouldn't have to. So let this book also be a letter to my future child: We understand. We know. Wonder away. Include us in your wonderings when you want to. Know that we love you. Know that we know you love us, too.

The international adoption process can take a long time. Although there's no way to be sure exactly when this little brother or sister from overseas will join the family, it's likely Griffin will be four or five when that happens. We can't wait to go to China together, all three of us, to bring home the newest member of our family.

* * *

Endless gratitude goes, as always, to the beta-reading geniuses who are Edie and Luci Paczkowski, Julia Zeh, and Emma Humphrey; equally endless thanks go to my critique group: Lisa Amowitz, Heidi Ayarbe, Pippa Bayliss, Linda Budzinski, Dhonielle Clayton, Lindsay Eland, Cathy Giordano, Trish Heng, Cynthia Kennedy Henzel, and Christine Johnson. I am so much obliged to Kru Brandon Levi of Evolution Muay Thai for letting me write about his other, secret life in Nagspeake. To Ann Behar and Lynne Polvino, who believed in this book when it was just a bad synopsis, I am forever indebted. To Barry Goldblatt, thank you for taking a chance on me. I hope to make you proud.

To Nathan, who loves me even when I am in worse shape than a bad synopsis, and to Griffin, the unlikely infant who actually lets me work on something other than his diapers — you are my favorite people, and I love you.